MW01074376

"Vampires Don't Exist"
By: Reyanna Vance
©2005
The United States Library of Congress

For:
Every one of my loyal fans…you all know who you are.
My sister, Amanda Cantrell, who was my first fan. I love
you very "muchly."
To the rest of my family, my parents, and my friends; all
who encouraged me to pursue my dream; you all know who
you are as well.
Thanks for the support, guys.

Introduction (a few words from the author)

This is the story of a young woman who finds herself in a house full of bloodthirsty, and lustful, vampires. This story shows her endured suffering and how she learns of the ways of the vampires of **Aimeric's** clan.

But be warned now: This story is *not* a happy one, full of love and laughter. It's quite frustrating and, at times, confusing. You may not even like the ending. I guarantee you will be frustrated with my plot twists and surprises. But it will be enjoyable just the same. You may even have trouble putting the book down. At least, I hope so.

This story is not for the weak minded or weak-otherwise. It is quite dark and some of the events could be considered disturbing. I advise you to read with caution.

I hope I don't disappoint you too badly, but please remember, this *is* just a **story** of fiction…as far as I know

(grinning).

-Reyanna

Chapter One: Attempted Suicide

Aralyn walked the streets of a, usually busy, city in New England. The streets were glistening, from a rain shower, which had happened earlier that night, under the orange lights that lit her path. There was an eerie glow from the lights reflecting on the thick clouds above her, making the late October night seem very creepy, as it might have been in a horror movie.

Aralyn pulled her jacket tighter across her chest as the wind's icy fingers reached out to touch her. She wasn't even aware that she had started crying again until she felt the warm tears running down her pale face to drop below onto the concrete beneath her black boots. Her raven hair fluttered in the wind as she walked, nearing the cliffs to the ocean. She could hear the waves already, crashing against the stone; they sounded quite angry.

Aralyn was only twenty years old and already she wished to end her young life. She felt as though she had nothing left to live for. Not since her mother and only sister had died in a car crash one year ago that very night. What was ironic about it was that the night her mother and sister had been killed, the weather had been exactly the same as it was now; foggy, dreary and cold.

Aralyn's mother and Claire, her sister, had been driving at night. It had been difficult to see and the roads had been wet and, according to police reports, Aralyn's mother had lost control of the car on a sharp curve and ran off the road, clipping a tree and causing it to roll a few times. The windshield had shattered and one of the larger pieces had gone through Aralyn's mother's throat. She had died shortly after, due to loss of blood from that and other cuts on her body; she had died even before the ambulance could arrive.

Claire had managed to use her cell phone to call 911, even with how injured she had been herself, but when the police arrived, Claire was gone. A trail of her blood had been followed into the woods, which were about fifty feet from the car, but then the trail suddenly stopped. Police and others insisted that Claire had gone unconscious from blood loss, or died, and animals carried her off to the trees before they could get there. They didn't come right out and say it, but they implied that her body had been eaten in that short amount of time. Aralyn had been skeptical. There was no way that even a pack of wolves could finish off a full grown human in only twenty minutes. There was just no way, or so Aralyn believed.

Aralyn had insisted Claire be searched for. Claire must have been alive, somehow. Perhaps someone had found her and carried her to their home, trying to give her help? But no one lived very close to where the wreck had happened. The police dedicated only a few hours in checking the area out. They weren't convinced she was alive anywhere so it had been left up to Aralyn. She herself had found nothing to indicate Claire was still alive. She had soon given up hope, as the others had, and admitted that her sister was gone forever.

It wasn't long before Aralyn had lost her father too. Oh sure, he was still alive, but overcome with grief for the loss of his wife and youngest child. He had tried to be strong and keep himself together for the sake of the daughter he still had, but soon, he fell apart and had a mental breakdown. He turned to alcohol as his comfort and became a drunkard. He lost his job and stayed at home all day, wallowing in his sorrows. He had let his appearance go downhill, let his house fall apart, and let his relationship with Aralyn become almost non-existent. The only time the two spoke was when they argued. Aralyn hadn't had much of a motive to get out and get a job before (she didn't care anymore about her life), her sister had been her best friend and her mother her second and now they were gone. But she had eventually been employed at a local market and found a place to live on her own only a few days ago. She was supposed to move in the next morning but now, she wouldn't have to worry about it.

She had nothing. Her friends had abandoned her when she needed them the most, saying she had changed too much after the accident. Who the hell wouldn't change? Was she expected to be a happy-go-lucky person after what she had been through? They could have at least given her time to heal. But they didn't. They had soon stopped calling her and asking to hang out with her. Even her best guy friend had decided she wasn't worth staying beside during her time of grief.

So what did she have to live for now? Nothing. She was always in pain. But soon, she would feel none of it. Maybe she would even be reunited with her mother and sister. She had always believed in God, though she wasn't a hardcore Christian, but she didn't know how suicides went over in the afterlife.

"It doesn't matter," she whispered to herself. She had reached the cliffs and was looking over the edge, into the dark water below. The waves foamed white at the crests right before they hit the rocks. "I will end it all now, no matter the consequences."

She licked her dry lips and tasted the salt in the air for the last time. Her chest heaving with her nervousness, she took one last deep breath and closed her eyes before stepping to the very edge of the cliff. Her boots hung over the edge, just barely, enough to knock a few loose pebbles into the furious ocean below. Holding her arms out as though they were wings, Aralyn opened her eyes to take in the view one last time. She wanted her last scenes of life to be anything but total darkness. The ocean, though angry at the rocks, was calm further out, gentle, soothing. She became at ease with her decision. In just a few moments, she would be calm, as the sea was. Her legs moved forward and she started to fall–no, fly. She was going to fly; all of her pain would be gone if she flew.

Before she could totally leave the ground, however, Aralyn felt a hand grab the back of her jacket and before she could fight back, she felt herself being thrown backwards and landing on the soft grass behind.

Soft though the grass was, she still hit hard and she could tell her ribs would be bruised. Aralyn struggled to take a deep breath and looked up to see who had interrupted her latest attempt to kill herself. She had tried several times before, she had tried cutting her wrists deep enough to bleed to death, but always, when she would get the knife close enough, she would chicken out and not be able to do it, she had tried taking pills, but she only managed to swallow four pain pills, which was hardly enough to kill her, and she had tried to swerve off the road, as her mother had done, but always corrected the car before it could crash. Now, she had finally summoned up the nerve to jump into the arms of the ocean and she was interrupted. Someone had decided to stop her. She could kill whoever it was.

She groaned and pushed herself up on her elbows, staring into the face of a stranger. It was a man she had never seen before. His features were soft and almost angelic. He had the brightest green eyes she had ever seen and his dark hair fell into them, adding a bit more mystery to him. He knelt down beside her before she could say a word.

"Are you alright? What the hell were you doing that close to the edge?"

He had a soft voice to match his features.

His manners didn't soften Aralyn's anger. She jumped to her feet, startling the stranger to do the same.

"What the hell did you do that for!" she screamed and shoved at the man as hard as she could.

It didn't do much to the man; Aralyn was weak from not eating enough in the past few weeks. The man looked at her, dumbfounded, for a moment and then realization struck.

"Oh, I get it. You didn't slip, did you? You wanted to die," he said.

Overcome with grief and weakness, Aralyn covered her face and began to sob, sinking back to her knees on the ground. The man followed her and placed a friendly hand on her shoulder.

"Don't cry. I'm sure that, whatever it is, it can be fixed. Killing yourself isn't the answer to anything."

Aralyn shook her head. Her problem couldn't be fixed. She would always feel this way. Things would never work out and she would never be herself again. It was going to take a long time for her to summon up the courage to take her life again. Feeling herself being cradled and then lifted off the ground, Aralyn moved her hands and looked into the eyes of the stranger. He looked sad for her. He carried her to a nearby tree and set her underneath it, so she could lean against its trunk, and then he sat next to her.

"So, do you want to talk about it?" he asked after waiting a few minutes.

Aralyn, who had started to soften a little, stiffened up and rudely responded, "I'm not going to sit here and confide in a stranger."

The man grinned.

"So I'm a stranger. That should make it easier for you."

"What do you mean?" Aralyn asked, annoyed.

"You don't have to worry about me telling on you or whatever it is you're worried about."

Aralyn wasn't sure what to say to that and before she knew it (and she wasn't sure *how* he did it) she found herself telling the stranger everything, about how her happy life had fallen apart a year ago. The man listened to her and was sympathetic but he didn't judge her or make her feel as though she had no right to be feeling what she was. He was sincere in all of his responses to her and he listened to everything she had to say without interruption.

After Aralyn had gotten most of her tears out, the two talked for a long time, as though they had been old friends. She found out that his name was Devin Parker and that he was a drifter; he moved from city to city, never settling in one spot. Devin somehow made Aralyn feel safe and secure again. He even made her smile a few times, which she hadn't done very much at all in the past year. He made her believe that there might be the tiniest bit of hope left in this world of hers; of solitude and darkness.

"Come on," Devin said a little while later.

He stood from the ground and held out his hand.

Aralyn was hesitant.

"To where?"

Devin smiled.

"I'm taking you home."

Aralyn narrowed her eyes a moment. Did she really want to go back? It would be so much easier for her to run and jump. But maybe she had been saved for a reason. Still hesitant, Aralyn reached up and took Devin's hand. He pulled her to her feet and kept his fingers locked with hers as he led her back towards the city.

Half an hour later, the two were under the streetlights, walking past the buildings that made up the downtown area of the city. It was quiet since it was so late at night and everyone *normal* was in bed. They didn't talk much more but Aralyn kept glancing at Devin out of the corner of her eye every now and then, wondering why he was so concerned about a stranger who was suicidal. After about the tenth time of catching her looking at him, Devin stopped walking and grinned at her.

"What?" he asked.

Aralyn shrugged, smiling, almost teasingly, and continued to walk on. Devin pulled her back by the arm, hard enough she gently hit his chest, and before she could stop him, his lips were pressed against hers. He had the softest lips she had ever kissed before, which wasn't that many, but she could tell they would have been soft to anyone's comparison. He only kissed her for a moment and then pulled away to see if she was all right with it. They smiled and Aralyn leaned in again, taking over this time. This kiss was more intense and the two were locked together in a tight embrace while their tongues found each other through their parted lips.

The moment was broken suddenly when Devin shoved Aralyn backwards, breaking them apart. She looked at him, confused, and saw that his eyes, which had been so warm at first, were now angry, as though a storm was raging inside of them.

"Fucking slut!" Devin yelled.

"Devin! What's wrong wi-"

The back of Devin's hand, colliding with her cheek, cut off Aralyn's words. She was knocked backwards even more and her back hit the bricks of an old apartment building that had been abandoned.

"Don't you *dare* use my name like that, whore!" Devin spat. He walked to her and held her against the wall, his fingers digging into her arms. "Women like you make me sick. You barely know me and already you want my cock! You thought the '*poor pitiful me*' act would work on me? You thought you could get what you want with me and then leave me like all the others have done?"

Aralyn, terrified, shook her head frantically.

"No, I'm not like that!"

"Well is *this* what you want, Aralyn?" Devin growled, ignoring her.

He smashed his lips against hers, which didn't feel so soft now, and his hand groped at her left breast. He squeezed her hard, painfully, and she cried out as best she could with his mouth over hers. Aralyn shoved him back, finding new strength in her desire to get away, and she tried to run past him but was soon thrown back into the wall. She hit so hard it knocked the breath out of her for a second.

Aralyn fought Devin and punched him in the stomach before trying to kick him in the shin. He ignored her punch, dodged her kick, and then caught her hand when she tried to hit his face. Devin held her down with one hand and produced a knife from his pocket with the other. She stopped struggling and kicking when he held the blade in front of her face.

"Try that again and I'll filet you," he warned in a dangerous whisper. He eyed her hungrily for a moment, his eyes going from her face to her breast, down the rest of her body, and back again. "Yes, that sounds excellent. Why not do it anyway?" he said thoughtfully, a sinister smile playing on his lips.

He took Aralyn's right hand in his and slowly ran the blade across her palm. Aralyn grimaced in pain and tried to pull her hand away but Devin held on to it tightly. He sneered at her terrified expression.

"What's the matter? I thought you *wanted* to die?" he asked.

Aralyn glared at him and turned her head away. She had wanted to die, yes, but not like this. He was going to make it a painful death for her. Jumping off the cliff, she would have been dead before she really felt anything. Aralyn turning away from him only infuriated Devin more and he grabbed her by her black hair and turned her head back to him.

"I want you to watch, bitch!" he yelled.

He tore the jacket from her body, leaving her arms painfully exposed since she was only wearing a black wife beater. Devin brought the knife to her right arm and then her left, making several cuts in her flesh. She cried out with each cut, but she wasn't able to run, Devin was using his body to hold her down and keep her still. She was trapped. Her tears fell from her eyes and the hot, liquid pain, hit her cold cheeks with every cut.

"Why are you doing this?" she cried several times.

What had happened to the sincere, sweet stranger that had pulled her from the cliff? If she lived through his torture, this would be another lesson learned in life; the sheep can turn out to be the wolf, no matter how things appear. Trust no one.

"Shh," Devin cooed, making another cut.

At this point, Aralyn was numb to the pain, having received so many cuts. Devin placed a finger of the knife wielding hand to Aralyn's lips, laying his cheek against hers.

"You'll see," he whispered.

He kissed her cheek, licking away some of her tears and then, to Aralyn's horror, he took one of her arms in his hands and brought it to his mouth and began licking away some of the blood. His tongue swirled around the cuts and he sucked up the blood, swallowing it. His eyes fluttered as he got some kind of sick pleasure from what he was doing.

"What the hell are you?" Aralyn whispered, wide eyed.

Devin's eyes snapped open and his expression hardened once more. For a moment, Aralyn thought he might hit her again. But he didn't.

"I'm not a fucking vampire, if that's what you're asking!" he spat harshly.

His expression softened once more, making him even more terrifying, and he ran a bloody finger along her cheekbone.

"Vampire's don't exist, sweetheart," he whispered sarcastically.

He started to raise her arm again but was suddenly slammed up against her body. Aralyn's back collided with the brick wall once more and knocked the breath from her lungs in a loud gasp. Her eyes widened at the sight before her. Standing behind Devin was a figure and it had its grasp tightly around Devin's midsection, holding him in place against Aralyn; she could feel bony fingers touching her stomach through her clothes. At Devin's neck was a mouth and there was blood running down his throat. The creature was sucking the blood from Devin's body and he was quickly losing consciousness. His eyes were bloodshot from the pressure and his breathing had become shallow.

"Guess I was wrong," he managed to whisper before his eyes rolled into the back of his head.

Aralyn tried to scream but it wouldn't come out; fear had paralyzed her and had taken her voice. Devin's life was literally being sucked away and she was forced to watch, unable to run, unable to scream. She could smell his blood and it made her nauseous. She couldn't manage to close her eyes either and was forced to stare into the cold eyes of the creature sucking Devin's blood. The creature was vibrating guttural, animal, moans into Devin's neck as it sucked. Devin's body had started to go limp so the creature pushed him even more into Aralyn to help hold him up. She felt like her lungs were being crushed and she could barely breathe.

Finally, the thing let go of Devin and let him fall to the ground. Aralyn heard him let go of his last breath and she saw crimson leaking out of two puncture marks on his neck. Devin was now dead.

Whether it was from her own blood loss, her hunger, or shock at what she had just been through and witnessed, or a combination of all, Aralyn felt her legs give out from under her and then darkness consumed her. She lost consciousness before she could get a good look at Devin's attacker.

***

Aralyn slipped in and out of consciousness, only vaguely aware that she was being carried somewhere by the creature. During one of her times of consciousness, she saw trees and buildings, flying past her in a blur. She was moving at speeds incapable of a mere human.

"But I am no human, am I, Aralyn?" the creature asked as though reading Aralyn's mind.

She was in such a daze that Aralyn wasn't sure if the voice was male or female, it sounded garbled to her, and she wasn't able to answer before she slipped into darkness once more.

The creature carried her through the city, blood flying from her arms as they dangled carelessly in the night, being carried off by the wind, while Aralyn's captor took her to a place unknown by most, deep in the forest.

Chapter Two: A Familiar Face

The room was dark, lit only by a small flame on a table beside the bed that Aralyn found herself in when she came to. She tried to push herself up but the pain from putting pressure on her wounded arms kept her from getting far and she fell back against the pillows, a soft yell escaping her lips. Bringing her arms up, she examined them in the dim light and saw that they had been wrapped, as well as her palm. Blood seeped through the bandages in spots, staining the white with browning blots. Someone had done this.

Who?

She looked around the room, hoping to find a clue that would give her even just a hint as to where she was. The walls appeared to be concrete, maybe those of a cellar or basement. There weren't any windows except for a very narrow slit at the top of the wall. Foil covered it, heavily duct taped around the edges to keep it in place.

All that was in the room was the bed she was laying in, the bedside table with the candle, and an old dresser, which had missing handles from some of the drawers. The bed wasn't anything special, just an old brass frame with an equally aged mattress that was sunken in the middle. Even though it didn't look it, the bed was actually pretty comfortable and hugged Aralyn tightly; securely. The black satin sheets felt cool on her body, which, she realized, to her horror, was naked.

Starting to panic, thinking of what might have happened while she was unconscious, Aralyn frantically looked around the room; searching for the door or any other way out. She found it in the shadows, just barely making out the edges, and the brass doorknob, in the candlelight.

Taking a deep breath, Aralyn grit her teeth, forcing herself to sit up, grimacing at the pain as the cuts seemed to rip open again. Blood rushed to her head and she was blinded for a few moments. It was only after she could see again that she felt shooting pain, and her cheek throbbing. She touched the tender flesh under her right eye and whimpered. It was bruised from where Devin had hit her.

Slowly standing from the bed, she pulled the top sheet off, to wrap around her nakedness. She steadied herself for a moment before making her way to the door where she saw more light flickering underneath. She reached out and turned the handle, slowly at first so she wouldn't make any noise, but as she pulled on the door to open it, she realized that she was locked in. Panic stricken, she shook the door violently, the sound rattling through the room.

"Let me out! Somebody, please!" she cried over and over again.

When it became clear that no one was coming to rescue her, she gave up, crying, and went back to the bed. She lay down and buried her face in the pillow, muffling her sobs. Where was she? Was she going to live? Did she really even want to? The door suddenly burst open, making her jump out of surprise, and interrupted her thoughts. Aralyn secured the sheet tighter and looked to the doorway where a figure stood in the shadows, watching her.

"Who…who are you? And what do you want with me?" Aralyn asked, her voice shaking.

"Who am I?" a gruff, female voice asked mockingly. "Maybe you need a closer look."

The figure hissed menacingly and quickly appeared beside the bed.

Aralyn shrank back against the pillows, terrified of what the woman might do to her. But as the woman neared the light and revealed her face, Aralyn gasped. She knew her. The face had changed over the last year; her skin was pale, her features flawless, her lips a dark crimson. But her eyes, those emerald green orbs, were the same.

"Claire?" Aralyn asked in disbelief.

Claire. Aralyn's sister, who had supposedly been killed in the wreck a year ago.

"The one and only," Claire responded with a wide grin.

Aralyn saw two sharp fangs, glistening with saliva in the candlelight, hanging over Claire's bottom lip.

"You…you're a…Claire, what happened?" Aralyn stuttered.

Claire's grin widened even more and became almost malicious.

"I'm a vampire now, Aralyn."

"How? When? God, Claire! You've been alive for this long-"

"Stop."

Claire held up her hand and then, when she was sure her older sister was going to stay silent, she gently sat down on the bed next to her. Aralyn watched her and noticed how her once blonde hair was now raven and fell around her shoulders in dark curls when it used to be straight and silky. Claire took her sister's trembling hand and held it against her left breast.

"You see? No heartbeat. I'm not technically alive," she whispered with a smile.

"Who…who did this…to you? And why?" Aralyn asked, barely audible.

She was trying to hold back her tears.

"Aimeric, my sire, did this to me. He saved me, Aralyn. When the car crashed, and mom went off the road, I hit my head against the dashboard. I was bleeding, very heavily. My life was slipping away. I looked over at mom; she was already dead; killed instantly. I lay in that seat, crying, and not wanting to even try. I wanted to die, the pain was too much to bear; I couldn't fight it.

"But soon, I felt my body being lifted from the car. I felt him licking away the blood on my head, which streamed down my face. He licked his way down to my neck and then I felt the pain of his teeth break my flesh and puncture my vein. I knew what he was and what he intended to do. I didn't want it. I screamed and pushed him away, wriggling free from his arms. I fell to the ground and crawled into the forest, trying to get away from him. He only laughed and followed me, saying I wouldn't be able to get away. He picked me up again and brought me here, where he finished the job.

"He drank from me, almost draining me entirely, and then he gave me a new life. He changed me, made me what I am now. I hated him for it. I hated what he had made me, but soon, I grew to love him and I learned to enjoy my life as an immortal; a child of the night. I couldn't be happier now, Aralyn."

Claire smiled warmly and, for a mere second, Aralyn thought she had her sister back. But soon, Claire's expression became cold again, showing what she really was; a monster.

"I am not a monster, Aralyn."

Claire stood up angrily and threw her sister's hand aside.

"I...Claire...I didn't," Aralyn stuttered.

She hadn't said that Claire *was* a monster. Claire was next to Aralyn again in a flash, leaning in close to her, only inches from her face.

"I can hear your thoughts. Do not lie to me!"

The look on Claire's face was murderous and her words came out in terrifying growls.

"If I'm so much of a monster, do you really think I would have saved you from that prick in the alley? No! I would have watched him beat you, cut you, even rape you. But I chose to help." A cold grin slithered onto her red lips as she seemed to be enlightened. "Maybe you need some time to think about how you should respond to me and treat me."

She stood straight up and, in a flash, was at the door.

"Claire! No, wait! Please! I'm sorry! Don't leave me!" Aralyn cried and scrambled to get out of the bed to run after her, but Claire disappeared and the door closed loudly. The locks clicked together just as Aralyn reached it. She banged her fists on the wood.

"Please! Claire! I'm sorry!"

She screamed for her sister, begging for her to let her out, but Claire didn't come back that night. Aralyn was horrified and, returning to the bed, spent most of the night crying until she found sanction in exhausted sleep.

Her sleep didn't last long. Creaking of the ceiling above woke her up. There were other people in the mansion. Why hadn't they heard her? Dust from the wood fell down on her and caught in her throat. She coughed and rolled over on to her side to escape the assault and her thoughts wandered. She was unable to get back to sleep because of them.

So Claire was a vampire? Aralyn's sister had changed so drastically. She had always been the opposite of Aralyn. Her figure had been small and fragile while Aralyn's was strong and filled out. Claire's hair had always been blonde silk cascading down her back and Aralyn's was wavy and dark. Aralyn had been the pale one, unable to tan, taking after their father. Claire had always had a beautiful tan and resembled the girls' mother. Now Claire was even paler than Aralyn, her hair was black and curly and her, once warm, eyes were now cold and evil.

A rapid scratching at the tiny window across from the bed distracted Aralyn from her thoughts. She figured it was just the wind hitting a tree branch against the window's glass but the scratching became more urgent and wouldn't stop. Cautiously, Aralyn rose from the bed, keeping the sheet around her body. The window was out of reach so she went back to the bed and pushed it underneath the window, which wasn't very far away since the room was so small. The legs of the bed frame scraped the floor and made a terrible sound, one which Aralyn was sure anyone in the house could have heard. But she didn't care. It might bring someone to her and she would be able to escape this prison.

Aralyn stood on the bed, and as the scratching became even more intense, peeled back a corner of the tape and tin foil. A surprised yell escaped her lips when she saw the two, glowing, yellow orbs staring back at her. The cat was just as startled as she was and took off into the darkness. Aralyn took a moment to calm her nerves and take a few deep breaths. The cat must have been trying to get inside in order to escape the chill of middle autumn.

Once she was calm again, Aralyn pulled back the rest of the foil and gazed outside. The room she was in was definitely underground, or at least most of it since the grass and soil was level with the window. All Aralyn's eyes could see were huge, old trees covering the property of wherever it was she was at.

There were no lights, only the soft beams of the moon, which was half full and shined through a break in the clouds. Most of the stars weren't visible through the overcast sky. The wisps of gray cotton moved over the moon and made it eerie to look at.

How long have I been here? Aralyn wondered.

It wasn't all that important of a question but what else could she think about at the time? She had already asked herself, too many times to count, what was going to happen to her and why she had upset Claire with thoughts she hadn't even realized she was thinking. There were only so many times she could ask the same questions, over and over. It became quite dull and depressing.

Aralyn's fingertips touched the cold glass and she remembered how sweet the fresh air was. She longed to breathe in its cool crispness. The room was musty and damp smelling; not at all refreshing to breathe. She might have tried to open the window but she could clearly see that it was tightly nailed shut. Besides, she had enough sense to realize that she wouldn't fit through it even if she had gotten it open, so she wouldn't be able to escape. The cat was probably even too big to fit through it. The little black creature never came back and Aralyn grew tired of looking out of her prison. She fell back on the bed and stared at the ceiling until her eyes watered. Then, forcing them closed, she drifted off to sleep once more.

***

Warm rays of sunlight caressed Aralyn's face, gently bringing her out of her slumber. She groaned and rolled over, her eyes landing on the pile of wax on the bedside table, which used to be her candle. It had burnt itself out sometime during the night. Aralyn pulled herself up and the bed creaked. The bandages pulled on her cuts with the movements and she winced and peeled back the white cloth enough to see one of the gashes. A thin scab had formed on all of them, but had been torn open again when she moved. Blood started seeping out once more. The cool air hit the cut and was making it sting so she secured the wrap around it once again and stood from the bed.

Aralyn's throat was dry. She would have given almost anything for a glass of water. The door was still closed and as far as she could tell, it was still locked. Her eyes found the dresser and she went to it and opened all of the drawers, hoping to find clothes; anything. They were all empty though. A heavy sigh found its way out of Aralyn's lungs and through her lips. Why had she trusted Devin? Why hadn't she told him to leave her alone and let her die? She had wanted to die. She *still* wanted to die. But the knowledge of her sister being alive (in one way or another) and the curiosity of where she was, kept her from taking her life at that very moment. She would probably have been too cowardly to try again anyway.

It all became too much for Aralyn. Picking up one of the dresser drawers, she yelled and flung it against the wall. The wood cracked and splintered, sending several pieces sticking out of the sides dangerously. Aralyn rushed to the door and turned the handle, jiggling it vigorously, trying to break it off. Her fists pounded the wood and she shook the whole door on its frame.

"Let me out, damn it! You sons of bitches!" she screamed. "Do you hear me? Claire! Stop being a coward and let me out of here! Talk to me!"

Blood spots appeared on the door where her fists beat. She had broken open the skin on her hands and she was bleeding. Aralyn didn't care about the sting on her fists, she gave the door one last, violent punch and fell to her knees, exhausted, hungry, thirsty, and frightened.

"Claire, what have you done to me?" she heard herself whisper, laying her head against the door.

Before she knew it, the moon was lighting up her room once more and then it was morning again. Gray daylight. The stubborn clouds had stuck around and didn't look like they would be leaving anytime soon. Aralyn was back in the bed after managing to drag herself into it the night before. This was how she was to die, she realized. Starvation and dehydration. She would perish alone in this bed that she had never known. She was content on giving up now and letting the Higher Power take her. But, what a cruel way to go. The pains of hunger became unbearable and her throat felt like it had been cut in several places due to the dryness.

Aralyn stumbled out of the bed and made her way to the broken drawer. She yanked a piece of the wood off and held the sharp point against her throat, her cheeks becoming wet with tears. She wouldn't die slowly of starvation.

"Forgive me," she whispered, closing her eyes tightly. She pushed the tip against her skin and, holding it there, began to sob violently. "Why the fuck am I such a coward!" she screamed, throwing the wood to the side.

She should have been able to kill herself in this situation. But that tiny bit of hope that the door would open kept riding on her mind and gave her doubts about taking her life.

A sudden hard and insistent pounding on the window stopped Aralyn's tears and she jerked her head around. The clouds had become too heavy and were dropping a furious sheet of water onto the earth and slamming it against the window. Aralyn jumped up from the floor and, tearing the sheet from her body, wrapped her fist up with it. Taking her protected hand, she climbed onto the bed and covered her eyes before smashing the window. She peeled away the broken glass and threw the sheet to the floor. Cupping her hands together, Aralyn held them out the window, gathering up the rain to bring to her mouth. She drank what she could, wetting her throat and soothing her tongue. She drank for as long as the rain fell down, not completely satisfying her thirst, but enough that she didn't feel so horrible. It was just a quick downpour and it was over just as suddenly as it had started.

Aralyn was unsure of how long she had been in that awful room, but when the door finally opened, she was so close to death that she no longer cared.

Chapter Three: 'Virgil'

Weak with hunger, her throat still dry and her skin itching where her cuts were trying to heal, Aralyn wasn't feeling up to rejoicing when the door creaked open that night. The wounds on her arms had been wrapped in the same cloth for however long she had been stuck down in that room. To her it seemed an eternity. She had been prepared to die, and silently prayed for it to come soon.

She lay still on the bed, weak and naked, covered only by the sheet. She almost seemed glued to the mattress. She heard the door open, but was too weak to roll over and see if it was Claire or not. She was too weak to even talk.

Aralyn felt someone sit on the bed beside her and then a cold hand brushed her hair out of her eyes and away from her face. The hand was strong and that of a male; not that it was rough but it wasn't as delicate as a woman's. The hand slipped under Aralyn's neck and down her back as the man lifted her into a sitting position and held her against his chest while also keeping the sheet around her.

"Open your mouth," a deep voice commanded.

Aralyn heard him but she didn't respond. She just stared straight ahead, her eyes lifeless. The man brought a cool glass to her lips.

"Come on, open your mouth and take a drink." His voice was softer, friendlier, this time.

The very thought of feeling cool liquid running down her throat was enough to convince Aralyn. It had only rained the one time and she wasn't sure how long it had been since Claire had left her. Aralyn parted her lips and allowed the man to tip the glass, pouring the soothing water over her dry tongue. As soon as it hit her throat, it gave her enough incentive to grab the glass and drink greedily.

"Not so much at once, you'll make yourself sick."

The man pulled back on the glass a little and Aralyn returned to calmly sipping the water until it was gone. She leaned back in the man's arms, still too weak to move much on her own and feeling comfort in his strong grasp.

"Are you hungry?" the man asked.

Aralyn nodded and he reached to the bedside table, and brought a bowl of fruit in front of her. She reached out and grabbed for it but he pulled it away.

"Same with the food. Don't go too fast," the man warned.

Aralyn looked up at him for the first time, peering into his dark brown eyes, which were flecked with red. The man, or rather, vampire, as he had fangs too, was incredibly handsome. Not only were his eyes mesmerizing, but his hard facial features and midnight black hair, which fell loosely to his chin, was enough to make any woman melt. Not to mention that his body was incredibly toned. Aralyn could see this through the silk pants and shirt he wore; they outlined almost everything. She didn't have the strength to form a crush on him, however. She was far too hungry for that. Aralyn's head moved slowly in a light nod in response to the man's warning and he handed her the bowl. Hard as it was, she took small bites and ate the fruit slowly, until it was gone. Aralyn was still hungry when she finished but her stomach was at least satisfied for now. Once she finished, the man gently let go of her and stood from the bed. Now strong enough to sit up on her own and hold the sheet over her bare body, Aralyn looked at the pale-faced stranger and peered into his dark eyes.

"Who are you?" Aralyn asked curiously.

"My name is Virgil," the man said simply.

"Where is my sister?" Aralyn asked.

"I'm not sure. She comes and goes as she pleases. Who knows when she will be back?" he responded, sounding bitter.

Aralyn sadly looked down at her lap. She felt guilty for being the reason Claire left, or so she assumed was the reason. She had offended her sister with thoughts she hadn't even been aware she was thinking. Aralyn wondered if Claire would ever come back for her or if she would be stuck in this strange place forever. Wherever "this place" was. Aralyn looked back up at Virgil as this thought came to mind.

"Where am I? And how long have I been here?"

"You've been here for almost a week now, and you're in Aimeric's mansion. We're in his basement right now."

"Aimeric?" Aralyn repeated. "The vampire who-"

"Turned your sister?" Virgil interrupted and finished with a soft chuckle.

"Yes," Aralyn whispered, looking down at her lap once more.

"He's the master of this house. He is now your master too, Aralyn. Until your sister returns…if she decides to," Virgil said, hardness added to his tone as he said the last words.

"'Master'? What the hell do you mean?" Aralyn asked, indignant.

Virgil chuckled and clasped his hands behind his back, staring at Aralyn and holding her glare as though he were about to receive immense pleasure from what he was about to tell her.

"You're under your sister's protection for now. But if she takes too long in coming back, which I'm sure she will, you will belong to Aimeric entirely and he won't be too easy on you. Not to mention, I'm sure most of us won't be able to resist tasting your sweet blood and unless your sister returns, you *will* be taken. Odds are, Aimeric will not protect you. You will be dead in no time, or maybe turned into Aimeric's pet. Who can say for sure?"

Virgil laughed again, making Aralyn's skin crawl.

"Well don't get any ideas. My sister *will* be back."

Though the words came from Aralyn's mouth, she wasn't sure she believed them herself; Claire had, after all, locked her in this room and left her to die. She wasn't the loving sister that Aralyn remembered. Virgil smirked and, unclasping his hands, held one of them out.

Aralyn glared at it and then at him.

"What?" she demanded.

"I thought you might like to come with me and get cleaned up. Maybe put on some clothes?" Virgil grinned and eyed her body, which was barely covered. "Or do you prefer the sheet?"

Still glaring, Aralyn hesitantly took Virgil's hand. He pulled her off the bed and helped her weak legs support her own weight. Aralyn hastily adjusted the sheet and then slipped out of Virgil's arms, walking to the door on wobbling legs. She hadn't liked Virgil's attitude and therefore was determined to walk on her own, even though she felt like a ton of bricks had fallen on her.

"Wait."

Virgil grabbed her arm as she went by.

Aralyn glared at him, silently asking what the hell he wanted while also scolding him for having the nerve to touch her.

"You don't want to go out there like that."

"Well how do you propose I *do* go out there? There aren't any clothes in here, I looked," Aralyn argued snidely.

Virgil smirked again and, without warning, pulled her against his chest. Aralyn gasped at how cold he was, even through the shirt, and began to struggle when his arm slipped around her waist.

"Stop that! This is for your own good!" Virgil yelled.

Aralyn stopped struggling and looked at him, half curious, half angry; willing to listen to an explanation, but ready to kick him in the privates if he tried anything.

"You need to pretend you're with me, otherwise, they'll pick a beauty like you clean before you can take two steps," Virgil explained gruffly.

Aralyn, blushing slightly at the "beauty" comment, started to ask what he was talking about but she closed her mouth again almost immediately. Virgil had started walking with her. He went through the door and into a dark passageway, lit only by torches. The cement walls were wet with condensation and mold, and moss grew on the chipped surface in some places.

The set of concrete stairs that Virgil led Aralyn up looked like they would crumble under even a small child's weight. They held though, surprisingly, and the two reached the top where a chipped, wooden door was closed. Virgil kicked it open and smirked at Aralyn as though she was supposed to be impressed by his "might." Aralyn rolled her eyes at his foolish attempt. Looking ahead in the room they had entered, Aralyn gasped, tightening her fingers around the sheet. They were in a huge living room that looked like it had probably been an elegant ballroom back in its day. But not now. The floors were dirty and the walls were stained with what looked like blood. They had holes in them and the old wallpaper was turning yellow and curling at the corners. Torn couches and chairs were arranged all around the room and centered around an old television.

What had made Aralyn gasp though were the people on the couches, in the chairs, and leaning against the disgusting walls. There were at least two-dozen, rough looking, men and women in the room.

More vampires Aralyn thought to herself.

She found herself clinging to Virgil with her free hand while the other made sure the private parts of her body were covered. The vampires smelled her untainted blood immediately and they also sensed her fear. They stopped what they had been doing; watching television, performing all kinds of pleasure on one another, or just leaning, casually, against the walls to watch everyone else around them, so they, male and female could stare at her.

Aralyn shook with fear and clutched at Virgil so tightly that her nails dug into the flesh of his back. He didn't seem to notice though and he held her tighter, protectively, eyeing the other vampires and giving them warning glares; this one was his. When they walked through the room, the vampires whistled and hollered at Aralyn.

"Well, well, look what we have here."

"She's beautiful."

"A virgin. Smells delicious."

"Aw, look how scared she is. How wonderful."

These were some of the comments Aralyn heard the vampires say, making her heart beat wildly and fearful. She was so terrified that her stomach was tied up in knots and the food she had eaten was threatening to come up. She hid her face in Virgil's chest and refused to look at any of their horrifyingly beautiful faces.

"You're not going to keep her all to yourself now are you, Virgil? " a squeaky voice with a British accent asked.

Virgil stopped walking and Aralyn risked a glance to see whom the voice belonged to. They had stopped at a set of stairs that curved up to the second floor of the mansion. A man was standing at the base of the stairs, blocking the way. He was a middle-aged man, maybe in his late forties. His face was long and reminded Aralyn of a horse. He had a slim nose, which ended in a sharp point and his beady, cobalt eyes looked down it, staring at Aralyn.

"Move out of the way, Morgan," Virgil sneered.

"Now don't be selfish, Virgil. Does Master Aimeric even know you brought out Claire's wench of a sister?" Morgan didn't give time to answer. "Of course he must 'ave. Even *you* wouldn't risk his temper over a piece of ass, not when you could easily find another out on the streets. Even so, why don't you give us a taste?" Morgan reached out for Aralyn but was immediately knocked to the floor by Virgil.

"Don't touch her! She's mine!" Virgil yelled.

Morgan's shell of security had broken and he was cowering pathetically. Aralyn panicked and began to cry out, thinking that this had all been a trap and Virgil was leading her upstairs to her death after he planned on doing God knows what else.

"Alrigh'! Damn, I'm sorry! Have her all to yourself!" Morgan whined, crawling away, giving Virgil room to pass by.

Aralyn broke out of Virgil's grasp and started to run away. He caught her arm and roughly pulled her back against him.

"Where do you think you're going? You can't escape! They're all just waiting for you, love," he growled harshly against her ear.

Aralyn screamed and Virgil picked her up. He slung her over his shoulder, the sheet just barely covering her rear.

"Let me go!" Aralyn screamed and pounded on his back.

She didn't have the strength to do any damage though and soon gave up as Virgil climbed the stairs with her. They reached the second floor and Virgil walked down a creaky, dark hallway. Aralyn heard a door click open and then slam shut before she was tossed onto a large canopy bed. She scrambled, terrified, into a sitting position and saw that she had been taken into a bedroom, lit only by the beams of a full moon, which had managed to find a way through a gap in the heavy, black, drapes. Trying to be menacing, Aralyn glared at Virgil with false fire in her eyes, which he saw right through. Anyone could have. Aralyn's whole body was shaking and Virgil was sure he could see the heavy beating of her mortal heart hitting her chest and vibrating the sheet.

"What the hell were you thinking? I told you to stay with me!" Virgil said angrily in a loud whisper.

"You intend on sucking me dry, don't you?" Aralyn sneered, her voice shaky and choked.

Virgil smirked.

"Now, now, love. Let's save *that* for the honeymoon."

"You know what I mean! You said I was 'yours'!" Aralyn hissed.

"Oh for the love of…" Virgil shook his head in frustration and threw his arms into the air. "I said that you were 'mine' so they wouldn't try and drain you! I didn't mean it!"

Aralyn suddenly felt foolish. Of course he had meant that; he had told her before they left the basement that she needed to pretend to be with him. She was too proud to admit she was wrong and apologize however, so she just averted her eyes to the bed and twisted the sheet around her finger. Virgil eyed her for a few minutes and then sighed, irritated, before he went to the other side of the room and opened a door. Aralyn glared after him as he disappeared through the doorway and a few seconds later, she heard water running into, what she guessed was, a bathtub.

After a minute or two more, Virgil came back out not saying a word, and went to a closet across from the foot of the bed where he rummaged around inside. He turned back to Aralyn and tossed a piece of black clothing on the bed beside her.

"Take your bath and then put on that dress. It's Claire's, but I'm sure she won't mind. When you're done I'll give you more to eat, so hurry up." Virgil's words came out harshly and then he stormed out of the room, slamming the door behind him making Aralyn flinch.

Maybe she should have apologized.

Sliding her legs over the edge of the bed and then moving off the mattress, Aralyn quickly made her way into the bathroom. She locked the door, not knowing if it would do any good at keeping anyone out, but figuring she should at least try. After making sure no one was hiding and waiting for her inside, she let the sheet fall to the floor and then stepped into the old fashioned, claw foot bathtub. The hot water covered her exhausted body and she sighed in content. For now at least, she was relaxed.

It was only after she was mostly submerged that Aralyn realized her arms were still wrapped in the bandages. She pulled the cloth back and grimaced, gritting her teeth, as the gauze pulled on the wounds, ripping off the scabs that had formed, and allowed fresh blood to seep. The air hit them and made them hurt even more. Aralyn took a moment to breathe and then began to pull the bandages off her other arm. Before unraveling them, she held her arm under the water, letting the gauze get soaked so that it would be easier to peel off. The water stung her cuts, bringing tears to her eyes, but she thought it was better than slowly pulling the scabs off. Once they were removed, Aralyn quickly washed her hair and her body, including the cuts, which hurt like hell.

She stepped out of the tub (the water was tinted red from the blood on her arms) and wrapped a towel around her glistening body. She went back into the bedroom to retrieve whatever clothes Virgil had tossed at her. Picking up the silky cloth from the bed, Aralyn examined it quickly before slipping the dress over her head. It was black with a red sequined rose stitched onto the right shoulder. The sleeves were short and puffy and the dress went down to her ankles. It was simple, but pretty. After she was clothed, Aralyn tossed the towel into the bathroom and ran her fingers through her tangled hair before cautiously approaching the bedroom door. She stopped and listened, laying her head against it for a few moments. She didn't hear anything so she turned the door handle and opened it.

The door was suddenly flung the rest of the way open from the other side, making Aralyn jump backwards and yell softly out of surprise. Virgil smirked at her and she breathed a sigh of relief that it was only him. Of course, feeling her heart ready to jump out of her chest, she didn't hold herself back from punching Virgil on the shoulder.

"You scared the shit out of me!" she said in a loud whisper.

Virgil laughed and grabbed her wrist as she went to hit him again for laughing at her. His smile faded as he peered at her bloody arm.

"You can't go anywhere until those cuts are wrapped," he said, sounding sincere.

"I...couldn't find anything," Aralyn admitted, blushing slightly at the softness of his cold hand holding her arm.

"Come here then."

Virgil led her back into the adjoining bathroom, where he rummaged through a few cupboards. He brought out rubbing alcohol and more gauze. Aralyn's eyes widened at the sight of the alcohol.

"You aren't going to use that, are you?" she asked.

Virgil looked at her dumbfounded for a moment and then smiled.

"No, I'm going to drink it," he said sarcastically.

He became serious when Aralyn glared at him.

"You need to clean the cuts or they'll get infected," he explained calmly.

Aralyn nodded but didn't respond in any other way, dreading what was about to happen.

"Give me your arm."

Aralyn surrendered one of her arms and Virgil gave her a mock sympathetic expression, making her even angrier, before he poured the alcohol over her cuts. The pain was blinding, breathtaking. She thought she might pass out. Gasping, Aralyn, tried to yank her arm free but Virgil held tight and continued to pour. He let the liquid soak into the wounds for a minute, grinning to himself at the tears Aralyn couldn't help but let escape. Finally, Virgil wiped away the excess liquid and wrapped her arm with the clean gauze.

"You're enjoying this, aren't you?" Aralyn asked angrily, seeing the amused expression on his face.

"Yup." Virgil smirked again and took her other arm. "You women just make too big a deal of things. It doesn't hurt *that* bad."

"How 'bout if I cut you up and then pour this shit all over your wounds? Then you could see how it feels," Aralyn snapped.

"Trust me, babe. I *know* how it feels. I've had a lot worse done to me," Virgil said, readying the bottle once more.

Aralyn continued to glare but didn't say anything and then grimaced when the blinding pain hit her again. She bit her lip to keep from crying out, though she could do nothing to stop a new round of tears. After both arms, and Aralyn's right hand, had been cleaned and re-wrapped, Virgil put away the supplies and turned back to her. She was still crying softly but trying to hide it by looking at the floor. Stepping up to her, Virgil raised her chin to look into her violet eyes. Aralyn turned her head and avoided him.

"Don't cry, I'm sure your sister will be back," Virgil said.

His voice was surprisingly soothing and serious.

"I'm not…crying…because of that," Aralyn said through her tears.

"Then what is it?" Virgil asked.

"I don't know! I guess my arms hurt…"

Virgil laughed and pulled her into a quick hug.

"You'll be fine."

Vampires Don't Exist by Reyanna Vance

He was still chuckling when they pulled apart but as he found her eyes again, his smile faded and he saw just how beautiful this girl, standing before him, really was. Aralyn saw his eyes as they looked into hers and she knew what he had intended on doing before he did it. Virgil brought his hand up, stroking her soft cheek and leaned in to kiss her. Remembering how her last kiss with a stranger ended, she turned her head before he could reach her lips.

Virgil stopped, inches from her cheek and sighed.

"I'm sorry."

"It's okay," Aralyn said softly, but refused to look at him.

There was an awkward silence between the two of them until Virgil finally took Aralyn's hand.

"Come on, I'll take you to the kitchen and you can get some more food to eat," he said.

Aralyn nodded and allowed Virgil to lead her out of the room. When they reached the top of the stairs, she pulled away, fearing the vampires downstairs.

"Don't worry. They've all gone out for the night to feed," he said, reassuring her and held out his hand again.

Aralyn took a deep breath and hesitantly took it. She sighed in relief when she and Virgil entered the old living room and saw that it was empty and the house was deathly quiet. Good. No more vampires. Virgil took Aralyn to the kitchen, which was in as bad of shape as the rest of the house, or what Aralyn had seen of it anyway. The walls had holes in them, as though someone had punched them, the lights on the ceiling were hanging by their wires, the countertops were dirty, and, like every other room in this mansion so far, blood stained the walls. Aralyn didn't want to think about how the blood got there but she knew without having to and it made her sick.

"I'm going to leave for a little while, but I will be back before the others," Virgil said, interrupting Aralyn's thoughts.

He opened an old refrigerator, took out a plate of fruit, and gestured for Aralyn to sit down at the splintered table in the center of the room. She sat, not caring that the table was dirty. She was only focused on her own hunger at the moment. Virgil set the fruit down along with some bread and Aralyn began eating immediately, hungrily. While eating, she wondered why there was such food in a house full of vampires. She soon came to the conclusion that these creatures probably liked to "play" with their food and keep them alive for a few days. She quickly shook the image from her mind.

"Where will you go?" Aralyn asked in late response to his announcement of departing.

Even if only for a little while, she was afraid of being left alone in the house. How could Virgil even guarantee that he would be back before the others?

"I have to...feed," Virgil responded, avoiding her curious violet eyes.

"You mean kill?" Aralyn sneered harshly.

Virgil stood up abruptly and slammed his fists on the table, making her flinch.

"We do what we have to in order to survive," he growled, inches from her face.

Aralyn stood from her seat, raising Virgil's line of vision to meet hers. She was tired of being afraid and wasn't going to allow this creature to intimidate her.

"You're all murderers," she whispered maliciously, her teeth clenched tight.

Virgil snorted in anger and grabbed her arm, digging his fingernails into her flesh. Without a word, he dragged her through the kitchen and back to the cellar stairs. He shoved her through the doorway, still not saying anything, and slammed the door shut behind her, two different locks clicking on the other side. Aralyn was left standing at the top of the crumbling stairs.

She spun around and pounded on the door, screaming at the top of her lungs, almost like a child being punished, "I hate you!"

She then turned back around and descended the stairs in a huff, steadying herself on the moss-covered wall. When she reached the bottom step, she heard an echoing cough and stopped dead still.

Someone was in the basement with her.

Chapter Four: Fear and Punishment

Aralyn gazed down the dimly lit (by torches) passageway and saw an old oak door at the end that she hadn't seen before. The reason being that when she had left her room with Virgil, she had gone right and the door was to the left. She hadn't seen anything except what had been ahead of her; she hadn't had the chance to explore any area of the house except for the places that she had been taken to. The door had metal bars on it as though it needed some reinforcement added. There was a tiny window at the top of the door, which Aralyn could see more flickering torchlight through.

Curiosity getting the better of her, Aralyn slowly began to creep forward, towards the door. She heard another cough, followed by, what sounded like sobbing. She had a bad feeling coming from her gut but, for some reason, she couldn't turn back. Her eyes were focused on the door and only the door. Until a rat scurried past her that is. It broke her line of vision with the door for a second and she yelped as it barely missed her toes. Gaining control again, Aralyn continued to the door. When she reached it, she pressed her ear against the wood, in a break in the bars, and listened. She heard more coughing, sobbing and soft, painful moaning.

Aralyn turned the handle slowly and entered the room. It was dark, only lit by one torch across from the door. A wall of stench hit Aralyn like a wave crashing over her head. She smelled blood, festering wounds, urine and feces, and not to mention the musty smell from lack of fresh air. It was nauseating and she had to cover her nose. She could hear more rats, and probably insects, scurrying above her in the rafters and also, below at her feet. She was careful to step lightly.

Looking up, Aralyn let out a loud gasp. Rope, tied in nooses, hung from the ceiling. There were chains, whips, and cuffs, hanging on the walls, all stained with blood. Just in front of her was a large, metal table with four, large, protruding spikes. They were positioned one at each corner of the rectangle and they too were stained and caked with blood and, what looked like, pieces of flesh. Next to the large table was a small, surgeon's table with several tools, sharp and dull, all having the same brown tinge of dried blood.

A torture chamber. Aralyn was standing in the middle of a true torture chamber. Her mind was telling her to run but Aralyn's body wasn't listening. She was paralyzed, her feet stuck to the floor. She couldn't run.

"Who are you?" a weak voice asked.

Aralyn turned her head to the right side of the room and saw two huge cages along the wall. The sight brought tears to her eyes. Inside the cages were humans, most in their teens or early twenties, male and female. They were all dirty and wounded in one way or another. Crusting wounds were on their arms, legs, faces, anywhere that was visible and probably more where they weren't. They looked so pitiful, Aralyn's heart reached out to them. They didn't look underfed, however. In fact, as far as weight went, they all looked pretty healthy. It suddenly dawned on Aralyn. These people were being well fed so they could be kept as pets. So they could be kept alive so they would be ready for torture whenever *whoever* wanted. Of course there were a few that were incredibly thin, as though they had given up and were waiting to die, refusing to fight to stay alive any longer and who could blame them in these conditions? What kind of person, or rather, *animal*, could do this?

The people were terrified. Some were huddled into the corners, hugging themselves while weeping. Others had appeared to have given up all hope in living and were lying on the cold, dirty floor as though just waiting for that last breath to escape them, so *they* themselves could escape this awful prison.

"Well?" the voice asked. It was a female, maybe the same age as Aralyn. "Who are you? Another one of *his* scum? Have you come here to get some sick pleasure like the rest-"

She cut off her own words, looking up, terrified.

Aralyn turned around to see what the girl was so scared of, ready to run if she needed to, which she was sure she would. Aralyn gasped again when she turned to find Morgan, the vampire from earlier, standing so close to her that she could smell his putrid breath, which reeked of blood.

"'aven't you ever been told not to go snoopin' around in a house that doesn't belong to you?" Morgan asked.

Before Aralyn knew what happened, Morgan had backhanded her so hard that she fell onto the floor and was being straddled by the vampire. He held her wrists down against the cold floor and Aralyn found it hard to breathe with him on top of her.

"Get off of me!" she screamed and struggled beneath him.

Morgan laughed. Some of the prisoners had scrambled to stand up and peer through the bars to see what Morgan would do to this mysterious girl. She obviously wasn't a vampire, they could tell that now. Probably another one of Morgan or Aimeric's pets; playthings. They watched anxiously to see what he was going to do.

Would Morgan rape her? Drain her? "Play" with her? He would probably do all three, though they shuddered to think in what order. Morgan was about as sick as they came.

"You're a feisty one, ain't ya?" Morgan said as Aralyn continued to struggle.

She couldn't do much since she was pinned and trapped beneath him, but she had to at least *try* and get him off of her. Morgan finished laughing and then his voice became dangerously low and he leaned down to Aralyn's neck.

"Let's see how you taste."

Morgan opened his mouth and licked at the flesh on Aralyn's neck, tasting the pulse beneath her skin first. He sniffed it and savored it for a moment and then Aralyn screamed when his fangs penetrated her, going deep into the vein. He drew out only a little of the blood first and then licked it away, moving his tongue all the way up to Aralyn's cheek. She cried out and struggled some more, even though it was useless. The vampire was just too strong for her. What was worse, Aralyn could feel a hard bulge against her abdomen. Morgan had become aroused on top of her and she doubted he would control himself. She just had to wait for the perfect moment to knee him and then get away. She stopped struggling, saving her strength for that moment.

Morgan was back at her neck, licking away more blood, now savoring the taste instead of the scent. He moaned deeply and began rocking slightly against Aralyn as though trying to tell his erection to "be patient," that he would satisfy the ache soon enough. Aralyn felt as though she would vomit and prayed he would hurry up and give her her chance.

"Morgan. That's enough," a deep voice smoothly, yet authoritatively, commanded.

In a flash, Morgan jumped off of Aralyn, wiping his mouth, and staring, terrified, at the doorway. Aralyn lifted herself up on her elbows and, through eyes that glistened with salty tears, she saw two icy, blue eyes staring at her. The eyes belonged to a man and he was leaning against the doorframe with his arms crossed. He was smirking.

"Master Aimeric, I- I'm sorry. I just wanted a little taste and I…" Morgan stuttered.

His cool exterior was gone. Morgan was terrified of the man in front of him. Aralyn wanted to know why. She wasn't sure if she had someone to thank for the interruption, or someone new to fear. Aimeric. Aralyn remembered the name as Claire's sire, the one who had turned her into a vampire.

"Leave us," the man ordered calmly, speaking to Morgan.

"Y-yes sir."

Morgan scuttled out of the room, careful not to touch Aimeric as he went by him. Groaning softly, Aralyn pulled herself the rest of the way up into a sitting position. She touched the place on her neck that Morgan had bitten and felt blood. It wasn't a lot, nothing to be concerned about, really, but it hurt like hell. When she looked up, Aralyn saw that Aimeric was staring down at her, a cold look in his eyes. Just looking at him, Aralyn was covered in chills. She had a feeling Aimeric was feared for a reason. She wanted to get away from him, away from those eyes, which looked as though they were made of ice.

Scooting away, wanting to put as much distance between herself and Aimeric as possible, Aralyn felt her back hit against the metal table. Aimeric chuckled, amused at her terror, and then, seeing that the prisoners were watching them both, he sneered.

"Get back to the floor like the animals you are unless you want to come out and *play*," Aimeric hissed malevolently.

They knew what he meant by "play," and they didn't want to encourage him. Every one of the prisoners moved as far back as they could in the cages and fell to the floor, making sure not to make eye contact with either Aimeric or Aralyn. Aimeric moved forward. His steps were soft, he didn't make a sound. His aura screamed evil and Aralyn's very soul was struck with fear. Her body shook the closer he came to her and she almost looked to be in convulsions when Aimeric reached her. He knelt down beside her, inches away and cocked his head to the side in mock sympathy. His jet-black hair, which went to his waist, fell into his eyes. He didn't bother to brush it away, he only stared at Aralyn through the gaps of the curtain and, terrified as she was, Aralyn couldn't look away. She was drawn into him. Aimeric only stared at her for a moment, a malicious grin playing upon his crimson lips, and then he reached out with icy fingers and ran them along the side of Aralyn's face, making her cringe.

"Claire has told me all about you," Aimeric said, his voice the falsity of an angel. "I fear, however, that her description of you was inaccurate. You're far more beautiful than she let on and, had I known that, I may have come to introduce myself sooner."

Aralyn wanted to give him a sarcastic response, something similar to, "gee, I'm sorry we weren't acquainted sooner, you seem such a joy to be around," but she couldn't find the words. She could barely breathe.

Aimeric's fingers ran down her face and onto her neck where the blood seeped out. He touched it and then brought the few drops to his lips, his eyes never leaving Aralyn's, and he licked it away, almost provocatively.

"You're delicious," he whispered.

Finally able to look away, Aralyn glanced at the prisoners, her breathing becoming heavy as she saw the terror in their eyes. This man was evil, she could sense it. It was the only explanation for her body's trembling and the prisoner's behavior. Aralyn wasn't looking at Aimeric, but she could certainly feel his eyes all over her. The feeling was disturbing. She felt violated. When Aralyn turned back to Aimeric, she saw that he was grinning.

"Are you afraid of me?" he asked, delight in his voice.

Aralyn looked at the prisoners once more. *They* feared him, why shouldn't she? Placing two cold fingers under her chin, Aimeric turned Aralyn back to him.

"I promised my dear Claire that I wouldn't allow harm to come to you and I always keep my promises, dear Aralyn. There's no need to be afraid…yet," Aimeric said.

"Yet?" Aralyn whispered, her voice trembling to go with her body.

Aimeric's eyes widened with delight.

"Ah, so you *can* speak. Oh, sweet Aralyn, your sister can't expect us to keep you alive forever. Especially not when she ran off and just left you here to tempt us." Aimeric licked his lips, staring at the puncture marks on Aralyn's neck. "Even *I* have weaknesses, and," he lowered his voice to an almost seductive tone, "your sweet, virgin, blood is one of them."

Aralyn began to cry, the tears falling down her cheeks, one after the other.

"Oh you don't have to worry right now. I won't harm you as long as you obey the rules," Aimeric said.

"Rules?" Aralyn asked in disbelief.

What was he? Some kind of tyrant?

Aimeric grinned.

"Yes. Rules. I make them and everyone here obeys them or they are punished."

Aralyn's face contorted in anger. She wasn't as afraid suddenly.

"Fuck you! I'm not going to agree to obey to some rules made by a bully, just so I can stay in this creepy house! I want out of this place now, I don't care what Claire says!"

Aimeric frowned, glaring at her and she glared right back at him. Fire seemed to consume the ice in Aimeric's eyes and before Aralyn knew what was going on, she was brought to her feet, her back shoved against the table, and Aimeric had his hard body pressed against her, his hands on either side of her, on the table.

"Wrong answer, *sweetheart*," Aimeric growled against Aralyn's cheek.

Aralyn was filled with fear once again, her sudden courage gone as quickly as it had arrived. Aimeric's tongue slithered out of his mouth and he quickly licked away the rest of the blood that had started to dry on Aralyn's neck. When he was finished, he looked back into Aralyn's eyes and grinned coldly.

"Perhaps you need to be made aware of what the punishments can be for those who refuse to follow them. And, Aralyn, my sweet, you aren't going anywhere, so you may as well get used to the idea of this being your new home and me being your master," Aimeric hissed.

He grabbed Aralyn, roughly, by the shoulders and took her to the wall next to one of the cages. Aimeric slammed Aralyn's body, hard, into the wall and cuffed her wrists into a set of chains.

"What are you doing?" Aralyn asked, her voice shaking again.

Aimeric's smile was reptilian as he ran his finger down Aralyn's neck and onto her breast where the dress didn't cover.

"I'm going to show you what will happen if you disobey," he said simply. Aimeric kissed her quickly, licking at her bottom lip, and when he pulled away, he was sneering. "Watch closely now," he said.

Aimeric clasped his hands behind his back and then walked back and forth between the two cages. Aralyn followed him with her eyes, wondering what he had in mind and what he had meant by "watch closely."

"Which one will it be?" Aimeric asked as though he were making a business deal.

"What?" Aralyn asked confused, though deep inside, she knew what he meant.

Aimeric sighed, irritated, dramatically.

"Which one will pay for *your* mistake?"

"You can't be serious!" Aralyn said.

Aimeric appeared directly in front of her, inches from her face, and she jumped at the sudden sight of him, the back of her head hitting the wall out of surprise.

"Oh, but I am," Aimeric hissed. "This is only one of the many ways I can punish you, my sweet."

"Don't call me that, you sick fuck!" Aralyn spat harshly.

The vampire chuckled ironically.

"Oh, how bold you are…But not for long. Once I am through with you, you *will* learn to respect me and hold your tongue and think *very* hard before opening your mouth to defy me." He waved a hand back at the cages. "Now, choose a 'playmate.'"

Aralyn shook her head.

"No. I won't."

Aimeric spun around and slammed his hands on either side of the wall, near Aralyn's head.

"Did you just say, 'you won't'?" he growled.

Aralyn nodded, trying to show courage even though her insides were torn up and in knots and she wanted nothing more than to just be away from this creature.

"Is that so?" Aimeric whispered. He stared at her for what seemed like forever, even though it was only a few seconds, his eyes challenging hers. "Since you're new here and don't know any better, *and* you don't seem to learn all that quickly, I'll let you get away with that once. And then, when you see what happens, perhaps you'll have enough sense to not go against me again," Aimeric said warningly.

He pushed off the wall and moved so quickly that Aralyn didn't see him, so to her eyes, it was as though he disappeared and then reappeared again in front of the first cage. Aimeric flung open the door, the hinges squealing and echoing through the small dungeon, and grabbed a young girl by the red flames of her hair and pulled her out. She was only about sixteen or so and she desperately tried to fight Aimeric.

Aimeric didn't even seem to notice her flailing though. Not at first anyway. Once the gate was shut again, he pulled the girl to his chest and began petting down her hair and swaying her in his arms. Aralyn watched curiously, but still terrified for the girl. The girl, to Aralyn's shock and amazement, had calmed down immensely. It looked like Aimeric was trying to soothe the girl, to let her know that she would be okay, but Aralyn's gut told her otherwise. She remembered from horror books and television shows how fictional vampires had some sort of mysterious power given to calm their victims before they killed them. Could this be what Aimeric was doing? Only days before, Aralyn would have laughed at such things. She, like so many others, had never believed before that vampires were real. They had always been characters in fiction. Now, she knew better and she wished she didn't. Aimeric held the girl's shoulders, pulling her gently from his chest, and looked into her eyes.

"You don't want to die, do you?" he asked in a mock sympathetic tone.

Red curls moved back and forth, vigorously, as the girl shook her head.

"No, please, don't kill me," the girl begged.

Aimeric ran his fingers through her hair and then cupped her face in his hands. He kissed her, sickeningly gently, and she seemed to melt into him, as though the two were lovers. She was in a trance, it seemed to Aralyn. There was no way she could actually be enjoying kissing that monster. Aimeric's hands slid down to the girl's breasts and he cupped and fondled them gently. She deepened the kiss and urged him to do more.

Aralyn didn't care to see any of that so she turned her head away and looked at the other prisoners. They were all still frightened. They knew what was going to happen.

"You won't die, my beauty. I'll make sure of that."

Aralyn heard Aimeric's voice and turned back to see that he was now leading the girl to the metal table. The girl's eyes were lifeless and she walked with Aimeric as though she didn't care what he was going to do to her. Aimeric picked her up and laid her down on the table. That was when she came back to life, when Aimeric released her. She started screaming and kicking her feet.

"No!"

The word came out of the girl's mouth over and over, becoming strangled with each cry, as Aimeric held her down and strapped a thick leather belt around her waist, holding her body against the surface of the table. The girl kicked as hard as she could, sending her heels slamming down on the metal, pounding the horrible sound all through the basement level of the mansion.

"What are you doing! Stop it!" Aralyn screamed.

Aimeric ignored her and continued to strap the girl, now working on her legs.

"Please! No! …No!" the girl begged.

Her voice was choked with tears.

Aralyn had begun crying too. She didn't know exactly what Aimeric had planned, but she knew it wouldn't be a good thing and she didn't want to see it. She closed her eyes tightly, sobbing quietly, and turned away.

"Aralyn, look at me," Aimeric demanded.

She shook her head, keeping her eyes closed.

"Watch, or I will make it last longer than it has to," Aimeric sneered.

Hesitantly, Aralyn opened her eyes and looked back at the girl and Aimeric. He had strapped the girl down completely now; she couldn't move. Her legs were confined at the ankles and her arms were strapped just below the elbow, over her head. The girl was raising her arms as best she could, which was only a few inches, and balling her hands into fists, trying to move the rest of her body. Aralyn glared at Aimeric, trying to cover her fear.

The room was deathly quiet, the air thick with anticipation, fear, and hate. Aimeric glared back at Aralyn and then took the girl's hand in his.

"Please, no…" the girl continued to sob.

"Watch, Aralyn," Aimeric hissed coldly, keeping eye contact with her. "Are you gritting your teeth, darling?" he then asked the girl.

The girl's sobs became harder.

Violently, Aimeric slammed the girl's hand down on the spike at the corner of the table.

"No!" Aralyn screamed at the same time the girl let out a blood-curdling shriek.

The spike was now protruding from the girl's palm, blood running down the sides and onto her arm. Aralyn cried for the girl, her sobs becoming louder. She turned her head again, not able to look at the horrifying sight before her. The girl had finally stopped screaming but she was breathing hard, in pain.

"You know I hate to do this to you, right?" Aimeric asked. He stroked the girl's hair and then added, bitterly, "It's all Aralyn's fault though."

"Please stop!" cried Aralyn from her place on the wall.

She still couldn't look at him, or the girl, but she could hear Aimeric walking towards her, taking slow, deliberate steps to intimidate her. She soon felt his breath against her cheek.

"You want *me* to stop?"

Aralyn turned to face him and he gestured to the girl.

"*You* are the one doing this to her!" Aimeric yelled.

"No! You are! Now let her go!"

"Telling me what to do, Aralyn? Have you not learned your lesson!" Aimeric yelled and angrily stalked back to the table, picking up the girl's other hand.

"Watch, Aralyn! Watch what *you* are doing to this girl!"

Aralyn shook her head.

"Watch or *you'll* be forced to do worse to her," Aimeric said, his voice now dangerously calm.

"Please, don't! I'm sorry! I won't defy you anymore, just let her go!" Aralyn begged, pulling on her restraints as though she might be able to save the girl if she were to break free.

Aimeric grinned coldly.

"It's too late for apologies, sweetheart."

Aimeric shoved down the other hand on its spike and, again, the girl's screams filled the room, making Aralyn nauseous.

Aimeric laughed loudly.

"What the fuck is wrong with you!" Aralyn screamed.

Aimeric was on her in a second, pulling Aralyn's head back by the hair.

"What the fuck is wrong with *you*, Aralyn?" Aimeric sneered. "It is you who are responsible for this girl's suffering, and if you do not obey the rules, you will be responsible for several more innocents' sufferings."

He let her hair go and her head fell forward until she held it up on her own again. She was determined to keep eye contact now and not let him control her entirely, but this time, she held in her words, not wanting the girl to have to go through any more pain.

"Now, are you ready to agree to the rules or shall I start punishing *you*?" Aimeric asked.

Aralyn looked at the girl. She was lying mostly still except for the occasional shudder of her arm and the slow rising and falling of her chest.

"Yes," Aralyn whispered.

"Good girl," Aimeric said and smiled.

He kissed her lips and for as long as they were pressed together, Aralyn felt a strange calm wash over her. The feeling was gone as soon as Aimeric pulled away, however. He went back to the girl and took the straps from her body. He then removed both of her hands from the spikes. The girl yelled each time, though it wasn't nearly as painful to listen to as before. Aimeric picked her up and nonchalantly tossed her back in the cage. A few of the prisoners ran to the girl and started tearing off pieces of clothing to wrap her injured hands in. Aimeric went back to Aralyn and raised her chin to look into her eyes.

"The rules are: Do whatever I say, *whenever* I say it. You will not talk back to me and you will not try and escape. If you do, you will be punished, just like that girl, maybe more painful, maybe less painful; it depends on my mood and how severe your crime is, but I promise, it *will* be painful. Are these rules clear to you?" Aimeric asked.

Aralyn nodded quickly, not wanting to anger him further.

"I can't hear you," he said dryly.

"Yes."

"Try again."

"Yes, Aimeric."

"Almost. Yes 'what' Aimeric?"

"Yes, Master Aimeric?" Aralyn guessed.

Aimeric grinned.

"Excellent."

Reaching over her, Aimeric unlocked Aralyn from her restraints. She fell against him, weak and exhausted from all that she had been through and witnessed. Aimeric held her up, taking in a moment to breathe in the scent of her blood at the place on her neck where the neck meets the shoulder. He then began to walk Aralyn out of the dungeon and out of the basement.

"I'm not a monster, Aralyn. I merely do what needs to be done in order to gain the respect that I deserve," Aimeric said when they reached the stairs.

Aralyn didn't respond, she knew she couldn't without making him angry again.

They reached the top of the stairs and saw that the door was ajar, left open by Morgan, apparently. Aimeric walked Aralyn through and as soon as they went into the living room, Aralyn raised her head, smelling fresh air. The front door was open and Aralyn could see the moon shining brightly outside. It looked so inviting, the outdoors. If she could reach outside, she could escape. She could be free.

"I wouldn't if I were you. I'm much faster than you could even *dream*," Aimeric said, hearing her thoughts. Before she could respond, or even think of responding, Aimeric added, "Virgil, leave the rat alone and close the door."

Aralyn looked around at the mention of Virgil and saw that he was next to the open door, holding Morgan, by the collar of his shirt, against the wall. He had apparently been threatening Morgan before Aimeric interrupted them. When his eyes fell on Aralyn, he loosed his grip and let Morgan slide to the floor. Virgil's eyes were dark and penetrating as he looked at Aralyn and then, coming to his senses, he nodded to Aimeric and closed the door, latching it to its twin.

Aralyn wanted to break free from Aimeric's hold on her and run to the sanctity of Virgil's arms. She wanted him to hold her and comfort her; she wanted to be free from the monster that was holding her now.

Once the door was closed, Virgil turned back to Aralyn and his eyes roamed her body, though not in a perverted way, it was more as though he were checking to make sure she hadn't been harmed. Aralyn's hair covered the wounds on her neck so she appeared to be, physically okay.

"Why are you back so soon, Virgil? There's still at least four hours left of darkness," Aimeric said, sounding amused.

"I…came back to make sure the girl wasn't going to try and…escape," Virgil answered, seeming slightly nervous.

Aimeric studied him a moment, listening to his thoughts, as he had done to Aralyn before. Virgil kept them silent though.

"Aralyn won't be trying to escape anytime soon, I've already made sure of that," Aimeric said. "As you can see, she is safe and sound."

Virgil nodded, clasping his hands behind his back.

"Yes, I see that. Would you like for me to take her off your hands and show her back to her room? So that you can go out now, Master?"

Aimeric chuckled.

"That won't be necessary. I've already fed and besides…" he looked down at Aralyn, cruelty in his eyes, "Aralyn will be spending the rest of the night with me."

Aralyn looked at Virgil, silently begging him to help her. Virgil's body was tense, and he looked like he was having a hard time keeping his fists unclenched. But he held back and instead forced a weak smile.

"As you wish. Is there anything I can do for you?" Virgil asked.

"No," Aimeric said.

"Then…I will be retiring to my room for the rest of the night," Virgil said softly.

"Really? So early?" Aimeric asked, sounding suspicious.

"I've been tired lately," Virgil replied.

"I see…Goodnight then," Aimeric said stiffly.

Virgil gave Aralyn one last, sympathetic, glance, as if to say he was sorry, and then he turned and, ignoring

Morgan (who was still on the floor) and the smug look on his face, disappeared upstairs.

Aimeric ordered Morgan to go through the mansion and make sure the windows were all covered for dawn and then he led Aralyn upstairs. Her stomach was tied up in knots and she thought she might throw up. Aralyn knew what Aimeric had in mind and she didn't want to do it. She had never had sex before and she didn't want this sick creature to be her first.

The room Aimeric took her to was completely dark; Aralyn couldn't even see her hand in front of her face. It was obvious that Aimeric didn't take any chances in letting the sun into his room.

"Stay here," Aimeric ordered and let Aralyn go.

She did stay, not knowing how she would be able to even try and escape in such pitch darkness. Aimeric would be on her before she could even find the door again and then who knew what he would do?

The sound of a match being lit brought Aralyn from her thoughts and a second later, the room gently glowed to life. Aimeric was lighting several candles on a dresser with a huge mirror on top. The mirror reflected the lights and also Aralyn herself since she was standing in front of it. She watched a tear roll down her own cheek in her reflection while Aimeric continued lighting.

What was she going to do? She couldn't risk the pain and punishment of another person. She would suffer for her crimes but she couldn't let anyone else. But she couldn't just let this monster take her innocence, either. But did she really have a choice? She looked around the room, hoping something inside of it would tell her something. Maybe she could find a weapon, though she didn't know what was true of the myths of vampires. She had heard vampires weren't even interested in sex, that they were just mindless killing machines, and that apparently wasn't true. So how would she know what would work to kill them?

Had she not been in the situation she was, Aralyn might have thought the bedroom was beautiful. Silk drapes, black and red, hung off the walls and also curtained a huge, four-post bed, which was covered in rich linen and fluffy pillows to match. Next to the bed was a slick, black, coffin. There was one myth that was true, apparently. The thought of sleeping in a coffin made her feel claustrophobic, though. The floor beneath her was beautiful, polished wood. This room, unlike the rest of the mansion, had been kept up and was actually clean. There were vases set around with black roses in them, but that was all, along with the candles; there was nothing else in the room that could be used as a weapon. There was a closet to the left of the bed and another door, probably a bathroom, to the right, but even if they had anything to use, Aralyn wouldn't be able to get there in time.

Aimeric lit the last candle and Aralyn saw him approaching her out of the corner of her eye. Her stomach was a cluster of butterflies. She wanted to run. She wanted the floor to open up and swallow her. She wanted anyone to come and rescue her.

But none happened.

The screams of the girl echoed in Aralyn's head as a reminder of what would happen if she tried to run. She stayed where she was; she couldn't let another person go through that for her. She knew she was no match for a vampire; she wouldn't be able to win if she fought him. Aralyn's mind was a swirling mess, she didn't know what to do except stand there and inwardly curse herself for her own weaknesses. Aralyn's nerves shook violently as Aimeric came up to her. He cupped her face in his hands for a moment, looking into her eyes, trying to gaze into her soul, perhaps, and Aralyn averted her eyes to the wall. Not saying a word to her, Aimeric lowered his mouth to hers, softly at first and then he deepened it, trying to urge Aralyn to part her lips on her own. She refused and tried to turn her head.

"Don't fight it, darling. Submit to me," Aimeric whispered against her lips.

He licked her bottom lip and then forced his tongue into her mouth. Aralyn remained still, refusing to allow Aimeric's kisses and touches stimulate her in any way. Aimeric took his tongue and returned it to Aralyn's bottom lip right before he bit it gently, drawing blood to the surface.

Aralyn cringed.

Aimeric sucked the blood for a moment while sliding his hand up and down Aralyn's side a few times before finally stopping on her breast. His thumb teased her nipple through the material of the dress.

Aralyn remained a zombie. All she felt was anger right now. She wanted desperately to hurt this man in some way, but she didn't know how she could. Aimeric finished the assault on her breast and, slipping his hands back down to Aralyn's hips, he grasped her hard and roughly pulled her against him. Aralyn gasped loudly at the unexpected collision but it was cut off when Aimeric parted her lips with his tongue once more, rubbing it against hers.

He then moved down her neck and Aralyn felt his fangs penetrate, and re-open, the wounds from Morgan. Aralyn cried out softly, tears coming to her eyes, as the pain returned. Aimeric sucked on the wound greedily for a moment, Aralyn starting to feel faint, until he seemed to realize what he was doing. He pulled away from her neck and went back to her mouth. Aimeric's arousal became obvious, trying to break through the wall of his pants. That was when the tears began to flow. Aralyn was going to be raped and she was helpless to stop it. The nagging feeling of something more horrible happening was keeping her from trying to fight. There was nothing more horrible than watching someone else suffer for what you have done, at least, that's what Aralyn thought.

Aimeric untied the strings of her dress and slipped it down her shoulder, kissing her warm flesh. He turned around and pushed her backwards until they got to the bed. Then, Aimeric picked Aralyn up and laid her down, crawling halfway on top of her while he unbuttoned his shirt with one hand.

"Please, don't do this," Aralyn choked out boldly.

"Shh, it will only hurt for a minute," Aimeric assured her, placing a finger to her quivering lips.

Aimeric didn't say anything else and Aralyn knew there was no stopping him. He would have his way with her no matter how much she could beg for him to leave her alone. Aralyn cried softly, not wanting to anger him, while he placed kisses against her cheeks, her lips and her neck, at the same time his hands pulled the dress down. As the flesh of her torso was exposed, Aimeric moved his lips to follow the material, kissing Aralyn as her body was exposed. Aralyn felt as though she was going to, literally, implode. Her muscles were tight, and seemed to be on fire from the anger she was feeling. Anger at herself, anger at him. Aimeric moved so that he straddled Aralyn's legs and lowered his head so he could suckle her nipples, which had involuntarily hardened as a response to Aimeric's tongue. He swirled it around the peaks for a few moments and then continued down Aralyn's waist. He continued to peel the dress from Aralyn's body, not seeming to notice how stiff and tense she was, or how hard her fists were clenched.

Or he *had* noticed and just didn't care.

Aralyn did not feel pleasure at all, no matter how much Aimeric tried to arouse her with his mouth and fingers. She couldn't be turned on by rape and that was what Aimeric was doing; he was raping her. Aralyn silently argued with herself. She asked if she was really going to allow this man –no, *monster* rape her, or let more innocent people suffer for her?

But then, Aralyn thought, remembering something Aimeric had said. He had said he would start punishing *her* for her crimes, didn't he? So maybe the innocents wouldn't be punished. Aimeric would punish her instead and she could deal with that, or at least, she thought she could. Anything would be better than this. Aimeric had started to undo his pants and that was when Aralyn made her decision. She would take the punishment, no one else, but she would *not* allow Aimeric to force her to have sex with him.

"Get off of me!" Aralyn screamed.

She pushed at his chest and rolled out from under him, launching herself off the bed. She pulled the dress back up, loosely over her shoulders, as she ran to the door. She reached out to turn the knob, but that was as far as she got. Aralyn was thrown into the wall, hard. Her back would surely be bruised.

"I warned you, didn't I?" Aimeric growled against her cheek.

The look on his face was murderous. He was seriously angered this time, not like before when his anger had seemed to be mostly sarcasm and a way to show Aralyn that he was in charge. The look in his eyes now were enough to make Aralyn want to curl up in a ball right then and there. Aimeric grabbed Aralyn's wrist and yanked her out of the bedroom, down the stairs, and to the basement. He went straight to the cages this time, not playing any games. He pulled a young man out, as though he were a rag doll, and threw him into the wall, locking him into the same chains Aralyn had been in only a short time before.

"No! Punish *me*!" Aralyn cried, horrified.

The cold wall was hit up against her back when Aimeric pushed her against it, right next to the man.

"I don't think so, *sweetheart*," Aimeric sneered against her lips. "I have something much better planned."

Aimeric jerked Aralyn forward by the back of her neck with one hand, and stood her in front of the man. Using his free hand, Aimeric picked up a bloodstained fire poker off the surgeon's table and thrust it into Aralyn's hand, using his fist to make Aralyn's fingers lock over it.

"Strike him," Aimeric commanded.

"No."

Aimeric roughly pulled Aralyn into his chest, as though to say *he* was in charge, not her.

"Strike him or we'll have to add another little playmate to our game," Aimeric said.

"I can't!" Aralyn cried.

"Oh, for God's sakes, Aralyn!" Aimeric screamed.

Using Aralyn's hand, with the weapon in it, Aimeric began to slash the man, putting deep cuts all over his torso. He screamed with every hit and soon became a bloody mess, the crimson dripping to the floor to make a small puddle at his feet. Aralyn sobbed as Aimeric used her fist to hit the man over and over, against her pleas for him to stop.

When Aimeric did finally quit hitting the man, there wasn't a clean spot on his torso. Probably two-dozen or so gashes covered the man. He would be lucky if he lived. Aimeric let Aralyn's hand drop and she let go of the poker, letting it clang to the floor. She covered her face with shaking hands, refusing to look at the man; at what *she* had done. The man gasped painfully, however, and changed her mind. She looked up and saw that Aimeric had run his hand over the man's wounds, collecting the man's blood on his fingers. Aimeric then turned Aralyn around to face him and he smeared the blood on her face and neck.

"Do you see what *you* have done, Aralyn? This is all your fault!"

Aralyn's salty tears mixed with the blood and she turned to the man, barely able to whisper, "I'm sorry."

"Oh, you're *sorry*? 'Sorry' won't heal his wounds, Aralyn! You're selfish! You let others suffer for you!" Aimeric said.

"No! *You* did this to him!" Aralyn screamed back, though she immediately wished she hadn't.

Aimeric yanked her head back by the hair, leaning down to her face.

"What was that?" he hissed.

Aralyn didn't respond.

"That's what I thought," Aimeric said and released her.

He unchained the boy and then threw him back into one of the cages, tossing him carelessly on the floor. As with the girl, the others ran to him and began to tend to his wounds. Some were even bold enough to glare at Aimeric, though he didn't see. He had turned back to Aralyn.

"Are you ready to go back upstairs, or should I bring someone else out?" he asked coldly.

Aralyn kept her eyes to the floor but nodded.

"Yes," she whispered.

"Yes, what?"

"Yes, Master Aimeric."

Aimeric took Aralyn back to the bedroom where he stole her innocence while she silently cried to herself and stared at the underside of the canopy over the bed, refusing to watch the sick expression of sheer pleasure on Aimeric's face as he moved inside of her after forcing his massive sex into her opening. It had hurt and Aralyn had wanted to scream at the pain he had brought on to her, but she didn't, not wanting to give him the satisfaction of knowing that he had caused such pain to her in the midst of his pleasure. Aralyn bit her lip and when she wasn't doing that, kept her jaw clenched, while Aimeric had his way with her, to keep from crying out loud. He licked away the blood he had smeared on Aralyn's face and neck, the metallic taste adding to his deep groans of bliss.

When he finished with her, he demanded that she accompany him in his coffin while he slept. She didn't say a word to him but climbed inside and laid on top of him while he sickly stroked her hair and back as though he truly cared for her.

Aralyn cried herself to sleep with the monster holding her.

Chapter Five: A Proposition

Stirring slightly at the soft stroking of her hair and cheek, Aralyn opened her eyes and harsh reality came back to smack her in the face. She had hoped that the night before had just been a horrible nightmare. She had hoped her entire experience with these creatures of the night had only been a nightmare. But Aralyn found herself still in Aimeric's arms, their naked bodies entwined together in his coffin. She blinked hard, trying to hold back the tears of realization; last night had actually happened.

"So soft…so beautiful. I would keep you forever," Aimeric murmured, his voice seductive.

Aralyn closed her eyes again, pretending not to hear him, and wishing she could be taken far away from this place. She was angry with Devin for pulling her away from sweet death. She was angry with Virgil for abandoning her the night before.

"Would you stay with me, Aralyn? Be my queen? I would give you everything you desire if you allowed me to turn you into one of us," Aimeric said, his hand falling to the small of her back.

Opening her eyes again, Aralyn said, through gritted teeth, "Do I really have a choice?"

Aimeric chuckled, his chest vibrating under hers.

"For a little while."

He opened the coffin lid and Aralyn stood immediately, wanting desperately to get off of him and out of that horrible box she had been forced to sleep in. Just as she went to climb out, she was pulled back onto Aimeric's lap and he planted a hard, dominating, kiss on her lips.

"I *will* have you forever. Your sister cannot stop me for me long," he said, looking into her eyes.

Aralyn glared at him and jerked herself up, not responding. Aimeric followed her out of the coffin and she could feel him watching her as she went to the clothing on the floor. Her movements were slow due to the soreness between her legs. She knew the pain was from the night before and the thought only increased her anger towards Aimeric. Without glancing at him, Aralyn pulled the black dress back on and went to tie the strings around her neck. Aimeric came up behind her, to tie the dress for her, and she cringed but let him help her anyway. Placing his hands on her shoulders when he was finished, Aimeric kissed her neck softly and trailed up and down it.

"I would love you for eternity. *Only* you if that is what you were to desire," he whispered into her flesh.

Aralyn only stared straight ahead at the wall and Aimeric smoothed her hair around her shoulders before he turned her around, kissing her forehead. She avoided his eyes and looked past his shoulders.

"You don't have to decide right now. You have plenty of time," he said, chuckling sardonically.

Turning his back to her, Aimeric bent down and pulled on his leather pants and then his shirt. Aralyn stood there, motionless, until he finished and then he took her wrist and led her out of the bedroom, like an animal on a leash, and took her downstairs, through the living room and into the kitchen. Aralyn saw, through a crack in one of the boards covering the window, that is was dusk again. She had slept all day in that damn coffin with Aimeric. Most of the other vampires hadn't risen yet but a few of them had and were sitting on the couches, and they watched as Aimeric dragged her past them. None of them dared to say anything to her this time. Not when Aimeric was the one with her.

When they reached the kitchen, Aralyn saw that Virgil was sitting at the table, looking stressed. His hands were at the sides of his head, massaging his temples and he was looking down with his eyes closed. He hadn't even notice that the two had come into the kitchen until Aimeric spoke.

"Virgil, tend to her wounds."

He gave the command and gently pushed Aralyn forward. Virgil looked up and Aralyn thought she saw a hint of relief in his dark eyes. He quickly hid it though and casually stood from his seat.

"Yes, Master Aimeric, as you wish," he said coolly, taking Aralyn's hand to lead her away.

"And keep an eye on her. I'm going out. If she tries anything, punish her," Aimeric added authoritatively.

Aralyn looked at Aimeric over her shoulder, giving him such a cold glare that it was amazing the room didn't frost over. Upon looking at him, she noticed something that she hadn't seen a few minutes ago, probably because she had refused to look directly at him for very long. Aralyn saw that Aimeric was paler than usual and his icy eyes seemed to have faded to a dim gray. He looked sick. Aralyn didn't feel sorry for him though. In fact, she wished he would turn to dust before her very eyes.

"Is that so, Aralyn? You wish to see me dead?" Aimeric asked, amused. He stepped up to her, holding her glare, neither of them blinking, and then he smiled coldly. "I'll try to remember that later," he said, cupping her face.

He kissed Aralyn tenderly, which made her stomach lurch. Virgil sensed her body tense up and squeezed her hand as though trying to comfort her. The vampire Aralyn had come to hate dearly pulled away from her lips, chuckling softly, and then he swept past her and Virgil with an arrogant air, going out the door into the on-coming darkness with two other vampire men following him.

As soon as the door closed, Aralyn fell to her knees. She covered her face and sobbed so hard that her shoulders shook. Virgil was immediately on his knees beside her, wrapping his strong arms around her, and cradled her against his chest. Aralyn allowed him to hold her for a moment but, then, realizing she was angry with him too, she shoved him away.

"What did he do, Aralyn?" Virgil asked, though the tone in his voice indicated he already knew.

She didn't answer.

Brushing her hair aside, Virgil's eyes swept over the puncture marks on her neck.

"He drank from you," he observed quietly.

"Yes! He drank from me! Morgan drank from me! You've allowed me to be passed around like a glass of wine!" Aralyn yelled, finally unable to hold in her anger, her fright, and her embarrassment.

Virgil clenched his fists and gritted his teeth.

"Morgan too? I'll kill him," he promised.

Aralyn shook her head, not feeling any comfort. She remembered the prisoners in the cages and sobbed harder.

"What is it, Aralyn?" Virgil asked, forgetting Morgan for the moment and only concentrating on her.

"You're all monsters…sick, disgusting, twisted and evil, *monsters*!" Aralyn spat harshly.

Virgil was silent for the next few moments, looking away from her as though he knew she was correct in her accusations. After what she had been through, Aralyn had every right to accuse them all of monstrosity.

"How long do you suffer those people before putting them out of their misery?" Aralyn suddenly asked

Virgil hesitated, looking ashamed.

"…You found it?"

"How could I not have? I heard them crying from my door! I'm surprised I didn't hear them sooner!" Aralyn finally looked into Virgil's eyes. "Do you know what he did, Virgil?" she asked accusingly. Not giving him a chance to respond, she said, "He tortured them. Two of them; a man and a woman. He tortured them before me and it was *my* fault! *Mine*!"

Her sobs began to shake her body again and she had started rocking back and forth on her knees, burying her face in her hands.

"It's not your fault. He would have gotten to them sooner or later, he just used you as his excuse this time," Virgil said soothingly and touched Aralyn's shoulder.

"He's a monster," Aralyn repeated. "Sick…twisted and… God! He was inside of me! This is your fault!" she screamed, looking up at Virgil. "Why did you leave me with him? Why did you let him have me?"

Virgil looked at her, his face stricken with guilt.

"There's nothing I could have done to stop him, Aralyn; he's too powerful; he would have taken you anyway," he whispered.

"You knew what he would do?" she asked.

Again, Virgil looked ashamed.

"Yes. It's not the first time he took a girl against her will."

Aralyn had figured as much.

"He drank from you, but when? And how much?" Virgil asked.

Aralyn's mind flashed back to the horrible night before.

"Right before he…" she couldn't say it.

"Was it only before? Not during or after?" Virgil asked.

Aralyn shook her head. While Aimeric was inside of her, he had gone to her neck a few times during the heat of his passion, but he stopped himself from biting and drinking any more from her.

"Just right before and he took enough to make me feel dizzy," she whispered, remembering the horrible feeling.

Virgil nodded.

"That explains his appearance this morning."

"What do you mean?"

He hesitated.

"Whenever a vampire…exerts himself," he was careful not to say too much on the sensitive subject, for

Aralyn's sake, "he uses a lot of the blood inside his body and has to replenish it quickly or, as you saw with Aimeric, he gets sick and dies within only a day or two. Since Aimeric drank from you before he…well, you know, and since he took enough to make you dizzy, that means he had already taken too much from you and so he didn't want to take any more afterwards or he would risk killing you. So he waited until tonight to replenish the blood used. That's why he looked sick."

"Why didn't he just take one of the prisoners? And why would he care if I was killed if he had already had his way with me?" Aralyn asked, disgusted.

Not that she cared about Aimeric's health, and not that she wanted anyone to die, she was simply curious because Aimeric had already proven that he didn't care about anyone but himself.

"He hates actually feeding from the prisoners. They're merely his playthings. He prefers to hunt for his food and save the prisoners for true emergencies. And…I'm sure he has more plans for you," Virgil said.

Knowing he was probably right, Aralyn looked away, the tears forming again. She covered her face once more and Virgil reached out for her, taking her into his arms. He didn't care if she pushed him away; he only wanted to comfort her. Virgil gently rocked her in his arms and held onto her, as though it were possible she could be swept away with the slightest breeze, and Aralyn leaned against him letting him comfort her since she had gotten all of her yelling out and was no longer angry at him. She was only afraid now. After a few moments of silence, and being held, Aralyn had calmed down enough to stop crying.

"Come on, we'll change your bandages," Virgil said.

He stood and helped Aralyn to her feet. They went upstairs and Virgil cleaned her wounds as he had done the night before, wrapping them in fresh gauze. Eyes still puffy from crying, Aralyn sat there silently while Virgil took care of her.

"Aralyn, I've made a decision," he said suddenly.

Aralyn raised her eyes, which had been staring, intently, at the floor, and looked at Virgil in response.

"I'm going to get you out of here. I promise," he said, clasping a metal safety pin to hold the bandages in place.

"How?" Aralyn asked hopefully.

"I don't know yet, but I'll think of something," Virgil said.

Their eyes held each other for a moment and then Virgil leaned over, close to her lips. He lingered there, waiting, and silently asked for Aralyn's permission to kiss her. She didn't push him away so Virgil brushed his lips against hers. Aralyn closed her eyes and let his soft lips gently graze hers several times in sweet, quick, pecks.

Unlike Aimeric, Virgil's kisses sent a warm sensation through her blood.

Unlike Aimeric, Virgil's kisses made Aralyn want more and melt into him.

Unlike Aimeric, Virgil's kisses were sweet and not demanding.

"My, my, what would Master Aimeric say if he knew you were kissin' his 'bride-to-be,' Virgil?"

He and Aralyn broke apart and looked from the bed they were sitting on in Virgil's room. Morgan stood in the doorway, casually leaning against the frame, with his arms crossed over his chest. He had amusement in his cobalt eyes and was looking at Virgil and Aralyn down the length of his pointed nose. Virgil was on the floor in a second, barreling for Morgan's throat. He grabbed him and shoved him into the hallway, hitting his back up against the wall.

"You will not say a word or I will snap your neck in two, do you understand?" he sneered, clenching Morgan's throat in his hands.

Eyes watering bloody tears, Morgan nodded vigorously and clutched at the hands around his neck. With one last intimidating shove, Virgil let Morgan go and he slid to the floor, sniveling, but in a cowardly manner. Morgan knew he couldn't win a physical battle with Virgil but he also knew that he had something to use against both him and Aralyn.

Virgil went to Aralyn and helped her stand from the bed before leading her out of the room. As they passed Morgan, Aralyn glared at him and Virgil sneered.

"And stay the fuck away from her."

The sniveling vampire only smirked.

Once in the kitchen again, Virgil fixed Aralyn some human food to eat, which she ate hungrily, having not eaten since the night before. Virgil sat with her but he didn't watch her. He was busy trying to come up with a plan to get her away from Aimeric. He looked stressed again. Aralyn knew he was thinking of Aimeric and becoming discouraged. Aimeric was too powerful for both of them. He would kill them if they tried to leave, or worse, he would keep them as his "play" things.

"What's wrong?" Aralyn asked, though she already knew.

She just wanted him to confirm it that way she could give an offer of suggestions. He seemed to be brought back to reality by the sound of her voice and forced a smile. Aralyn noticed he was beginning to look sickly, as Aimeric had. His skin was like ash and his eyes were darker than normal. His lips also looked dry. Being overly stressed was another form of exertion, even for a vampire, Aralyn guessed.

"Nothing you need to worry about right now, just eat," Virgil said sincerely.

Hesitating at first, Aralyn did as he told her; she was still very hungry after all. When the plate was clean, she looked at Virgil sympathetically.

"Don't you need to um…feed?" she asked.

She still hated the idea of living off of humans but she knew Virgil only did it to survive, unlike Aimeric who tortured and killed for fun.

Virgil smiled.

"Don't worry about me."

"Yes. Don't worry about him. He isn't worth it and doesn't deserve any concern you can give."

Virgil sat up straight and Aralyn's insides twisted together, threatening to squeeze everything she had just eaten until it spilled from her mouth, when they heard Aimeric. He had only just now returned and was glaring at Virgil coldly, jealously. Virgil held back his anger and looked back at Aimeric.

"Back so soon?" he asked curiously.

Though refusing to look at him, Aralyn saw Aimeric grin from the corner of her eye.

"I just couldn't stay away from this beauty," Aimeric responded, coming up to stand beside Aralyn.

Her fists clenched together as he smoothed his fingers through her hair.

"You may leave us now, Virgil. For God's sakes, go get something to eat, you look horrible," Aimeric said, chuckling.

Virgil forced a laugh and stood up.

Aralyn's eyes rose to meet his and Virgil's seemed to say, "Just a little longer, I promise."

As if to say she was "his" and *he* owned her, Aimeric smoothed Aralyn's hair behind her ear and away from her neck. She longed to take the knife in front of her and plunge it into his chest but she doubted that would do anything except make him angry.

"I guess I'll...be back in a little while," Virgil said, hesitating.

With one last apologetic glance at Aralyn, Virgil left her there at the table, alone with Aimeric once more. The Master vampire went to a chair across from Aralyn and sat down, not saying anything for a long time. He only leaned back in the chair and gazed at Aralyn with a smug look plastered on his pale face. His cold blue eyes watched her violet ones, only blinking every now and then. They traveled down to her lips, her neck, and then to her breasts.

"Are you going to sit there all night or are you going to come to me?" Aimeric finally asked.

Aralyn's head shot up and she glared at him.

"I am not a dog that will come to its master when he returns home," she said, her voice shaking, yet there was some strength to it.

She kept her eyes in line with his and waited for his threats.

He laughed.

"Very well then, *I* will come to *you*."

He stood and coolly went to her side. Aralyn's body was visibly shaking again from anger, fear, and disgust. She averted her eyes to the floor, stubbornly refusing to look at him. Aimeric's hand snaked out to touch her face and his other went to her waist and pulled her from her seat. He slid a finger under her chin and turned her so she would look at him. Aralyn saw that he didn't look sick any longer. His face was filled out and his eyes looked brighter. Aimeric had been regenerated by whomever he had killed that night. Cupping her face in his hands, Aimeric ran his thumb over her cheek (she flinched at the icy touch of his fingers) where there was still a faint bruise from where Devin had hit her a few nights before.

"I never did ask you, what happened to your face?" His hands moved to her bandaged arms. "And your beautiful flesh...who did this to you?"

Stubbornly turning her head again, Aralyn answered, "It doesn't matter, he's dead; Claire killed him."

Aimeric chuckled at the harsh tone Aralyn used when speaking to him and also at the mention of Claire.

"Yes, that does sound like my Claire. I had her once and then she decided she didn't like men and only preferred to kill them," Aimeric said thoughtfully.

Aralyn didn't answer him. She wasn't going to have a real, civilized, conversation with this creature she so loathed. Gently turning her chin, Aimeric pressed his lips against hers, softly pecking them while she remained still. His tongue slithered onto her neck and lingered over the scabbed puncture marks, tasting the dried blood, while his arms drew her closer and pulled her against him. His hands moved to her rear and gave it a gentle squeeze. Aralyn stood there, motionless, and didn't respond to his kisses and then the tugging of her bottom lip with his teeth. However, when she felt his arousal against her abdomen, she pushed him away.

"I'm still hungry," she lied, avoiding his hungry eyes, which she could feel roaming her body.

He looked her over for a few seconds and she thought he would be angry with her and force her to have sex with him again. But he didn't.

"Very well, go ahead and eat some more…build up your strength." Aimeric helped her into her seat and leaned down to whisper seductively, "You're going to need it."

Aralyn's stomach was, once again, twisted in knots. She knew what he was implying. She didn't show her nervousness though as she served herself some more of the food Virgil had placed on the table. Aimeric watched her with a lustful grin on his face, taking in every detail of how she ate. She deliberately ate slow, taking more time than needed in order to postpone what Aimeric had in mind for as long as she could; she did not want to go back to the bedroom with him. After a few moments of her deliberate, slow chewing, Aimeric leaned forward on the table.

"Do you have any idea what you do to me?" he asked, his voice a sultry growl.

Aralyn slowly, almost robotically, turned her head in his direction and glared for a good ten seconds before going back to the food, picking through, since she wasn't hungry, and taking small bites.

"You shouldn't force yourself to eat, my love, you'll make yourself sick," Aimeric said smugly, knowing all along what she had been doing.

Aralyn gagged on the food in her mouth and fresh tears were brought to her eyes. She threw the fork down and covered her face, sobbing. She couldn't help it. She didn't want this disgusting creature inside of her again. The thought literally made her sick. Aimeric chuckled and stood up, pulling Aralyn out of her chair, and brought her, gently, against his chest.

"Come now, is it so bad? Do you really find me so repulsive?" he asked.

Wanting to push him away, but not knowing what he would do to the prisoners, Aralyn allowed Aimeric to hold her tightly, swaying her from side to side, and brush her hair down. It was all just a sick game to him. He would have his way with her until he grew bored and then he would kill her.

"How long do you plan on keeping me alive?" Aralyn asked bitterly through her tears.

Aimeric stopped chuckling and held her out in front of him, taking her hands off her face, and brushed a strand of black hair from her eyes.

"I would love you for eternity. I've already told you that." He paused thoughtfully before continuing. "I don't know what it is about you, Aralyn, if you were any other girl, I would have snapped your neck by now for all of the trouble you've caused me, despite Claire's wishes. But you,

you're different somehow. You draw me to you. I don't know if it's your beautiful expressions, or your constant rejection of me, or maybe a combination of both, but you have me in a trance over you."

"Don't say that," she said.

"Why?"

Aralyn finally looked Aimeric in the eyes and saw something different in them; they seemed softer, kinder. But she didn't care. She wasn't going to fall for his tricks. He was a monster and that's all there was to him.

"You still hate me?" Aimeric asked, the cold grin back on his face.

Aralyn's jaw clenched so tightly that the words were barely coherent as she said, "I...loathe you."

Aimeric laughed for a moment, amused, but then his eyes turned murderous and he grabbed her arm, jerking her through the living room, up the stairs and to the bedroom. She pulled on his arm but didn't fight him any other way. No matter how disgusted she became with him, she wouldn't allow him to get so angry with her that he would hurt others for her sake again. Once in the room, Aimeric slammed the door and took Aralyn by the shoulders, growling into her lips.

"Here is what's going to happen: We are going to make love and it's going to be together this time. There will be no crying. You can whimper, you can moan, and you can scream your pretty little lungs out, but it had better be out of pleasure *only* or you will be punished, and by 'you,' I mean everyone down in that basement. Do I make myself clear?"

"No...please-"

"*Do I make myself clear*?" Aimeric interrupted and emphasized each word.

Aralyn shook her head, shoving him away from her. She didn't look back. She flung open the bedroom door and ran downstairs to the front door. The crisp, night, air welcomed her with open arms and she ran out into them.

I'm sorry, I'm sorry! Aralyn said over and over in her mind as though the prisoners would hear her.

Once again, the weakness had won. She knew Aimeric would be dangerously angry with her and he might kill everyone in the cages this time. She had tried so hard to keep harm from coming to them, but hearing Aimeric say she had better *enjoy* him raping her again had been too much. She momentarily lost sympathy and caring for others. All she knew then was to get away from Aimeric. She knew she would regret abandoning them later, but for now, she was only focused on escaping. Her cheeks became cold from the wind sweeping over them, which were wet with tears, but she didn't care; she was free.

Bare tree branches reached out and clawed at Aralyn's face and arms as she ran. Warm blood soon trickled down her cheeks, contrasting with the cool air. It was dark. Where was she? Which way should she go? Where was the road? Was there even a road? She couldn't see anything in this dark forest. Rocks and twigs on the ground prodded at Aralyn's bare feet, but she didn't seem to notice. She needed to find a way out. She couldn't hear anything of comfort. No street traffic, no horns, nothing. She just ran straight forward, wanting to put as much distance between herself and the horrible mansion as possible.

She had no idea that Aimeric was simply humoring her.

Aralyn's screams filled the dark forest when Aimeric appeared directly in front of her. She would have fallen down had he not reached out and grabbed her by the upper part of her arms. His fingernails painfully dug into her.

"Did you really think you could get away?" Aimeric sneered.

"Let me go! Please!" Aralyn cried, trying to break free from his grasp and escape him once more.

He held her tight.

"I don't think so. You'll be lucky if I don't take you home and play with you. You're lucky you're so goddamn beautiful. You're lucky you feel so *fucking* good," he growled.

Aralyn felt the wind whip up around her and in an instant, she was back in the bedroom with Aimeric.

"No more games! I'm losing my patience with you," Aimeric said.

Aralyn didn't have a chance to say anything; his lips were against hers before she could take another breath. He kissed her hard, almost violently. Whatever gentleness he had intended on using, if any, had disappeared. He moved up her face, kissing and licking away the blood from the tree branches and the tears she had cried and *was* crying at the moment. His mouth moved back to hers and his hands went to her rear, squeezing it as he picked her up. He lifted her onto the bed and wasn't gentle at all as he crawled on top of her. He thrust against her a few times, over their clothes, and raked his fingers through her hair.

Aralyn's whole body was tense and she grimaced with every kiss he laid on her. She turned her head away when he tried to kiss her mouth again.

Pulling away, Aimeric raked his fangs over her lips.

"Respond to me," he hissed.

He held her head in one place, so she couldn't turn it again, and parted her lips. His tongue crudely found hers and he literally took her breath away this time. Fear took over and Aralyn tried to kiss him back, so as not to anger him again, but she knew she didn't do it very well since she was sick with the idea of what was happening. Aimeric didn't seem to care though. He sat up, bringing her with him, and wrapped her legs around his waist. He finally pulled his mouth away from hers and moved to her neck.

Aralyn sucked in the breath that had been stolen. Aimeric brushed his lips against the scabs on Aralyn's neck, lingering there, sniffing the dried blood. Aralyn saw a far away look in his eyes and figured her blood was pulling him into some kind of trance again. He wanted to take more from her.

Please don't... she thought to herself but didn't dare say it.

Hearing her thoughts, Aimeric's head jerked up to look at her and, coming back to himself, he kissed her hard and slid his hands down her sides. He brought the dress up to her waist, rubbing her thighs, and then he moved up to untie the strings. He lifted the dress off of her and went back to kissing her throat, his hand groping one of her breasts at the same time. Aralyn gritted her teeth against Aimeric's shoulder, trying desperately not to feel anything but hate for him. But as his thumb and fingers tweaked her nipples and his tongue slid up and down her throat, she couldn't help but feel a wave of pleasure ripple through her body. Heat pooled in her abdomen and then went even further down. Her muscles clenched and tightened with anticipation. Why? Why was she feeling this? Tears of guilt slowly rolled down her cheeks and she hoped Aimeric wouldn't see them.

He didn't.

Aimeric lifted Aralyn up so that she was kneeling in front of him and his mouth took over on her breasts. He nipped at her and sucked on the hardened peaks while he slid his hands up and down her back. She held in the whimpers of pleasure she wanted to release, refusing to admit that he was causing this feeling inside of her; the aching that she longed to stop. Aimeric laid her back down on the bed and began to lick down her midsection. He moved to her left thigh and kissed down, then over, and Aralyn's breath caught in her throat the closer he got inside of her thigh where the flesh was most sensitive and then she let it out and shuddered slightly when his tongue barely grazed her sex. Aimeric only licked once and then he kissed and licked both thighs, going back and forth, teasingly.

Why was Aralyn feeling this way? Why was she feeling such pleasure? She hadn't felt this way at all last night when Aimeric raped her the first time. Maybe because he had gone so fast the night before that she didn't get the chance to feel anything? Or maybe he was doing something to her mind, making her believe she wanted him to continue. She remembered how he had manipulated the girl in the basement right before he tortured her.

Her thighs were glistening with saliva now and her heart had begun to beat faster, her breaths coming in raspy puffs, but she still continued to hold in the moans she wanted to release. The ache became more and more and she soon found herself actually *wanting* him to keep going.

Stop it she told herself, her tears starting to fall harder.

She didn't want to like this; she hated this monster.

Aimeric's hands slid up behind her legs to grasp her rear and Aralyn felt him take his tongue off of her. Before she could decide if she was happy he had done so, or disappointed, Aimeric growled.

"I said no…*crying*."

The last word came out harshly and he pulled her down the bed a little so that he could plant his face between her thighs. His tongue darted out in quick motions, lapping against her sex. Aralyn gasped loudly and her heels dug into the mattress of the bed. Her fingernails went to the skin on Aimeric's shoulders and the back of her head fell into the pillows. As Aimeric's tongue moved vigorously against her, drawing onto it the juices from deep within, Aralyn used all the willpower she had to keep from screaming out. She tore her fingers from his shoulders and instead clenched the bed sheets together in her hands while her breathing came in shuddering gasps due to the fire surging inside of her. She tried to take her mind off of what he was doing to her and, instead, tried to focus on the underside of the canopy over her head, silently begging for her body to not respond. It wasn't listening though and she was on the verge of letting it all out; screaming seemed like a sweet release.

Aimeric moaned into her, sending vibrations against her core and that was enough to send her over the edge. Her body shuddered and she moaned loudly, closing her eyes. Aimeric pulled away from her and she tried to catch her breath and desperately tried to control the beat of her heart, along with her breathing.

But Aimeric wasn't finished with her

"I can't stand it anymore."

Aralyn opened her eyes at the sound of Aimeric's voice. He was hurriedly tearing off his clothes and she saw that he was fully aroused, his member hard and ready for her.

"I need you now," Aimeric growled.

He hurriedly lowered his body onto Aralyn's, grabbing her legs and wrapping them around him once more. His throbbing head met Aralyn's opening.

"No..." she breathed, though she didn't really mean it.

"What did you say?" Aimeric growled warningly against her ear. "You had better correct yourself now, Aralyn."

He thrust into her, hard, and Aralyn gasped out of pleasure and pain, though mostly pain since she was still pretty tight.

She did manage to mumble an incoherent "yes," and then more as Aimeric moved inside of her. He brought her hands over her head and smashed them into the pillows, his fingers entwining with hers, their nails digging into each other's skin. Aimeric moved inside of her, hard. Each motion of his penetration made her body writhe and when she felt his tongue against her ear, she let out a loud moan. He covered her mouth with his and she closed her eyes tightly but kissed him back eagerly. She was enjoying this; she didn't *want* him to stop. The thought made her sick. What could she do?

Virgil.

The thought entered her mind and she used it, mentally making the men switch places. Virgil was making love to her, not Aimeric. She moaned loudly into his mouth and Aimeric (Virgil) quickened his pace. Aralyn's hips moved to meet his every thrust and she didn't try to keep any more of her emotions inside.

"…God…Aimeric…" she breathed.

Aralyn's eyes flew open. Why had she said his name? She had been thinking of Virgil.

"Yes," Aimeric rasped in response. "It is me who is doing this to you."

He thrust harder and she yelled softly.

"You remember this, Aralyn."

He sat up on his knees, bringing her up with him and thrust still harder.

"I am the only one who can make you feel this way. Do you understand?" he growled against her neck, sucking on the flesh. She didn't respond right away so he moved to her mouth and demanded, "*Do* you understand?"

He thrust harder, growling deeply into her lips.

Gasping, followed by a loud moan, Aralyn locked her legs tighter around his waist and breathed, "Yes."

He continued to move inside of her, and she moved along with him; their bodies moving in perfect synchronization. Both of them were glistening with sweat, Aimeric's tainted red with blood, and their hair stuck to the backs of their necks and cheeks.

Finally, after several teases from Aimeric where he would slow his pace, sometimes stopping entirely, when

Aralyn came close to an orgasm, he let her have it. She felt her climax take over her body and she arched her back, letting out a scream.

Aimeric bit into her neck and sucked out some of her blood (she didn't care at that moment) while continuing to pump into her as her entire body shuddered one more time, this time longer and more violently, and then he followed her; groaning into her neck at his own release.

The two fell back on the bed and Aimeric took a moment to rest on Aralyn's chest while she caught her breath, gasping hard for it. After a moment, Aimeric pulled out of her, eliciting another soft moan, and then he rolled over on his side and pulled her to his chest. He kissed her softly along her cheek, her neck and the parts of her arms that weren't bandaged. He held her tightly, refusing to let her go.

Aralyn bit her lip, trying not to cry now that the passion and heat was over, but the tears fell anyway. They were tears of guilt. She was angry for allowing herself to feel any kind of pleasure from this creature.

"That wasn't so bad, was it?" Aimeric asked against her ear and then nipped at it softly.

She was too ashamed to respond to him and only closed her eyes, giving in to sleep.

Chapter Six: Sadie and Mabel

A few hours later, Aralyn woke up to the sound of low, rumbling, thunder and hard rain beating on the windows. She turned her head slightly and saw that the clock on the wall pointed to ten thirty-seven in the morning. The room was still dark as night, however, due to the boards on the windows and the heavy curtains that covered them. Not to mention the skies were obviously thickly covered with storm clouds so it would probably still be dark in the room, no matter what.

Aralyn was still in Aimeric's arms, both of them still nude, but his hold on her wasn't very tight so he must have still been asleep. She didn't quite understand why they had slept in the bed and not the coffin. She thought vampires always slept in coffins. It wasn't that important to her though so she didn't think on it long. She quietly turned her head to see that Aimeric was indeed still asleep. His head lay against her shoulder and his eyes were shut tightly. Cautiously shifting her weight, Aralyn slid out of the bed and silently prayed that he wouldn't wake up.

Halfway to the bathroom, she hit a weak spot in the floorboards and it creaked loudly. Cringing, she stopped and waited for Aimeric to move, inwardly cursing herself for making noise. He didn't even stir though. Silently breathing a sigh of relief, Aralyn stepped around the rest of the weak spot, or what she hoped was the rest of it, and went into the bathroom, softly closing the door. She knew she wasn't safe, Aimeric could come in at any time he wanted, but she still felt relieved with the door between them. At least she would hear him opening the door. Maybe.

Aralyn turned on the hot water to the shower, wanting eagerly to rid her body of Aimeric's scent. Even with him in the other room, she could still smell him; the metallic scent of blood mixed with his natural, male, scent.

She stepped into the shower, moved under the water, and took off her bandages as they became wet. The shower was a little too hot at first, but she forced herself to stay under it, wanting to make sure she was properly cleansed. She cried as memories of the night before came back to her in quick flashes. Why had she allowed herself to feel such pleasure with that monster? She shouldn't have responded to him as she had done; it had been wrong. She had told herself not to give in and she ended up doing it anyway. But, she realized she'd felt like she didn't have that much control over her own senses and feelings; they had just come out.

After washing her flesh for the fifth time, she finally turned off the water. Her body was slightly burned and splotchy from the heat mixed with how hard she had scrubbed, but she didn't seem to notice. After wringing out her long, ebony hair, Aralyn wrapped a towel around her body and, after taking a breath, hoping Aimeric was still asleep, she turned the doorknob and opened the door. Aimeric was awake leaning back on his elbows on the bed (He looked tired since he usually didn't rise until near sundown). The silk sheets covered his nakedness and his dark hair curtained his shoulders. His blue eyes fell on Aralyn as soon as she stepped out of the bathroom, and he smirked at her while gazing upon her towel-covered body. The parts of her skin that weren't covered glistened with the tiny beads of water she had missed.

"I had hoped you would wait for me and we could shower together," Aimeric said smoothly.

Aralyn hung her head and averted her eyes to the floor.

"I...I'm sorry. I woke up and couldn't get back to sleep."

"No apology is necessary. Just wake me up next time."

Aralyn looked up at him for a moment but when she saw he had stood from the bed, she turned her head quickly, and avoided looking at his naked figure. She sensed him walking towards her and a few seconds later, he had his fingers under her chin, and turned her so she had to look into his eyes. He smiled and kissed her lips softly.

"Good morning, my love," he said.

She forced a quick smile and mumbled, "'Morning."

Aimeric smirked and then reached down, taking her arms, and gazed, thoughtfully, at the cuts on them.

"These would heal in an instant if you became one of us," he said, more to himself than to her.

Aralyn yanked her arms free.

"No thank you."

Aimeric chuckled and kissed her forehead.

"Go find something to wear in the other room and then come back here… And don't try anything funny, Aralyn," he warned before going past her, into the bathroom.

Once Aralyn heard shower water running, she sighed and left the room, glad to be free of him for at least a few minutes. She quickly went out into the hall and literally bumped into Morgan. He had a wide grin on his narrow face as he steadied her.

"Ah, Miss Aralyn. Or should I say…" he paused to bow to her, "'My Queen.'"

He laughed and Aralyn glared, shoving past him.

"Where do you think you're going?" Morgan asked, grabbing her arm.

"Let go of me," she said dangerously low.

"Yes, let go of her."

Aralyn felt the familiar guilt from the night before, creep up on her when she saw that Virgil was standing beside her, glaring, dangerously, at Morgan. He reached out and shoved Morgan's hands off of Aralyn.

"I was just gonna make sure she wasn't goin' to run away!" Morgan snapped, indignant.

"I doubt she would be going anywhere dressed...like that," Virgil said, his eyes roaming Aralyn's body, barely covered by the towel.

She blushed slightly.

"I was just going to find some clothes when he stopped me."

Virgil nodded, understandably and said, "Come with me."

He took the hand that Aralyn wasn't using to tightly hold the towel up, and led her away, leaving a scowling Morgan behind. When they reached Claire's room, Virgil opened the door and led Aralyn inside. He quickly closed the door and then, bringing Aralyn up against him, pressed his lips to hers in a passionate kiss. She started to melt into him and open her mouth so he could enter but then she gently pushed him away.

"Virgil, I can't...if Aimeric saw..." Her words drifted away.

She didn't want to think of what might happen to either of them, or anyone else, if they were caught.

"I know. I'm sorry," Virgil said, ashamed for not being able to control himself.

He stepped away, hoping the gap between them would cool the feelings he had of wanting to throw Aralyn to the floor and make love to her right there.

"Have you thought of a way to get me out of here?" Aralyn asked desperately.

"I have an idea, but I can't tell you anything yet," he said softly, turning his back to her; the gap wasn't working.

Aralyn looked at the back of him sadly for a moment, still feeling guilty for what she had done with Aimeric and for now, just pushing Virgil away.

"Will you come with me?" she asked suddenly.

Virgil turned around, surprised.

"If you want me to, yes."

Aralyn smiled and took a few steps forward to embrace him.

"I want you to" she said into his chest.

He held her for a moment and then, kissing the top of her head, let go and gently pushed her backwards.

"You should get dressed now," he said.

Aralyn nodded and went to the dresser, which she assumed was Claire's, pulling out a few items of clothing; a pair of black leather pants and a red band t-shirt. She looked shyly at Virgil and he nodded, taking the hint, and turned around while she put the clothes on. Aralyn let the towel drop and then quickly pulled them on.

"I have to go back to him now…he's…expecting me," she said softly when she was finished.

Virgil turned back around and took Aralyn's hand in his, pressing his lips gently against her fingers.

"I will get you away from him, I promise," he whispered.

She nodded and Virgil led her out of the room, though it was obvious he didn't want to let her go back to Aimeric by the look on his face and the tension in his body. When they reached the Master vampire's room, the door opened and Virgil dropped Aralyn's hand immediately, thinking it was Aimeric. They both breathed a sigh of relief when they saw Morgan, but instantly became suspicious; he had a smirk plastered on his pasty face.

"What are you up to, worm?" Virgil sneered.

"Nothin' at all," Morgan responded nonchalantly, and walked off.

Virgil glared after him and then ran his finger along Aralyn's cheek.

"Be patient, okay?" he said.

She nodded again and, after a moment of Virgil looking like he desperately wanted to kiss her, he left, going in the same direction Morgan had gone. Aralyn took a moment to gather her nerves and then she turned the handle on the door to return to Aimeric. Before she could turn it all the way, however, the door flung open and Aralyn was pulled inside. Aimeric slammed the door shut and then shoved her onto the bed, straddling her legs and pinning her arms down. All he had on was a pair of pants, his chest was naked and had a few drops of water trickling down his sides and his hair was wet from the shower as well.

"Morgan tells me you and Virgil have gotten quite close," he sneered, pushing her wrists into the mattress.

"It's nothing, I swear!" Aralyn said in a frightened whisper.

"He saw the two of you kissing!" Aimeric growled.

She didn't have an argument for that. She turned her head to the side, guiltily.

"Have I not been clear on the rules, Aralyn? Have I not been clear on what would happen to you!" he yelled.

"I'm sorry!" she said, tears shining in her eyes.

She looked at him and silently pleaded for forgiveness.

"I don't believe you. I think you need another reminder," he said harshly.

Aimeric pulled her off the bed and flung open the door, leading her down to the basement.

"No! Please!" Aralyn yelled.

He ignored her, dragging her through the dark passageway, and took her into the prison cell.

"Aimeric, please, don't hurt anyone!" she said desperately.

"Shut up! I'll teach you not to whore around," he growled.

"But I didn't...I only kissed him, I swear!" she said, trying to pull her arm free from his death grip.

Ignoring her cries, Aimeric threw her against the wall and chained her arms down. He left her there and, not saying another word, stormed out of the cell.

"What are you going to do?" Aralyn yelled, terrified. "Aimeric!"

She heard him climb the stairs and then his voice boomed through the house.

"Mabel! Sadie! Get down here!"

Aralyn waited a few minutes, straining to hear anything. Aimeric soon returned with two female vampires. One was tall and thin and had light blonde hair, almost white, which hung past her rear. Her eyes were shocking green and her skin was ivory. She wore just a black mini skirt and a top that barely covered her small breasts. The other girl had short, purple colored hair with red tips. She was shorter than the blonde and her figure was sportier. She had several eyebrow piercings, plus her lip and nose were pierced. Her skin was also ivory and she was wearing contact lenses to make her eyes look feline; they were yellow with a black slit for the pupil. She wore a short black dress with black fishnet hose and a pair of black boots that zipped up to her knees.

The two girls hung onto Aimeric's arms, running their hands up and down his chest, while keeping their eyes on Aralyn. The purple haired girl licked her lips and Aralyn saw another piercing on her tongue. Aimeric glared at Aralyn for a moment and then, turning to the purple haired girl, he said, "Mabel."

He kissed her hard and the two of them licked at each other's tongues for a moment before he turned to the other girl.

"Sadie."

Aimeric kissed her the same, running his hand over her breast, while she cupped his pants. When they pulled apart, Aimeric gently pushed both girls forward; towards Aralyn.

"I want you both to teach her a lesson; do what you will," Aimeric said.

He sat down on the table, waiting for the girls to begin their work.

"Stay away from me," Aralyn warned the vampire women.

"What are you going to do about it?" Mabel challenged.

Aralyn looked over at a smirking Aimeric.

"What are you going to have them do?" she demanded.

"Whatever they want," he answered in a sneer.

Aralyn shrunk back against the wall, rattling the chains as Sadie and Mabel came to stand directly in front of her, trying to get as far away from the women as she could but, knowing that her efforts were useless, she started to cry again. Was there no end to her suffering?

Sadie started first, moving to stand on Aralyn's left, ignoring her tears, and ran her cold hand over Aralyn's face.

"Such a pretty little thing," she said.

Her hand fell down Aralyn's neck and onto the puncture wounds. She leaned down and sniffed the wounds and then looked over at Aimeric and grinned.

"She's already been tasted?"

Aimeric nodded and waved a hand.

"Help yourself."

Sadie quirked an eyebrow.

"Really?" Turning back to Aralyn, she whispered, "My, my, you *must* have been bad for Master Aimeric to offer *us* a taste."

Mabel moved to Aralyn's other side.

"What did you do? Fuck another man?" she asked with a soft laugh.

Out of the corner of her eye, Aralyn saw Aimeric glaring at her from the table; Mabel had hit it pretty close according to him. The blonde vampire brushed back Aralyn's hair on the other side of her neck and examined it.

"Hmm, this side is clean," she observed. She grinned at Mabel. "What should we do about that?"

"No," Aralyn said, frightened, and tried to shake the women off.

"Oh, what's wrong? Are you scared?" Mabel asked with mock sympathy.

"Best not to struggle, *love*," Aimeric hissed.

Aralyn cringed as she felt both, Sadie and Mabel, start to lick her neck, tasting the blood underneath her skin. Mabel's fangs entered her vein first and Aralyn gasped loudly and then grit her teeth.

"Does that hurt?" Sadie asked, amused, as Mabel drank. "Allow me to distract you from the pain," she whispered sensually.

She moved to stand in front of Aralyn and then ran her hands over Aralyn's breasts, pushing her body against hers. She lowered her mouth to Aralyn's and aggressively kissed her, forcing her tongue onto Aralyn's.

Shaking the chains even more and struggling to get Sadie off of her, Aralyn moved her head from side to side but all she accomplished was Mabel's fangs tearing even further into her flesh. Sadie followed Aralyn's movements and continued to kiss her while Mabel stole her blood. Aralyn could hear Aimeric chuckling and then, after a few moments, Mabel finally pulled away, wiping her mouth free of the blood that dribbled down. She took a moment to slowly lick the crimson liquid from her fingers, while eyeing Aralyn, who was still being kissed, and then, she whispered to Sadie, "Your turn."

Sadie pulled away from Aralyn, licking her lips, and smiled.

"It's about time."

Already feeling slightly drowsy from blood loss, Aralyn leaned her head against the cold brick, trying to keep her eyes from closing. She felt her own, warm, blood trickling down her neck.

"Brace yourself, sweetheart," Sadie said, moving her tongue to the other side of Aralyn's neck.

She raked her fangs over the vein and tasted the scent first. Mabel took one of Aralyn's arms and scraped her fingernail across it, bringing little drops of crimson to the surface. She smiled at Aralyn's drowsy expression.

"I haven't had enough," she explained.

As Mabel brought the arm up to her mouth, Sadie's fangs penetrated Aralyn's neck. Aralyn screamed and she balled her hands up into fists though she didn't have enough strength to move the chains. It seemed like forever that the two women were latched onto her, drinking her life source without caring how Aralyn felt. Yet, Aralyn didn't really blame them, it was Aimeric that she hated even more now.

After a few moments of sucking part of Aralyn's life out of her neck, Sadie moved to her arm and did what Mabel was doing; Sadie sliced open one of Aralyn's already existing cuts and began to slurp at the blood that surfaced. If it weren't for the chains holding her up, Aralyn would have slumped to the ground at the weakness she was feeling at that moment. She could feel herself slipping into darkness and she welcomed it. Her head bobbed a moment and then her chin fell to rest on her chest. After only a few seconds, Aralyn felt her chin being raised and she managed to flutter her eyes open, looking into the eyes of Aimeric. He was blurry and his words echoed as though he were far away.

"Have you learned your lesson yet?"

Aralyn shook her head drowsily and as best she could.

"Get away from me...just let me die..."

"I don't think so, my love," Aimeric said.

He pulled the women up from their positions on the floor. They had both fallen to their knees in ecstasy when they had begun drinking from Aralyn's arms.

"Thank you, ladies. I'll call you back down if I need anything else," Aimeric said to them, kissing them as he had done before.

Both girls smirked and then left the prison, leaving Aralyn alone with Aimeric and the prisoners, who had become curious and came to the gates to watch as Aralyn was being tortured. When Aimeric stood a moment ago, however, they had all run to the back of the cell.

"Don't make me do this to you again, Aralyn," Aimeric said as he undid her cuffs.

Aralyn mumbled a few words that were incoherent but Aimeric heard them in his mind, "Fuck you."

He laughed as she collapsed against him, almost entirely unconscious now.

"Later, my love," he promised.

Aimeric gathered Aralyn up into his arms as she slipped into total darkness.

Aimeric carried the unconscious Aralyn up the crumbling stone steps, her head resting against his chest. Her blood was almost intoxicating as it trickled out of the wounds on her arms and neck and stained his shirt, but he kept his craving for her under control. It was true that her blood was no longer the sweet virgin blood it had been before but it was still better than most humans he had fed from. Like so many other differences the humans had, the taste of their blood varied.

Aimeric carried Aralyn through the living room where Morgan, Sadie, Mabel, and Virgil, along with a few other vampires, were conversing. Virgil, as usual as of late, looked angry and worried, hounding the other vampires with questions, which Aimeric had no doubt were about Aralyn.

"What did you do to her?" Virgil asked when he saw Aimeric carrying Aralyn's limp body.

"Nothing that concerns you," Aimeric sneered. He began climbing the stairs. "I'll deal with *you* later."

Chapter Seven: Declaration

Virgil watched Aimeric take Aralyn up the stairs and then he verbally pounced on Morgan.

"What did you tell him?" he growled, baring his fangs.

"Only the truth of wha' I saw," Morgan said simply.

"I'm going to fucking kill you," Virgil said.

Sadie and Mabel hissed at him disapprovingly and Morgan smirked.

"You can't do nothin' to me; I'm under Aimeric's protection. You kill me, he kills you. Then who would poor, sweet, little Aralyn run to?"

Virgil angrily shoved Morgan backwards, knowing he was right.

"You're going to pay for this," he promised, pointing a finger at him, before he stalked to a closet near the front door and pulled on rain boots followed by a cloak and then a rain jacket.

"What the hell are you doing?" Sadie asked.

"None of your business, whore!" Virgil snapped angrily.

Sadie smirked.

"*Your* whore at one time…or have you forgotten?"

Virgil glared at her but didn't respond and then he turned to the front door.

"You're begging for Aimeric to kill you, aren't you?" Mabel asked.

"I don't care what he does to me! I won't let that girl suffer anymore. I'm going to find Claire!" Virgil announced in a loud whisper.

He went outside into the pouring rain, thankful that the clouds so thickly covered the sun.

"You're a fool!" Morgan called after him, closing the door.

Virgil didn't care if what he was doing was foolish; he had to save Aralyn from Aimeric before he destroyed her. Not just physically, but mentally as well. Aimeric had literally sent hundreds of girls to insane asylums simply for his own sick pleasure, keeping them alive, allowing them to suffer in so many ways before he sent them back to their families as some sort of sick joke. The girls would wake up screaming in their beds at night and would be in such a frenzy that their families couldn't calm them down.

Virgil couldn't let this happen to Aralyn.

He trudged through the mud and went through the forest until he came to the edge of the city. The rain never let up the whole time, but that was a good thing. By the time Virgil knocked (more like pounded) on the door of a large mansion, he was exhausted. After several minutes, the door finally cracked open and a soft gasp followed before Virgil was pulled inside.

"What the hell were you thinking? You could have been killed!" the person said.

"I had to come, Orrin," Virgil gasped.

"In the daytime? The sun may be covered today but that doesn't mean you are entirely protected, Virgil! Look at you!" Orrin scolded.

"It's important. I don't know if I would have had enough time to wait until dark, I don't know how much time I have even now. Once Aimeric finds out I left, he'll be furious as it is."

"What's so damn important that you would risk the sunlight? *And* Aimeric's temper?" Orrin asked.

"A girl," Virgil responded.

Orrin scoffed and folded his arms over his broad chest.

"I might have known."

"And besides, the sun isn't out," Virgil pointed out.

"Those clouds could break at any moment," Orrin argued.

"Doubtful," Virgil replied.

Orrin shook his head in dismay.

"When are you going to learn that you just aren't as powerful as I am?"

"Don't get cocky; you're one of the lucky ones," Virgil said.

"Not so lucky. My 'luck' can also be a curse," Orrin said.

"Only because you allow it to be," Virgil replied.

"Maybe…" Orrin said quietly.

After a moment of silence had passed between the two of them, Orrin clapped Virgil on the back.

"Well, come in to the kitchen and I'll give you a nice, hot cup of blood and you can tell me why you're running around outside during the day and risking…Aimeric's temper."

There was a harsh tone when Orrin said Aimeric's name.

Virgil nodded and followed Orrin to the large kitchen, which was way more up to date than the one in Aimeric's mansion. The whole house was up to date and it was clean.

"Everyone else asleep?" Virgil asked, sliding into a chair at the cherry wood table.

"Yup. That's what *normal* vampires do during the day," Orrin said sarcastically, sticking a mug into the microwave.

"I guess my clan isn't normal then," Virgil remarked, remembering everyone who was awake at the mansion.

"I could have told you that. That's one of the reasons I left," Orrin said, shrugging.

"You're lucky he let you go so easily," Virgil said.

"I was a bother to him," Orrin replied.

Virgil nodded, laughing softly.

"I remember. You did cause some trouble, didn't you?"

"It was worth it. Aimeric disgraces us all. He kills not only vampire kind, but his own clan members; I'm lucky he didn't kill me," Orrin said.

The microwave beeped loudly and Orrin took the mug out, placing it in front of Virgil.

"Thanks," Virgil said and took a drink.

His face contorted in disgust; old blood never tasted as good as fresh but he needed it.

"No problem. Now, tell me, what is so important about this girl? Who is she?" Orrin asked, sitting across from him.

"Her name is Aralyn," Virgil began.

"You mean Claire's sister?" Orrin interrupted.

"You've spoken to Claire? When? Is she here?" Virgil asked, looking around.

Orrin shook his cloaked head.

"Not anymore. She came to talk to me about…never mind, it's not important."

"Do you know when she will be back? Or if she will be at all?" Virgil inquired.

He would have pressed on and asked Orrin what it was that he and Claire had been discussing, but Aralyn was the only thing on his mind at that moment.

"No. I don't know."

"She's lucky that Aimeric hasn't figured out that this is one of the places she comes to on her little vacations," Virgil said bitterly.

Orrin was now a member of a different clan than Aimeric's. And to vampires, clans were the only family they had and if a vampire was caught contacting members of other clans he, or she, could be punished by death or however his master deemed justifiable. Virgil himself was risking a lot by being there.

"She knows the risk and it doesn't bother her, or so she says," Orrin said, shrugging.

"Claire has been strong since day one. She's only been a vampire for a year but she already acts like she knows everything," Virgil commented.

"The new ones always do. And then it hits them what their life really is and a lot can't handle it. I'm sure you went through a state of depression shortly after you were turned," Orrin said.

Virgil nodded.

"It was thirty years later when I should have been aging and turning gray that it hit me that I was immortal, or the closest thing to it," he said.

Orrin nodded in understanding and another long moment of silence passed before Orrin spoke up again.

"So what is this girl having done to her?"

"Aimeric is destroying her," Virgil said angrily.

"He's destroyed a lot of mortal women, and men for that matter. Why is she different to you? Because she's Claire's sister? I'm sure Claire will handle everything when she returns to that house. That woman even has the balls to question Aimeric," Orrin finished.

"He will destroy her *before* Claire returns!" Virgil said, raising his voice.

"So let him! It's not your problem!" Orrin said.

Virgil sighed, leaning back in his chair, and rubbed his face.

"Oh…I see," Orrin said, studying him, as realization dawned. "You're in love with her, aren't you?"

"Yes," Virgil said quietly.

"Leave it alone. Forget her. If Aimeric has already claimed her, which I'm sure he has, she may as well be dead to you."

"No!" Virgil pounded his fists on the table, not caring if he woke the vampires up. "I will not forget her,

Orrin; I'm taking her far away from Aimeric. But I need Claire to get her away from him first."

"What do you mean?"

"I'm not sure exactly myself. I just think that if Claire was there, Aimeric would back off of Aralyn a little and I could get her away easier…fat chance though, right?"

Orrin nodded in agreement.

"But still, I have to try anything that might work," Virgil continued.

He stood from the table and set the empty mug down.

"Where are you going?" Orrin asked, worried.

"Back to Aralyn. I came here looking for Claire, she's not here, so now I am going back."

"Virgil, that's crazy. You're already weak. At least wait until sundown," Orrin protested.

"She may need me now. Besides, I don't want to put your clan in danger. Aimeric is already pissed at me, if he finds me here, who knows what he'll do? As for being weak, I feel fine. The blood helped, thanks."

Orrin sighed, following Virgil to the door.

"I hope this girl is worth it."

Virgil looked at him, his hand on the doorknob.

"She is," he replied, pulling the door open, and stepped onto the porch.

The rain had turned into a light mist but the clouds were still thick.

"Take care, my friend," Orrin said, closing the door.

Virgil nodded and stepped off the porch and on to the wet grass. On his way back to the mansion, his mind wandered. How could he save Aralyn? He knew Aimeric would keep her alive for a little longer, but would it be enough time? He needed to come up with something quickly. Where would they go? How would they stay hidden? Aimeric had vampires run away in the past. Except for Orrin, he had pursued them all and found them, making them pay for it. He had waited for a while until they thought for sure that they were safe and then he went to them and brought them back to the mansion to torture them; keeping them barely alive for weeks, or sometimes, even months. One of his ways of punishment was letting the sun fall on them long enough to burn them but not kill them, and then he would do other, horrible, things to them, before he finally killed them.

Orrin had been right about Aimeric; he was a disgrace to all vampire kind. No vampire was innocent. No vampire had *not* killed a mortal at least once, some had become so disgusted with themselves that they refused to feed off humans and only feed from animals and rodents, but they had always tried one human once in their undead lives. But Aimeric was close to being Satan himself. He had killed thousands, including vampires. He did have weaknesses, yes, but no other vampire had been able to find them yet, besides what they themselves were weak against. Aimeric was one of the strongest undead that had ever walked the Earth. How was Virgil going to rescue Aralyn from that?

Virgil wasn't weak by any means, compared to mortals and most other vampires, in fact, he was second in strength only to Aimeric in his own clan, but compared to Aimeric himself, Virgil may as well be an insect under Aimeric's boot.

"Well, well, look who's back."

Virgil had been so deep in thought that he hadn't realized he had come upon the mansion. And there stood Aimeric, leaning against the door. He was heavily cloaked to protect his flesh from the daylight that even *he* was weak against.

"Relax, I only went for a walk," Virgil said casually, stepping up to the door.

He wouldn't show his fears, his doubts, his frustrations; not to Aimeric.

Aimeric smirked.

"You must have really needed it to risk the sun," he said coolly. He knew Virgil was lying. "I wonder...what could have upset you so much?" Aimeric asked him dryly.

"Is she dead?" Virgil sneered.

"Ah, so it *is my* Aralyn that you got so upset over," Aimeric said.

He straightened up and opened the door, gesturing for Virgil to go inside.

"*Is* she dead?" Virgil repeated, not moving.

Aimeric grinned.

"She's sleeping. Sadie and Mabel wore her out."

Virgil's fists clenched tightly along with his jaw, he knew what the girls had probably done to Aralyn. He wanted so much for the sun to break through the clouds so that Aimeric would burn, even if it meant he burned along with him, at least Aralyn would stand a chance then.

"I would re-think things if I were you, Virgil. You can't win against me in *anything* we compete for," Aimeric sneered, seeing Virgil's fists clenched tight.

With a scowl on his face, Virgil ignored Aimeric and stepped into the dark house. It wouldn't do any good to argue with him right now.

"Oh and Virgil?" Aimeric called.

He turned around, still glaring.

Aimeric smiled, an evil gleam in his cold eyes.

"Aralyn belongs to *me* and *only* me. I hope your punishment will make you think twice about touching her, or even *thinking* of touching her, again."

Two pairs of strong hands grabbed Virgil's shoulders from behind.

"Take him downstairs," Aimeric ordered coldly.

Chapter Eight: A Few Moments in Heaven

Aralyn heard painful screaming in her sleep. Torturous screaming, as though someone was being slowly killed. The sounds made her blood curdle and her eyelids twitch in her sleep. Her body stirred with each yell until one finally made her jump up in bed, gasping loudly. Aralyn then realized that she hadn't been dreaming; the screams had been real.

"Good evening, my love," Aimeric said, sitting up behind her.

His arms snaked around her naked shoulders and his hand rested over her left breast as his cold lips found the skin on her neck and lightly began pecking it. Aralyn was in Aimeric's bed, though she didn't remember how she had gotten there. The silk sheets that were covering her had slipped down to her waist when she sat up but she didn't care at that moment; she didn't even care that Aimeric was touching and kissing her. She was only focused on the screams so her eyes scanned the room, searching for the source of the cries she had heard.

"What is that?" she finally whispered hoarsely, due to her dry throat.

"Never mind," Aimeric said, still kissing her. "Come downstairs with me, I'm sure you're hungry. Thirsty too; you've been asleep for three days now."

"What?" she asked in disbelief.

"You were quite weak; apparently the girls took too much of your blood," Aimeric said, chuckling into her hair.

Aralyn didn't laugh; she didn't think it was funny. Her anger raged inside of her again when she remembered what Aimeric had done, or rather, allowed to have happen, to her the other day.

"Come on, let's get you something to eat," Aimeric said, pulling her off the bed.

He smirked at her naked body before throwing a robe over her shoulders and tying the belt around her slim waist. He tied it roughly, pulling her forward as he closed off the gap in the front of the robe, so that her hands hit up against his chest.

"I trust you have learned your lesson?" he asked and turned her head to the side to look at the puncture marks on her neck.

The movement pulled the scabs on the clean skin and Aralyn grimaced.

"Aralyn?" he asked, demanding an answer when she didn't show any sign of agreement.

"Yes," she said softly.

"Good."

He kissed her deeply and Aralyn forced herself to kiss him back, though her stomach was churning. She wanted to know what was going on, where Virgil was, and who was screaming so she thought it best to comply with Aimeric's wishes and if he wanted a kiss, then she would give it to him. Pulling back, he smiled and touched Aralyn's bottom lip with his thumb.

"Good girl. Now come."

He took her hand and led her downstairs to the kitchen where he sat her down at the table before going to the counter to chop up various fruits. He set the pieces on a serving plate when he finished slicing them. At the sight of the juices leaking out of the fruit, Aralyn's stomach rumbled and her mouth watered. She hadn't realized how hungry she was until then and her eyes seemed to be glued to the fruit as she anxiously waited for Aimeric to serve it to her.

While waiting, her thoughts wandered. She didn't hear the screaming anymore and almost asked Aimeric about it, and also about Virgil, but, catching herself at the last second, she just waited quietly with her hands in her lap. She didn't think it wise to ask about Virgil; Aimeric would get jealous and angry.

Finally, the plate was set in front of her along with a fresh glass of orange juice and then Aimeric stood behind her while she hungrily ate and drank the juice in three gulps. Cold hands massaged the tense muscles in Aralyn's back, moving up to her shoulders and then when Aimeric reached her neck, and his fingers got too close to her bruised wounds, she winced. Hearing her soft gasp, Aimeric pulled Aralyn's hair gently to the side and ran his fingers over the bumps on each side of her neck. His hands slid down her shoulders and came to rest at her sides as he knelt beside her.

They looked at each other for a moment; Aralyn's expression was anger covered up by curiosity and Aimeric's was thoughtful. Pushing himself up to her lips, he brushed his against them softly and then looked at her again.

"I can make the pain go away forever," he whispered.

She leaned back in her chair and turned her head slightly so he wouldn't kiss her again.

"I need more time," she said quietly.

Of course she didn't have any intention of letting him turn her into a vampire, but she thought that if he thought she was thinking it over, he would leave her alone long enough for Virgil to come up with a plan so the two of them could escape together. Aimeric stared at her intently, trying to read her mind so Aralyn tried her hardest to keep Virgil out of it so Aimeric wouldn't get suspicious. She tried to keep her mind blank, though she wasn't sure if she could actually keep her thoughts hidden from Aimeric. If she hadn't succeeded, Aimeric gave no indication. He only smiled and kissed her one last time before standing up.

"As you wish. I will be leaving for a while, I haven't fed since you passed out," Aimeric said, pouring her some more orange juice.

"Why?" Aralyn asked, confused.

He set the cup down and looked at her, a very serious expression on his face.

"I was worried about you so I stayed to watch over you."

Aralyn looked at him for a moment, as though he had spoken a foreign language, and saw that he was starting to look sickly from lack of feeding, but she still couldn't bring herself to feel sorry for him and after only a few seconds, she didn't even believe that he had been worried about her. If he had stayed to watch over her, he had only done it to make sure no one else touched "his" property while "it" was unconscious. Seeing the look on his face, Aralyn quickly brushed those thoughts aside. Aimeric had pried into her mind again and heard everything she had just thought and now he was looking angry.

"I'm sorry," Aralyn said.

He shrugged.

"You can't help what you think I suppose…at least not right now…"

Something in that last statement told Aralyn that it was a warning and that she had better try her hardest to control her thoughts.

"I have made it clear to everyone here that you are off limits, so, unless something happens to me," he smirked, obviously thinking the idea absurd, "you are safe. I want you to go upstairs when you are finished eating and rest some more; your mortal body is still healing."

Aralyn nodded, taking another bite of a strawberry slice.

"I have ordered that Morgan watch over you and make sure you don't try and…escape." Cupping her face in his hands, Aimeric looked down at her and smiled, a warning, sardonic smile. "But that shouldn't be an issue, should it, my love?"

"No, Master Aimeric," she said, looking into his eyes to show she was serious.

"I didn't think so," he said, stroking her cheek with his thumb.

He turned around and glided to the kitchen doorway.

"Morgan!" he called into the living room. "Get in here!"

A few seconds later, the vampire bounced into the kitchen, looking like a favored child.

"Yes, Master?" Morgan asked, smirking at Aralyn.

Oh, how she would love to beat that smirk off his narrow face.

"I'm leaving now. Watch her," Aimeric said, going to the front door. He paused when his hand touched the doorknob. "Oh and Morgan?"

"Yes, Master?"

"*Don't* touch her," he warned and opened the door, letting a wave of fresh, cool air enter the stuffy house.

He went outside and pulled the door closed behind him.

Morgan turned to Aralyn after Aimeric left, looking disappointed, which Aralyn couldn't help but smirk at, feeling it was her turn. Morgan glared, murderously, back at her and then sat down to watch her eat. It got annoying after a few bites.

"Can I help you with something?" Aralyn asked snidely.

"Nope," Morgan responded simply.

She rolled her eyes and finished off the juice before hurriedly eating the rest of the fruit while she also tried to ignore the petty man before her. Aralyn thought it was amazing that she could hate someone more than Aimeric, but it was true; she wished to see Morgan's death before

Aimeric's. Wanting to get away from him, she stood from the table, intending to go upstairs, when the door to the basement slammed and seconds later, a big, bulky vampire came into the kitchen, supporting a very bloody Virgil.

Aralyn gasped.

"Oh my God, what happened to him?"

Virgil was shirtless and only wearing a pair of tattered and torn pants. His torso was covered in blood from, what looked like, whip marks.

"First of all, I would refrain from using that name in this house or Aimeric will let you have it," the large vampire began. His voice was deep and threatening sounding, but it also held a hint of stupidity. "Second of all-"

"Second of all, Virgil was punished for touchin' you!" Morgan interrupted and fell into a fit of exaggerated laughter.

"I don't like being interrupted!" the other vampire growled.

Carelessly tossing Virgil to the floor, the big vampire grabbed Morgan up by the collar of his shirt and growled something else to him, which Aralyn didn't hear; she wasn't paying attention to them. She rushed to Virgil's side and pulled his head onto her lap.

"Virgil. Wake up."

He groaned and opened his eyes at the sound of her concerned voice, bringing a hand up to touch her cheek.

He chuckled softly.

"Don't worry about me, love. I heal pretty quickly. These should be almost gone in only an hour or so."

"This is my fault," Aralyn whispered, a tear rolling down her cheek.

Shaking his head gently, Virgil whispered, "No, it's not. It's partially Morgan's fault, but mostly, it's mine. I knew he would want you, Aralyn. I should have stayed away from you. I'm so sorry." He looked into her violet eyes and then asked, "What did he do to you? He wouldn't tell me."

As though her wounds reacted to his words, Aralyn felt a sharp pain run through both sides of her neck, but she shook her head, not wanting Virgil to worry about her.

"Nothing really…"

He frowned, obviously not believing her, and opened his mouth to say something but Morgan, who had worked out whatever was going on between him and the other vampire, cut him off.

"Hey, whore! What do you think you're doin'?"

"Don't call her that!" Virgil spat.

"Shut up!" Morgan growled and then looked to Aralyn for an answer.

"He's hurt and bleeding! I can't just leave him here on the floor," Aralyn said defensively.

Using all of her strength, which wasn't very much at that moment, Aralyn pulled Virgil up to sit in one of the chairs at the table.

"I'll tell Aimeric," Morgan threatened.

"Go ahead!" Aralyn dared as she wet a cloth.

She took it over to Virgil and gently cleaned his wounds.

"Don't worry, honey; it's not his blood," the big vampire said.

Aralyn glared at his back as he left the room, chuckling at his own joke.

Morgan exaggerated another laugh.

"Isn't Wes a riot?"

Ignoring Morgan, Aralyn continued to dab at the cuts on Virgil's chest until he took her hand.

"Sweetheart, really, I'm fine now. Look, I've already stopped bleeding," he said gently.

Looking from his chest, to see that he was right, and then to his dark eyes, with tears shining in her own, Aralyn whispered, "I'm sorry."

Virgil smiled and wiped away the tear that fell from her eye.

"Don't be, I'm fine."

Aralyn gently wrapped her arms around Virgil's neck, careful not to touch his wounds, not caring if Morgan saw the two of them. Virgil kissed her cheek and secured his arms around her as well.

"Oh well, this is interesting. Master Aimeric will love to hear this, I'm sure," Morgan said thoughtfully.

Virgil glared at him and, before he could stop her, Aralyn jumped up, grabbed a knife from the table, and spun around, plunging the blade into Morgan's chest. The vampire looked surprised at first as though he didn't think Aralyn had it in her to do something like that.

But it didn't matter.

Smirking, Morgan pulled the knife from his chest. "Nice try."

"Aralyn, come on, sit down," Virgil said softly.

Glaring at Morgan, Aralyn obeyed and slowly sat in the chair across from Virgil.

"How do you feel?" she asked.

She couldn't ask him what she really wanted to, not with Morgan there. She wanted to ask him if he had found a way out of this hell yet, but she knew she would have to be patient.

"Better," Virgil responded.

"Are you sure you aren't in any pain?" Aralyn asked, looking, worriedly, at the bloody marks on his torso.

"Yes, I promise," Virgil said.

"Are you hungry?" she asked.

"I'm fine Aralyn."

"Really? No offense, but you don't look it. I mean, if you are hungry, I could…I mean you can…" she stuttered, not sure if she really wanted to say it.

"I know what you're trying to say and the answer is 'no.' I'm not going to drink from you," Virgil said sternly.

Morgan scoffed from behind her and mumbled something, neither of them heard.

"But if it will make you feel-"

"Aralyn, no," Virgil interrupted sternly.

She slumped back in her chair and he smiled.

"Thanks for the offer love, but I could never drink from you and besides, you're still too weak anyway."

"Hmm, 'love,' I'll be sure to write tha' one down," Morgan muttered.

Aralyn sucked in an angry breath of air, trying to keep calm.

"Just ignore him," Virgil said softly.

"Easier said than done," she mumbled.

Virgil laughed softly.

"I know."

Suddenly remembering that she was supposed to go to bed when she finished eating, Aralyn stood from the table.

"I have to go. Do you need any help up the stairs?" she asked, concerned.

Virgil shook his head.

"No, I can walk on my own now."

"Okay," she said, hesitantly nodding. "Goodnight then."

"Goodnight, Aralyn."

The two held each other's gaze for a few moments and then Aralyn turned to leave, shoving past Morgan, and went up the stairs to Aimeric's bedroom. Morgan was at her heels, following her up.

"Don't you have somewhere you could be?" Aralyn hissed, rounding on him once they got into the bedroom.

"Aimeric told me to keep an eye on you so tha's what I'm doin,'" Morgan said snidely.

Sighing, and wanting to get away, Aralyn went into the bathroom and slammed the door in Morgan's face just as he tried to enter behind her.

"Don't try anything, wench! I'll be right out here!" he yelled, and gave the door a quick hit.

Jumping only slightly at the loud sound, Aralyn sighed and ran water into the tub. She untied the robe and let it fall to the floor and then she unraveled the bandages on her arms. The cuts had healed mostly now so she doubted she would have to wrap them again. The scabs were starting to fall off, leaving only scars; reminders of what had happened when she had trusted a stranger.

It seemed like so long ago that Devin had pulled her from the Cliffside, but in reality, it had only been a few weeks. She turned off the water and stepped into it, grimacing slightly when it touched her skin; she had let it get a little too hot. She washed quickly, not wanting to be in the water long, and then pulled the plug to drain the tub. After a quick blotting with a towel, she put her robe back on and, taking a deep breath, she went back into the bedroom to face Morgan.

He was leaning against the bedpost, smirking at her.

"Did you enjoy your bath?"

"It got me away from you for a little while, so I would say so," she said coolly.

"I see," Morgan said, nodding.

He eyed her body and took in her form as though he were memorizing it to keep forever locked into his mind. Starting at her face, which was framed by wet locks, he traveled down to her neck and breasts. She hadn't dried herself entirely so droplets of water had caused the, black, silk robe she was wearing to stick to her skin, outlining her nipples, and they also made the bare part of her chest glisten in the torchlight. The rest of the robe hugged every curve of her body.

"You look...absolutely satisfying," Morgan said in a sultry whisper.

He pushed himself off the bedpost, and kept his lust filled eyes on her. His hand stretched out to touch her arm, to pull her forward, and Aralyn stepped out of his reach.

"Aimeric said not to touch me," she sneered.

Morgan's fists clenched tightly but he stepped back, knowing she was right.

"I am tired, and I want to go to sleep so leave," Aralyn demanded.

"You can sleep with me in here, go ahead," Morgan said, waving a hand towards the bed.

Aralyn's face contorted into anger and she stepped forward.

"Leave now," she said through clenched teeth.

"Make me," Morgan said childishly.

Aralyn lunged forward and grabbed at his shirt, intending on forcefully shoving him out of the room; the very sight of him made her angry and she wanted him out. His looks were not comforting; she didn't feel safe at all with him around. She doubted she had the strength to throw him out, he was a vampire after all, but she had to try at least. Morgan caught her by the wrists and shoved her backwards.

"Enticing bitch!" he hissed.

"I wasn't inviting you to touch me, you piece of filth! I want you out!" Aralyn yelled.

Morgan chuckled and turned his back on her to pull down the covers on the bed.

"You are something else, you know that? Honestly, I don't know why Aimeric keeps you around, you're just a-"

With a swift hit on the back of the head from an iron ashtray, Morgan fell to the floor, unconscious. Aralyn stared at his still form for a moment, in shock that she had knocked him out. She had only intended on hurting him. She wanted to cause him pain, knowing that he could do nothing to harm her back; so it turned out Aimeric was good for something. How could Morgan be this weak?

"Shit, what do I do now?" she muttered to herself.

She set the tray back down on the dresser and then turned back to Morgan, lightly kicking his leg to see if he was really out; she still couldn't believe a conk to the head would really knock a vampire out; she was surprised it had happened. Aimeric was going to be mad if he came home to see she had knocked Morgan out; he would think she was up to something. He might punish her, Virgil, or anyone else. She couldn't let that happen, but what should she do? She did the only thing she thought she *could* do. She decided to see if Virgil could help her.

Quietly opening the door and sneaking out into the hall, Aralyn glanced both ways before she hurriedly ran to Virgil's room. She knocked softly on the door and opened it a crack, whispering his name.

"Aralyn?" Virgil asked, sitting up in the bed he was laying in. "What are you doing? Are you crazy? You're going to get caught."

Aralyn went further into the room.

"I need your help."

He was off the bed in a second.

"Why? What's wrong?" Virgil asked, concerned.

"Just...follow me," Aralyn said, opening the door enough for them both to fit through.

When they got to Aimeric's room, Virgil sighed in dismay, seeing Morgan lying on the floor.

"What happened?"

"He made me mad," Aralyn said sheepishly.

"How did you knock him out?" Virgil asked in disbelief.

Aralyn showed him the ashtray.

"I didn't think it would actually knock him out...Aimeric's going to be pissed."

Virgil nodded.

"Damn Morgan and his weaknesses."

She stood there, slightly embarrassed at the trouble she had caused, while Virgil looked at Morgan thoughtfully, coming up with some sort of plan to get out of this one.

Finally he looked at Aralyn and said, "Stay here. I'll be back in a little while. If Aimeric comes back before I do, just...tell him that Morgan tried to touch you or something, that should make him understand."

Aralyn nodded and watched Virgil leave, closing the door behind him. She really didn't want to run into Aimeric's arms and cry "rape" if he happened to get home before Virgil could get back, but if it would keep anyone from getting punished, except Morgan of course, then Aralyn would do it if she had to. She paced the room, waiting and hoping it would be Virgil she saw come through that door when it opened, and watched to make sure Morgan wasn't going to wake up on her.

***

After about half an hour had passed, the doorknob turned and Aralyn held her breath. She released it when Virgil stumbled in, helping a human, a male of about thirty or so, walk with his arm under the man's shoulder. The man was mumbling words and his sentences were slurred.

"What are you going to do with him?" Aralyn asked curiously.

"He's drunk," Virgil grunted, and shifted the man's weight in his grasp.

"I see that, what are you-" Aralyn gasped, stopping in mid-sentence, seeing two holes on the man's neck as Virgil lowered him to the floor.

"What...did you drink from him?" she asked.

"Yes," Virgil responded, reaching for Morgan.

"Why?"

"Aralyn, please don't ask me questions right now. Help me with Morgan."

Hesitating for only a second, Aralyn went to Virgil's side and helped him take Morgan to a chair by the window. Virgil made Morgan slump over the side of the chair, his arms dangling over the edges, and then he went back to the human man and dragged him to the foot of the chair, at Morgan's feet. Kneeling beside him, Virgil looked at Aralyn.

"You might not want to watch, love."

She turned her head, closing her eyes; she had a good idea of what he was about to do. Virgil used one of his long fingernails to slice open the man's wrist, luckily the man was so heavily intoxicated that he didn't seem to notice. Picking the man up again, Virgil held the bleeding wrist over Morgan's mouth and let the crimson liquid trickle into it. In his sleep, Morgan tasted the blood and opened his mouth further, allowing it to pour inside and onto his tongue.

"Hey...are you...doing...what?" the drunken man asked, scrambling up his words.

Virgil ignored him but Aralyn, hearing the man, risked a glance to see what Virgil was doing.

She scoffed in disgust.

"Couldn't you have at least knocked him out first?"

"He doesn't care, he doesn't even feel it," Virgil said.

It was true, the man had only been curious before. Now, his eyes fluttered as he slipped into unconsciousness himself. Whether it was from lack of blood or from the alcohol, neither Aralyn nor Virgil knew for sure.

"So, what's your plan exactly? What are you doing?" Aralyn asked.

Morgan had begun to moan in his sleep from the taste of the blood.

"You're not going to like it," Virgil said.

"Just tell me."

"I went to the basement and brought him out, gave him some hard stuff, and then I brought him up here. Morgan drinks his liquored up blood, and becomes drunk himself. That will explain to Aimeric why he's unconscious, and even if he's not by the time Aimeric returns, he'll be drunk enough that anything Morgan says will go in one ear and out the other," Virgil said.

Thinking Morgan had had enough, Virgil let the human fall to the floor.

"So, why did you need to drink from him first?" Aralyn asked

"To make sure enough liquor was in his blood," Virgil replied.

"How come you aren't drunk?"

"I only had a little," Virgil responded with a smile. His smile faded as he remembered something. "Look away," he advised Aralyn.

"Why?"

"You're full of questions tonight, love," he said smiling again. "I need to bite him a few more times to make him look 'played' with. That's how Morgan feeds."

Feeling her stomach churning again, Aralyn nodded and, disgusted, looked in the other direction. She cringed when she heard Virgil's fangs penetrate the flesh in five different places; the sound was a quick slurp and then, when the fangs were pulled out, it sounded as a tin can did when its lid was popped off by a can opener.

"Aralyn, you can look now…Aralyn?" Virgil asked.

She heard him, but didn't move.

"What's wrong?" he asked, coming up to stand beside her.

"I just…wish he didn't have to die," she said softly, knowing the man would be dead in a few minutes if he wasn't already.

How did this man's dying justify what she had done to Morgan? She had wanted to avoid this; it wasn't any different than what Aimeric would have done.

"Sweetheart, he would have been dead in no time anyway. Aimeric never keeps them for very long. Trust me, this was probably the best way for him to die; it was fairly quick and he didn't feel anything."

Aralyn nodded but she still felt guilty for it.

"I'm glad you came to me though; it shows me that you really do trust me," Virgil said, touching her arm.

She looked at him and saw that he was being sincere.

"I do trust you, Virgil."

He smiled.

"I was actually hoping to talk to you again tonight," he continued. "I know how to get us out of here but it will have to wait until tomorrow, after Aimeric leaves to feed, so we'll have more time before the sun rises."

"Really!" Aralyn asked, almost losing control over her emotions and letting out a yell.

She wanted to scream and jump around the room. She didn't even care to ask *how* Virgil would get them out of there. She trusted him and that was all she needed. She stopped herself from getting too excited and instead, threw her arms around Virgil and hugged him tightly.

"I'm glad you're so happy about it," Virgil said, laughing softly, holding her.

Pulling away enough to look into his eyes, she smiled.

"Of course I am."

He returned the smile briefly before lowering his lips to hers, kissing her softly. Closing her eyes, Aralyn responded and kissed him back, opening her mouth to welcome him inside. He complied and their tongues touched together. Aralyn started to pull back at first, tasting the metallic flavor of the remnants of the blood in his mouth, but he held onto her, kissing her more passionately and she soon forgot the taste and melted into him. Aralyn felt the heat spread through her body and she could tell that she wouldn't be able to let him go until it was cooled.

He must have felt the same way because he stopped kissing her and laid his forehead against hers so he could whisper, "You have no idea how much I want you right now."

Barely able to, Aralyn nodded.

"Yes, I do."

Her words were enough to convince him and he pressed his lips against hers again. She closed her eyes once more and soon felt as though she was floating in space. When she opened them again, she saw that it had been true.

"Where are we?" she asked, pulling away from Virgil to gaze around the room.

The ceiling was low and slanted and pieces of old furniture were thrown around the room along with boxes filled with, what could only be described as, junk.

"We're in the attic," Virgil said.

"How did you do that?" Aralyn asked.

Leaning down to her neck, he whispered, "A magician never reveals his secrets."

She smiled as his lips gently pecked at her flesh. Pain shot through her when they touched the bruise around her wounds, however, and she pulled away, wincing.

"What is it?" Virgil asked, concerned.

"It's um…nothing," she lied.

Brushing her hair to the side, Virgil found the scabbed holes in her neck.

"Is this the only one?" he asked.

Aralyn could hear the anger in his voice when he spoke.

"No," she said softly and then pulled her hair back so that he could see the other side.

Aralyn heard him sigh angrily and then Virgil turned her around and, cupping her face in his cold hands, kissed her softly.

"I'm going to get you away from him, I promise. We'll leave tomorrow, no matter what."

She nodded and Virgil ran his fingers through her hair, smoothing it out.

"If it hurts too much and you don't want to make love right now, I understand; I can wait for you for as long as it takes," he whispered sincerely.

Aralyn wrapped her fingers around Virgil's, which now rested on her shoulders.

"I want you now," she whispered.

Virgil nodded and Aralyn saw that he seemed relieved despite what he had said. She pulled him down into another passionate kiss and Virgil gently slipped off her robe before pulling her to the floor. They made love quickly, knowing that they didn't have much time before Aimeric would return, and held in their verbal emotions of pleasure, fearing they would be heard. During her climax, Aralyn found it extremely difficult to hold in her cries, wanting to scream out her feelings for the man she had fallen in love with in such a short time; she knew she loved him, even though they had only known each other for less than a few weeks; the thought of living without him brought her feelings of wanting to die.

To silence her whimpering, Virgil covered her mouth with his after huskily whispering, "Be quiet, darling."

Once his release followed hers, they laid on the floor in each other's arms for a few moments, taking time to recover, before Virgil would have to take her back to the bedroom.

"Aralyn, no matter what happens, you have to know that I love you," Virgil said after a few moments of silence.

He knew the risk they were taking then and would be taking the next evening and he knew of the consequences if they were caught.

"You can tell me that tomorrow night when we're far away from here," she responded.

He kissed her forehead but didn't say anything else. They dressed and re-appeared in the bedroom a few minutes later. Morgan was still asleep in the chair, blood crusted along his chin.

With one last kiss goodbye, Virgil said, "I will come for you tomorrow after Aimeric leaves."

Aralyn nodded and, as Virgil went for the door, she stopped him by calling his name.

"What?" he asked confused.

"I *do* love you too," she said.

Not able to resist, Virgil rushed back to her and stole another kiss.

"You can tell me that tomorrow night when we're far away from here *and* after I've made love to you the *right* way."

He winked and then finally left the room, leaving Aralyn alone with Morgan and the corpse. She shuddered when she saw the body again and started to climb into bed, hoping that she could forget them both if she closed her eyes. Before she could make it onto the mattress, however, the door opened and Aralyn went deathly pale.

Chapter Nine: Death of the Undead

"What the hell happened in here?" Aimeric demanded.

Since Aralyn and Virgil had forgotten to come up with an explanation, Aralyn quickly responded with the first thing that came to mind.

"Um, I came out of the bathroom earlier and found him like this," she said, trying to keep her voice calm.

Aimeric eyed her skeptically and stepped further into the bedroom.

"How long had you been in the bathroom?" he asked, obviously trying to get information out of her to piece together.

"About half an hour, maybe?" she guessed. "I took a bath."

"I see that; your hair is still wet," Aimeric remarked. "How long have you been out of the bath?"

Trying to cover up the fact that she was getting nervous, Aralyn said, "Twenty minutes or so," as best she could, though her insides were shaking.

"Why are you just now getting into bed?"

She didn't have to think to answer this question.

"When I came out, the sight disgusted me and I had to leave. I only just now got the courage to come back in," she said.

"And where did you go?" he asked.

"Just out in the hall," she said.

Aimeric approached her, taking deliberately slow and intimidating steps.

"Why do you seem so nervous?" he asked.

"The...the blood..." she stuttered, waving a shaking hand in the direction of the unconscious human. "It's making me nauseous-" Aralyn gasped as Aimeric grabbed her by the upper part of her arms and held on to her tightly.

"You aren't planning anything, are you, Aralyn?" he asked in a warning whisper, showing his fangs.

"No, of course not," she breathed, looking into his eyes, on the verge of tears.

His grip loosed but he still held onto her.

"Good. That's very good, Aralyn, because if you were, that would be extremely foolish," he said, the same harsh tone in his words.

He eyed her coldly for a moment and she desperately tried to keep her thoughts hidden and out of his reach. Not saying anything else, Aimeric let her go and then turned around to face the mess on the other side of the bed. Aralyn inwardly sighed in relief and watched Aimeric go over to Morgan. He grabbed Morgan by the shirt and jerked him up out of the chair, growling a rude awakening.

"What the hell are you doing sleeping on the job?"

Morgan's eyes shot open and the terror appeared instantly on his face.

"I…what's going on?" he asked confused.

Aralyn's heart dropped as she realized Morgan wasn't drunk; Virgil hadn't given him enough blood, either that or it had worn off already.

"What's going on?" Aimeric mocked.

He threw Morgan to the floor next to the body.

"You decided to have a little snack on duty and passed out! That's what's going on!"

Morgan stood on shaky legs and pointed a finger at Aralyn.

"No! She hit me!"

Aimeric smirked at Aralyn over his shoulder and then turned back to Morgan.

"I doubt that."

"She did!" Morgan argued. "Bitch hi' hard too!"

As soon as the words fell from his lips, Morgan knew he had gone too far and could do nothing as the back of Aimeric's hand collided with his cheek, knocking him to the floor.

"You will not speak of her in that manner again," Aimeric hissed.

Morgan bowed his head.

"You're right, Master, I apologize."

"Get out of here and take this *thing* with you."

Aimeric kicked the body to the side and Morgan stumbled to pick it up. Morgan glanced at Aralyn, though he didn't dare glare at her like he wanted to, and carried the body out of the room. Aralyn stood there, stunned that Aimeric had actually defended her against Morgan, just for calling her a name, as Aimeric closed the door. She wasn't sure what to say to him but she didn't have to say anything; he didn't exactly give her the chance.

"Come here," Aimeric commanded.

She obeyed and, on shaky legs, went to stand in front of him. He touched her arms cautiously, looking them over, and then, in one swift motion, he tore the robe from her body. It wasn't a sexual act though; Aimeric was looking over her body as though checking for bruises or cuts or anything else.

"I saw into Morgan's thoughts; he pushed you, did he do anything else? Hurt you? Touch you in any way?" he asked, anger lacing his words.

"No," Aralyn said softly, shaking her head.

She couldn't believe how protective Aimeric was being after all that he had done to her himself, *and* allowed Mabel and Sadie to do. Then it made sense. Aimeric was the only one allowed to do anything to her because she was "his," at least until Claire came back, *if* she ever did. It was similar to the logic of an older and younger sibling: The older one could pick on the younger one but no one else dared to or they would have to answer to the older one. Aralyn watched Aimeric look her over and for a split second, she thought she saw his eyes burn with rage, but it must have been her imagination because he looked at her and smiled.

"You seem to be okay," he said.

"Yes."

Aimeric leaned down and kissed her several times, pulling her naked body against his. He moved to her neck, going up and down it, letting the tip of his tongue touch her every now and then.

Aralyn gently pushed him away.

"Not now, Aimeric, please; I'm tired," she said softly, daring his temper.

He looked at her and there was that fire in his eyes, but, again, it only lasted for half a second.

"Very well, get into bed then," he said.

Aralyn nodded and, thankful that he didn't start screaming at her and force her to have sex with him again, climbed into bed and pulled the sheets up to her chin, laying her head on the pillow. The mattress shifted under Aimeric's weight as he settled himself next to her, his chest against her back, wrapping his arms around her.

"Just...go to sleep now, my love," he whispered, kissing her shoulder.

Her eyes did feel heavy, sleep sounded good right now, so she closed them and soon after, she was off in another world, dreaming of the life she and Virgil would have together...

A cold chill woke Aralyn up a few hours later. Her body trembling, Aralyn saw that she was no longer in Aimeric's arms and her covers had been pulled, or kicked, off. She didn't care that Aimeric wasn't there, but she did want her covers back, so she sat up to retrieve them and as she went to fall back down on the bed, she heard soft groaning; painful groaning.

Dreading who it was, Aralyn slid out of bed and picked her robe up off the floor, quickly slipping it over her shoulders and tying the belt. It was still dark outside; Aralyn knew this because the clock on the wall only read five-thirty in the morning. Quietly descending the stairs, Aralyn followed the echoing groans to the basement, knowing that's where she would probably find Aimeric. She remembered how angry Aimeric had been with Morgan, maybe he was torturing him? Aralyn had thought she wouldn't care if that happened to Morgan but now that it was a possibility, she didn't really want it to be; the groaning sounded too painful. She snuck down the stone steps, which led to the dungeon, and opened the door. As the torchlight revealed who was chained to the wall, Aralyn gasped and ran inside.

"Virgil!"

A strong hand yanked her back by the wrist and then she was enshrouded in his arms, locking her tightly in his grasp.

"Good evening, my love!" Aimeric hissed sardonically into her ear.

Wes, the large vampire from before, stepped out of the shadows and grinned at Aralyn, as did Morgan, who slithered out opposite Wes.

"What did that son of a bitch tell you?" Aralyn asked through gritted teeth, glaring at Morgan.

Aimeric hit her back up against his chest and growled against her ear, "He didn't have to tell me anything! Do you think I couldn't smell him all over you, you fucking whore?"

"Leave her alone," Virgil managed to say, though his voice was strained, struggling to raise his head to glare at Aimeric.

Virgil's body was covered in fresh whip marks, all over this time instead of just on his chest, he even had a few on his face.

"I'll tell you when you can speak," Aimeric growled dangerously and then nodded to Wes.

Wes returned the nod and then hit Virgil with a whip across the neck. Virgil yelled through gritted teeth and fresh blood tears fell down his face. Salty crystal ones streamed down Aralyn's.

"Not to mention, that little setup of yours was pathetic," Aimeric continued. "Morgan's scent wasn't on that human anywhere; only Virgil's was. That got me suspicious anyway and then, I smelled you, my *love*. I almost went crazy right there, but then I decided I would have a little fun with both of you first."

"Don't hurt her! It wasn't her fault! I am responsible for everything!" Virgil said.

Aralyn could see that it pained him to talk and that pained her in return knowing that it was her fault. She should have just let Aimeric come home to see that she had knocked Morgan out and she should have told Virgil that they could wait one more night before making love; she should have known that Aimeric would be able to tell right away what they had done. Aimeric walked with Aralyn to stand directly in front of Virgil. Virgil raised his head again to glare at Aimeric; his eyes were almost on fire, such rage burned within them.

"Do you honestly think I would harm this beautiful flesh?" Aimeric asked him, running his hands across Aralyn's cheeks, her throat and then onto her arms.

Virgil sneered through his bloody tears and Aralyn shook Aimeric's hands off of her but he only placed them back around her shoulders and waist.

"I can forgive *you*, Aralyn. You're only a weak human who probably succumbed to Virgil's mind willing," Aimeric whispered against her neck, nuzzling her hair. "But you, Virgil," he continued, hissing the words, jerking his head up so that his icy stare locked with Virgil's hate filled expression. "I cannot forgive you. You've been trying to manipulate me this whole time she's been here, trying to get Aralyn away from me."

"Because you don't deserve her!" Virgil snapped harshly. "Look what you've done to her before and what you're doing now!"

"Virgil, no," Aralyn whispered, shaking her head.

Both men ignored her though.

"You're in no position to be scolding me," Aimeric sneered. Stepping backwards with Aralyn, and keeping his eye on Virgil, he said, "Wes?"

"Yeah?" the vampire asked.

Wes had a face that resembled a pig. His nose was pushed in on a round face, his eyes were small and beady, and his blonde hair was cut in a buzz.

Aralyn could almost hear the smirk in Aimeric's voice as he said, "Do your worst."

"My pleasure," Wes replied, going to stand directly in front of Virgil.

"No," Aralyn said through gritted teeth, struggling.

"You're not going anywhere," Aimeric said, holding her tight.

"Master, I want to do something," Morgan spoke up, glee filling his voice.

"Get out, Morgan. I don't need you down here anymore," Aimeric hissed.

Looking hurt, Morgan hung his head and shuffled out of the room, going back upstairs.

"I want you to watch closely, Aralyn," Aimeric sneered against her ear. "I want you to watch this and then ask yourself if it was worth it to allow another man to fuck you."

"He didn't *fuck* me," Aralyn sneered. "*We* made love; something you and I will never do."

Aimeric's hold on her tightened to the point where it was hard for her to breathe and she gasped as his strong arms crushed her own chest against her lungs.

"You better not say another word like that to me again or I will make you regret it," Aimeric warned, and then, raising his head to look at Wes, he asked, "What's taking so damn long? Strike him!"

Wes nodded and hit Virgil with the whip across his chest, his legs, his arms, and his face. With each hit, Virgil screamed in pain, and with each scream, Aralyn's tears fell harder onto Aimeric's arm.

"This is what will happen to any man who touches you without my permission," he said to her.

Virgil's screams and the sound of the whip tearing his flesh was making Aralyn sick and weak; if it weren't for Aimeric holding her up, she probably would have fallen to the floor. She tried to cover her eyes but Aimeric held her hands and arms down. She tried to look away but Aimeric turned her head back and ordered her to watch. After only a few minutes Virgil was so covered in blood that he was unrecognizable. His dark hair was stuck to his face, matted in blood.

Wes eventually put the whip down, but he wasn't finished. Taking the same fire poker that Aimeric had used a few days ago, Wes held the tip of it in the flames of the torch and then stabbed Virgil's arms over and over with it. He screamed, a shrill sound that chilled Aralyn's blood, and she squeezed her eyes shut, feeling like she was going to be sick. She struggled again, trying to reach Virgil and help him somehow, but Aimeric kept his arms around her, stopping her from moving even a foot, and he laughed loudly at her futile attempts.

"Stop it! Please! Let him go!" Aralyn begged.

Some of the prisoners' curiosity had won them over and, despite the fact that Aimeric was in the room, they had come to the edge of the cells to watch Virgil's torment. They had been thrilled at first, most of them, to see that a vampire was going to endure some of the same suffering they had gone through, but even *they* had started to get sick at what Wes was doing.

He was now pulling out Virgil's fingernails, one by one, with a pair of pliers. It seemed Virgil had run out of screams because he was only whimpering and groaning now. Aimeric allowed Aralyn to sink to her knees, and he fell to the floor with her as she sobbed into his arm, which was loosely around her neck.

"Please...stop," she repeated weakly.

"I could go on with him forever, Aralyn. He can't die from these wounds alone; he heals too quickly. If you want his suffering to end, you have to promise to be mine forever...*only* mine...become one of us," Aimeric said, nuzzling her hair and neck.

"I promise! Just let him go!" Aralyn said without hesitation.

She didn't want Virgil to suffer anymore.

"A promise, to *me*, is unbreakable, Aralyn, and by that, I *could* mean death," Aimeric said warningly.

"I know..." she breathed, her heart dropping even further than it had already.

But if becoming a vampire, and belonging to Aimeric, would be what it took for Virgil to be let go, then she would do it; she couldn't bear to watch him suffer any longer. Aimeric looked at Wes, who was looking back at him over his shoulder, waiting for the next command.

"You heard her, Wes, end his suffering," he said sardonically.

Knowing that Aimeric was up to something by the tone of his voice, Aralyn raised her head to see that Wes had put down the pliers and was taking an old axe from the wall. She used all her strength in trying to stand, her muscles straining in her legs while she tried with all her might to struggle free from Aimeric.

"No!" she screamed.

Aimeric pulled her back down to her knees, and crushed her back against his chest again. Virgil knew what was going to happen so he used the last bit of his strength to look as deeply into Aralyn's eyes as possible and whisper, "I love you." He barely had enough time to say it before the axe sliced his head clean off his neck.

Aralyn watched, in shock, as Virgil's severed head fell to the floor and then, a moment later, turn to dust, along with his body. Aimeric began chuckling, followed by Wes, until the two filled the room with echoing laughter. The prisoners had started to back up in the cages at that point, probably fearing that Aimeric would go after one of them next.

Finally coming back to herself, Aralyn shoved at Aimeric as hard as she could and, this time, since he was preoccupied with laughing, she caught him off guard, and she jumped up, and ran for the door. She reached it, and then the old staircase, running up to the living room, and to the front door. As she opened it, a hand slammed it shut again and Aimeric grabbed her arm.

"Breaking your promise already, my love?" he sneered.

"Get away from me, you sick, son of a bitch!" she screamed.

He pulled her up to sneer against her lips, "*You* are not in charge here."

Out of the corner of her eye, Aralyn saw a collection of old swords, which were in an umbrella stand. Kneeing Aimeric hard in the crotch, she got him to drop her to the floor and then she quickly ran to the stand and grabbed one of the swords. Not taking the time to think and realize it wouldn't do any good, she plunged the sword into Aimeric's chest before he could grab her again, and then she opened the door and fled outside as Aimeric yelled in pain and out of anger. She let a breath of air escape when she saw the morning sun, rising into the sky.

Chapter Ten: Through Her Eyes

Aimeric, his face contorted with rage, slammed the door shut, after almost being burned by the sun, and yanked the blade from his chest. He spun around on his heel and chucked the blade, hard, towards the wall of the staircase leading to the second floor. The trajectory of the blade ran into an obstacle, however, that being another vampire, who had been on his way upstairs. The blade caught him and pinned him against the wall. The young male looked down at his chest, the hilt sticking out of his sternum, and then grinned stupidly at Aimeric.

"Nice shot," the young one said.

"Fuck off, Bryce," Aimeric growled, not in the mood for humor.

"Right…I'll just uh, get this out of here." Bryce said.

He groaned, pulling on the blade until he was free from the wall, and then, tossing it to the ground, he took off upstairs.

Aimeric went to the door, trying to decide if it was worth the risk to see if Aralyn was still outside or if she had managed to get very far away already. His hand went back and forth, from the doorknob to his side, and he paced a few times. If it were possible, his nostrils probably could have produced smoke as angry as he was.

"What are you going to do, Master?"

Morgan had come out of the kitchen, looking concerned that Aralyn had been able to escape; he had watched from the doorway.

"I can't do a damn thing right now, can I?" Aimeric snapped. "Fucking sun!" He paused, thoughtfully. "But she won't get away with this…she'll be back here soon."

"Should I tell the other vampires to get ready to hunt for her tonight?" Morgan asked.

"No, that won't be necessary; I will handle her," Aimeric said. A smirk slithered onto his face and he added, "Maybe I'll have some fun with her first."

Morgan chuckled softly, relieved to see Aimeric's humor starting to return.

"I'm going to my room. Make sure I am not disturbed. I need to concentrate so I can make sure she doesn't do anything stupid," Aimeric growled, going for the stairs.

"Yes, sir," Morgan said.

"If I am disturbed by anyone, I will be punishing *you*," Aimeric added.

Morgan nodded and watched Aimeric go upstairs.

As soon as he was out of sight, Morgan cocked his head in a mocking manner and repeated in a child-like voice, "If I am disturbed, I will punish *you*."

Rolling his eyes, Morgan began to make the rounds to pass on the message to the other occupants of the mansion *not* to bother Aimeric for anything.

In his room, Aimeric settled himself into his coffin, though not to sleep. He needed to concentrate, he needed quiet. He closed his eyes and willed a mental connection with Aralyn, searching for her. He could hear her thoughts (she was crying still), and he used them to lead his mind to where she was. She was running, still only in a robe, into the city.

After a while, when the sun was bright, she came upon the other side where a small house resided on a hill. Aimeric used her mind, her eyes, to show him everything. The house had potential, but lack of care had left the paint peeling and the window in the door broken. The porch needed to be swept, and the yard needed work. Tall weeds and grass grew all around the house and in the gravel driveway where sat an old Ford; Aralyn's father's truck.

Aralyn's thoughts told Aimeric that the house and the yard had become like this when her mother had died and Claire had been presumed dead. Her father had given up, not caring anymore, not taking care of anything except Aralyn and then even that had lacked. Aralyn climbed the steps of the porch and the door squeaked on its hinges as she went inside.

Her shaky voice echoed in Aimeric's mind.

"Dad?"

The house was dirty on the inside too. Empty beer cans and bottles lay all over, cigarettes in dirty ashtrays sat on the tables, and trash overflowed in the kitchen. There were even cobwebs on the ceiling.

"Don't go into the bedroom, my love," Aimeric murmured and he saw her stop; she had heard him.

Aralyn spun around in the hallway, her breath trembling, and she looked for Aimeric. Her frightened eyes darted all around her, down the hallways and on the ceiling. She calmed herself after a moment, thinking his voice had been her imagination and she was being paranoid. She continued through the house until she came to a door that was cracked open.

"Dad? Are you in here? It's me, Aralyn..." she said in a small voice and gently pushed open the door.

Through Aralyn's eyes, Aimeric saw her father, lying across the bed with a gun in his hand. In his head lay the bullet and blood stained the sheets. Aralyn covered her mouth and quickly backed out of the room, but her eyes stayed on her dead father. She was stuck to the floor, looking into the bedroom. Her breathing filled Aimeric's ears; she was starting to hyperventilate.

"Leave, my love," Aimeric said.

Aralyn jerked her head up at the ceiling and her back hit the wall. She then turned and ran, forgetting Aimeric for now, out the front door, and to a nearby shrub where she bent over and spilled all the contents of her stomach, which wasn't much. She started to cry again, wiping her mouth with the sleeve of the robe.

"Come to me, Aralyn."

"No! Leave me alone!" she screamed to the air.

She looked at the house once more, coming to a decision that only she and Aimeric could hear. Aimeric let her run, watching, through her eyes still, as she fled down the hill, past the trees and around the city to the Cliffside, which she had become so familiar with. She didn't think about it this time and her feet carried her to the edge. Aimeric heard her; she wanted to die again; her father was dead now and she didn't believe she could live without Virgil. Aimeric's fists clenched over his chest and jealousy raged in his cold, dead, heart.

"Get away from the cliff," his harsh voice ordered right before she reached the edge.

Aralyn felt her legs lock up and she fell backwards on Aimeric's command.

"Now get up."

"I can't…" she said, sobbing.

"Get up and find some warmer clothes, Aralyn, before you freeze."

"Why can't you just leave me alone?" Aralyn whimpered, holding her head in her hands.

"Come on, sweetheart, get up," Aimeric said in a soothing tone.

She obeyed and slowly stood.

"Now go get your clothes."

"I can't go back there," she whispered, remembering her father.

"Then come back here."

"No," she said firmly, becoming angry again. "I will never come back to you."

"Never say 'never.' You will love me eventually. I will make you *think* you love me until you actually do if I have to, though I would prefer you do it on your own," Aimeric hissed.

She began to cry even harder.

"Why are you doing this to me? Find someone else! Just leave me alone!"

She sobbed for a few more minutes, lying in the grass, until she realized that Aimeric hadn't said anything else to her in a while. Slowly standing, Aralyn looked around cautiously. The air surrounding her was still and calm, the only sound Aralyn could hear was the waves crashing against the rocks below her. She stopped crying and wiped her eyes. Aimeric watched her still; he only made her think that he had left her.

She shivered, hugging herself, and started to walk away from the cliff after glancing at it once more. Aimeric's mind followed her inside of her own and he watched her as she made her way back into the city once more. She received several strange looks from the people she passed since she was only in a robe but she didn't notice or care. The sun was bright, since it had become nearly noon, and Aralyn had to shield her eyes as she walked; she hadn't been in the direct sunlight in a while so it hurt her. She went to a duplex in the center of the bustling city and knocked on the door. Reading her mind, Aimeric knew that this was where one of her former best friends lived; a male.

"Come on, Brian, open the door," Aralyn said softly, laying her hand against it.

Jealousy burned in Aimeric's cold blood again and he almost told Aralyn to turn around until he saw her hand go to the doorknob and then she turned it, letting herself in.

"Brian!" she called.

He wasn't home. The house was empty except for a white cat that was lounging in the sun on a windowsill. Aralyn pet the animal quickly, scratching it behind the ears, before going into one of the bedrooms and rummaging around in the dresser drawer. She found a few of her old sweat shirts and a pair of jeans that she had brought with her, shortly after her mother had been killed, when she spent the night at Brian's a few times to get away from her dad's drunken yelling. Aimeric heard her as she wondered why Brian kept her clothes for her after the huge argument they had had the night she tried to kill herself, right before she had been brought to Aimeric's mansion. That was when she had lost Brian as her best friend and also when she had decided that she was completely alone.

Aralyn let the robe fall to the floor and quickly slipped on the pants; they were baggy, since she had lost some weight over the last few weeks, but they would be fine for the time being. She pulled on a black sweatshirt and then gathered up two more shirts for later, stuffing them into a plastic bag, which she found in the kitchen. She threw the robe away, not wanting to be reminded of Aimeric.

Aimeric smirked when he heard her think that.

Grabbing a few items of food from Brian's cupboards in the small kitchen, Aralyn pet the cat once more and then left the house. She closed the front door and then casually walked down the sidewalk, taking a few small bites of a fruit pastry. She didn't know where she was going to go, maybe look for Claire. Of course, maybe she didn't really want to see her sister. Claire had, after all, abandoned her and left her with Aimeric in the first place.

Aimeric watched Aralyn all day, not letting her out of his reach for one second and not letting her have any other thoughts of suicide; he had to keep her safe until he could get to her. She didn't try to contact any of her other, former friends, thinking they wouldn't want to see her. She went to the park and thought about what to do and where to go. Aimeric smiled to himself, hearing her fears of him finding her and taking her back. She tried to think of places to go that he wouldn't be able to find her, and then she wondered how she would get to them.

She had decided she would try to get away from New England and go somewhere west, maybe Arizona. But she didn't know how she would get there. Would she be safe from Aimeric? Or would he find her? Surely he wouldn't go out of his way to bring her back. He wouldn't travel that far, would he?

Before she knew it, the sun had begun to set.

Hearing her heartbeat faster as she saw the sun lowering over the lake in the park, Aimeric smiled to himself again; he could sense her fear of knowing what the setting sun brought; darkness and with darkness came the vampires. Aralyn's heart pounded in her chest and drummed against Aimeric's ears. She stood from the bench, grabbing the bag with her extra clothes, and started to head back into the city, thinking he wouldn't be able to find her as easily amongst a crowd.

Aimeric sat up in his coffin, opening his eyes, and laughed.

"It's time, my love."

Chapter Eleven: A Whisper in the Shadows

Yawning, while cautiously looking around, Aralyn hugged herself in the cold, huddling against the concrete of the interstate overpass she was sitting under. She wanted to sleep, she hadn't since that horrible morning, but she knew that the vampires came out at night, and she wasn't going to risk being caught off guard by any of them. It was only at that moment she thought she should have tried sleeping during the day so that she could be more aware that night, but it hadn't crossed her mind before; she had been too preoccupied earlier, trying to think of where she could go. That was another thing she could have done. She could have tried to get out of the city during the day but that thought had never crossed her mind either since she had been so busy trying to decide *where* to go and what to do. She cursed her foolishness.

She also didn't understand why she had let Aimeric stop her from jumping off the cliff and she didn't understand even then why she couldn't bring herself to take her life. Why had she lost control of her own body just because Aimeric spoke? It didn't make sense. What did she have to live for anyway? Her whole family was dead, except for Claire but she may as well have been too. Aralyn's only love had been brutally murdered, and she was fighting to keep hidden from the monster that had killed him. She didn't know then that it was Aimeric manipulating her mind to keep her from killing herself and also clouding her mind so she couldn't think straight. She also didn't know that it was Aimeric manipulating her mind now to get her to stand and walk down to the street.

Feeling compelled, Aralyn moved her feet, leaving behind the bag, which was empty now; she had put on the t-shirt under the black sweatshirt and the blue sweatshirt over the black to keep herself sheltered from the chill of mid-autumn. The moon was full, or at least, close to it, and had dark wisps of oncoming rain clouds sweeping across the light; painting an eerie picture above her. She walked with her head down, not wanting to make eye contact with anyone outside. She wasn't exactly in the best of neighborhoods. Hearing leaves rustle behind her, Aralyn turned slightly and peered into the trees. She didn't see anyone so she kept walking.

"Aralyn..."

The wind whispered her name, or so she brushed it off as the wind after checking all around her and finding no one. She felt icy eyes penetrate her soul; they wouldn't leave her. Quickening her pace to a jog, Aralyn moved further into the city, hoping the tall buildings would close her in and make her feel less vulnerable. They didn't; they made her feel trapped. She frantically looked above on one of the buildings, feeling even more violated by those eyes. Shaking her head in dismay, Aralyn backed away.

"No," she whispered.

Aimeric was standing on the roof of one of the buildings, looking down at her and grinning coldly.

"Stay away from me!" she screamed.

Several people around her stopped walking and looked at her like she was crazy for a moment before they continued on to wherever it was that they had been going. Aralyn looked back at the building and yelled softly out of fear and frustration; Aimeric was gone again. She still felt him nearby though so she started to run, not knowing where she was going, but not wanting to stay in one spot either. She ran until she reached the park again. She ran onto the bridge, over the river, stopping abruptly in the center, her breath catching in her throat, when Aimeric appeared directly in front of her. He grabbed her shoulders before she could attempt to run again.

"Did you honestly think you could escape?" he sneered.

"Let go! Help!" Aralyn screamed, flailing her legs and trying to pull her arms out of Aimeric's grasp.

He swung her around so she was trapped between the rails of the bridge and his body. Her back hit the rails fairly hard but she didn't notice.

"You can call for help all you want, but they can't stop me," Aimeric whispered menacingly. "Do you remember your promise, Aralyn? Do you remember how we both agreed it was unbreakable? How I would have every right to kill you if you did break it?"

She nodded, her hair falling into her eyes. She didn't care if he killed her now. She almost wished he would, though she was afraid of how he would do it.

"And yet here you are, trying to break it and run away from me," Aimeric said.

"You lied to me! You said you would let him go," she argued.

"Do not call me a liar. I did let that poor excuse for a vampire go," Aimeric snarled.

"You killed him!" she spat.

"Is death not a release?" he asked, amused.

Aralyn looked away and clenched her jaw. Thinking for only a second, she looked back at Aimeric, daring him with her eyes.

"Then release me too; kill me."

Aimeric leaned down, close to her lips, and snarled, "Your mortal body *will* die, but it will not be a release; you will belong to me forever."

Straightening up again, Aimeric wiped away the tear that had fallen from Aralyn's eye.

"You will soon forget he even existed; I will make sure of that," Aimeric said coldly.

"I will not forget! He will be with me in everything I do. Even when you take me to your bed, he will be with me there," Aralyn said, her voice a dangerous growl.

Aimeric chuckled, shaking his head, and then, in a flash, his hand was across Aralyn's cheek, forcing her head to the side. She turned it again, slowly, holding a hand to her left cheek where he had hit her, and glared at him.

"You never learn, do you, whore?" Aimeric asked, taking her arm.

The world spun around Aralyn and in a second, she and Aimeric were back in the mansion.

"Not even back in the house and already you need to be punished again," Aimeric mumbled, dragging her to the basement.

Wes was already down there when they arrived, mentally torturing the prisoners by cracking the whip against the cell bars. With each hit, they all flinched back. Aimeric pushed Aralyn against the brick wall and cuffed her hands in the chains.

"Do you want me to strip her first, Master?" Wes asked, grinning.

Aimeric spun around and knocked the whip from the vampire's hands.

"You will not break any flesh on her body!" Aimeric yelled.

Wes shrunk back in fear, even though he was twice Aimeric's size.

"Then what did you bring her down here for?" he asked stupidly.

"I have other ways to punish her, but she is not to be *physically* harmed!" Aimeric growled. "Now, get out!"

Still confused, Wes tossed the whip to the floor and turned on his heel to leave the basement. Turning back to Aralyn, Aimeric touched her lips with a finger and then brushed back her hair to stroke the cheek he had hit, which was beginning to bruise.

"I'm sorry. I will never do that again; I hate to distort your beauty," he said softly.

She jerked her face away, not wanting him to touch her.

"Will you always hate me?" he asked, looking into her eyes.

She glared at him and whispered, "Go…to…hell."

He leaned in close to her, pressing his hard body against hers and, twirling a strand of her hair around his finger, said, "I'll let that one slide."

Aimeric kissed Aralyn briefly and then stepped away to leave.

"Sweet dreams, my love," he said, closing the door with an echoing bang, leaving her in darkness.

Aralyn laid her head against the cold, brick wall and closed her eyes. Seeing Virgil's head rolling to the floor, they shot open again and a tear fell down her cheek. She wasn't sure if she would ever get that image out of her head; she doubted it as long as she was down in the prison he was killed in.

"Hey."

Turning her head in the direction the soft voice had come from, Aralyn saw that the girl from before, the one that Aimeric had first punished in front of her, was standing at the edge of the cage.

"I'm sorry you're down here," she said softly.

Aralyn shook her head, more tears spilling from her eyes.

"You don't have to apologize for anything. I should be apologizing to you. If it weren't for me, you wouldn't have gotten hurt before."

"No. It's not your fault. He would have done it sooner or later; you were just his excuse for that time," the girl said.

Aralyn looked at her sadly.

"What's your name?" she asked.

"Emma."

"That boy...is he still alive?" Aralyn asked softly, remembering the other one she felt responsible for.

"Yeah, I'm still here."

He was sitting against the bars near the back of the cage.

"I'm so sorry," Aralyn said.

He shrugged.

"Like she said, it wasn't your fault. That bastard is sick and twisted."

Standing up, he looked at Aralyn through the bars.

"My name's Toby."

"I'm Aralyn."

One by one the prisoners gave their names to her and she spoke with them and listened while they told their short tales of how they had gotten caught and brought to Aimeric's mansion. Aimeric hadn't caught hardly any of them himself; they had mostly been brought by the other vampires and then given to Aimeric. And every one of them all said the same thing at the end of their story, or at least similar: "I was always told that vampires didn't exist, that they were a fairytale."

Before she knew it, Aralyn was fast asleep, exhausted from the events that had happened the morning before up until then. Her dreams haunted her, repeating Virgil's death over and over until she woke up in a cold sweat. She tried to stay awake, but gave in to sleep again and started the whole process over.

***

She spent three days down there with the prisoners, shooing rats away with her feet so they didn't try to nibble her. Her wrists had gotten sore, and had started to bleed, from struggling when Aimeric would come down and touch her; she hated him touching her. He came down to feed her and give her water mostly so she wouldn't get sick. He hand fed her, since her arms were chained, and frequently asked her if she had learned her lesson yet, or if she needed more time to think. She always answered him sarcastically and always ended up having to spend another night downstairs, shivering in the cold with her back against the bricks; it was a good thing she was wearing three shirts or she might have froze to death. Aimeric kissed her whenever he wanted to but he didn't do anything else to her, saying he would save that for when he could "do it right."

Morgan had come down every night at sunset to feed the prisoners and then again right before dawn. He also supplied them with blankets so they wouldn't freeze. Aimeric kept his prisoners well fed and well taken care of in order to make sure they had enough energy when he wanted to "play" with them, which he did twice while Aralyn was down there. He didn't do much to them but he made sure Aralyn knew what he was capable of. He mostly just drank from them in various places (his favorite seemed to be from the wrists) while they were chained to the wall next to Aralyn. She had always gotten sick at her stomach and turned away. She had remembered Virgil saying Aimeric didn't usually feed from the prisoners unless he had to, so he must have done it just to get to Aralyn in another way and make her have another reason to want to get out of the basement and come back to him.

Each time Morgan came down he smirked at Aralyn and made sarcastic comments, some vulgar, about how she was chained to the wall. He never came close enough to touch Aralyn, he knew better, but on the forth night, Morgan became brave enough to stand directly in front of her after he finished feeding the prisoners. He had a mischievous look in his eyes.

"Wearing all of that clothing is hiding your figure," he observed coolly.

She glared, but didn't respond.

"Maybe we should do something about that," he said.

"Don't come near me," Aralyn warned.

"Why not? No one's here to stop me right now; Aimeric's out feeding early."

"I don't give a damn about Aimeric! You just better not touch me!" Aralyn screamed.

Smirking, Morgan deliberately ran his finger between her heavily covered breasts.

"Oops." He looked at the cuffs around her wrists and shook his head slightly in dismay. "I wonder how we'll ever get those shirts off with these on?"

"Get away from me," Aralyn growled.

"I know!" Morgan said, enlightened, and ignored her demand.

He stepped back and, using his fingernails, ripped the first sweatshirt. The torn pieces of cloth dangled at Aralyn's sides.

"You're being stupid, even for you, do you think Aimeric won't be able to smell you if you do anything to me?" Aralyn said.

"So I'll give you a bath when I'm done," Morgan said.

"I don't think that will work."

Morgan jumped what seemed like a mile into the air and his cool attitude quickly disintegrated and turned into fear. Aralyn's hateful glare at Morgan turned into a smirk as she saw Aimeric standing in the doorway of the prison, not because she wanted to see him, but she was glad to see Morgan frightened and caught.

"What the hell are you doing, Morgan?" Aimeric asked.

"N…nothing," he stuttered in response.

Aimeric calmly walked over to Morgan. He always seemed scarier when he was calm. He reached out and grabbed Morgan by the throat, his fingers locking tightly around Morgan's neck. Morgan's eyes watered bloody tears.

"'Nothing' hell," Aimeric whispered chillingly. He released Morgan, throwing him to the floor. "What makes you think you can put your filthy hands on *my* property?"

"I'm not your-" Aralyn started to protest bravely.

"It's best if you stay out of this, my love," Aimeric sneered before turning back to Morgan. "Well?" he demanded.

"I'm sorry Master! I can't help it sometimes! She lures me to her! I think she's a witch and has me under a spell!" Morgan said, defending himself.

"This is your last chance, Morgan. If you touch her again, I will lock *you* down here next. Now get the hell out of my sight," Aimeric growled.

Morgan scrambled to get out of the basement, running for the stairs, and when he reached the top, he slammed the door.

"Now, you," Aimeric said, stepping up to stand in front of Aralyn. "Are you ready to come back to a warm bed? Have a decent meal?"

"Why did you let him go? Why is Morgan always the one you let off the hook?" Aralyn asked, ignoring Aimeric's question.

She was more curious than anything though when she said the words, she realized they came out child-like, like she was a young kid, feeling pushed aside by a younger sibling being favored.

"He's harmless, Aralyn," Aimeric said. "All I have to do is speak and he cowers like a dog and does whatever I order."

Aralyn looked down at her torn shirt.

"He doesn't seem harmless to me."

"Do you want me to kill him? Because I can," Aimeric offered, though his tone indicated he only asked to make her feel better.

"No," Aralyn sneered. "You would enjoy that too much."

Aimeric chuckled. He then stepped up to her, snaking one arm around her neck and the other around her waist.

"You don't have to be jealous of him," Aimeric said, kissing down her neck.

"I'm not. I would just like to see *him* locked up down here; he's the one who deserves it," Aralyn said, trying to ignore Aimeric.

"He doesn't disobey me," Aimeric said caustically, taking his lips off of Aralyn's neck to look into her eyes.

She averted hers to the floor, or what she could see of it anyway, with Aimeric so close against her.

"Well?" Aimeric asked.

"What?"

"*Are* you ready to come back upstairs without an attitude?"

Aralyn hesitated, thinking it over. His offer sounded very inviting. She could use a bath, and warm blankets on a soft mattress sounded close to Heaven at that moment. The food sounded most enticing, however. All she had had to eat was a few slices of bread each day; that was all Aimeric had given her. A warm meal, fresh fruit, cool water and juice, it all sounded wonderful. But she wasn't sure if she was prepared to trade her body for the nourishment of real food and the luxury of a bed and bath, which, she was sure, was what Aimeric expected.

"Aralyn?" Aimeric asked when she didn't respond.

"Yes," she said quietly.

Aimeric smiled and reached up to unhook the cuffs.

"What the hell is going on here?"

Aimeric stopped what he was doing, he hadn't even gotten the first cuff off yet, and Aralyn looked up and breathed a sigh of relief and surprise.

"Claire!" she said, happily.

Vampires Don't Exist by Reyanna Vance

Her sister had finally returned.

Chapter Twelve: The Return

"I said I didn't want her harmed, Aimeric!" Claire hissed from the doorway before stepping further inside.

She went to stand beside Aimeric, looking at him, silently demanding an answer. As soon as she got close enough, Aimeric reached out and grabbed her, throwing her hard into the wall beside Aralyn.

"And I've told you so many times before that *you* don't tell *me* what to do," he sneered. "I've played your little game and kept her alive and away from the others for a little while, but I'm through; she belongs to me now and I'll do as I wish."

Claire only smirked at him, undisturbed by his sudden outburst.

"Besides," Aimeric continued, "she tried to escape."

He let Claire go and stepped away from her. Claire ran her tongue over her fangs enticingly before moving to stand beside Aimeric. They both looked at Aralyn, who wasn't sure what was about to happen, why they were both looking at her the way they were, as though trying to figure out what they should do with her. Aralyn didn't know what to say, if she should say anything at all, either, so she just looked from one to the other cautiously. Claire folded her arms over her chest. Aralyn felt like she was on display.

Finally, letting her arms fall to her sides, Claire strolled up to Aralyn and casually looked her over, rolling up the sleeves of her torn shirt to check her arms, turning her head and running her fingers along the healing puncture marks on Aralyn's neck, and touching the tender spot on Aralyn's face where she had been bruised by Aimeric's hand. She examined Aralyn's bleeding wrists and then stepped back with her hands on her hips, gazing at Aralyn while Aralyn gazed back. Then, without warning, Claire slapped Aralyn, hard, across the face, over the bruise she already had, bringing fresh tears to Aralyn's eyes; they pooled at the edges but didn't fall.

"Ungrateful bitch! I saved you! I took you in! I rescued you from being raped, tortured and beaten and probably murdered and you show your appreciation by trying to escape?" Claire snarled.

"You rescued me?" Aralyn repeated in a low voice, laced with malice. "Isn't it ironic how you saved me from those things and brought me here where they happened anyway!" Aralyn's voice rose with every word until she was screaming the last ones, almost to the point of being incoherent.

Claire looked at her, amused, and Aimeric glared. Aralyn took a moment to calm her voice, also taking a breath, before she continued, since no one else was saying anything.

"I've *been* raped, kept here as a prisoner, tortured in more ways than one, and I've been close enough to death so many times that I wish it would come already! I wished it before, but never so much as I do now! Do you think I *like* being here? I mean, God! At least if you would have left me with that dumb fuck you '*saved*' me from, I would be dead by now!" Aralyn yelled.

"You can't mean that; you don't want to die," Claire sneered.

"Why the hell wouldn't I?" Aralyn challenged, the tears finally falling down her cheeks.

"I've heard enough," Aimeric said sternly.

Aralyn flinched when he stepped towards her, going past Claire. He returned his arms around her, gently rubbing the small of her back through her clothes. He gently kissed away the tears that had fallen and then looked into her eyes; something in his wouldn't let Aralyn look away this time.

"Do you really hate it here that much?"

His voice was surprisingly soft and free of sarcasm.

"What do you think?" Aralyn asked, still unable to tear her eyes away from him.

"I'll make it better for you, my love," Aimeric whispered and brushed his lips against hers.

He finished freeing her arms from the chains and she wrapped them around his neck, allowing him to help her stand. Aimeric held her close against his chest, his arms around her waist to keep her steady. Claire watched them for a moment and then went up to Aralyn and cupped her face in her hands.

"I'll make it better too," she promised.

Claire kissed Aralyn's forehead and then turned on her heels and went to the cage, calling Emma over to the gate. The girl obeyed and went to the bars. Claire took the girl's hands through the bars and examined them, unraveling the bandages to peer at the wounds on her palms.

Smirking at Aimeric over her shoulder, Claire said, "You had fun without me."

"Claire, what's happened to you?" Aralyn asked in a horrified whisper.

Had that been the old Claire, she would have been sick just by looking at the girl's wounds. Not paying attention to Aralyn, Claire tangled her fingers into Emma's hair and pulled her face against the bars, kissing her deeply and slipping her tongue into the girl's mouth. Totally under Claire's mind manipulation, Emma kissed her back eagerly. Aralyn looked away, not caring to see that side of her sister. But not looking at Claire meant looking at Aimeric, who, since he was holding her, was only inches away from her face.

"Your sister is a different woman than you used to know," Aimeric said.

"And *you* made her that way," Aralyn said bitterly.

Aimeric only smiled.

The hinges on the gate squeaked and Aralyn looked up again to see that Claire was taking Emma out of the cage.

Claire smirked at Aimeric and Aralyn.

"We won't be back for quite some time; I trust you won't need anything, Aimeric?"

"No, we will be spending most of the night in bed. Aralyn needs her rest," Aimeric said.

Aralyn's stomach knotted, she doubted Aimeric only planned on making her rest. He probably intended on wearing her out first. Claire nodded and winked at Aralyn, leading Emma away, while the prisoners watched Emma go sadly. The two women went out the door, and disappeared from sight. After they were gone, Aimeric looked at Aralyn and took a moment to run his thumb over her swelling cheek. She was a mess. Her body hadn't been free of cuts and bruises since she had arrived at the mansion; by the time old ones healed, new ones replaced them. Aralyn's hair was also matted from not being brushed or washed in the last four days.

She winced at his touch and moved her head to the side.

"Please don't," she said quietly.

Aimeric nodded, removing his thumb, and then, picking her up in his arms, he carried her upstairs to the bathroom. He turned on warm water to fill up the claw-foot tub and, while it was filling, he helped Aralyn slowly peel off her torn shirt and other clothes. He turned off the water and then helped her step into it where he washed her, careful not to irritate or re-open any of the cuts she still had. He washed her hair for her as well. He was gentle and not overbearing in any way, which shocked Aralyn. She wasn't quite sure what to think of this side of Aimeric. When he was finished, he took her hand, kissing her fingers, and pulled her up, out of the water, to wrap a towel around her. He was still gentle when he dried her off and then he put a new robe around her shoulders. It was white cotton and made Aralyn feel extremely relaxed. Aimeric ran his fingers through Aralyn's wet hair and kissed her gently.

"Is that better?" he asked, smiling.

"Yes…thank you," Aralyn said hesitantly, still not sure what to make of his sudden change in behavior.

Was he up to something or just trying to get her to change her mind about him? It wouldn't happen.

Aimeric took her to the large canopy bed and gently set her on the mattress against the pillows. He then released all of the drapes around the bed, except for one side. He disappeared into the bathroom again for a moment and then returned with a wet washcloth and a few bandages. He sat down next to Aralyn and first, wrapped her wrists where they had been bleeding, and then pulled her onto his lap, placing the washcloth, which was cool, against her face where Claire had hit her. She had been hit in the same spot three times in less than a month, twice in only four days. Again, Aimeric's touch was soft and gentle and Aralyn actually found herself relaxing in his arms and leaning further against his chest; forgetting everything he had done if only for a little while.

"I've ordered Morgan to bring your food up. He should be here in a moment or two," Aimeric said, softly kissing her forehead.

She nodded and grimaced slightly as he moved the cloth around her bruise.

"Do you really hate me, Aralyn?" Aimeric asked after a moment's silence had passed between them.

Aralyn wanted to say "yes," and ask him how he could even ask her that after all he had done to her. But somehow, she found it hard to say so, instead, she blinked away a tear, thinking of Virgil, and shrugged.

"I don't know. I don't understand how you can be so gentle like you are now and then…" she paused, her eyes stinging with more tears. "Why did you kill him?" she bravely finished.

"I was jealous," Aimeric responded simply. "Somehow, he had managed to make you fall in love with him and yet, you hated me."

Aralyn felt her fists starting to clench. She wanted to jump up and scream at him, tell him *why* she had fallen in love with Virgil. She wanted to tell him how Virgil hadn't raped her and forced her to obey rules, and how he hadn't tortured people to teach her a lesson. But she was too exhausted, and too weak, to stand and yell, so she was forced to only think these things. Her body was tense though.

"Is that what would make you happy? Accept me, Aralyn? Do you want me to wait until you are ready to make love? Not give you so many rules? Release the prisoners?"

Aimeric had prodded into her mind again.

Not knowing how to respond, she stayed silent and wrung her hands in her lap. He could be tricking her, getting her to ask him to do these things and then he would become angry and say she was telling him what to do and punish her or the prisoners again.

"I would do all of those things for you," he continued when she didn't respond. "I don't know what it is about you, Aralyn, you've been nothing but trouble for me, but somehow, I feel real love for you. At least, I think it's real. I've never felt this way about anyone during my undead life."

Aralyn looked up at him, into his eyes, and, for once, they seemed sincere and warm and she felt herself being pulled into them. She knew she shouldn't believe him. Torture and rape were not things someone did if they loved the other person. So why did Aralyn want him to kiss her? Why was she waiting eagerly for it? Aimeric lowered the cloth and moved his lips to touch hers, not hard and demanding, as he had done so many times before, but passionate and loving, leaving her craving more from him. For the first time since she had been there, Aralyn willingly wrapped her arm around his neck and pulled him closer, kissing him back just as passionately. She felt only him and it was as if her mind was drawing a blank and only telling her to melt into him; she knew of nothing else.

Soft knocking on the bedroom door briefly interrupted their kiss and Aimeric moved his lips off of hers long enough to call, "Come in."

He continued to kiss her and moved to her neck as Morgan opened the door and stepped inside with a tray of food. He brought it to the bed and Aimeric straightened up (Aralyn was disappointed he had taken his lips from her), taking it from him, and set it on Aralyn's lap. Morgan then moved to the end of the bed and clasped his hands together behind his back as though waiting for something.

"Do you think you're going to get a tip? Get the hell out!" Aimeric roared.

"Yes sir," Morgan grumbled and left the room, looking hurt.

After Morgan was gone, Aimeric had Aralyn sit up against his chest, instead of lying down, as she had been doing, and he hand fed her the food on the tray. Something about it was erotic and Aralyn felt feelings well up inside of her that she never thought she would feel for this creature before, she wanted him to touch her and kiss her, she wanted him inside of her; she certainly did not feel like herself. Once all of the food had been eaten, Aralyn became very drowsy and, feeling totally serene and comfortable, fell asleep in Aimeric's arms.

Aralyn's sleep was dreamless, which was unusual for her; she had been having terrible nightmares. When she woke up hours later, she was on her side with Aimeric's arm draped over her. He was asleep beside her. She didn't understand why they hadn't slept in the coffin since that first night. Though they were covered still, Aralyn heard rain pounding hard against the windows, angrily demanding to break through the glass and the armor of curtains. She felt strange, almost as though she was forgetting something important. Feeling cloth on her wrists, she raised her arms and, seeing that they were bandaged, wondered why they were. She couldn't remember what had happened and why her wrists needed to be wrapped that way. The movement on her side of the bed, even though it was soft, woke Aimeric. He stirred slightly at first and then, when he saw that Aralyn was awake, secured his arm tighter around her thin waist and kissed her hair.

"Good morning, my love…or should I say evening?" he asked, looking at the clock on the wall; it was five-thirty pm. "I hope you slept well," he added in a soft whisper.

Aralyn turned around to face him and smiled. She wrapped her arms around his neck and curled her fingers in his hair to greet him with a deep, passionate, kiss. Not surprised by her sudden change in behavior, Aimeric pulled her against him and deepened the kiss even more, sliding his tongue across her bottom lip, until she opened her mouth, making it so that their body's craved to be touched by one another. Aralyn locked one of her legs with his and pushed him over onto his back where she straddled his hips and removed the silk nightgown she was wearing. Aimeric grinned and brought his hands up to her breasts, gently massaging her nipples. Aralyn let him play with her for a moment, throwing her head back and moaning softly, and then she leaned down and kissed him, biting playfully at his lip, before moving down, over his chest. She kissed down his torso and stomach and rubbed her hand over his member with slow, gentle strokes. He was slowly hardening in response to her touches. When her mouth got closer to his organ, she moved to his thighs and let the tip of her tongue run over him, barely touching his flesh.

Sometimes gentle touches were more effective than hard and urgent touches. Aralyn had never gone down on a man before but she didn't seem to be having any trouble in knowing what to do, almost as though she were being guided somehow. Aimeric started groaning softly in response to her and his hands went to her hair. He closed his eyes and let her continue. She moved to one of his testicles and gently licked it, before taking it into her mouth. She was careful not to handle this part too hard though since it was so sensitive. His member hardened even more, which was what Aralyn was hoping for. She took her mouth and moved it to lick up the shaft, teasing him right underneath the head before she closed her lips around it. He was moving, barely, against her throat, and massaging her scalp while she worked on him. She swirled her tongue and flicked it around the head, eliciting more groans from Aimeric. She began to move her mouth up and down over the shaft, her hands massaging his thighs, her thumbs circling the inner part. As Aralyn began to suck on the head, she brought her hands to the base of the shaft and pulled down on it while her tongue and mouth continued to work him. He was close to coming and Aralyn knew it. She took her mouth off of him and smiled devilishly at him. She started to crawl back on top of him, after teasing him, and after she had straddled him once more, Aimeric took her around the waist and flipped her over, onto her back, so that he was in charge.

"Bitch," he hissed against her lips, annoyed that she had stopped right before his release.

Aralyn just smiled again and he kissed her hard, his hand going to rub against her clit. She began wriggling underneath him, moaning loudly, and once she was wet enough, Aimeric thrust into her and she cried out in pleasure and pain, but mostly pleasure. The two made love for as long as their bodies could handle. Aralyn willingly gave herself to him that time; without a fight, without tears, and without forced cries of satisfaction. Everything was real, or so it seemed.

Lying in each other's arms afterwards, Aimeric kissed the length of Aralyn's arm and then went to her ear and whispered, in a raspy voice, "I love you, Aralyn."

She heard him but she didn't respond; her thoughts were elsewhere with that feeling of forgetting something.

"Aimeric?" she asked thoughtfully.

"Hmm?"

"Did something…happen last night, or…maybe a few nights ago…something significant?" she asked, thinking, trying to remember herself.

"Yes," he purred. "We made love, just like today."

Taking her lower lip into his mouth, Aimeric bit it gently and drew a few drops of her blood onto his tongue before he stood from the bed. Aralyn rolled over and watched him dress.

"Where are you going?" she asked, forgetting her strange feelings.

"I need to feed, but I'll be back soon," he replied zipping up the black, leather, pants he had pulled on. He also threw on a black, button up, shirt, leaving the top two buttons undone.

He leaned down to kiss her goodbye.

"Go wherever you want in the house but stay inside. You're protected from the vampires here but if you go outside alone, I can do nothing for you."

Aralyn nodded and Aimeric left the bedroom, closing the door quietly behind him. Falling back on the bed, that strange feeling increasing, her mind began to wander. She heard Aimeric's voice from downstairs, yelling something to Morgan, and then the front door slammed shut. Aralyn was up from the bed in a flash, instantly sickened by what she had just done with Aimeric willingly and even initiated. Her memory came pouring back to her from all sides and she remembered what Aimeric had done to Virgil. She saw his head fall to the floor and her own screams echoed in her mind. Somehow, Aimeric had been able to make her forget Virgil, temporarily, and, at the same time, make her believe she was in love with Aimeric himself.

Feeling as though she would throw up, Aralyn ran to the adjoining bathroom and waited, in front of the toilet, for the feeling to disappear. It did after a few moments but she was still disgusted with herself and she could still smell Aimeric all over her so she ran the shower water and stood under the hot stream for several minutes, scrubbing her body hard to rid herself of his scent. She was crying as she stepped out of the tub and wrapped a towel around her mildly burned body. She went to Aimeric's closet, hoping to find something she could wear. She found a long, flowing, black dress that had the slightest bloodstain at the neck; apparently from one of Aimeric's previous victims. It was all she could find that would fit her so, as much as it sickened her to wear, she put the dress on and tried to ignore the bloodstain. She took a quick look at herself in the mirror on the dresser and saw that her eye was black from both Aimeric and Claire hitting her. She angrily turned from the mirror and left the room. She did not want to be in it and reminded of the events that had happened just a little while ago with Aimeric. She still couldn't believe she willingly had sex with him and even *wanted* it. It wasn't like before, when she simply gave in and felt the pleasures of the flesh, this time, she *started* it. Did that make her just as sick as Aimeric?

As soon as Aralyn exited the bedroom and went into the hall, she ran into Morgan. His eyes filled with lust instantly when they landed on her chest, which was enhanced by the corset style top of the dress. Grunting in disgust, Aralyn shoved past him and headed for the stairs.

Morgan grabbed her arm as she went by and she spun around, yanking it free.

"Aimeric said not to touch me!"

Morgan looked angry enough to hit her and he did raise his hand but then quickly lowered it, knowing what Aimeric would do to him if he hit her.

"What is going on out here?"

Aralyn turned to the annoyed voice and saw that Claire was standing in the doorway of her bedroom, which was two rooms down from Aimeric's. She was only wearing a thin black robe that barely covered her curves.

"Claire," Aralyn breathed, still shocked that she was looking at her long lost sister, no matter how drastically she had changed in the past year.

"Morgan," Claire said, her long black curls swaying across her back as she stepped out of her bedroom.

She ignored Aralyn, going past her, and sashayed up to Morgan, aggressively pulling him against her, smashing his chest against her breasts, and kissed him hard. She licked at his lip and Morgan grabbed her rear and tried to pull her tongue into his mouth with his teeth. They went at each other like this for a moment and then Claire pulled slightly away.

"Hasn't Aimeric told you before not to play with his 'pets'?" she asked against his lips. Then, pushing him away, she laughed. "You're so stupid sometimes, Morgan."

Morgan stared at her, surprised at first, until he began to glower and then, a deep growl emitted from within his chest and he muttered, "You're a fuckin' tease."

He shoved past her and retreated to the first floor, leaving Claire, still laughing, and Aralyn, who was looking at Claire, uncomfortable and confused. Once he was gone, Claire turned to her sister. Aralyn was looking at her, speechless at how seductive she had become. Before, Claire had always been too shy to even *talk* to a member of the opposite sex and now, they were just her playthings.

"What are you doing out here, Aralyn?" Claire sighed.

"I was…I'm not sure. I guess I just wanted to get out of the room," Aralyn said.

"Yeah, I guess it could get boring," Claire said, nodding.

She didn't seem to care though. She turned and went back to her bedroom.

"Wait!" Aralyn called as the door started to close.

"What?" Claire asked and opened it again.

Aralyn took a few steps forward.

"I, um…don't you need to feed?"

She didn't really care, she was just desperate to talk to her sister; she had missed her for so long. Claire laughed again, almost childishly.

"No. I already had my meal. Can't you tell? Look at how I *glow*!" She threw her head back, continuing to laugh, almost maniacally.

Aralyn had noticed that there seemed to be a little bit of color in Claire's flesh where it hadn't been before; an after effect of feeding off the warm blood of a human, Aralyn guessed.

Seeing the confusion in Aralyn's expression, Claire stepped aside and waved a hand nonchalantly.

"I ate the girl," she said. Then, giggling again, she added, "In more ways than one."

Aralyn gasped, suppressing a scream, when she saw that Emma was lying, naked, on the floor, with the life completely drained from her body. Aralyn covered her mouth and backed into the wall of the hallway, sliding down to the floor, disgusted, yet unable to look away from the body, as had happened when she had seen the body of her and Claire's father.

"It's such a shame I got so hungry after my orgasm. That girl pleased me like no other." Claire sighed dreamily and then shrugged. "Oh well."

Aralyn was finally able to squeeze her eyes shut. It didn't do her any good though; the girl's dead form appeared on the backs of her eyelids. She couldn't get the image out of her mind. She wasn't sure if she would ever be comfortable with what her sister was.

"Oh, Aralyn," Claire sighed.

Aralyn opened her eyes and saw that Claire was now kneeling beside her.

"We're not monsters, dearest. We need to live, in a manner of speaking, too," she said. Brushing Aralyn's hair down she added, "This is how we live. You understand that, don't you?"

"I…just need some time to get used to it," Aralyn said quietly, not wanting to offend her sister again and have her leave.

She didn't want to be alone with Aimeric again.

Claire laughed.

"Of course you do." Suddenly enlightened, Claire pulled Aralyn to her feet. "I have an idea. You can come along with Aimeric and me when we go hunting tomorrow. That way you can see how we survive."

Aralyn's blood boiled in rage at the mention of *his* name and she jerked her arms free of Claire.

"I will not be going anywhere with that monster!" she spat.

Claire grabbed Aralyn's neck and pushed her into the wall.

"Aimeric is your Master now, Aralyn. He has claimed you as his. You will learn to respect and obey him, as you will me. Have you not learned anything of his temper yet?" she asked, sneering against her cheek.

She let go of Aralyn's neck and pulled her into a tight embrace that pushed the air, which Aralyn had been holding, out of her lungs.

"You're special, Aralyn. He wants you to be his companion for eternity. You should feel honored," she whispered. Holding Aralyn out in front of her, Claire smiled. "Do you understand that he is your Master?"

Aralyn nodded slightly and averted her eyes to the floor. She knew she was his now. There was no escaping him or her fate. He had caught her twice when she tried to escape. He had somehow forced her to have sex with him that would be considered consensual. She had, after all, been the one to start it and she certainly hadn't told him no. How was he able to do that? She would never be free of him. Unless…

"Good. Now, you should go get something to eat. You'll need your strength. Aimeric is always aroused after he feeds," Claire said, laughing, and gave Aralyn a gentle push towards the stairs. Aralyn hesitantly descended them, going for the kitchen, and Claire went back to her room.

She ate quickly, not really having much of an appetite. As she stood from the table, she felt almost as though she was being called to the basement; something was drawing her towards it. She went down the stone steps and into the cold basement, hearing whispers as she approached the door to the prison.

The voices quickly hushed when she creaked open the wooden door and then, when she stepped inside, someone whispered loudly, "It's Aralyn!

The prisoners stood from their concrete seats and pressed their faces against the bars.

"Aralyn! You're alright!" Toby said and held his hand out to her.

She rushed over to him and took his cold fingers in hers.

"Are you hurt again?" Aralyn asked, worried.

"No. Nothing new," Toby responded.

"Aralyn, where is Emma?" a young woman asked.

Aralyn dropped Toby's hand and turned from them. "I…I'm sorry…she's dead," she said quietly.

To Aralyn's surprise, sighs of relief filled the room.

"Thank God!" one breathed.

"What?" Aralyn asked, appalled, spinning around to look at them again.

"Aralyn, her suffering is over, and better yet, she was not turned," Toby explained, excitement filling his voice.

Before Aralyn could respond, the prison door flew open and Aralyn saw that Aimeric was standing in the doorway. Her head was beginning to cloud again and she was having trouble concentrating. As Aimeric came closer to her, she held her hands against her head, fighting her own mind as her memories strained to be kept inside. She forced herself to keep Virgil's image in her head and what Aimeric had done to him so that she wouldn't become Aimeric's puppet. But it was no use. His image was fading from her mind, no matter how hard she tried to keep it.

"Don't try to fight it; it's useless," Aimeric said, taking slow steps towards her.

The prisoners backed further into their cages the further Aimeric went into the room. By the time he walked past them, they were all huddled near the back.

"What are you doing to me?" Aralyn whimpered as he pulled her towards him and rested his hands on her hips.

"Just a little mind manipulation. Your attitude, and rejection, was fun at first, but now, I'm tired of it, Aralyn. If you would have obeyed and respected me from the beginning without a hassle, I might not have had to resort to this, but you're much more fun and *satisfying* when you want what I want," Aimeric said, pressing his lips against her cheek. "Now tell me why you're down here."

"I…just wanted to talk…to someone," Aralyn said drowsily.

He didn't really seem to care and, bringing his hands up to either side of Aralyn's head, Aimeric kissed her lips several times and pushed her against the wall. She whimpered again when her vision became even more hazy and her memories started to fade away until she had no recollection of anything that had happened; all she knew was Aimeric and she was only focused on kissing him back. Her lips urgently responded to his and she brought his tongue into her mouth and sucked on it for a moment until Aimeric pulled away.

"I need you tonight," Aimeric whispered against her lips before kissing her hard again. "I need you to become one of us."

"Do it," Aralyn mumbled, not really aware of what she was saying.

She whimpered again, pulling him back to her mouth. Aimeric kissed her a moment longer and then he moved to her neck and licked the flesh where the vein pulsed underneath. Holding her hand against the back of his head, so his lips stayed against her neck, Aralyn urged Aimeric to sink his fangs into her. He complied and she gasped when she felt them penetrate her skin and fall into her life's vein. Aimeric sucked at the wound, drawing out her blood, but only for a few seconds.

He pulled away suddenly, all urgency lost, and he stared, thoughtfully, into Aralyn's violet eyes. She looked at him, confused.

"I have a better idea, my love," he whispered and licked her bottom lip before pulling away to look at her directly again.

Aralyn ran her own tongue on her lip, tasting the blood that Aimeric had had on his tongue, and whispered, "What?"

Aimeric cupped her face in his large hands and kissed her once more, this time gently, lovingly, and then he began to lead Aralyn out of the prison.

"I've always wanted a child, Aralyn. But vampires cannot have children," he said, thoughtfully.

After opening the door first, Aimeric picked Aralyn up and carried her up both sets of stairs, to the bedroom. He laid her down on the bed and pulled the covers over her.

"Get rested, you're going to need it," he whispered and kissed her briefly.

As he went to pull away, Aralyn held onto his neck and kept him there, sliding her tongue into his mouth; she wasn't quite satisfied yet. Aimeric humored her for a few minutes, kissing her back, and then he pulled away, smirking.

"There will be plenty of time for that later. Right now, rest. I will be back in a while," he said and left the room, closing the door behind him.

As soon as he was gone, Aralyn, again, came back to herself and cursed loudly for wanting him to penetrate her again. She rolled over onto her side and let, yet, more tears fall from her eyes. It seemed she was doing a lot of crying lately. She cried softly and thought about what Aimeric had said about a child. What had he meant? What was he planning? Where had he gone? She asked herself these questions over and over in her mind and tried to come up with an explanation without wanting to admit the possibilities, until she fell asleep. In sleep, she could dream and when she dreamt, she was free.

Chapter Thirteen: A New Face

Aralyn woke up the next morning, shortly before noon, alone in the bed and still wearing the dress from the night before. The room was still dark, only a sliver of sunlight was able to sneak through a crack in the boards since the curtains were partially open. Groaning as she sat up, Aralyn held her hand to her head, feeling the leftover ache from all the crying she had done the night before. She slid her feet over the side of the mattress and lumbered towards the bathroom, her eyes staying on Aimeric's coffin as she went by it. She had no idea if he was inside or not, but she wanted nothing more than to rip the boards off the window, throw the lid off, and take pleasure in watching Aimeric burn to ashes from the sun's rays.

But not knowing if she had the strength, as well as not being aware of how long it took for the sun to affect a vampire, kept her from doing it. As far as Aralyn knew, Aimeric could get to the curtains before the sun could burn him and then who knew what he would do? So she just passed by the coffin and went to the shower. It seemed that was all she did lately; shower and sleep. When she wasn't under Aimeric's control and being forced to have sex with him that was.

Now that Claire was back, Aralyn didn't want to go into her room to find clothes, unsure of what, or who, she might find in there, so she put the black dress back on and thought about what she could do. She had already tried escaping twice and that had only caused her more trouble, along with other innocent people; she didn't care about herself so much as the others who would suffer because of her if she disobeyed again. There was only one other thing she could possibly do and she needed a little while to summon up the courage to do it.

Deciding she needed time to think her plan over, Aralyn left the bedroom and began to wander through the

167

mansion. She hadn't seen much of the house and since she had some time to kill, she decided she would look it over.

Aralyn spent most of the afternoon looking through the house, wandering the dark halls and peeking into the bedrooms that weren't locked. She found nothing of particular interest, just coffins and cockroaches. When she came to Virgil's old room, she couldn't bring herself to look inside so she went right past it.

The huge house, which was probably a few hundred years old, hadn't been taken care of over the years. The walls were dirty and cracking, the carpet was worn and covered with an inch of dust, cobwebs hung from all over above her, and rats and roaches scurried about in almost every room. The roaches bothered Aralyn the most and she tried to avoid them at all costs, hurrying down the hallways and hoping she wouldn't step on any of them with her bare feet.

Aralyn wondered why the vampires stayed in the coffins all day when they could easily roam the mansion. The house was dark enough, since the windows were all boarded up or covered with tin foil, that she didn't think they would be bothered. But then, maybe it was just because they were used to sleeping all day and staying up all night.

Brushing past the cobwebs that reached out and touched her face, Aralyn opened a door on the third floor and snuck inside. She found the room to be an old science laboratory, or something of the like, seemingly untouched for years, just like most of the rest of the house. Aralyn curiously looked around. She had to cover her mouth when she saw animal body parts and whole rodents floating around, preserved, in jars on shelves. Feeling sick, and not wanting to discover anything else in the room, Aralyn quickly backed out and shut the door.

Her back hit someone and she let out a soft scream. Turning around quickly, her heart pounding, Aralyn expected to see Aimeric behind her. She sighed in relief when she saw that it wasn't him.

"Oh, I'm sorry," Aralyn said, looking into the soft brown eyes of a young, female, vampire.

The girl's skin was dark, the color of coffee, and her hair was pure white and silky, trailing past her rear. A short, black, mini skirt showed off her long, slender legs and the red halter-top she wore enhanced her medium sized breasts. But she didn't look sleazy; she was very beautiful.

"What are you doing up here?" the girl asked, her voice surprisingly soft and childlike.

Her expression was emotionless and her eyes held Aralyn's, almost as though she was looking deep into her soul.

"I was, uh, just looking around. I'm sorry if I intruded, or if I'm somewhere I'm not supposed to be. I was bored an-"

"Shh."

The girl placed a finger over Aralyn's lips. "I was just curious. Not many wander up here…but then…not many are given the chance, are they?" Her lips broke into a smile. "But you…you're special aren't you? The Master has kept you alive for a long time."

Aralyn was finally able to look away from the girl's eyes and avert hers to the floor as she softly said, "I don't want to be; special or alive."

"But you are anyway. Aimeric has chosen you to be his eternal lover. He's never even considered it before, always going from one woman to the next, killing her when he's through. He's even had a few men. You should feel honored, especially since he's going to make you the mother of his child," the girl said.

Aralyn's eyes shot back up.

"What did you say?" she asked the girl in alarm.

The girl giggled.

"Oh, I guess you'll find out about that later. Forget I mentioned it."

Aralyn couldn't forget, her mind would be preoccupied with what the girl had said until she knew for sure what Aimeric was planning, but Aralyn knew the girl wasn't going to offer anymore information on the matter, so she asked, instead, "Who is Aimeric? What is he? Why does he have so much power over me?"

"That's strange…usually one would formally introduce themselves before talking so casually," the girl said, almost in a singsong voice.

Aralyn looked at the girl, confused, wondering if she was actually serious, after all they had been talking only a moment ago.

Shaking it off, she said, "I'm sorry. My name is Aralyn."

"I'm Cora," the girl said, smiling, amused.

"Nice to meet you," Aralyn said hesitantly.

Cora nodded and then, placing her arm around Aralyn's shoulders, she began to lead her away while answering her questions.

"Aimeric is a Master Vampire; our leader. He was the first vampire of our specific clan after he made a deal with Satan and was turned. Satan turned him into one of his followers and told him to make more for his army. Aimeric is powerful. More powerful than the rest of us *because* he is our Master; the first created of this clan. There are many vampire clans, but I won't get into that right now. We're talking about Aimeric.

"He is able to manipulate your mind, make you believe things that you never would have thought before, along with any other mortal's mind. He does it when he wants, and how often he wants because he is different from the 'lesser' vampires. Lesser vampires, like myself and the rest of the others here, only have the power to scan minds and calm our victims. We don't have the power to will you to think how we want you to; that's only Aimeric and other vampires like him; Masters," Cora finished.

"But, if he could control me, or manipulate me, all along, why didn't he do it from the beginning instead of having me disobey him?" Aralyn asked, confused and angry, as the two descended a flight of stairs.

"I'm sure he just wanted to have some fun with you first, to see how you would obey without his influence over you. He loves watching his victims struggle and also, with you disobeying so often, from what I hear, he was able to have a real excuse, in his eyes, to torture some of the prisoners," she responded.

Aralyn knew this was the truth, Aimeric had said to her before that "her attitude was fun for a while." Clenching her fists out of anger, Aralyn thought of something else.

"Does he have to be near me to control me? Why do I always snap out of it when he leaves?"

Cora laughed again.

"He only wants you to *think* that. You didn't hear this from me, but he can manipulate you wherever you are, no matter how far away from you he is. The only time he could lose control would be if he were preoccupied with something else."

"Like what?" Aralyn asked curiously.

"Like…" Cora hesitated, thinking. "If he was engaged in a battle with another vampire…something like that."

Aralyn nodded; that information might help her later.

"Did he 'make' all of you?" Aralyn asked after a moment.

"In a way, yes. He is connected to all of us in one way or another. He turned a few of us and then that few turned a few others and so on and so on. In the three hundred years that Aimeric has been a vampire, our clan has grown to about forty or fifty."

"That's all? In three hundred years?" Aralyn couldn't help but ask.

"We can't turn a lot of mortals very often. It would unbalance the three realms of Heaven, Earth and Hell. Satan only wants an army for the battle of Armageddon, not an implosion of the world," Cora said chuckling again.

Aralyn nodded, feeling entirely comfortable with the girl. Cora wasn't like the other vampires at all; she didn't give off that evil vibe that Aralyn felt around everyone else. Cora was different somehow. Aralyn just didn't know what it was that made her that way. The two made it back to the second floor and stood at the door to Aimeric's bedroom. As Aralyn reached for the doorknob Cora pulled her back.

"Come with me. I want to show you something."

Confused, but glad to get away from Aimeric for longer, Aralyn let Cora lead her downstairs towards the basement. When they passed through the living room, Aralyn looked at the clock on the wall and saw that it was sunset, or at least, close to it. A few of the vampires were already awake, lounging on the sofa. They were waiting until it was safe to go outside.

A few of them hissed at Aralyn as she went by, trying to scare her, but she knew she was safe under Aimeric's protection, and didn't let them get to her. Sadie was one of the vampires awake and, when Aralyn caught her eyes, she licked her lips and grinned seductively. Turning her head, Aralyn scoffed, trying to ignore Sadie, and focused on where Cora was taking her. The young vampire woman opened the door to the basement and took Aralyn down to the prison.

Aralyn started to open her mouth in order to ask Cora why she was bringing her down here but, seeing Aimeric standing in the middle of the room with his hands clasped behind his back, she hesitated and then demanded, instead, "What's going on?"

Perhaps she had been wrong about Cora. Why had she led her to Aimeric? Aralyn looked at the girl questioningly but Cora wasn't looking back at her. Instead, she was glaring, hatefully, at Aimeric.

"There. I brought her down here like you said, now let me go hunt," she hissed spitefully.

Aimeric grinned coldly and then waved a hand towards the door, dismissing Cora, giving her permission to leave. With a quick apologetic glance in Aralyn's direction, Cora spun around on her heel and left the prison, leaving Aralyn alone with Aimeric and the prisoners.

<u>Chapter Fourteen: Pick One</u>

Aralyn refused to move and stayed in one spot, staring fiercely at Aimeric; the creature she so loathed. He calmly walked over to her and took her arm.

"What are you doing!" Aralyn asked, spitting out the words.

"Temper, Aralyn," Aimeric warned patiently, taking her to stand in front of one of the cages. He stood behind her, resting his hands on her shoulders, and whispered in her ear, "Pick one."

"No," she whimpered, falling to her knees, all of a sudden weakened from fear and disgust. "Aimeric, I haven't done anything! Please don't hurt anyone!"

He chuckled softly, pulling her back up to her feet.

"Not for that," he said.

She stopped the tears that had threatened to fall and turned her head to look at him.

"For what then?" she asked.

"Pick the one whom you think will give us a beautiful and healthy child," Aimeric said in a low whisper, kissing her cheek.

"What? You can't be serious," Aralyn breathed, shaking her head in disbelief.

"Oh but I am, Aralyn. I would do the job myself, of course, but, as I already told you, I can't, so," he waved a hand in front of her towards the cage and repeated, "pick one."

Aralyn looked through the bars and saw that three healthy looking young men were standing in the cage. She could see they were in great physical shape since all they were wearing was a pair of sweat pants each. They all had broad shoulders and different skin tones. One was darkly tanned with short, sandy blonde hair, which fell into sea green eyes. The second one was paler than the first and had short, black hair and silver eyes. The third had long, curly dark hair down to his shoulders and dark eyes against a lightly tanned and chiseled face. They all looked confused and seemed to be in a trance; they were being manipulated by Aimeric.

"I can't...please don't make me do this," Aralyn said and stepped backwards, hitting Aimeric's chest, shaking her head.

"Fine, Aralyn! I will choose for you, like always," Aimeric said loudly, making her flinch.

His arm slid around her neck and he opened the door to the cage where he yanked out the dark haired one with silver eyes. Aralyn stepped out of the way and watched, fearfully, as Aimeric closed the door, keeping hold on the young man. Aralyn bit her lip, like she always did when she was nervous, knowing what was going to be ordered of her.

"What's your name?" Aimeric asked once the gate was secure again.

"Darren," the man responded in a monotone.

His eyes stared straight ahead.

"Well, *Darren*, you are going to make love to my Aralyn here until she conceives, and then I'm going to kill you because I cannot allow another man to touch her and get away with it. Do you understand?" Aimeric asked casually.

Aralyn couldn't hold in her sobs as the tears poured from her eyes to land on the stone, cold, floor at her feet.

"Yes," Darren answered.

Aimeric nodded his approval and turned to Aralyn, cupping her face in his hands.

"Try not to enjoy it too much," he said dryly, placing a few kisses on her lips.

Sorrow and fear were replaced by anger and loathing once more and Aralyn flung herself away from Aimeric.

"I am *not* going to do this!" she yelled.

"Get over here, Aralyn," Aimeric said, his voice low and dangerous.

She shook her head.

"I am running low on my patience with you. I will give you one minute to come to me on your own," he warned.

Aralyn's eyes darted all over the room, searching for any kind of weapon she could use; she was no longer afraid of killing herself and she would do it this time. Spotting an old arrowhead, it's sides chipped and worn, on the surgeon's table, Aralyn grabbed it and brought it to her throat.

"I would rather die," she hissed and started to slide it across her neck.

"Drop it, Aralyn!" Aimeric yelled before the blade could go too deep.

The tool fell from Aralyn's hands. Before she could reach for it again, Aimeric was on her in a second, slamming his body against hers, and hitting her back into the wall, holding her in place. The prisoner's watched from the corner of their eyes and silently prayed that he wouldn't harm her but they dared not to look at Aimeric or Aralyn.

"You better not try anything like that again or I will do it for you, only I will make it slow and extremely painful. Do you understand?" Aimeric hissed, inches away from her face.

"I don't care!" she snapped.

"Oh, I think you would. I'm not talking a few hours of suffering, *sweetheart*. I'm talking about weeks, even months, of excruciating pain; I've done it before," he said.

Her chest rising and falling with the deep breaths she took, Aralyn angrily eyed Aimeric; she knew he was serious.

"So let's try this again: *Do* you understand?" Aimeric asked patiently.

Aralyn nodded, her jaw clenched tightly, tears shining in her eyes.

"Good."

The pressure on Aralyn's chest was released and Aimeric stepped slightly away from her, allowing her room to breathe. He brought his hands back to her face and lowered his mouth to hers. Tensing at the feel of his lips, Aralyn jerked her head to the side at first. Aimeric calmly turned her back and kissed her hard, thrusting his tongue into her mouth, and she slowly came under his control. Aralyn moved her hands to his waist and held on to him so she could hungrily kiss him back and Aimeric moved his hands to her back so he could unzip the dress she was wearing. His tongue slithered down her throat and licked away the blood that had surfaced from the cut she had inflicted on herself. Moaning softly in response, Aralyn pushed her body up against Aimeric's letting him know that she wanted him *now*. She felt his sex begin to harden against her, but he didn't hurry in anything he did, which was starting to drive her almost to the point of insanity.

Slowly, the dress fell to the floor and Aimeric touched his lips against her flesh in every place he knew would heighten her sexual senses. He didn't miss one spot and she soon began whimpering. Her body ached for him and she wrapped her fingers around his sex, rubbing him through his clothing. She felt him tremble slightly at her touch, but other than that, he didn't let her know she was affecting him as much as he was affecting her.

When the dress finally fell all the way off, and the heat between Aralyn's thighs was almost unbearable, Aimeric stepped away from her and pushed Darren forward in his place. Darren obediently took over, kissing her, as Aimeric willed, and placed her on the table while she fumbled with his pants, trying to hurriedly remove them. Pulling Darren onto her, Aralyn kissed him urgently and felt him harden almost immediately against her thigh. He

177

didn't take his time with anything and thrust into her. Aralyn coiled his hair in her fingers, holding onto him, while he moved inside of her, rapidly, and threw her head back, moaning loudly.

Aimeric stood to the side and watched to make sure the two didn't do any more than what was necessary. Once Darren had spilled his mortal seed into Aralyn, Aimeric threw him back in the cage by his hair and, taking off his shirt, he placed it around Aralyn's quivering shoulders and carried her upstairs where he eased his ache as well

This happened every night for the next two weeks. Aimeric would lead Aralyn into the prison where he aroused her and manipulated her mind before letting one of the three men take her while he watched to make sure they didn't do too much. He watched to ensure that there was no foreplay (he did that), too much kissing, and also to make sure it didn't last any longer than necessary.

Aralyn's feelings for Aimeric were still spiteful and she hated him when he wasn't manipulating her, or so she kept telling herself. As much as she hated to admit it, she could feel herself starting to see him differently. Something about him, which she couldn't explain, was mixing up her feelings and making them go in all different directions; she blamed it on the mind manipulation anyway, even though she knew that when she was thinking these thoughts, she was in control of her own mind, but they could have been after thoughts from the mind controlling. How did she really know she had control of her own mind, after all?

The thought of continuing to try and take her life had crossed Aralyn's mind only once more but she had quickly pushed it aside knowing that she could very well be taking two lives now instead of one, and while she hated the idea of having a baby that wasn't conceived out of love, she knew it wasn't the child's fault and so she didn't want to harm it.

Morgan continued to taunt Aralyn for the next two weeks, when Aimeric wasn't around, having even more reason to antagonize her since he knew that she was being forced to have a baby. Aralyn tried her hardest to ignore him and walk away, but a few times she had lost her temper and snapped at him, which only made Morgan more obnoxious.

Claire stuck around longer this time and took joy in teasing Morgan when he antagonized Aralyn, which Aralyn was grateful for. If Claire knew anything about what Aimeric was having Aralyn do, she kept her thoughts to herself because she never brought it up and neither did Aralyn; she didn't like talking about it.

On the last night of the second week, Darren was chosen, once again, to make love to Aralyn and after he had finished, Aimeric grabbed him off of her by the hair and sunk his fangs into his neck, draining him of his life. He left the other two, the blonde one, Ethan, and the other, Joseph, alive in case he still needed them; in case Aralyn wasn't pregnant yet and they needed to continue after her cycle.

It had been Aimeric's jealousy that had killed Darren. He didn't like how much he had seemed to please Aralyn. Once Darren's body had gone limp, Aimeric let him drop to the floor and finish dying while he took Aralyn upstairs and made love to her, harder, and longer. He wanted to accomplish everything Darren hadn't and so much more. He succeeded and, by the time the two had finished for the night, Aralyn had filled the room with cries of pleasure and her breath felt as though she had lost it forever and would never return. She fell asleep on top of Aimeric shortly after, with him clutching her black hair, which was matted against the back of her neck.

Chapter Fifteen: The Night Out

Soft stroking from Aimeric's hands woke Aralyn from her dreamless sleep the next evening after their last round of lovemaking. Aralyn raised her head to look into Aimeric's eyes, which appeared unusually warm. She smiled at him and then pushed herself up to softly press her lips against his.

"Would you like to go hunting with me tonight?" Aimeric asked when they broke their kiss.

Aralyn hadn't gone yet, as Claire had suggested. Since Aimeric had been so persistent on Aralyn conceiving, he had postponed taking her out. This night was the first, in the last two weeks, that Aralyn wasn't to have sex with either man downstairs. Aimeric had decided she needed a break and also, he wanted to wait and see if it was necessary to continue. He didn't want Aralyn having sex with another man if she didn't have to. He was sure he had figured everything out right and as long as he was correct, Aralyn's menstrual time was due in the next couple of days. If Aralyn wasn't pregnant, then Aimeric would have her continue to have sex with one of the two men that were left, every night again until a few days before her next menstrual time and repeat the cycle until she was pregnant.

Still partially under Aimeric's mind manipulation, Aralyn nodded in agreement, which Aimeric smiled to in response. The two rolled out of bed and dressed quickly before going downstairs. Aimeric had gotten Aralyn her own wardrobe in the last two weeks and he picked out the clothes she wore that evening, which were, a black leather corset that pushed Aralyn's breasts up into voluptuous cleavage, a black and red plaid skirt that was cut low, resting on her hips, which also showed off part of her flat stomach. Aimeric had completed the outfit by presenting her with knee high boots, which zipped up Aralyn's calf to her knee. She let her long, raven, hair hang loose, trailing down her back. Aimeric was dressed in his usual attire; black leather pants and a black button up shirt with long sleeves. The two met Claire at the front, double, doors. The house was mostly empty already since the other vampires were already out hunting.

"Ready to go?" Claire asked, smirking.

Her clothes were unseen, covered by a long black coat she had on. A pile of black curls sat on top of her head, fastened with a few hair clips, a few strands falling into her mischievous green eyes. Nodding, Aimeric led Aralyn out the door by the small of her back and Claire followed them.

Waiting on the circular drive was a slick black limousine. The engine was running and the headlights were on, showing the fog in the air, ready to go. Aimeric smoothly opened the door and ushered the two women inside before crawling in after them. A strip of dim lights bordered the roof, like tiny stars, and illuminated the leather seats while also placing a soft glow on the three of their faces.

"Aralyn and I will be stopping at the park," Aimeric said to Claire, pulling Aralyn onto his lap while the car slowly pulled away and left the mansion's drive.

Ignoring the oncoming conversation, Aralyn pulled Aimeric's hair to the side and, placing one arm around his neck, lowered her lips to touch the cold flesh of his throat.

"I trust you will be fine without us for a short while?" Aimeric continued, looking at Claire.

She chuckled.

"I hardly think I need a companion to hunt anymore, Aimeric. I've done fine on my own before."

So you have," Aimeric mumbled.

Claire smirked and crossed her legs, showing the black fishnet stockings she wore, which disappeared into the buckled ankle boots on her feet.

"Why the park?" she asked.

"I'm going to show Aralyn how others hunt first and the club would be too much of a distraction; too much happens there at once," Aimeric responded, kissing Aralyn quickly as her lips reached his for a brief moment before returning to his neck.

"Good idea, I suppose," Claire said, nodding.

Aimeric smirked in response and then brought Aralyn's chin up so he could kiss her mouth again. Their lips stayed together and their tongues entwined for the rest of the ride to the city.

When the car finally stopped in front of a brick building with only a few, blacked out, windows, Aimeric waved in a gesture which commanded Claire to leave the car.

"What? You don't trust me to have you dropped off first?" she asked in mock innocence.

Aralyn looked at her from Aimeric's lap, slightly amused.

"Not with my car, no," Aimeric replied with a sly grin.

Smirking at both of them, Claire opened the door and stepped outside. After a moment of wriggling, she bent back down and tossed the coat back into the car and her outfit for the evening was revealed. She was dressed enticingly, no doubt to attract her victims. Over the fishnets, she wore a pair of red leather short shorts that barely covered the cheeks of her rear. Her top was a tight, knit, black, shirt with a yellow collar. A pair of leather suspenders was hooked at the bottom of the shirt to the shorts.

"No need to rush, I'm quite hungry tonight," she said before stepping back out into the night.

"Don't worry about *that*," Aimeric replied as she closed the door.

Aralyn watched her sister, through the tinted windows, sensually walk up to the entrance and saw she was immediately let inside by the bouncer, winking at him as she walked in.

"It's all a part of the game," Aimeric whispered in Aralyn's ear before he gently nibbled it.

"What is?" Aralyn asked as the car pulled away.

"Seduction," he whispered.

Grinning, Aralyn turned back to him and placed a hard kiss on his lips. He returned it for a few minutes before breaking apart again.

"We dress to attract, we attract to catch, and we catch to feed," Aimeric continued.

"Is the process any different when you want to turn someone?" Aralyn asked curiously.

"Not really. Most of the time, the decision to sire a mortal comes at the last few moments of their lives when they beg for us not to kill them."

"But I'm sure a lot beg for that…surely you can't uh, *sire* all of them, can you?"

Aimeric grinned.

"My, you're inquisitive this evening, darling."

"Isn't that why I am here? To learn about you and other vampires?" Aralyn asked pointedly.

"You're right; that is why you are here. A lot beg, yes. I suppose it depends on the vampire's mood at the time and their intentions afterwards. Sometimes, vampires feel sorry for their victims when they beg for their lives; not me, of course, but others," he said and chuckled softly before continuing. "Or, a vampire will sire a victim to keep as a pet; a toy. An object to hunt for him, to boss around, or, in most cases, to have for pleasurable desires."

For a brief moment, Aimeric released Aralyn's mind to hear her response to that. Her eyes grew dark and she frowned, leaning away slightly, but she didn't make a move to escape his lap.

"To keep…as a pet and for pleasurable desires," she repeated softly, almost sounding hurt. "Like what you're doing with me?"

Aimeric placed his hand on the back of her neck, bringing her into a soft, yet passionate, kiss.

"No. You are no toy and you are no pet," he assured her softly after pulling away enough to look into her eyes.

It was obvious that she didn't believe him by the look she was giving. Pulling her into another kiss, Aimeric listened to her thoughts to find out exactly why she didn't believe his words. Aralyn didn't believe him because of what he had been doing since she had arrived; controlling her mind, forcing her to do things; it was all an act of tyrannical ownership. She felt like she was on a leash. And in all reality, she was. But at that moment Aimeric was not manipulating her, and yet, she was willingly kissing him back and just as passionately. The car slowed to a stop and Aimeric broke the connection between their lips once again.

"We're here," he said.

Aralyn nodded and climbed off of his lap so she could follow him out of the car. Shivering slightly under the clear, chilly sky, Aralyn looked into the center of the park and saw several couples, and a few loners, sitting on the benches around the playing equipment and leaning against the trees.

Placing Claire's coat around Aralyn's shoulders, Aimeric whispered against the side of her head, close to her ear, "You are free tonight; I will not pry into your mind or manipulate you as long as you don't give me a reason to. Stay with me and remain calm, no matter what you see."

At the sound of his voice, and his breath against her cheek, Aralyn closed her eyes and nodded. She didn't like the idea that his voice, his breath, his touch, aroused her with the simplest of each.

"Keep your voice down if you want to speak and don't make it obvious what we are here for," Aimeric added softly, pecking her cheek.

With another quick nod, Aralyn was led toward the children's playing equipment, by the hand that Aimeric had grasped.

"Remember, we are only lovers out for the evening, so act like it," Aimeric said, helping her climb onto the merry-go-round.

It wasn't hard to pretend and Aralyn hated to admit it. But the mood was right. The night was beautiful and the temperature was perfect to be secured in the arms of a lover, no matter how cold they were, and that's exactly where she was; in the arms of her lover. Aimeric was leaning against one of the poles, sitting in the center of the merry-go-round, and Aralyn was against his chest, laying her head on his shoulder, trying to convince herself that her developing feelings for the vampire were only an after effect of all the mind manipulation he had done.

"Can you tell me which ones are the vampires?" Aimeric asked, looking ahead at some of the figures talking amongst themselves.

Aralyn concentrated on the people, trying to pick out the ones with the most vampiric characteristics, or what she had seen so far of the vampires at the mansion and what she remembered from books and movies. She mentally ruled out the ones wearing crosses or any other religious accessories or clothing. Along with religious appearance, Aralyn decided that anyone wearing clothes that were traditionally considered "normal" and covered the fleshy areas, were human. She picked out three rough looking figures and pointed them out to Aimeric, guessing that they were the creatures of the night.

"Only one of them is," Aimeric said in response. "Vampires are not always 'dressed to kill' because not all humans are attracted to that kind of thing."

He pointed discreetly.

"The ones by the tree, wearing the silver chained crosses, are vampires that belong to another clan; the crosses are probably symbolic of that clan since some think they need such things."

"I thought-"

"Vampires fear crosses?" Aimeric interrupted, amused.

He had heard it all too often before. He had had several victims whip out a religious piece of jewelry to try and scare him off. He then "taught" them not to believe what they read in books or saw on television.

Aralyn nodded.

"That is only a myth. Garlic, holy water, and crosses hurting any of us are all just ideas that priests came up with to make the villagers from long ago feel protected. The myths have been ongoing for centuries. But most of them are untrue."

"What *is* true?" Aralyn asked.

"Cutting off the connection of a vampire's head from its body and being exposed to the sun for too long are the only ways to kill a vampire. A stake works sometimes, but only on the weak ones. "

Nodding, Aralyn listened while watching the two, male and female, by the tree. They were pretending to converse while watching around the park, out of the corners of their eyes.

"They have decided on their prey. Do you see how they're discreetly approaching that couple over there?"

"Yes," Aralyn said softly, watching with interest.

The vampire couple said something to the mortals and the four laughed together. The two humans, also male and female, nodded to something the female vampire said and then began to follow them into the trees. Before she could ask anything, Aralyn felt her body being thrown through the wind, or so it seemed as everything, trees, grass, and people, sped by in a half second until she appeared with Aimeric behind a tree, near the couple.

"First, the seduction," Aimeric observed from behind her, not bothering to explain how they had come so far from the merry-go-round in only a second.

With Aimeric's arms keeping her in place, Aralyn looked ahead, around the tree, and saw the male vampire had held his hand out to the female mortal and brought her to his lips while the female vampire did the same to the human male. The vampires had worked their charms, so to speak, and it was all too familiar to Aralyn. She should have been upset because she knew that these two humans were helpless against these creatures of the night, as she had been and still was, but she wasn't upset; if anything, she was intrigued as to how the vampires would do their work. Her violet eyes watched curiously as the vampires both inconspicuously moved to their victims' necks.

Thinking she could handle watching that part, Aralyn continued to observe, but as soon as the fangs penetrated the flesh and the blood started to run down the mortals' throats, along with hearing the painful gasps, which emitted from the victims, she had to turn her head. She grasped Aimeric's shirt and kept her eyes hidden in his chest until the grotesque sounds of the vampires' drinking died down. Aimeric didn't say anything, but he held Aralyn tightly around the waist and kept his eyes on the couples.

After a few minutes of cringing, Aralyn heard the bodies drop to the ground with a soft thud and then she felt herself being turned around. Aimeric moved her so she could see the male vampire wipe blood from his chin and then lick his finger while he eyed the girl. When the two jumped on each other, locked in a crushing embrace, smashing their lips together, high on ecstasy from the taste of the blood, or so Aralyn assumed since that was how Aimeric behaved after feeding, Aimeric took her arm and led her away and the two vampires started to moan loudly, not caring that they were in a very public place. What could anyone do to them, anyway?

"Blood is a drug to us. It fills us with warmth and ecstasy like nothing else and arouses us more than almost anything, as you already know," Aimeric said as they walked.

Aralyn saw him glance slyly at her from the corner of his eye and she rolled her eyes, knowing that he was referring to his own reaction of the blood.

"Aren't they afraid people will find the bodies?" Aralyn asked quietly and kicked away a twig that had fallen to the ground from one of the trees.

Aimeric shrugged.

"The authorities just blame it on wild animals when they find bodies, and hide the fact that the flesh was mostly untouched, and the body drained of blood, from the public." He smirked and added, "After all, in this day, vampires don't exist. Or so they think…"

Reaching the car again, Aimeric let Aralyn inside before sitting next to her and giving the order to the man in the front to drive. For the rest of the ride back to the club, Aralyn sat, silently staring out the window, and watched as the city lights went by. She couldn't believe how naïve humans were that a body with two puncture marks at the neck, drained of blood, could be passed on as an animal attack. But she knew it was true.

Aimeric had been right; most people in this day didn't believe vampires were real.

Chapter Sixteen: The Club

When they arrived back at the club, Aimeric led Aralyn straight inside, going right past the bouncer without even a glance. The bouncer did nothing to stop Aimeric; he was familiar with him and knew not to say a word. Immediately welcomed by the loud music and flashing strobe lights, Aralyn felt uncomfortable inside and grasped Aimeric's hand to keep him from wandering away from her; not that he really would, but it made her feel better being in such a place. The floor was alive with young dancers and the air was filled with smoke and the scent of alcohol.

Aralyn scanned the room quickly and saw that Claire was sitting on one of the bar stools, talking to a young woman. The woman was beautiful, of course, and listening to Claire talk, nodding her head. Aralyn didn't have time to think about going over to her though because Aimeric had already started to lead her up a set of stairs to a balcony on the second floor that overlooked the dancing men and women.

While Aimeric took a moment to look around, searching for a table, Aralyn watched her sister from over the rail. Claire was now leaning over, kissing the girl softly, and licking at her bottom lip. The two women stood after a moment and Claire followed the woman through the room and to a side exit, both disappearing outside into the night. Aralyn didn't even want to *think* of what Claire might be doing to the woman so she turned her head back to Aimeric just as he had started to walk again. He had found his table and took Aralyn to it, helping her to sit in the corner booth before sliding in next to her.

He kissed her neck softly and whispered, "Watch me and then wait for my signal."

She nodded and Aimeric leaned back in his seat so that his icy orbs could scan the room below. Aralyn watched him and followed his line of vision when his eyes finally stopped moving. They landed on a young man, a boy, rather, of about sixteen years of age. He was obviously wasted on drugs, most likely speed or another amphetamine. His eyes were unfocused and he was dancing wildly, by himself, unaware of anything going on around him except for the music. Head shaking, seemingly out of control, his, black, purple tipped, spiked, hair stayed in place while the numerous chains he had on his body rattled, which included the chain he had attached from his left ear to his nose.

"Stay here," Aimeric ordered and stood from the table.

Aralyn's eyes followed him as he descended the stairs, into the crowd. She was distracted for a moment when she saw Claire out of the corner of her eye. Claire was coming back in through the door on the side of the room, wiping something off of her chin that Aralyn could only guess was blood since she was alone again. The woman was nowhere to be seen. Claire spotted Aralyn on the balcony and winked at her before going back to the bar, this time to start a conversation with a male. Aralyn looked back at Aimeric and saw that he was standing behind the boy, whispering something to him from over his shoulder. The boy smiled faintly and nodded, allowing Aimeric to lead him towards the same door Claire had just come from. No one had noticed that some of the people were disappearing before their very eyes, out the side exit. Aralyn found it odd but then figured it was because most of them were so wasted or having so much fun that they weren't paying attention.

Aralyn turned her head and started to follow Aimeric's movements, with the boy, but something else caught her eye. A figure, with pure white hair, down to his waist, was standing in the shadows a few feet away, looking at Aralyn intently. Since he was covered by the darkness in the corner of the balcony, Aralyn could barely make out his masculine figure, arms crossed over a broad chest, and blood red eyes. When he saw that he had caught Aralyn's attention, he smirked at her.

Aralyn, come here.

Aimeric was calling to her mentally, and she turned her attention back below where she saw that he was standing with the boy, still whispering to his smiling face, but keeping his stern eyes on Aralyn. She hurriedly stood and glanced at the mysterious man again. She was taken aback when she saw he was gone. She stood there a moment and searched for him, but she didn't see him. She wondered if him being there had just been her imagination. There *was* a lot of smoke in the room and it was hot, so maybe she had been seeing things.

Get down here, Aralyn.

Aimeric's voice was hard and stern this time. Knowing that he was getting impatient, Aralyn quickly brushed her thoughts about the man aside for the moment and rushed down the stairs towards Aimeric's waiting hand. He grabbed her, pulling her against his side, while he led the boy with his other hand.

"What took you so long to come to me? What were you doing?" Aimeric growled in a low voice, leading the two away.

"I thought I saw someone, I'm sorry…" she whispered, frightened at the look in his eyes.

He was back to looking cold and dangerous, like what he had looked like that first night when he tortured Emma. Aralyn shrunk back slightly and then glanced at the boy when she heard him humming softly to himself, totally oblivious as to what was happening or what was going to happen to him.

"We'll discuss this more later," Aimeric hissed, pulling both of them towards the door.

Vampires Don't Exist by Reyanna Vance

He opened it and the three inconspicuously slipped outside, which wasn't hard to do since no one had been paying attention to them in the first place. The alley, where they were at, was obviously never used, except to empty the trash. It was dark and abandoned and looked like something out of a scary movie. Aralyn stood off to the side and leaned against the building, crossing her arms, to watch Aimeric as she had been brought to do; to observe the ways of the vampires and better understand them.

Aimeric smoothly ran his hands up the boy's chest and neck, curling his fingers in the stiff hair on top of his head. He leaned down and licked the boy's neck while gently massaging the bottom of his scalp. The boy's glossy green eyes fluttered in ecstasy and he held onto the back of Aimeric's shirt, tilting his head more. Aimeric ran his tongue up and down the boy's neck and then, smirking at Aralyn over his shoulder first, he turned the boy's head and touched his lips to the boy's in a hard and forceful kiss. The boy responded by pulling Aimeric closer to him and thrusting his tongue into Aimeric's mouth while shamelessly hitting his pelvis against Aimeric's thigh. Aimeric reached down and gently tugged on the boy's hardened cock a few times through his pants. The boy moaned into Aimeric's mouth. Not sure of how to respond or what to think of the scene before her, Aralyn moved her eyes around the alley while Aimeric humored the boy. Her stomach churned when she saw an ash pale hand dangling over the side of one of the dumpsters. It was Claire's victim from earlier, or so Aralyn assumed; she wasn't about to go over and check.

Another moan from the boy took Aralyn's attention away from the dumpster. It was a mixture of pleasure and pain. Aralyn looked to see that Aimeric had moved to the boy's neck, his fangs deep into the boy's vein while his hand still teased the boy's cock. The boy had gripped Aimeric's hair and closed his eyes at the feel, and pain, of the vampire's fangs, but too lost in ecstasy to think of what was going on. Aimeric was gently sucking at the wound, moaning into the boy's neck, allowing the crimson to fall onto his tongue and run, smoothly, down his throat. Aralyn cringed and turned away again.

Watch. You have to get over that little phobia of yours, said Aimeric's mind, going into Aralyn's.

Holding her arm across her stomach, feeling as though she would be sick, Aralyn forced herself to watch but tried to drown out the guttural moans that were now coming from Aimeric's throat as he sucked out the blood. The boy's moaning faded and his body went limp and started to slide to the ground. Aimeric held him up until he had had his fill and then he tossed the body down to the ground. The boy's breathing became slow wheezing and then, closing his bloodshot eyes, he let go of his soul.

"Did you notice that I let him go before he was fully dead?" Aimeric asked, his voice a lusty growl.

Aralyn nodded, staring at the body, unable to tear her eyes from it.

"We cannot keep drinking when the heart stops beating or we will die. And also, we cannot drink too much blood in one night or we will become drunk and sick," Aimeric said.

"Uh huh," Aralyn said, not really listening.

She only looked away from the body when Aimeric appeared in front of her and pushed her against the wall. She felt his arousal and knew what he wanted. As he went to kiss her hard, she pushed him back.

"Wait," she said, staring at the blood that was trickling down his chin.

"What?" Aimeric asked, annoyed.

"I want...let me..."

She couldn't say it, so she answered him by pushing herself up on the toes of her boots and, closing her mouth around his chin, she sucked away the blood leftover from the boy. She wasn't sure why she had done it, except that she was curious as to how it tasted and why it affected the vampires the way that it did. Other than almost gagging on the crimson liquid, she didn't get a chance to decide what she thought of the taste. Aimeric was impatient and in a hurry to have his way with her. The feel of her hot tongue on his chin had been too much to contain his sexual desire any longer. He shoved her harder against the wall, kissing her roughly. He pulled up the skirt she was wearing and ripped away her underwear while Aralyn worked on freeing his erection. Once he was released, Aimeric used the brick wall behind them to brace on and Aralyn wrapped her legs around his waist. Aimeric thrust into her and they both let out a loud gasp, followed by soft moaning.

"The blood," Aimeric gasped. "Warms our bodies and works as a natural stimulant for us."

He thrust quicker.

"It arouses us quickly," he panted.

"Yes," Aralyn gasped, agreeing.

That was always how the blood affected him and it didn't surprise Aralyn; she was used to it by that time and wasn't complaining.

Their lovemaking was over quickly but when it was over, Aralyn's fingernails were streaked with blood from where she had been grasping onto Aimeric's neck. He didn't seem to notice, or care. Before going back into the club, the two straightened their clothes and Aimeric licked the blood away from Aralyn's fingers. Aimeric left the body in the street, not caring who might come across it and not bothering trying to hide it in a dumpster as Claire had done. While Aimeric led her through the club, towards the main entrance, Aralyn searched for her sister.

"Where's Claire?" she asked Aimeric, not seeing her.

"She'll show up sooner or later. Come on," Aimeric growled and shoved through the crowd of people. He took Aralyn outside where the limo was still waiting for them.

"We're leaving without her?" Aralyn asked, worried.

"She does this all the time, Aralyn. You should know this by now, now get in," he responded, annoyed, as he opened the car door.

Aralyn hesitantly climbed inside, not wanting to upset him further, but she wasn't able to forget about worrying about her sister; Claire may have been a vampire, but that didn't mean that Aralyn couldn't worry about her. Pulling the door closed, Aimeric slid in next to Aralyn.

"Take us home Frederick," he ordered, gruffly to the driver.

Frederick nodded his chubby, baldhead and the car pulled away. Aralyn looked at the driver thoughtfully; he didn't look like a vampire.

"He isn't," Aimeric said in response to the question she hadn't had the chance to ask yet.

"Why do you..." Aralyn began.

"Not kill him? Torture him? Turn him into one of us?" Aimeric finished for her.

She nodded and looked down at her lap.

Shrugging, Aimeric responded, "You never know when you might need a ride during the day. Freddy and I have an agreement. He promises his loyalty to me, and the secret of our existence, in exchange for my protection."

"Oh, I see," Aralyn said softly.

Aimeric looked at her thoughtfully for a moment, and then, sighing softly, he pulled her head down onto his lap.

"Lay down. You're tired; I can see it in your eyes."

She nodded in agreement; she really was tired. She lay down on his lap, sprawling her long legs across the back seat and closing her eyes. She was almost immediately asleep.

Chapter Seventeen: Feelings Revealed

The soft cooing of a baby woke Aralyn up and she found that she was in a strange bed in a dark room. She couldn't see anything at first. Her mouth was dry and she was still tired; exhausted. Pulling back the sheets that covered her body, Aralyn saw, through the nightgown she was wearing, that her skin was still stretched from her pregnancy. She had given birth a few hours ago, that much she remembered. The cooing turned into impatient crying and Aralyn looked across the room to where the cries were coming from. In the corner, under a silver beam of light, which came from an unseen force, there was a bassinet that held the crying newborn.

Aralyn's motherly instincts immediately kicked in and she was off the bed in a second, rushing to the baby. She felt scared almost, like the child was in danger and she had to get to it. She wanted to protect it and hold it in her arms. Always.

However, when she reached down to pick the child up, she drew back and screamed, frightened. The baby's face was stained red from crimson tears and tiny, pointed, fangs hung below his lip. Aralyn stared at the crying, monster-child, wondering what to do. What had happened to the child? Why was it like this? She didn't want to touch it.

"It's disgusting, that you would allow this to happen to your own baby."

Aralyn spun around and saw the man from the club; the one with the white hair and blood red eyes.

"I didn't-"

"You did! You were the child's protector! He instinctively trusted you because you are his mother and you *let* this happen to him!" the man yelled, interrupting her.

"Who are you? Why are you here?" Aralyn demanded.

"You will find out soon enough," he hissed before he disappeared.

With angry tears in her eyes, Aralyn spun back around to the bassinet, her fingers clenching tightly to the sides. She hadn't allowed this to happen! She didn't even know exactly what *had* happened! How dare that bastard confront her? Her tear filled eyes looked down into the bassinet and she saw that her son had stopped crying and was staring up at her with a knowing look in his eyes. He knew she was his mother, his nurturer. Aralyn noticed his eyes were different colors; one was hers, violet, and the other ice blue, belonging to Aimeric. The baby kicked his legs and cooed, smiling up at her. He wanted to be picked up. Aralyn touched his face. His ivory skin was so soft.

She smiled and whispered, "You're not so strange are you? I think mommy over-reacted for a moment; you're beautiful."

Aralyn reached into the bassinet and gently picked up the, almost weightless, infant. She kissed his soft, dark hair, and rocked him in her arms until he fell asleep.

"Aralyn. Wake up. We're home."

She stirred at the gentle shaking Aimeric was doing to her shoulder. He pulled her up and she looked at him stupidly for a moment, not sure of where she was at.

"What is it?" Aimeric asked, frowning.

"Nothing," she said softly and shook her head; she had been dreaming and that had been all.

Aimeric's frown deepened but he opened the car door anyway and led her inside the mansion. A few of the vampires had already returned and were lounging around in the living room, watching television mostly. Two, both males, were arguing about something, probably unimportant. One sneered something evilly and the other one shoved him. The one shoved, shoved the other back and they ended up falling to the floor in an all out punching match. Neither of them had noticed Aimeric had returned. He slammed the door, making his presence known since they had been too absorbed in their fight to sense him.

"Knock it off!" Aimeric yelled as the door latched shut with a loud boom.

Both men jumped up from the floor, a look of terror in their eyes. The other vampires stopped what they were doing and looked at the four of them, then, seeing the two at fault for their interruptions, glared angrily at the two men.

They both hung their heads, and, in unison, mumbled, "Sorry."

Aimeric glared at them coldly, keeping them in place by using the authority of fear, by only a look in his eye, as he led Aralyn upstairs. Once they reached the bedroom, Aralyn started to make her way to the bathroom to change into sleeping clothes for the rest of the night. Aimeric pulled on her arm and yanked her back. Startled, Aralyn turned to face him and she saw that he was angry, clenching his jaw.

"What?" Aralyn asked softly.

She had no idea what she could have done, why was his temper flaring?

"Why did it take so long for me to get your attention tonight at the club?" he asked sternly.

Aralyn lowered her eyes to the floor. She had thought, and hoped, he had forgotten about that. He hadn't said anything in the car, why had he brought it up now? Perhaps because she had been so tired then. She wasn't sure what she should say. Aimeric might get jealous and get the wrong idea if she told him that it had been a man who had caught her attention before. Her mind wandered to earlier when she saw the white hair and those red eyes staring back at her from the corner of the balcony. That same man had haunted her dream in the car too. She had the feeling he knew her and wasn't going to leave her alone.

"I see," Aimeric said, reading into her open mind again.

"If he comes near you again, come directly to me and tell me where he is. Do not talk to him. I don't want you having anything to do with him," Aimeric ordered sternly.

"Who is he?" Aralyn asked.

"None of your concern, it's not important. Now go get changed."

Sighing inwardly, disappointed that Aimeric wasn't going to tell her anything, Aralyn nodded and went to the bathroom. It was no use trying to argue with him. She quickly showered and then slipped into a silky, red, nightgown that went just past her thighs. After brushing her hair, Aralyn turned the knob on the door and stood in the doorway, watching Aimeric thoughtfully. He was standing at the edge of the bed, deep in his own mind, thinking of something that Aralyn knew he wouldn't be sharing with her anytime soon. He looked so serious, so stern, at that moment. Something was troubling him.

"Bed or coffin?" Aralyn finally asked, breaking the silence and officially announcing her return, though she was sure he knew she was there before.

Aimeric turned and looked at her for a moment. His eyes lustily traveled her slick figure as she leaned against the frame, but then they grew dark and he came back to himself and waved a hand at the coffin.

"I'm going in the coffin. You can have the bed," he said gruffly.

Aralyn frowned, confused. He had never given her a choice before as to where she would sleep and if she was given the choice, it was for both of them. Aimeric had never asked her to not accompany him in slumber.

"You mean…alone?" Aralyn asked, sounding somewhat hurt.

"Is that a problem?" Aimeric returned moodily.

Something about the white-haired man was *definitely* bothering him. Aralyn bit her bottom lip and looked down at the floor.

"I guess not," she said.

Aimeric scoffed.

"Are you saying you *want* me, a 'monster,' as you've put it so many times before, to lay with you? You never did willingly before."

Aralyn raised her head, glaring.

"What's wrong with you?"

Aimeric scrunched his eyebrows, disapproving her tone, and took an intimidating step forward.

"You're getting quite free with your words lately. Perhaps you need another reminder of who is in charge and who asks the questions?" he growled.

Aralyn looked away from his cold eyes.

"No. I'm sorry, Master Aimeric."

He eyed her for a moment longer and then brushed past her, into the bathroom without another word. Aralyn stood there for a moment, still in the doorway, listening to Aimeric irritably yanking his clothes off and running the shower water. The curtain was soon yanked back as well and then he disappeared behind it.

Tears were stinging her eyes as she pushed off the doorframe and made her way to the bed. She pulled the covers up and sighed, snuggling under their warmth. The tears rolled down the bridge of her nose and fell onto the sheets as she lay there, asking herself why Aimeric was so angry and why she was even crying about him. If anything, she should be glad that his arm wasn't around her and that she didn't have to pretend to love him that night.

Vampires Don't Exist by Reyanna Vance

The shower water stopped after a few minutes and the soft glow of the light in the bathroom went off and then Aralyn heard Aimeric step across the floor, settle himself into his coffin and shut the lid softly. Even though she knew she should be able to, and she was even disgusted with herself for feeling this way, Aralyn couldn't get to sleep without being in Aimeric's arms. When he had his arms tightly around her, she felt safe, like she couldn't be harmed. That night she felt vulnerable and easy to violate, like everything that *could* possibly harm her would. She hated that she had become dependant on Aimeric and expected him to protect her when most of the time, since she had arrived, it had been he who had harmed her. She knew he wasn't manipulating her mind at that moment, so it wasn't he who had influenced these feelings on her. Was she really growing, did she already *have,* feelings for Aimeric? There was no way. Not after all he had done to her, all that he had stolen from her. If she were to have feelings for Aimeric, that made her just as disturbed as him, right?

Finally, after what seemed the rest of the night, and not being able to sleep, Aralyn stood from the bed, slipped on a robe, and went downstairs towards the kitchen. Maybe a snack would help; she hadn't had anything to eat that day. On the way down, she opened a window shutter and peeked outside. It was morning but the sky was dreary and gray and heavy rain poured down from the clouds above, reducing visibility considerably. The house was deadly quiet since everyone was in bed or their coffins, but something didn't feel right. She felt eyes watching her as she went to the fridge and took out a carton of orange juice. Cautiously, she looked around while she poured a glass for herself. She didn't see anyone, but the feeling was still there and continued to haunt her while she drank. It was eerie; that feeling of someone watching you.

Despite that spooky feeling, Aralyn was unexplainably giddy. She just felt excited about something that she didn't know anything about, like something good was going to happen. She had no explanation though, that night hadn't exactly been very joyous. She stood from the table and gasped when her eyes met the familiar blood red ones.

The man from the club had appeared right in front of her. Should she scream for Aimeric? Aimeric had told her not to talk to the man, yes, but she wasn't going to get any answers from Aimeric and that's what she wanted: Answers. She decided to hold on calling for Aimeric for now.

"Who are you? What's your name?" she asked quietly after she regained control of her nerves and slowed her heartbeat from the initial shock of the man's sudden appearance.

"My name is unimportant, Aralyn," the man responded in a soft voice.

"You know mine," she pointed out.

Face cracking into an amused smile, the man responded, "Yes, I do. Fair enough then…my name is Orrin. I was a friend of Virgil's."

"Virgil," Aralyn said softly.

She remembered how they had made love and made plans to escape, and then his head rolling to the floor. She shook the image from her mind. Virgil was gone now, no sense in dwelling.

"And what are you doing here? Are you a vampire?" Aralyn asked.

"Half actually."

"Half? How?" Aralyn asked, confused.

"The same way your baby is going to become half," Orrin responded, a serious sternness to his tone.

Taking a step back, aghast at what he had just said, Aralyn breathed, "Baby? What are you talking about? It's only been two weeks…I don't even know if I'm-"

"You are," he interrupted.

"How do you know?"

"Call it a gift. But I'm not here to give you this news. I'm here to try and stop you from making a mistake and…to rescue you."

"Rescue?"

"Yes. To take you away from this hell…from Aimeric."

Away from Aimeric? It's what she had wanted since the night she had first met him. He had raped her, mentally tortured her, starved her, killed the man she had fallen in love with, messed with her mind to make her forget that she had even *known* that man for a while, and forced her to conceive the baby she just found out she was carrying by forcing her to make love to three different men, among many other things. He had been horrible to her and he still was a lot of the time. So why was she so reluctant in accepting this man, Orrin's, offer?

"Come with me, Aralyn. Don't let him corrupt your mind further or your baby. That's right, Aralyn, y*our* baby, not Aimeric's," Orrin said.

Aralyn slowly began shaking her head.

"I don't even know you…I can't trust you."

"Why not? I'm offering you freedom. Isn't that proof enough that you can trust me?" Orrin took a step towards her before he continued. "You don't deserve this life. Neither does that child you're carrying. You can't let Aimeric turn this baby into what I am. It's not a life to live. I am an outcast among humans and vampires because I am not fully either of them. The clan I am with was gracious enough to accept me for who I am; I got lucky. But there is no guarantee of how your child will be accepted if you allow this to happen. Please…come with me, Aralyn."

She stepped backwards, realization dawning on her, her eyes growing wide.

"I can't…" she whispered, shaking her head again. "Why?"

"Because…I…I love Aimeric," Aralyn said, shocking even herself.

Orrin grabbed her shoulders roughly.

"What are you thinking! He's a cold-blooded monster! A killer! You're disillusioned! He's messing with your mind! Come with me and Claire and you will realize that!"

Aralyn's eyes widened even further.

"Claire? What are you planning?"

Seeing the look on Orrin's face, she knew he realized he had said too much. Backing away, Orrin shook his head.

"Please…forget I said that. Aimeric would kill her if he knew," he begged.

"Knew what?" Aralyn asked desperately.

She was tired of having things kept from her.

"Nothing! Just forget it. Aralyn, if you love your sister, forget it. Don't even think of it, or he'll know!" Calming his frightened voice, Orrin swallowed and added, "Aralyn, listen to me. You don't love Aimeric. You only think you do because that is what he has molded into your mind. Please…reconsider?"

"No…I know how I feel…I do love him."

Orrin sighed and started to protest but he stopped short and strained to listen to something that Aralyn wasn't able to hear. His eyes widened and he didn't even utter a sound. He disappeared without a word and left Aralyn confused, turning around to search for him. Her stomach flip-flopped when she saw Aimeric, casually walking into the kitchen.

"What are you doing down here?" he asked, eyeing her suspiciously.

"I couldn't sleep and I was hungry," she responded, trying to read his expression so she could see if he was still in a bad mood.

She wondered why he was up so early and if he had heard Orrin but she stopped thinking, remembering what Orrin had said, and didn't dare ask him, about it. Aimeric studied her a moment, and she knew he was probing her mind, looking for anything she was keeping from him, so she desperately tried to keep Claire, Orrin, and the news of the baby blocked from him. She didn't want him to know she was pregnant yet because she knew that he would want to know how she knew so soon and then she would have to tell him that it had been Orrin who had told her. A cold grin crept onto Aimeric's face and he glided over to her, raising her chin to look into her eyes.

"Is that so?" he asked in a low, seductive whisper.

Is what so? Aralyn thought desperately.

"Do you want me to say 'I love you too' Aralyn?" he asked, his voice sarcastic and mocking.

She averted her eyes to the floor, feeling ashamed for her newly revealed feelings for this horrible man. Still, she was relieved it was those thoughts he had found and not the others.

"Are vampires even capable of love?" Aralyn returned, daring him.

"Vampires are capable of a lot of things. We can be very passionate, very emotional, and very deep. It all depends on the man or woman, and who they were before they were turned, and also who they wanted to *be* deep inside. Even the new characteristics, physical features, of the newly transformed, depends on the man or woman before and who they wanted to be." His mocking tone was replaced with stern sincerity, like she had offended him and he needed to defend himself.

"So…what kind of man were you?" Aralyn asked, looking into his hard eyes finally.

They narrowed and Aimeric frowned.

"Please don't be upset with me for asking…I only want to know who you were, who you are now…I want to know *you*."

Aimeric's hand had fallen to her hip at that point and he smirked.

"You want to know who I am? Come with me and *I'll show you*."

He was daring her, she could tell by his menacing stare, by the tone of his voice, how he had hissed the words, and by his tightened grip on her hip. Aralyn didn't want to be intimidated by him, not when she was so close to finding out about him and his past, so she slowly nodded in agreement. With a triumphant, and cold, grin, Aimeric took her by the waist and led her out of the kitchen; towards a place where Aralyn had no idea even existed until now.

Chapter Eighteen: Psycho

Aimeric took Aralyn through the living room, past the stairs on the right side, and down a darkened corridor which Aralyn had never been down before. He passed by several closed doors until he finally came to a stop at one at the very end of the hallway. It looked like it should be a closet or something; it was so far away from everything else. Still holding Aralyn around the waist, Aimeric reached above the door and felt around on top of the frame until he found what he was looking for, which was a small iron key. He used the key to unlock the door and open it.

Aralyn's heart pounded inside her chest as she stepped into the room, her bare feet hitting the cold, wood floor. She was nervous. She was afraid of what Aimeric was taking her to see. With Aimeric, it couldn't be good.

The room looked like it was supposed to be some sort of office. There was a huge mahogany desk in the middle of it on an expensive looking, imported rug, with a comfortable looking, black office chair behind it. On the desk was a stack of papers, a pencil cup and other office supplies. Behind the desk was a huge bookshelf, which lined the wall, filled with all kinds of different books. Some were science books, and others were grammar. One shelf was filled with fantasy and fairytale stories. All of the books looked to be very old but well taken care of over the years. There was a fireplace on the right side of the room and all kinds of trinkets ran the length of the mantel and small statues sat on the floor around it. Some were angels, which Aralyn thought odd, and others were gargoyles. There was even a centaur in the middle of them. This was the first room in the mansion, besides Aimeric's bedroom, that looked to be taken care of and cleaned on a regular basis. It was nothing like the rest of the house.

Before she could take another step inside, Aralyn heard Aimeric curse loudly and then he left her side,

rushing for the window. The curtains had been pulled open
and there was no foil or boards covering it. It almost looked
like someone had left them open deliberately. Aralyn
thought Aimeric was extremely lucky that the sky was so
thick with the heavy rain clouds that day, covering the
sun's rays, or else he might have been burnt instead of just
feeling a slight sting. He quickly slammed the shutters
closed and pulled the heavy, navy blue drapes across to
cover them. Aralyn thought she heard him mumble,
"Cora," but she wasn't sure. She wasn't really concerned
with her anyway at the moment. She looked at Aimeric,
concerned.

"Are you alri-"

"Do not ask me such a foolish question, Aralyn!"
Aimeric snapped, interrupting her. "Number one, if I
weren't alright, I would be a pile of ash right now on the
floor. Number two, I hate being asked if I am alright; it
makes me feel weak."

"I'm sorry. I just…I don't know," she lied, looking
to the floor.

She had been about to say she just cared for him
and didn't want him hurt, but she didn't because she didn't
want to admit it. She wished she could make the feelings
she had for him go away. He obviously didn't care for her.
To Aimeric, she was only an object; a thing to take to bed
when he needed physical pleasure, a thing to boss around
and control, a thing to grow a child for him so he could take
it away from her when it was born. Why couldn't she hate
him as she had before? Even though she was looking at the
floor, she could still tell that Aimeric's eyes were on her
and he was violating her mind again. She could feel him.
She wished he would stop that too. Aimeric stepped across
the room and touched her hair, gently smoothing it out.

"I don't think of you like that. And the child will be
ours, I won't take him from you."

Vampires Don't Exist by Reyanna Vance

She jerked her head up at the sincerity of his voice and saw that his eyes looked different; they looked warmer, somehow, like he really meant it. That look only lasted for a second though and his expression darkened once again, remembering why he had her in this room. He dropped his hand from her hair to her wrist and grasped it once more, leading her over to the bookshelf. Taking a large, black book, with a dragon's head on the side, Aimeric revealed a lever behind and pulled it down. The shelf clicked, the sound of a lock unlatching, and Aimeric gently pushed it to the side, showing the secret of a long stairway, which led to an underground tunnel. Probably an old hideout that people used to use during war times.

Aralyn was nervous, frightened even, but her curiosity overwhelmed her and she found herself descending the stairs. Aimeric caught her arm and stopped her. She looked at him questioningly.

"This is my secret. Do not tell anyone anything you are about to see. To you and everyone else here, this place does not exist. Do you understand?" Aimeric said.

He held a hidden warning in his expression and the tone of his voice, letting her know that the consequences would be painful if she breathed one word, about what he was about to show her, to anyone.

"I promise," Aralyn said, not having to pretend to be afraid.

Nodding his approval, Aimeric closed the bookshelf behind them and led Aralyn down the stairs. Since the shelf shut out any light, which hadn't been very much anyway, to the tunnel, they were locked in darkness so thick that Aralyn couldn't even see her hand when she waved it in front of her face. Claustrophobia set in and Aralyn felt her throat begin to close up. Digging her nails into Aimeric's hand because of how tight she was gripping it, she started gasping for air and even stumbled a few times on the steps that he was leading her down. Once they reached the bottom, she was in such a frenzy, breathing so hard, that she feared she would pass out. Her back was suddenly shoved against a wall and she felt Aimeric hold his body against hers, his cold hands cupping her face and his breath touching her lips.

"You are in no danger here, Aralyn. I am here with you; there is no one else, except maybe a few mice. I can see everything that is happening down here and I will not let you be harmed…now calm down," Aimeric whispered, touching her lips with several, assuring, soft pecks.

She did calm down after a moment, her breathing became normal, and Aimeric took her hand again, but that wasn't enough for her. Taking her hand out of his, Aralyn slid her arm around Aimeric's waist and laid her head on his bare shoulder, feeling relieved when he secured his arm around her, holding her tight to his side. She still felt a little frightened so she closed her eyes for the rest of the walk down the long passageway, even though she couldn't see anything anyway. She felt more in control that way, like if she opened her eyes, she would be able to see something dangerous coming for her and if that were true, she would rather *not* see it.

Neither of them said anything as they walked. Aralyn could smell the dirt and must attached to the walls and the floor. She could feel it too, the dirt, as she walked, on the bottom of her feet, along with tiny rocks. A few sharp ones were in her path and stung the bottoms of her toes with their sharp edges. She wished she had thought to put on shoes before being led down here. But then again, she hadn't known that Aimeric would be taking her underground where she would need shoes. They finally stopped and Aralyn heard the release of a doorknob before being taken a few more feet across the dirt floor.

"Brace yourself," Aimeric warned, letting go of her.

She smelled the metallic odor of blood and her stomach churned at the thought of what might be down here in the dark. Aimeric moved away from her and she heard a light switch flick on and the room was illuminated in a dim light from a loose bulb hanging from the ceiling. They were in a small room that had probably been used for storage long ago for water and food. At that moment, however, it had an old, wooden desk, a metal file cabinet and a wobbly looking table in the corner. The floor was dirt and the ceiling's rafters were covered in gray soil and dust. The first thing about the walls that Aralyn noticed was that there were messages written on them in a strange color of ink, or paint. Aralyn next noticed the walls themselves were a strange color; a dim gray with, what looked like, black stitches painted on, in different places to look like patchwork.

"This is where I used to spend a lot of my time. I came here to think, brood, and feel sorry for myself," Aimeric said, chuckling softly.

Not sure what this had to do with the man that Aimeric used to be, but still interested, Aralyn stepped forward to read some of the messages on the walls.

"To live is to die," and "Darkness is my light," were two that she read before looking closer at the ink. Her stomach flip-flopped as she examined the ink. The ink wasn't *ink*. It was dried, crusty, blood. The words had been written when the blood had been fresh and now it had dried to a rusty brown color. Aralyn bravely reached out and touched the blood, running her finger through the word "live." Crusted specs of brown, from the letter "I" came off on her finger, but that wasn't what sickened her to the point of wanting to throw up, and her whole body shaking. The wall had felt rubbery when she touched it.

"Hu…human…"

She stuttered the words, her eyes misting over and her hands beginning to shake even more. She couldn't form the words to finish her sentence.

"Human flesh," Aimeric confirmed, nonchalantly, coming up to stand behind her. "Preserved and sewn together with wire, laced with their hair, to make the perfect 'wallpaper.'"

Feeling nauseous, Aralyn slumped over and covered her mouth to keep from throwing up.

"I did this before I was turned," Aimeric continued.

"You're...disgusting," Aralyn choked.

Aimeric laughed.

"Yes. That's what mother and father said when they found this room too. They're over there." He pointed and Aralyn choked even more on the tears that had started flowing from her eyes; tears of disgust, and tears of fright.

"I had to kill them or they would have sent me away. You see, Aralyn, even as a mortal, I was...different. Psychologists these days would probably say that I didn't get enough love as a child; they're probably right. I was ignored most of my childhood, but I don't believe that's what caused my...unique idea of art," Aimeric said softly.

"This isn't art! This is mental disturbance!" Aralyn screamed, straightening her back to look at him. Her face was wet with tears.

"Do not raise your voice to me, darling," Aimeric said, taking her arm so he could lead her to the desk.

Ignoring him, Aralyn jerked her arm free and went to lower herself into the chair. She didn't want him touching her.

"I wouldn't if I were you," Aimeric warned smoothly.

Turning to look down at the seat, Aralyn scoffed in disgust and moved to lean against the surface of the desk instead. The chair was upholstered in human flesh as well. Aralyn sat on the desk, closing her eyes, trying not to look at the walls or the chair, and brought her knees up to her chest, resting her head against them. She ignored Aimeric's hands when they started to pet her hair down, thoughtfully.

"I was always fascinated by the flesh of a human's body, Aralyn. I thought it was beautiful, but, unfortunately, the beauty of the skin didn't always reflect the individual person. People, humans, are greedy, self-loving creatures that don't always deserve the beauty of their own skin, hair, and eyes. I did the world a favor and rid it of the people who were ugly inside and put their physical beauty to good use. Sometimes, they were even still alive when I started to skin them," Aimeric finished thoughtfully.

"God…" Aralyn groaned, leaning away from his touch.

He didn't seem to hear her though, or notice she had leaned out of his reach.

"I preserved the skin so that it wouldn't dry out and crack, then I sewed it together with the wire and hair and plastered it onto my walls. I know it's hideous to you, it was to everyone else who found it too, though they weren't alive long enough to tell about it…don't worry though, that won't happen to you," he said, returning his cold fingers to her cheek.

"You really are a monster," Aralyn said quietly, not caring at that point if she made him angry.

He wasn't angry though.

Aralyn sensed the smirk in his tone as he responded, "A monster that you fell in love with." He brushed back her hair and caressed her neck. "*Do* you still love me?"

Aralyn's stomach tightened and she was sickened even more, when she immediately thought "yes." She didn't want to admit that to herself though. She shook her head in denial, looking up at him with hate in her eyes.

"No…no! I hate you! You deserve to rot in hell for what you've done!"

Aimeric quickly leaned over her, causing her to fall back on her elbows.

"Don't lie to yourself sweetheart. We both know that you still love me, no matter what I've done in the past.

You can't help yourself, it's the human in you," he breathed against her face.

She glared at him, but didn't say anything, and Aimeric straightened up to continue his story.

"I changed when I met *her*; I haven't used human flesh to decorate with since..."

Aralyn looked at him curiously.

"Who?"

"Caitlin. I fell in love with her right before I was turned three hundred years ago. She was seventeen, the daughter of a noble. We met at a Christmas party when I was twenty-seven. She taught me that, in spite, of the ugliness people held inside, most also had at least one good quality. For example, the raging drunk had a gentle side where his children were concerned, the gossiping woman had a warm heart for a sick neighbor, that sort of thing. We used to sit under the stars together and talk so intimately with one another."

Aralyn watched Aimeric's eyes focus on the flesh covered ceiling as he went back to those nights in his own mind.

"She never found this place and I was glad she didn't because I knew she would have reacted horribly to it, just like all the others. I deliberately kept it from her. And for the first time, since I had put up the first patch of skin, I felt guilty, ashamed, after realizing what she had told me about people was true.

"It was then that I decided I would never take another human life again, and I didn't, not as a mortal. Guilty I felt, yes, but I still couldn't bring myself to destroy the room I had worked so hard on and was so proud of."

He paused and looked at Aralyn, but she stubbornly turned her head away.

"Three weeks after I had met Caitlin, there was an accident. It was the middle of winter and one of my family's horses had gotten out and stepped onto the frozen lake in a weak spot. She fell through and was drowning and, while trying to save her, I ended up drowning as well. I went to hell, of course, but I wasn't ready to die at that point so I begged Satan to let me come back to earth. He agreed, but on his conditions; I had to become one of his followers and serve him. I agreed and he turned me into what I am now."

Aimeric looked at Aralyn again and grinned.

"A 'monster,' as you say."

She scoffed and his smile widened.

"I loved my new life, so much that I went to Caitlin in order to turn her so we could be together forever. But she refused and, in tears, begged me not to take her. She was a holy woman and didn't want to disappoint her god. I was angry at first and wanted to kill her for refusing my offer but I couldn't because I still loved her. So, instead, I asked if I could make love to her once before leaving her life forever. She said no at first, saying that it would be a sin in many ways, but after a few moments of my touch and kisses, she gave in because she loved me just as much; it was our way to say goodbye," Aimeric said quietly.

Aralyn was watching him closely. He turned his head to look at the ceiling once more, deep in thought. About *her*. About Caitlin. Suddenly feeling incredibly stupid, Aralyn narrowed her eyes. Here she was, in love with a man, a psychotic one at that, and he still loved this Caitlin. Her doubts returned. Aimeric didn't love her, she was just a replacement. He was still in love with Caitlin and probably regretted not turning her against her will.

"I did love her," Aimeric said in response to Aralyn's thoughts. "She was beautiful. She had long hair, the color of sand, and her skin was like porcelain. Her face was soft and her eyes were the brightest green anyone could ever imagine. She had a heart of pure gold. I left her after taking her love, never to bother her again, and let her get on with her life. She did. She married a few years later and had three children. I left her alone but I never stopped watching her, protecting her. I watched her grow into an old woman while I stayed in the body of a twenty-seven year old. My only regret is that I couldn't do anything to save her, sixty-six years after we made love, when she fell. She had a bad hip at that time and fell down a flight of stairs. It broke her neck and she died instantly," Aimeric said, keeping a soft tone.

Aralyn wasn't sure what to say. She was jealous, though it still sickened her to admit it, to hear him speak of this girl who had grown into an old woman and was dead. If Caitlin had agreed to be turned so long ago, she would still be with Aimeric, not Aralyn. He wouldn't want her if he still had Caitlin, or if he did, he would have killed her by now. She kept her jealousy to herself, hiding it from Aimeric, and stayed silent, waiting for him to go on.

"Caitlin changed me for life. I never did skin another human, I only continued to preserve this room. But, becoming a vampire still re-awakened the fascination I held of hearing their screams. It's like a drug to me…or sweet ecstasy. That is why I keep my pets in cages, to hear them scream whenever I want."

Aimeric shifted his gaze to Aralyn, almost daring her to say anything to reprimand him, to tell him how disgusting he was then, as a human, and now, as a vampire Master. She didn't though; she only looked away and scoffed lightly, disgusted.

"The point of me telling you all of this, Aralyn, is not to boast, what you call, monstrosity, but to make you understand that even a, sick and twisted, human-monster turned vampire can love; passionately, deeply, and with every ounce of his black soul. My love for Caitlin will never cease, and I will never forget her, but you must know now that I have a new love. I love you very deeply and knowing that you love me, even if what I do, and did, disgusts you, makes my love for you even stronger than I thought possible."

He touched her, softly caressing her long strands of ebony and the warm flesh on her face before he rested a firm grip on her shoulder. He leaned down and kissed her mouth gently.

"I would gladly die all over again for you," he whispered, kissing her again.

Aralyn flinched back and then jumped off the desk and rushed to the door.

"I want out of this place…now," she said softly, yet determined, keeping her eyes on the floor, not wanting to even look at Aimeric.

She heard him sigh softly and a few moments later, he was at the door, opening it for her. She might have stomped out and run away if it hadn't have been for the fact that she couldn't see where she was going. Aimeric switched off the light and took Aralyn's hand, leading her back through the darkness. She remained silent.

"You won't have to return to this room, but you wanted to know who I was, and who I am, *me*, so I showed you. Remember that Aralyn; it was *you* who asked," he said harshly while they walked.

"I wish I hadn't!" Aralyn ground out bitterly.

Aimeric didn't say anything else to her, not even a threat, and he took her back upstairs, through the mansion and to the bedroom. Once they were inside, Aralyn immediately left Aimeric and rushed to the adjoining bathroom to spill the contents of her stomach into the toilet. For only a moment she wondered if her pregnancy was already giving her symptoms but she quickly brushed that idea aside; it was too early. Her getting sick was pure disgust at what she had just seen, and heard from Aimeric, mixed with disgust for herself at her feelings for him still, if they were in fact *her* feelings. She didn't rule out Aimeric's mind manipulation this time. Who could willingly love a monster like him? Maybe she should have followed Orrin after all and kept her baby from Aimeric. After a while she would surely forget her feelings for the creature. But what if they were caught? Remembering what Aimeric had done to Virgil, Aralyn had to open her mouth to be sick again. How could she love Aimeric? He was cold and cruel; a disgusting animal that enjoyed watching the innocent suffer. How could she stay with him and allow him to help raise her child? She couldn't answer any of the questions she asked herself.

She stood from where she had been sitting on the floor and rinsed her mouth in the sink, cupping her hands to bring the water to her lips. She rinsed out her mouth and then, halfway turning, looked at the closed door, which led to Aimeric, who was no doubt waiting for her on the other side. She wasn't ready to see him again so she sat down on the floor and leaned her head against the counter, closing her eyes. She hadn't slept at all the night before and she wanted it so bad; her eyes were dry and scratchy because of the lack of sleep, in addition to the tears that had fallen and were *still* falling.

The door was rapped on just as she was on the verge of falling into her dreams.

"Come out of there, Aralyn. You can't hide away forever; you need to rest."

Aimeric opened the door and pulled her reluctant body to its feet. She shook him away and took herself to bed, laying down on her side and pulling the covers up to her chin while closing her eyes. She cringed when Aimeric lay down next to her, his chest against her back, and draped his arm over her, securing her tightly against him.

"Go to sleep now," he whispered, kissing her neck.

Not responding, Aralyn sighed inwardly, thankful that he didn't expect anything of her for the rest of that day, and kept her eyes closed until she drifted far away from the monster holding her.

Chapter Nineteen: Harsh Accusations

That afternoon, as she slept, Aralyn's dreams were filled with screams of the innocent, blood dripping off the walls, and human flesh hanging from the ceilings, followed by her own self running towards Aimeric, screaming for him to give her back her baby. All of this happened in the deepest depths of space, where there was no light, no sky, and no ground; she had just been running in space, in a dark hole.

Aralyn stirred, waking up to cold lips pressing against the flesh of her neck. Aimeric was trying to wake her up by kissing her and rubbing up and down her side, his hand sliding smoothly over the silk nightgown and robe she was still wearing. Once he saw that Aralyn was awake, his kisses became more intense against her neck and shoulder and he started to roll her over, placing a leg between hers. He went to kiss her lips but she shoved him away and rolled back over on her side, putting her back to him again.

"Are you denying me, Aralyn?" Aimeric asked warningly.

She didn't respond and he sighed, heavily, irritated.

"Perhaps I should have waited to show you my room. Forgive me, I thought you were stronger than that; I thought you could *handle* it," he said coldly against her ear.

She still didn't say anything.

"Giving me the silent treatment? Very well. I will play your game, but only for a little while. When I come back, I expect you to respond to me. If you don't...well," his voice became even colder, "consequences must be considered."

Aimeric rolled off the bed and slipped on a silky, button up, black shirt. Even though her back was still to him, Aralyn felt his eyes on her as he dressed. He was angry with her and he was glaring at her back. He pulled on a pair of pants and then his boots. The air in the room was tense and deathly quiet except for Aimeric's dressing.

"I'll be back later," Aimeric snapped, leaving the room and closing the door.

As soon as he was gone, Aralyn looked at the clock on the wall. It was 7:21 in the evening, past sunset; she had slept all day. She was still tired though, so she closed her eyes and tried to get back to sleep. She was just on the verge of it again when the door was knocked on and then opened softly before Aralyn had a chance to tell whoever it was to "go away." Aralyn looked over her shoulder and groaned as Morgan came into the room, carrying a tray of food.

"What? Did he send you to watch me again?" she asked, irritated.

He chuckled, stepping into the room, and closed the door.

"No. He sent me to feed you."

He walked over to the bed as Aralyn sat up, rolling her eyes, and his eyes traveled down to her chest. Seeing his line of vision, Aralyn looked down and saw that her breasts were almost fully exposed since the robe had come open and the nightgown she was wearing had slipped down. Glaring, she pulled the robe closed and Morgan grinned at her again. She hadn't seen much of the sniveling vampire in the last few weeks since she had been with Aimeric for most of the time, and then in her room, recovering from all the love making she had been forced to do. She hadn't missed him and she certainly wasn't happy to see him now.

"Here ya go. Lots o' calcium, and vitamins, for the baby," Morgan said, amused, and set the tray over Aralyn's lap.

He loved rubbing it in, Aralyn's situation and lack of choice. She looked down at her lap to examine the food.

On the tray was a plate of sliced oranges and strawberries, a piece of buttered toast, and a tall glass of milk.

"He knows about the baby?" Aralyn blurted out without thinking it over first.

She hadn't really heard him, not paying attention to his annoying voice, until now, when she played over what he had said in her mind again. She was startled that he had said something about the baby, how could either he or Aimeric have known? Morgan looked at her, confused, and raised a suspicious eyebrow.

"He knows you *could* be pregnant." He looked at her harder. "…Are you hiding something?"

"I…no…of course not" Aralyn stuttered, unconvincingly. Seeing the look of skepticism on Morgan's face, she quickly added, "I had a dream and was confused for a moment."

Morgan looked at her a moment longer, still seeming slightly suspicious, but thinking that a dream was acceptable.

"Whatever…eat and drink up," he said, gesturing to the tray.

"I don't like milk," Aralyn said plainly.

"I don' care if you don' like it. Aimeric said to make sure you eat healthy an' that's what I'm doin.'"

"You're such a little lap dog," Aralyn sneered.

He looked angry at first, but then smirked.

"Look who's talkin,' love."

Aralyn was tempted to throw the milk all over him. She didn't though; she knew she had to drink it. She really did hate it though. To Aralyn, milk smelled like the cow it had come from and tasted what she imagined the stomach to taste like. She held her nose and drank it quickly; for the baby she knew was growing inside of her, *not* for Aimeric.

Once she was finished eating, she ordered Morgan to leave her room. He took the tray and did leave, but he smirked at her the whole way out. After he had left for good, Aralyn got up from the bed long enough to shower and dress into another nightgown; she didn't feel like getting up for good. Lying back on the bed, Aralyn covered her eyes with an arm and thought about everything that had happened to her in the past month and a half or so. After that, she thought about Aimeric and wondered if he would make her have sex with either of the two men left before she felt it was safe to tell him that she was pregnant already. He had given her the next week off, and possibly the next after that, to see if her menstrual period would show up or not. She wondered if it would. She had heard that women sometimes get their period still for the first month or so of pregnancy.

As she lay there, thinking about all of this, the giddy feeling returned suddenly, despite her depressed mood. She guessed it was her body responding to her pregnancy, which was also something she had heard; that women sometimes know they're pregnant just from a feeling. Maybe this was the feeling they got.

She heard the bedroom door open and removed her arm from her eyes to see Aimeric standing there, watching her. She watched him too as he closed the door and then turned his mischievous eyes back to her while casually unbuttoning his shirt. He pulled it off and tossed the material to the floor before working on his boots, which he tossed aside as well.

"Are we talking yet?" he asked sarcastically.

"Do you *want* me to talk?" Aralyn returned harshly.

Aimeric smirked, working on his pants. He tossed them aside and stood at the foot of the bed, naked before her. Aralyn let her eyes roam his body and she felt an electric shock pulse through her veins; just the sight of him was enough to arouse her and it sickened her. She wanted him against her, she wanted to feel his flesh sliding against hers and feel him inside of her again.

"Actually, talking isn't really what I had in mind," Aimeric said huskily, crawling on to the bed.

He kissed her hard and she pushed at his chest but her heart wasn't really in it.

"You want this just as much as I do, Aralyn, I can hear your thoughts," he rasped, nipping at her bottom lip while his hands worked on undressing her.

"No…" she whimpered, though her body was responding and writhing underneath Aimeric as he touched her.

He rolled them both onto their sides and brought Aralyn's leg up around his waist and kissed her mouth hard, thrusting his tongue against hers. She gasped as he pushed into her and then she started to moan softly as their bodies moved together. She didn't want to admit that they were moving together though so she bit her lip, when Aimeric's mouth moved to other parts of her body, and whimpered, trying her hardest not to show, verbally, what she felt.

"Let it out…scream…don't be ashamed to admit, and react to, what I do to you," Aimeric growled against her lips.

She tried to ignore his words but she couldn't ignore what she was feeling. Her fingernails dug into Aimeric's arms.

"You love this, don't you?"

She whimpered, keeping her eyes shut tightly.

"Don't you!" Aimeric demanded again.

"Yes…" she finally breathed.

"Say it then."

"…I love…what you do…to me," she said, gasping.

"Scream for me, Aralyn."

She did. She yelled loudly and moaned his name over and over until they both released, and both were satisfied. She put all she had learned of him into the back of her mind and didn't allow her information to interfere with her feelings. Aimeric was cruel and he was sick, but for some reason, she didn't think she cared anymore. She loved him and love can blind a person.

***

The first real sign of Aralyn's pregnancy came to her three weeks after that night she had shamelessly screamed out during Aimeric's making love to her. She had been sleeping in his arms when she was violently awakened by the sick feeling in her stomach. Barely making it, she had to run to the bathroom and vomit, throwing up twice before she flushed the mess and was able to return to bed. After she rinsed her mouth and washed her face, she went back into the bedroom, drowsily holding onto her mid-section.

Aimeric was sitting up in the bed, looking at her curiously.

"Are you alright?"

She nodded slightly.

"Are you pregnant, Aralyn?" he asked as she crawled back into bed.

He had thought she might be for the past couple of weeks since that's how late her time of the month was. In addition to being late, he had noticed other changes in her. She had always seemed to be tired no matter how much sleep she got, and also, whenever he touched her breasts, she had winced and complained that they were sore.

"Yes," Aralyn whispered, closing her eyes.

Pulling her against his naked chest, Aimeric kissed the top of her head.

"Good. We can release our men then. We'll do it tonight."

Aralyn wasn't really paying much attention to him; she was still tired and trying to go back to sleep. It didn't matter though since he seemed to be talking more to himself than to her anyway. She fell back asleep only a few moments later and when she woke up again, it was because she had gotten a chill and when she opened her eyes, she found out why.

She was alone in the bed.

Slipping on a robe, Aralyn cautiously left the room to look for Aimeric, peeking around the corners and looking down the hallways before advancing further. For some reason she had a bad feeling.

She wandered the halls upstairs first, only coming across a few of the other vampires that lived there. They ignored her mostly when she asked if they knew where Aimeric was, either that or they, rudely, told her that, "he apparently didn't want her to know, so it was none of her business." Aralyn left them, glaring, and continued searching through the large house, peeking into every room that wasn't locked, but finding nothing except for furniture and coffins. When she got to Aimeric's second room, the one with the underground tunnel, she stopped outside the door. She did not want to go into that room; she wanted to forget it even existed. Just the thought of what was behind that bookshelf made her nauseous and she had to steady herself on the wall for a moment. Once the wave had passed, she softly knocked on the door, refusing to open it even though she knew where the key was to unlock it. She waited a few minutes but no one answered, so she turned to leave. She stopped shortly when she saw Mabel standing there in front of her, looking at her curiously.

"What are you doing here?" she asked.

"I'm looking for Aimeric," Aralyn responded.

Mabel smiled evilly.

"He's in the basement."

Before Aralyn could ask what he was doing down there, Mabel turned on her heels and sashayed to the front door, down the long hall, and outside into the night. Aralyn stared after her, even when the door had closed, wondering why she had seemed so cheery about Aimeric being in the basement. And then it hit her; the basement. Aimeric was probably torturing more innocent victims. Without thinking it over first, Aralyn ran to the cellar, flung open the door, and descended the staircase. She saw that the prison door was already open so she peered inside cautiously. Aimeric was standing with his back to her and in front of Joseph, one of the mortals who had had sex with her so she could conceive. He was chained to the wall. Aralyn's stomach flip-flopped when she saw him and she looked to the left and saw Ethan, the other mortal, hanging from the ceiling by a noose. He was still alive, but very bloody and seemed out of it, unaware of much that was going on around him. Joseph suddenly started screaming and drew Aralyn's attention back to him. She saw that Aimeric had taken a pair of pliers and was twisting fishing wire around one of Joseph's fingers so tightly that it cut past his flesh and was working on the bone. Silently gagging, Aralyn noticed that the rest of his fingers had already been cut off that way and were nothing more than bloody stumps on his hand. She closed her eyes and covered her mouth for a moment, trying to regain her composure, until she heard Aimeric growling out words.

"Did you enjoy your time with her? Was it worth it?"

"You *made* us do it! You sick fuck!" Joseph screamed, gritting his teeth.

He was also salivating from the pain.

"Aimeric, stop!" Aralyn yelled from the doorway.

She didn't care if she was being foolish, she couldn't let this continue.

"Stay out of this, Aralyn," he hissed back at her, still twisting the wire.

Joseph screamed loudly; the wire must have gotten more of the bone.

Ignoring Aimeric's demands, Aralyn rushed into the room and grabbed his arm, making the pliers fall to the floor.

"Please stop! They only did what you told them to do!" she pleaded.

When she had first grabbed his arm, Aimeric turned on her, the look on his face scathing and she thought for a minute he might hit her. But, seeing the pleading look on her face, his expression softened, though his voice was still hard.

"I said from the beginning that they would die for touching you."

"So then kill them! But don't suffer them first!"

Aralyn couldn't believe she was begging for Aimeric to kill the men, but she knew he wouldn't let them go and a quick death was better than being tortured.

"Are you trying to tell me what to do?" Aimeric growled.

"No," Aralyn said without hesitation. "I am begging you; please, Aimeric, end their suffering now."

"Are you asking this of me because you care about them?" he asked jealously.

"No. Not like that. I do care, yes, but only because they are aware of everything you are doing to them. They can *feel*, Aimeric. I…couldn't imagine…"

"If I stop, you will be happy?" he asked.

"Yes."

He hesitated, staring stiffly at Joseph out of the corner of his eye while Joseph glared back at Aimeric through the tears that had sprung to his eyes. Suddenly, Aimeric pushed Aralyn to the side and jumped on Joseph's neck, sinking his sharp fangs into him. The back of Joseph's head hit the wall behind him, but he met Aralyn's eyes with his own and mouthed "thank you" right before he became limp in the chains. When Aimeric started growling into Joseph's neck, making animal sounds, Aralyn had to turn her head away

A few minutes later, she heard the release of a rope and then a loud thump as though something heavy had hit the ground. Halfway turning, Aralyn saw that Aimeric had released Ethan from the ceiling and was now attached to his neck, sucking out his life source the same as he had done to Joseph. Ethan whimpered underneath him but he was already mostly dead anyway so he barely knew what Aimeric was doing to him. The sight and smell of the blood leaking out of the corners of Aimeric's mouth made Aralyn feel even sicker but she didn't want to leave yet, she wanted to be sure Aimeric would make sure they were dead. She looked at the wall, where Joseph's body was still chained. His head was slumped over and all color had been drained from his body; he was dead. When she turned back to Aimeric she saw him jerk himself off the floor, finished with Ethan, and look at her angrily. She flinched back when he stormed up to her, leaning close to her face.

"Do not ask anything else of me anytime soon. I was generous today, but do not expect me to wrap myself around your little finger, Aralyn; *I* am still in charge here," he snarled.

Aimeric pushed past her and left her in the dungeon, angrily climbing the stairs and slamming the door when he reached the top. Letting the breath escape, which she had been holding, Aralyn sank to her knees on the cold floor, gaining control of her nerves again. Once she had done that, or at least, most of it, she stood on shaky legs, her eyes switching back and forth from both bodies. She gagged, seeing the fishing wire still stuck in Joseph's finger and felt a twinge of guilt for loving the man that had done it. Again, she wondered if she truly did love Aimeric, or if he still had her under his control. She had thought before that she truly did love him but how could she? How could she be in love with someone who was capable of causing so much pain?

Why was she constantly asking these questions? He gave her great pleasure in bed, but she knew that that wasn't what had brought out her feelings for him. Either she was crazy, believing he was different around her, gentler, or she *was* still under his control; she doubted the latter though. His eyes, which could be so cold to others, seemed warm to her now. She knew he truly cared for her. His touch and kisses were enough to send her into an ecstasy she had never known before, not even the one time she had made love with Virgil. Aimeric's domination over her was a sick turn on and she felt disgusted with herself when she thought this; almost wanting to run after him to beg him to take her over and over until her needs were fulfilled. So was it love, lust, or lack of control?

Still somewhat lost in her thoughts, Aralyn looked up to see the prisoners, who had decreased in number over the last few weeks, staring back at her questioningly. Some had died recently from wounds and sickness. To her relief, Aimeric hadn't brought anyone else in to replace the ones who had died yet and she hoped he wouldn't for a long time; ever if possible. One of the ones who had died, which she was greatly saddened about, was Toby. His wounds had become infected and, not able to be properly cared for, the infection had won.

"So…you're pregnant now, Miss Aralyn?" one girl, about fifteen, Aralyn had forgotten her name, asked.

Aralyn nodded guiltily.

"And do you honestly believe that that monster up there is capable of loving another man's child?" a man of about thirty asked, harshly.

"We may have had help, but the child is *ours*," Aralyn defended haughtily.

"How could you, Aralyn? You hated him! You wanted to see him dead as much as we do, and now you're *defending* him? You actually *love* him?" the man asked.

"I can't help it," Aralyn said quietly.

"You're just as sick as he is," the man said, shaking his head, and walked away from the bars.

"Leave her alone! She's just confused!" the girl jumped to Aralyn's defense. She looked at Aralyn pleadingly with tears in her eyes and added, "Aren't you? Tell me he still has you under his control?"

Aralyn hesitated, looking, sadly, at the girl and the rest of the prisoners. They were waiting for her answer. How could Aralyn make the girl, and everyone else, understand when she didn't know what she really felt herself? She couldn't answer and she couldn't look at their accusing faces any longer; she had to get away. Aralyn ran for the door, stopping abruptly when it opened and Morgan came in with a mop and bucket of water.

"Where are you off to in such a hurry?" he demanded.

Ignoring him, Aralyn shoved by and ran up the stairs to her and Aimeric's bedroom. She had wanted to run into his arms, but the room was empty so she flung herself on the bed instead and cried until she fell back asleep again.

Aralyn woke a little while later, to someone softly stroking her hair, and sat up, expecting to see Aimeric. Surprised, she gasped, letting out a soft squeal of glee, and jumped to her knees, throwing her arms around Claire. Claire hadn't been back to the mansion since that night at the club, which seemed so long ago; Aralyn had started to fear that she would never see her sister again.

"Oh there, there…did you miss me?" Claire asked, half mockingly, and patted Aralyn's back.

"Yes, I did," Aralyn admitted.

Claire smiled and held Aralyn out in front of her, looking her over for cuts and bruises.

"I see he's taken better care of you this time," she remarked dryly.

Aralyn nodded.

"He has."

Claire's face broke into a smile and she took Aralyn's hands.

"I hear we're going to have a baby."

"Yes," Aralyn said quietly, feeling guilty, remembering the prisoners and what they had said to her.

Suddenly becoming alarmingly serious, Claire lowered her voice.

"Do you have any idea what Aimeric intends on doing to you and the baby when you go into labor?"

Aralyn shook her head, feeling confused.

"I see…so he hasn't told you anything on the matter yet," Claire mumbled. She lowered her voice even more and added to herself, "I suppose he's waiting to tell you until you're far enough along so that you can't abort it."

"What is he going to do?" Aralyn asked.

Claire shrugged.

"I'm not sure it's my place to tell you, dear sister."

"Why? Stop playing these games and hiding things from me, Claire! What does Aimeric have planned? And who the hell is Orrin? Why does he want me to-"

"Quiet!" Claire hissed, holding a finger up to Aralyn's lips, straining to listen around her.

Aralyn stayed silent and waited.

"He's coming. I will talk to you more later, but do not mention Orrin again," Claire warned before disappearing from the room.

As she did, Aralyn looked towards the door, hearing it open, and saw that Aimeric had returned, from wherever he had been, and was standing in the doorway.

"Aimeric, what happened?" Aralyn asked, seeing burn marks on his hands and arms.

She almost jumped from the bed and ran to him but, remembering his pride, stayed where she was.

"It's nothing. I just got a little too close to the fire," he said, stepping inside, and closing the door.

He went into the bathroom and Aralyn heard water running from the sink for a few minutes before he came back out.

"What fire?" she asked cautiously.

"You're asking an awful lot of questions lately," he growled, irritated.

"I'm sorry," Aralyn said, looking down at her lap.

She heard him sigh and then felt him sit on the bed next to her.

"I torched my room," he said after a moment of silence.

Aralyn looked at him and her eyes shot the question, "why" since her mouth couldn't seem to do it.

"I know it upset you, and I don't want you to be upset with the baby, it isn't healthy for him or you," Aimeric answered.

Aralyn sat there, in shock, stunned that he would destroy that awful room that he was so proud of, especially when she hadn't asked him to do it, just for her sake.

"And...I'm going to release the prisoners," he continued.

She thought she might fall over and faint at that very moment when she heard him say that.

"Only until you have the baby. Then I will find more if I want," he added stubbornly.

Aralyn couldn't hold it in any longer. She reached up and threw her arms around Aimeric's neck, embracing him tightly, lovingly.

"Thank you," she whispered, pulling away.

"Don't get used to it," Aimeric said gruffly, kissing her quickly before they shared another hug.

She knew he would probably never change fully and she knew he would most likely do things in the future to hurt her or make her angry and wish she hadn't ever admitted she loved him, but for now, he had changed the tiniest bit for her and she knew Aimeric loved her. This, Aralyn knew for sure.

Chapter Twenty: Betrayal

It was several months later and Aralyn was only a few weeks away from her due date. Not much had changed in the many months that had passed, except Aralyn no longer doubted her feelings for Aimeric. She often regretted loving him, especially when he showed the monster side of himself, but, as she had been told before by a good friend, "you can't help whom your heart loves, even if he *is* a psycho." Aralyn had added that last part.

During these months, Aralyn had experienced what it was like to have a child growing inside of a woman. She had connected with her baby from the beginning; even before she had first physically felt it move, she had felt it spiritually. Though the child was not conceived out of love and even though Aralyn had been appalled at first, at the thought of having a baby for a vampire, she now wanted the child more than anything in the world. The baby was *hers* and, the man she had fallen in love with, Aimeric's. She knew most people might say it wasn't possible for a woman to fall in love with a monster. A monster that had raped her from the beginning, a monster that had raped her even again, by forcing her to have sex with other men in order to fulfill his own selfish desires for a child. It wasn't love, it was control and Aimeric was doing the controlling. That's what people would say. But Aralyn didn't care; she knew what her heart felt.

As the baby grew, so did Aralyn's belly. It was now a size that could very possibly rank enormous. Aralyn loved her baby and she loved being able to feel it move and to feel it connected to her, but she was getting tired of being pregnant. She wanted to hold her baby in her arms and listen to it breathe, cry, and see it smile. Not only that, but Aralyn was uncomfortable. She always found herself too hot, her legs and feet and back constantly ached it seemed. Her feet were swollen a lot of the time and she found it difficult to even move. But she knew she would have to be patient and wait until the baby was ready. She did hope it was soon though.

Aimeric had kept his promise. He never did bring another human into the mansion to torture during Aralyn's pregnancy. The dungeon was empty and had been for a long time. Aimeric had released every prisoner without fear of them telling anyone what they had been through. No one would believe them. He never brought up the flesh-covered room either, knowing how it made Aralyn sick. He had become warmer, to Aralyn anyway, especially when they were alone. Some nights, they would just lay in each other's arms, talking about everything and nothing. Though he had become warmer, he still was in charge and Aralyn knew that. He had reminded her a few times, though he wasn't as harsh. That could just have been because he didn't want to be rough with her during her pregnancy, but Aralyn didn't think so. It didn't really bother her though, Aimeric's domination over her, she wasn't one to make her own decisions anyway, not in the last couple of years. Not that she liked being bossed around, but to her, she didn't really see it as being bossed around, she just, simply, *didn't* care.

Aralyn often wondered about Orrin, the half vampire, who had told her she was pregnant in the beginning. He hadn't come around again since that night in the kitchen. Aralyn wasn't really disappointed, in fact, she was mostly relieved, but she was still curious as to why he had given up so easily after he had seemed so determined to get Aralyn to leave Aimeric. The thought had crossed Aralyn's mind that Aimeric had found Orrin out and had killed him. She hoped with all her heart that that wasn't what had happened; she hoped Orrin had simply given up. She didn't dare ask Aimeric about him though. She had asked Claire, however, a few times, about the strange vampire. But every time Aralyn brought up his name,

Claire brushed her off or changed the subject, telling Aralyn not to mention him again. Aralyn did give up after a while and stopped asking about him.

Claire, like Aimeric, had changed a little. She was more considerate of Aralyn's feelings and didn't leave the mansion for long periods of time like she used to. The most she had stayed gone was a couple of days. The two had become closer, like the sisters they used to be when Claire had been alive. They had long talks, they laughed, and they reminisced together. On the days when Aralyn had to stay in bed, Claire usually sat with her and the two would eat together, sharing memories. They spoke of the vacations their family used to take together and how much fun they had always had when they were kids, before their lives had fallen apart that dreary night in October. Aralyn never told Claire about how their father had given up and became an alcoholic, not caring about anything. She had the feeling that Claire knew anyway, though. Aralyn did tell Claire about how their father had killed himself months ago. Claire had already known. She didn't seem too upset about it though. Aralyn didn't really blame her. Not that they didn't love their father, but even Aralyn hadn't really thought about his death much. She wasn't sure if she had just gotten used to losing people she loved and she was numb to the pain, or if it had been because of the time frame when he had killed himself. At the time, Aralyn had been too busy trying to get away from Aimeric that she hadn't really had the time to think about it and then she had struggled with her mixed up feelings for the vampire and now, she was busy trying to get ready for their baby.

Aralyn wasn't sure why Claire had suddenly changed. Maybe she had decided Aralyn needed her to help prepare her for motherhood. Maybe Claire had felt guilty for what she had done to Aralyn in the beginning. Whatever it was, Aralyn wasn't sure if she would find out. She didn't really care though. She was just glad to have her back, or mostly back. Claire was kinder and caring, yes, but she was also still a vampire. She seemed more human again though. In fact, except for when she had to leave to feed, Aralyn often forgot that her sister had become a vampire. Aralyn trusted Claire with every ounce of her own life.

In the mansion, life for Aralyn was pretty much routine still, but she didn't really mind, especially being pregnant. Most of the vampires ignored Aralyn, going on with their nightly lives, barely noticing her, which, she also didn't mind. Except for Morgan, of course. He was still as sniveling as ever. He was a great annoyance to Aralyn and she often asked Aimeric why he hadn't killed him. Aimeric had always responded the same, "He's a good servant." Aralyn had always rolled her eyes. Not that she really wanted Morgan to die; she just didn't see how Aimeric could put up with him. She wouldn't have complained if Morgan was banished to somewhere far away, though. He always found a way to antagonize her, make her feel bad and uncomfortable. This, of course, was only when Aimeric wasn't around. When Aimeric was, he would always turn back into the coward he truly was and suck up to Aimeric as much as he could get away with. Morgan also blamed Aralyn for "ruining his fun" since Aimeric had released the prisoners on her account. With Morgan, Aralyn had grown quite accustomed to the phrase, "fuck off" and used it whenever Morgan brought the prisoners up to her. He usually responded with some vulgar remark, unless Aimeric was nearby, but he *would* leave her alone; he had actually learned to not *keep* antagonizing.

Cora was rarely seen at all in the mansion. The whole time that Aralyn had been there she had only seen the girl five times, including their first encounter. She barely left the house to feed and mostly stayed alive off of the rats that ran around upstairs in the walls. She only took human lives when she felt too weak and needed replenished; when the rats weren't enough.

When Aralyn had asked Aimeric why Cora was that way, he told her that it was because she had only been a vampire for about thirty years and was one of the ones who had become depressed after being turned and was still getting used to the idea, deciding if she liked the thought of immortality, or the closest thing to it. He had said that for the first fifteen years of her new life, after her sire had turned her, she had stayed in the laboratory most of the time, experimenting with rats and anything else she could get a hold of until she grew bored and decided she liked art better. The laboratory hadn't been used by anyone else and had been abandoned by Cora when she went to drawing and painting. She was quite the artist and could draw and paint just about anything. Aralyn had only seen a few of her works, after she had stumbled into Cora's bedroom one day, which were a few sketches and canvas paintings lying against the walls and against easels, mostly of young, bleeding, women crying bloody tears, but Aralyn thought they were beautiful. Others, however, would probably think the art was disturbing or scary, but Cora obviously didn't care. Aralyn had only been allowed to admire the paintings for a few moments, however, before Cora had asked her to leave, claiming she wanted to be left alone.

Aimeric had also told Aralyn that Cora hated him since he was the Master Vampire, even though he wasn't the one who had actually sired her. He was still head and responsible for the clan, so she turned her hate to him. Cora's sire, after turning her, had abandoned her and left her at the mansion. Aimeric had had him hunted down and killed for leaving the clan without permission.

Whenever Cora and Aimeric were in the same room together, they ended up arguing and Cora usually stomped back upstairs. Aralyn asked Aimeric why he had allowed her to live, since taking pity on someone wasn't really his style. He had responded that she wasn't worth his time since she didn't cause any harm to anyone else, though he had told her before that she deserved to die. Aralyn didn't like hearing that part; she thought Cora was probably just hurting and felt alone and needed someone to trust.

That was why Aralyn now found herself climbing the stairs to the third floor, towards Cora's room. She had been thinking of Cora all that day for some reason and decided she would try and talk to the girl, get her to open up a little and trust Aralyn so that, maybe, she would feel better about being a vampire.

Claire and Aimeric had gone out to feed for the night, taking Morgan with them, which was a rare occurrence, but one that Aralyn was happy about. A few of the other vampires had stayed in, not interested in going out that night, but they all mostly stayed downstairs around the television, as always. Aimeric's clan wasn't exactly energetic most of the time.

Aralyn was on the third floor now, wandering down the hallway, which had been cleaned up. The whole house had been cleaned up at the request of Aralyn. A few months ago, she told Aimeric that she didn't want to raise a baby in such a mess because it was hazardous. Aimeric had agreed and put the vampires to work, replacing wallpaper, dusting, and cleaning the floors and walls. Most of the blood was gone, but there were still stains in a few places. Blood was hard to get out. All of the wood pieces in the house, door framing, floors, furniture, had all been polished. All of the windows had new shutters, instead of tinfoil, and newer curtains so that the mansion didn't look so run down. Aralyn was pleased with the difference.

Coming to the door, Aralyn stopped in front of it and went to knock, she didn't want to be rude and just open the door. She stopped though, before her knuckles could hit the wood, hearing voices on the other side of the room, and listened to what they were saying. The first voice Aralyn heard, no doubt, belonged to Cora.

"She's only got a few weeks left!"

"I know that, Cora."

The second voice sounded familiar, it was a man, but Aralyn couldn't place where she had heard him before.

"What if she goes into labor and you aren't here? Will you be able to make it back in time?" Cora asked in an accusing tone.

"Labor can take many hours, even a day or so, especially with the first child; I'm sure I can make it back here if you call me through telepathy," the man responded.

"There *are* exceptions. Labor can also only take a *couple* of hours, even *with* the first child."

"I'll be here, Cora. I promise."

It wasn't Aimeric speaking, but who else would be concerned about Aralyn going into labor if not the father? She strained to listen, pressing her ear against the door.

"I think it would be best if you move in here, Orrin," Cora said flatly.

Orrin! Why was he at the mansion now when he hadn't been around for so long? And what were he and Cora planning?

"I can't! Aimeric would feel my presence here and then we would all be found out!" Orrin replied haughtily.

All? Who else was involved in whatever was being planned?

"I suppose you're right," Cora said dismally.

"It will be fine, Cora. Everything will work out," Orrin assured her.

She sighed.

"Why do you always have to be so optimistic?"

"It's just who I am."

Another sigh.

"Once she goes into labor, we won't have much time. Surely Aimeric will turn her right away."

Aralyn's breath caught in her throat. Aimeric was going to turn her when she went into labor? Why? What was the point of doing it then? Aralyn forced herself to keep listening, promising she would think more on that matter later, right now, she needed to find out what these two were up to.

"He can't do it too quickly or it will kill the child," Orrin said.

"Are you sure you want to save the child? This would be a lot easier if we didn't have to time it just right to be certain to disrupt the turning," Cora said.

"I would never ask that that little, innocent, life to be forced to go through what I went through. I have been shunned most of my life, accepted only by my clan-"

"Claire and I have accepted you," Cora interrupted.

"Only you two, and a few select others, including Virgil, but that doesn't make up for the pain I have felt, for the beatings I have endured because of jealous rages that I have the powers a vampire has, but few of the weaknesses," Orrin said.

"Right. You have the power, so why don't you fight back?" Cora asked.

"My heart won't let me."

Orrin's response was so simple, yet so passionate, Aralyn started to feel sorry for him and even found her eyes getting teary.

"That is one thing I envy of you; a heart. I-"

Aralyn heard Cora take a sharp breath and then the room went silent for a split second, right before the door was yanked open and Aralyn was pulled inside the room.

"What did you hear?" Cora demanded angrily, digging her nails into Aralyn's arms.

The dress that Aralyn was wearing was short sleeved so Cora's claws went right into her flesh. Cringing and wincing, Aralyn stared back at Cora and then looked at Orrin. His red eyes were staring back at her pleadingly.

"I…nothing," Aralyn finally stuttered.

Cora swung her around in a half circle.

"Do not lie to me!"

"Cora."

Orrin touched her arm, giving her a silent warning with his expression.

Cora looked at Aralyn's frightened face, and the tears in her eyes, and then at her swelled belly and reluctantly released her. Aralyn took in a breath and rubbed at her bruised arms and then looked at her fingertips when she felt warm liquid. They were stained with blood; Cora's nails had broken the skin on her arms. Orrin took Aralyn's shoulders and led her to a chair, helping her sit in it.

"What are you two planning? You're not going to try and take my baby, are you? Is Claire in on it?" Aralyn asked, the words flowing out of her mouth, one after another.

"Calm down," Orrin began. "We aren't going to take your baby from you. We want to take you *and* the baby away from Aimeric."

"Orrin!" Cora scolded loudly.

He glanced at her over his shoulder.

"It's fine, Cora. She won't tell Aimeric, no matter what she thinks she feels for him." He turned back to Aralyn and added, "Right?"

Aralyn hesitated, knowing that he was right; she didn't want Aimeric to hurt either of them. But she wasn't going to leave Aimeric either.

"I'm not leaving him," she said stubbornly, avoiding the question.

"He's going to turn you, Aralyn! As soon as you go into labor, that way the baby will be half turned and become his instead of the human who impregnated you."

So that was why Aimeric wanted to turn her when she went into labor. She stood up, not easily due to her belly, and faced Orrin.

"So what?" Aralyn challenged. "I told him a long time ago to turn me, before I even got pregnant! If the baby is half turned too, it doesn't matter; we'll be a family."

Orrin sighed, rubbing his temples.

"Dear Lord, what has he done to you?"

She glared at him.

"Do you know what you will be doing to this baby?" he asked after a moment.

"I heard you say that you have the powers but few of the weaknesses, and since the baby will only be half, she or he will still age, am I correct?"

He nodded.

"Yes, he will age, but slower than a full human."

"Then what would be so horrible?"

"If you heard that, then surely you heard me say that I was beat numerous times for only being half?"

"Aimeric and I will teach him to fight back," Aralyn said simply.

She saw Orrin's jaw clench out of frustration but he held in whatever argument he had for her.

"Very well, Aralyn. If this is the life you truly wish to have…I would just hate to have to see you raise a child on your own…should something happen to Aimeric. My offer to take you away still stands for now, but once the child is born, you are on your own."

He took her arm and led her across the room, towards the door, as she started to protest.

"What do you mean by 'should something happen to Aimeric'?" she demanded as she was pulled towards the door.

Orrin ignored her and opened it, gently pushing her out into the hall.

"Goodbye, Aralyn. I hope you come to your senses soon; you don't have much time left," he said, closing the door.

Aralyn held up her hand and stopped the door from latching.

"Tell me what you plan on doing or…I'll tell Aimeric," she said, though not very convincingly.

Orrin smiled sadly.

"No...you won't."

The door latched without another word and Aralyn was left standing in the hall, irritated, knowing that Orrin had been right; she couldn't tell Aimeric and risk having them tortured and killed. She cursed softly to herself and then went back downstairs to her room.

<u>Chapter Twenty-One: Lesson to be Learned</u>

Once she reached her and Aimeric's bedroom, Aralyn went straight to the adjoining bathroom and washed the cuts on her arms from Cora. They burned a little still but they weren't bleeding anymore. Once they were clean, she went back into the dark bedroom, not turning on a light or lighting any candles, and sat down on the sofa at the end of the bed, biting her thumb nervously as she thought of what Orrin had said. He had definitely been right about one thing; Aralyn would not tell Aimeric anything unless she believed he was in real danger, which she didn't think he was. Aimeric was the strongest of all the vampires in the mansion. The others literally cowered before him. She didn't want any unnecessary killing, which she knew was what would happen if she told Aimeric what she had heard earlier. So, instead, she promised herself that she would keep an eye out for anyone else acting suspicious and watch Cora closer as well. She wasn't sure if she would be able to stop anyone, but at least, if she kept an eye out, and listened to what was going on around her, she would be able to decide when and if she should tell Aimeric anything.

The door started to open and Aralyn quickly reached up and pulled a blanket from the back of the sofa and wrapped it around her shoulders, not wanting Aimeric to see the cuts on her arms; she knew he would be angry and demand to know what had happened. Then what might he do to Cora? She leaned against the sofa and put on a fake smile as Aimeric entered the room, the moon beams from the opened curtains bouncing off his jet-black hair.

"What are you doing sitting here alone in the dark, my love?" Aimeric asked.

She shrugged.

"Thinking…"

Aimeric paused a moment to unbutton the first three buttons of his shirt and then he sat down, next to Aralyn, drawing her into his arms, and nuzzling her neck. His hand went to her belly and he circled part of it with his thumb. Aralyn sank into his chest. He was warm, he had just fed.

"About what?" he asked.

"Names for the baby," Aralyn lied.

"I see…" he said thoughtfully and then sat up straight.

"Aralyn?"

"Yes?"

"What happened to your arm?"

She turned her head, alarmed, and saw that the blanket had slipped down, showing the bruising cuts. She wasn't sure what to say, but she didn't have to say anything.

"Stay here," Aimeric growled, seeing into her mind.

He stood, angrily, from the sofa, and stalked towards the door.

"Aimeric! What are you going to do?" Aralyn called after him, but he ignored her, leaving the room, and slamming the door.

Aralyn cursed herself for not being able to block her thoughts and almost ran after him. But she stopped herself, not wanting to risk Aimeric's temper this close to the end of her pregnancy. She didn't want to put any stress on the baby. She fell back on the sofa, cradling her baby, and prayed, silently, that Aimeric wouldn't harm Cora or find Orrin.

***

After falling asleep again, Aralyn woke up as the sun started to rise, gently caressing her face to bring her out of her slumber. Once she realized it was the sun, and not a dream, she gasped loudly and, in a panic, thinking Aimeric was still in the room, ran to the window and slammed the shutters and curtains closed. She had had them open the night before to enjoy the moonlight and had accidentally fallen asleep, forgetting to close them before. She breathed a sigh of relief when she turned around and saw that Aimeric wasn't in the room. At least he was safe. However, *not* having him in there with her was unusual and it got her mind wandering again. Where was he? She hadn't seen him since he had stormed out on her, looking for Cora.

What if Orrin and Cora had fought together and found a way to catch Aimeric off guard? What if they had somehow overpowered him? Worried, Aralyn rushed to the door, flinging it open, and quickly descended the stairs down to the living room. She was halfway down the stairs when she heard Aimeric's voice and she loudly breathed a sigh of relief, knowing he was okay.

"Let this be a lesson to all of you! This is what will happen if anyone turns against me!" Aimeric said loudly, in an authoritative tone.

On that last sentence, relief turned to fear and Aralyn hurried the rest of the way down the steps where she came into the living room, amongst a crowd of vampires, every resident of the mansion, and they were all circled around something in front of the huge window right at the bottom of the stairs. The whole first floor of the house was dark except for a few candles lit around the living room. It almost looked like some kind of a ritual was taking place. Still standing on the last step, Aralyn looked around, over the tops of the many heads, and saw that Aimeric was standing to the left of the window, his hand on the cord that would open the heavy curtains. Directly in front of the window was Cora and she was tied to a wooden stake on a makeshift stage. She was naked and her dark skin was covered in whip marks. Blood dribbled down her neck, arms, torso, and legs, to the floor. Aralyn gasped, horrified, knowing what was going to happen. She pushed through the crowd, trying to reach Aimeric on the other side of the room. She had to stop him.

"All of you in the front might want to step aside," Aimeric said loudly.

The crowd divided down the middle, separating to each side of the room, out of the window's path, leaving Aralyn standing in the center. She stopped in the commotion and looked at Cora, who was only a few feet in front of her. The girl had been tortured for a long time. She was bleeding heavily and looked like she would beg for death at any minute. Their eyes met, Cora's filling with, fresh, blood tears and looking at Aralyn apologetically, for only a second before Aimeric violently threw open the curtains, sending a stream of light from the morning sun onto Cora's body. Terrified and surprised, the other vampires hissed and ran into shadowed corners of the mansion in order to escape the sun's violating fingers.

"I told them to move, didn't I?" Aimeric mused.

Out of the corner of her eye, Aralyn saw that Aimeric was smirking at Morgan, but she couldn't look directly at either one of them; her eyes remained on Cora as the girl's body began to smoke. Aralyn tried to look away, but for some reason she couldn't, her eyes were glued to Cora's. Cora was now gritting her teeth but refusing to cry out. She kept her pride, though Aralyn couldn't see how. The girl was in an immense amount of pain.

Feeling someone watching her, Aralyn finally managed to turn her head towards Aimeric. He was watching her, having only just spotted her when the crowd had cleared. They stared at each other, Aralyn's expression questioning and disgusted and Aimeric's eyes cold and hard. The rest of his features remained emotionless, however. Their gaze didn't last long. When Cora had finally given in and started screaming, Aralyn turned her attention back to her. The young vampire's skin was literally melting off of her frame and her dark eyes were bulging in their sockets until they finally imploded and a gooey substance, of which used to be her eyes, began to run down her cheeks.

This was all Aralyn could stand to watch. She had to get away. She had to rid her head of the horrible image and rid her ears of the screaming. But she couldn't move very far. Her feet wouldn't work, her nerves were too shocked. She was barely able to move, only making it far enough to prop herself up on the wall, covering her mouth and closing her eyes. She tried very hard to block out the screaming but failed miserably. Her insides were churning. She could feel Aimeric looking at her but she refused to look back. It was times like these where she wished she could make herself fall out of love with him. During his times of tyranny, she wondered *how* she could possibly stand to be with him? How was someone, even a vampire, capable of performing such heinous acts?

The room went dark again and Aralyn opened her eyes, but didn't look at any one person. She kept them on the floor, staring at the carpet, listening to what would happen next. Cora's cries had faded and Aralyn knew she was dead now. The whole room was deathly silent, for what seemed an eternity, until a low chuckle emitted from Morgan, followed by a few others, until the room finally filled with loud laughter. Aimeric wasn't laughing though. He went to Aralyn and wrapped his arm around her shoulder, pulling her off the wall and against his chest to support her since her legs had seemed to be giving up on her. Disgusted, she almost pushed him away, but she knew she needed him to help her walk back to the stairs. She wouldn't be able to make it up them on her own. Risking a glance around the room, as she was being led away, Aralyn looked up and immediately wished she hadn't. She saw a pile of ash under the window, which used to be Cora. The ashes also lay in a bloody puddle. Holding back the want to throw up, Aralyn turned and buried her face into Aimeric's chest.

Aimeric stopped at the base of the stairs and faced the room. Aralyn looked up again, avoiding the ash pile, and caught Morgan's snickering expression. She glared hatefully at him; somehow she figured all of this was his fault. He must have helped Aimeric in some way or another. He probably brought Cora to Aimeric and started this whole disgusting display of tyranny. Aralyn searched for Claire but didn't find her, which added to her worry and discomfort.

"I'll say it again, since *some* of you came in late," Aimeric said loudly.

Aralyn looked up and saw him looking down at her. This speech would be for her benefit. For some reason, Aimeric felt he had to explain why he had just killed Cora.

"It seems, the late

Cora was plotting against me and was going to have me killed. It doesn't really surprise me; I've known she's hated me, and herself for that matter, for a long time now. She wouldn't tell me who was with her in her little plot but I found out anyway," Aimeric said. He paused a moment and then added, "Cora always *did* have a feeble mind."

A few vampires laughed lightly and then the room became quiet again and Aimeric continued.

"Our old *friend*, Orrin, and my precious Claire would have been her accomplices. They have run away now, apparently sensing Cora's mistake. If any of you see either of them, tell me immediately. Do not harm them. They will be for *me* to deal with."

Tears sprang to Aralyn's eyes; she knew Aimeric would not show Claire any mercy.

Please...stay away, Claire, Aralyn thought.

Aimeric shot a warning look down on her, but Aralyn didn't care and she let her tears fall freely.

"That is all. If any of you find either of them, tell me," Aimeric repeated before leading Aralyn up the stairs.

The vampires mumbled agreements as the two of them disappeared and then their voices faded out as Aimeric reached their bedroom and the two went inside.

"Crying for your betraying sister, Aralyn?" Aimeric sneered and pushed her inside, closing the door behind them.

He looked at her angrily, waiting for a response, but she didn't give it right away. She was exhausted and needed to sit down so she took a moment to lower herself onto the sofa before answering.

"I just don't want her to die," she said quietly.

"So you would prefer she kill me?" Aimeric hissed.

"No!" Aralyn yelled without meaning to. Seeing Aimeric's warning expression, she lowered her voice and added, "I don't want either of you to die. I don't want any more killing at all, Aimeric, and I especially do not want to have to choose between you and my sister."

"There were a lot of 'I don'ts' in there, Aralyn; aren't you being selfish?" Aimeric asked stubbornly, walking across the floor to stand beside the armored window as though he could see outside.

"Not wanting people to die is *not* being selfish," Aralyn boldly argued.

"Are you implying Cora's punishment was unjust?" he spat at her.

"Yes," Aralyn said without hesitation.

Aimeric took an intimidating step forward and, glaring, said, "Well, *you* do not have the authority to make that call."

"What you did was horrible and disgusting, Aimeric!" Aralyn yelled.

She wasn't sure where this new bravery was coming from, but she refused to let it slip away now.

Daring Aimeric's temper even more, she added, "How could you?"

"Do not question me, Aralyn," Aimeric growled.

"Stop it. Stop threatening me," Aralyn said, her fists clenching the cushions of the sofa.

Aimeric stepped the rest of the way up to her and, from behind the sofa, took Aralyn's hair and pulled her head back enough so he could sneer into her lips.

"Don't think that just because you're pregnant you can talk to me like that. I'm still in charge here, over you and everyone else in this house. Don't make me do something I might regret later."

"Don't kill her," Aralyn said, ignoring his threats.

Releasing her hair, Aimeric jerked himself away from the sofa and paced the room with his hands clasped behind his back. Aralyn watched him, waiting. She wasn't sure what he was thinking. For a moment, she thought he almost looked guilty.

Finally, Aimeric looked up at Aralyn, the cold still holding to his eyes.

"I'm not going to promise you that I won't kill her if she returns. She has betrayed, and plotted to kill me; death would be a just punishment. If you can't handle that, then perhaps you should die with her," he bit out.

Aralyn stared at him in disbelief, eyes watering again. She was overly sensitive because of the pregnancy and that last sentence had hit her like a bullet to the chest.

"You would kill me too?" she asked, hurt.

Aimeric hesitated before letting out a frustrated sigh.

"No. You know I wouldn't. But you still can't expect me to do nothing about Claire."

"Will you search for her?" Aralyn asked.

He moved across the room to sit beside her on the sofa, taking her chin to look into her eyes.

"Not if you ask me not to."

"Please don't," Aralyn begged in a soft whisper.

Aimeric nodded, looking only slightly disappointed, he hadn't really expected her to agree for him to search for Claire, and let his hand fall off of her face.

"I meant what I said though; don't think you can talk back to me anymore and get away with it," he added sternly.

Aralyn sighed, leaning back against the sofa, and looked away from him. She was frustrated. Why did he have to add that last part? Why did he feel he had to control her so much? She didn't understand. Aimeric surprised her though when he gently pulled her to his chest and laid back on the sofa with her, kissing her forehead. He was being gentle and loving. Maybe he actually felt guilty.

"Go to sleep now; you're looking exhausted," Aimeric whispered against her forehead, kissing it once more.

Aralyn didn't object. Being so far along in her pregnancy, she was always tired and exhausted it seemed. She nodded and, closing her eyes, snuggled into Aimeric's chest. She was soon fast asleep.

Aralyn.
What?
The time is coming. I can sense it. Are you ready?
For what?
To leave Aimeric.
No! Claire, stay away!

Aralyn was being gently shaken and slowly pulled back into reality. She jumped up, confused.

"What?" she mumbled.

"You were dreaming, talking in your sleep," Aimeric said, holding her up and looking at her questioningly. "What were you dreaming about?"

It hadn't been a dream; Claire had been talking to Aralyn while she slept. Apparently she and Orrin were still planning something and Claire knew the baby would be coming soon. But how did she know that? Sliding out of Aimeric's arms, and off the sofa, Aralyn turned her back to him and thoughtfully rested her hand on her belly. She wasn't sure what to say; she didn't know what the two were planning, but she knew it wasn't going to be good.

"Aralyn?" Aimeric asked sternly, wanting an answer.

"N-nothing," she stuttered, unconvincingly and bit her lip, trying not to think of Claire and give her away.

"Aralyn," Aimeric began, standing up behind her. "If you know something...if that bitch-" he stopped and cleared his throat. "If *Claire* has contacted you, you had better tell me now," he finished warningly.

"She hasn't!" Aralyn said, a little too quickly.

"Do not lie to me!" Aimeric roared, grabbing her arm.

"I won't let you kill her!" she screamed back.

"So she *is* planning on returning? How stupid is she?" Aimeric asked harshly, more to himself than to Aralyn, ignoring her tone.

"She isn't stupid!" Aralyn defended. "She cares about what happens to me and the ba-" Aralyn gasped loudly, stopping in mid sentence, and grabbed Aimeric's hand to steady herself so she wouldn't fall to the floor from the blinding pain.

Aimeric held her up, suddenly looking concerned, instead of angry.

"What is it?"

"I think I've gone into labor," Aralyn responded painfully.

Chapter Twenty-Two:
A Life Begins, Another Ends

Several hours later, Aralyn was in bed, yelling in pain, as yet another labor contraction hit her. She yelled longer this time than the last; she was getting close to delivering. Once the wave had passed, she fell back on the pillows, gasping for breath, and released Aimeric's hand, which she had grabbed when the contraction hit her. He was standing beside the bed, dabbing her sweating forehead with a cool, damp, cloth in between waves.

"Stop touching me!" she hissed at him, irritated. "And get him the hell out of here!" Aralyn added turning her glare to the foot of the bed where Morgan was standing with his arms crossed, leaning against the bedpost.

He was smirking at her, loving every second of seeing her in so much pain. Aimeric glanced at Morgan from the corner of his eye while still dabbing Aralyn with the cloth, ignoring her other harsh demands to stop touching her.

"Morgan, leave," Aimeric said coolly.

"Fine. But can I speak with you Master? Out in the hallway?" Morgan asked.

Aimeric glared, annoyed, and then, sighing, he looked at the female vampire, on the other side of the bed, who was helping assist Aralyn with labor and delivery.

"How long?" he asked.

"Not long now, maybe ten or fifteen minutes," she responded, shrugging.

"Fine."

Aimeric kissed Aralyn's forehead quickly, promising he would be back in only a minute or two, and then left with Morgan.

"What the hell do you want?" Aimeric growled, closing the door, after they had reached the hallway.

"To remind you that you ought to be turning her soon, don't you think?" Morgan asked, starting off strong but stuttering on the last words.

Aimeric sighed angrily.

"How many times do I have to tell you, before it penetrates that thick skull of yours, that I have to wait for exactly the right moment or I risk killing the child?"

"Alright! Jeez, I just thought you might need a reminder, what with all the stress you've been under-"

"I hardly think I could forget about this!" Aimeric roared, opening the door. He lowered his voice to a hissing whisper and added, "Now keep an eye out for that treacherous bitch!"

Morgan nodded and Aimeric went back into the bedroom.

"Aimeric! Don't-"

Aralyn's terrified words were cut off when Orrin held a knife to her throat.

"You shouldn't have left her alone!" Orrin said triumphantly.

Before Aimeric could get one curse word or threat out, the door slammed closed and Claire jumped on his back, trying to bite his neck, growling ferociously and scratching at his arms and chest. The assistant to Aralyn was now dead on the floor. Her neck had been snapped and she would soon only be a pile of dust. Aralyn and Orrin watched, nervously, as Aimeric struggled with Claire and tried to fight her off. He rushed back into a wall, hitting Claire's back against it hard, trying to stun her so she would fall from him but she held her arms tightly around his neck and her legs wrapped around his waist.

Aralyn could sense Orrin's worry and felt the cold steel touch her neck a few times due to his shaking hand. She wasn't worried about being killed though. She didn't believe Orrin would be able to kill her, what would be the point of this poor "rescue" attempt? But Aralyn *was* worried about Claire. Aimeric didn't appear to have the advantage at the moment due to the surprise attack, but she was sure that he would gain the upper hand soon enough and Aralyn knew she could do nothing to help either of them, not in the position she was in at that moment.

The door suddenly burst open and, for the first time since she had known him, Aralyn was glad to see Morgan and sighed a breath of relief. He ran at Claire with a candelabra and hit her hard on the back of the head with it. She hissed and jumped at him, her claws out, ready for blood. Before she could swipe at Morgan, or do anything else, however, Aimeric turned on her and knocked her against the wall, holding her down with his own weight.

"Bitch!" he yelled.

"Claire!" Orrin said at the same time and watched, alarmed, as the two vampire men started to gang up on her.

"Don't kill her!" Aralyn screamed.

Aimeric shot her an angered glance over his shoulder. How dare she ask him not to kill Claire when the bitch had come to do him in?

Aralyn suddenly screamed, throwing her head back and gritting her teeth, as her uterus tightened once more. Her fingers clawed into the bed sheets. Aimeric started to go to her but a punch in the back of his head from Claire changed his mind. He turned around and slapped Claire across the face. Morgan kicked her side. Orrin glanced from Aralyn to Claire, trying to decide if he should aide his comrade. She wouldn't be able to fight off both Aimeric and Morgan, for long. Aralyn was still in bad shape and obviously not a threat so Orrin made up his mind and ran to help Claire. Raising the knife in his hands, he went to hit Aimeric in the neck, hoping to stun him if nothing else and give Claire a chance to break away for a moment and regain her bearings. But Aimeric sensed him and spun around in time to knock the blade to the floor.

Aimeric growled fiercely, enraged beyond anything he had ever been before, his fangs bared viciously, and he locked his fingers around the silver haired vampire's throat.

"Did the two of you really believe you could kill me?" he sneered.

Morgan had gained full control over Claire, twisting her arm up around her back to hold her in place with one hand, the other holding her around the neck. He was waiting for Aimeric's orders. Claire looked very defeated already. She had several cuts on her face and blood tears in her eyes.

"It was all worth a try to kill you," Orrin sneered back at Aimeric, his eyes also becoming bloody with his tears; tears of defeat.

"My question is, why now? Why your father?" Aimeric growled deeply.

"I wasn't about to let you destroy two more lives! We've wanted to kill you for quite some time now. It seemed only right to try and save Claire's sister and *her* baby. We had to wait for the right moment, when you would be distracted and miss your chance on turning the child at least. And you, Aimeric, may be my creator, but you are *not* my father!" Orrin spat.

Aimeric only grinned evilly, enjoying how worked up Orrin got when he mentioned him being his father. The two glared at one another for a moment and then Aimeric looked at Claire over his shoulder. She was looking at him with fierce green eyes.

"And you? I thought you had forgiven me…I must say that you hid your thoughts well."

"I've always hated you! I never forgave you for what you have done to me!" Claire said, her dark curls a shaken mess, hanging in her eyes.

She tried to shake off Morgan, but she had been weakened from the fight and wasn't strong enough.

"I wanted to die!" she continued when she realized she couldn't escape. "I was in so much pain, and I had lost my mother already and you took me anyway!"

Aimeric laughed loudly.

"So that's what this is all about? A grudge? You are angry at me for giving you eternal life, Claire?"

"You gave me eternal hell!" she snapped back.

"And you, Orrin," Aimeric continued, looking back at him. "You are angry because I prolonged your life? Gave you the powers of a vampire, yet few of the weaknesses?"

"You gave me a curse! To suffer twice as long in this world of discrimination and segregation."

"You hate this life so much?" Aimeric snarled, jerking Orrin forward by the collar of his shirt. "I can take it away just as easily."

Aimeric violently snapped the bones in Orrin's neck and threw him to the floor next to the female vampire's ashes. Orrin never even had the chance to try and fight Aimeric; it had all come too fast.

"Son of a bitch!" Claire screamed, looking at Orrin's body.

"Aimeric! It's coming!" Aralyn cried desperately from the bed, gasping for breath and moaning in pain.

Hearing Aralyn say this must have been enough for Claire's strength to return because she suddenly jerked herself free from Morgan and jumped in front of Aimeric as he made a rush over to Aralyn. She hissed and swiped his face with her claws, drawing blood. Aimeric didn't seem to notice the scratches, but Claire's attempt had angered him even more and he grabbed her by the hair, throwing her backwards into Morgan.

"Keep her still!"

Morgan nodded and elbowed Claire in the back of the neck, knocking her to the floor. As soon as she fell,

Morgan was on top of her, holding his knee in the center of her back to temporarily paralyze her.

"Get the fuck off of me!" Claire screamed, trying to move underneath him.

He ignored her though.

Aimeric made it to Aralyn's side and sat beside her, brushing her hair back out of her eyes. He calmed his voice to a soothing tone.

"Aralyn, my love, are you ready?"

"Yes, do it, please," Aralyn begged, still in immense pain.

"No! Aimeric, stay the fuck away from her!" Claire yelled.

"Shut up!" Morgan hissed, applying more pressure to her back with his weight.

Aralyn looked up at Aimeric pleadingly and he moved his hand to brush the hair away from her neck.

"Calm down," he whispered, lowering his lips to hers.

She couldn't calm down though. She was in pain and another contraction was causing her body to tense her muscles and grit her teeth. She barely felt like she could breathe and when she could, her breaths came out in loud gasps. Aimeric grabbed her hand and she squeezed it. He kissed her softly to calm her with his own mind and to, hopefully, ease her pain. Her breathing slowed and she stopped writhing. A wave of calm washed over her and she could barely feel her labor now. She melted into Aimeric and kissed him back lovingly.

Aimeric moved to her neck, keeping her calm with the touch of his fingers on the side of her face, and then he penetrated her flesh with the sharp points of his fangs. This woke Aralyn up and her body came back to life with, yet another squeeze of her uterus, and she whimpered loudly as Aimeric drank from her. With both, the pain from labor and Aimeric's teeth in her neck, Aralyn could feel herself starting to pass out from the pain. It was too much for her and she cried out a few times, tears rolling down her cheeks. Her fingernails clawed at Aimeric's arm and her body tried to protest, writhing underneath Aimeric.

After a moment, the pain started to disappear and Aralyn became numb to everything. She was suddenly very tired. She stopped crying and her breathing slowed to only wheezes. Her eyes drooped and her arm fell back on the bed. She was just barely hanging on at that point. Her vision became clouded because she was trying so hard to stay awake. She could barely make out Aimeric's figure as he pulled away from her. He took his fingernail and sliced open his own wrist. Aralyn could hear Claire's muffled screaming of protest, as though coming through from a radio station with bad reception.

Aimeric held his wrist over Aralyn's mouth, allowing his blood, his life, to drip onto her lips. Tasting the horrible blood on her lips, Aralyn tried to turn her head away but Aimeric pulled her back and forced her mouth to close over the wound.

"You have to drink, Aralyn, or you will die," he said in a stern voice.

She moaned in protest but began to suck away at the wound anyway. She gagged a few times but then, as she got used to the taste, she could feel her body becoming energized once more. She began to drink from Aimeric greedily, wanting to stay alive, wanting to feel her energy come back. After a few moments, Aimeric pulled his wrist away and Aralyn sat up quickly in the bed, suddenly screaming. She gasped and pushed as hard as she could and a few moments later, a baby's cries filled the room.

"No!" Claire screamed as Aralyn fell back on the pillows.

Aralyn's pain was not yet over with. She cried out and her body writhed as it began to die, Aimeric's blood working through her system, killing every organ inside of her. She felt immense pain, shooting all through her veins and into her eyes. Hot tears rolled down her cheeks. What had she allowed to have happen to her? Had Aimeric tricked her? Was she going to die? She coughed up blood and, rolling over onto her side, dry-heaved violently. Her nerves started to go out of control and her body shook. She tried to sit up but lost the strength to do so. She finally gave in and everything went black.

Aralyn woke only a few minutes later, feeling energized, more than she had ever felt before. Her pain was completely gone. Her vision was no longer cloudy. Slowly, she drew herself up and peered down at her body. She was thin again and her skin flawless. There was no sign that she had ever been pregnant. There were no stretch marks where there had been before and her stomach was flat, which she could see through the nightgown she was wearing. Aralyn brought up her arms and gazed at them, trying to find the scars she had gotten from Devin cutting her so long ago. She couldn't find them; they had disappeared entirely. She turned her gaze back down. Not only were her blemishes and scars gone, but also, other aspects of her body had changed. Her breasts were perkier and rounder than they had ever been. Her body was toned nicely. She moved the bed sheet aside and brought her leg up. It was smooth, as though just waxed, and as soft as a baby's skin. She had become what she had always pictured herself to be. In her eyes, *this* was perfect, what she wanted to look like, who she wanted to be.

"How do you feel, my love?"

Aralyn looked up at Aimeric. He was standing over her with a bundle of blankets in his arms, grinning down at her. She smiled back and fell onto the pillows dreamily, giggling softly.

"I feel…great."

She sighed in contempt and then, turning her head slightly, she saw the amazed look on Morgan's face and the hurt look on Claire's. Aralyn's sister was looking back at her from the floor, defeated more than she had ever been, with blood tears in her eyes. Her jaw clenched, out of anger, out of hurt. They stared at one another for a moment, Aralyn not sure of what to say, and then, suddenly, Claire's expression turned vicious and she somehow managed to escape from Morgan. She jumped up and slashed her claws across his eyes. Morgan yelled in pain and stumbled backwards. It all happened so fast; Aimeric was holding the baby and wasn't able to stop Claire in time and Aralyn sat up too late to defend herself; Claire jumped on the bed and, before anyone could stop her, she violently grabbed Aralyn's head and pushed her backwards, snapping her neck.

Aralyn never even felt it. She fell into darkness once more…

Chapter Twenty-Three: A Journey to Hell

Hearing painful screams, Aralyn opened her eyes slowly, and coughed. Her lungs felt closed up, like they were stuck together. She was sweating; it was hot and the heat was suffocating. She sat up, still trying to rid her throat of the smoke, and took in her surroundings. Wherever she was, she was underground, surrounded by rock walls and ceilings. Smoke overtook the air and pools of liquid fire were all around her. The screams she had been hearing came from the many people in the fire. There were thousands, men and women, and they all struggled to get out of the pools but there was an invisible barrier around the edges, keeping them in the lava. Their skin was covered in boils and burns. That was, where they *had* skin. Some of them were just masses of muscle. This was because their skin would melt off of their bodies, chunks falling off, into the fire, until every inch of it was gone. Their screams echoed, out of synch, throughout the caves. It was a horrible noise to take in. Once their skin fell completely from their bodies, followed by their muscle, and they had turned to just a skeleton, their skulls fell under the fire for a few seconds and then they popped back up again, completely regenerated. They bobbed in the fire for a moment with fresh muscle and skin on their arms, torsos and faces, and then their flesh began to boil again.

It was an ongoing cycle, never to end. They were regenerated only to start the process of painful melting all over again. And they were all still alive, in a way, to feel all of it. As Aralyn stared around her, not sure if she should be disgusted or curious, but nevertheless enthralled with what was going on before her, a figure began to emerge from the smoke ahead. She soon found her attention drawn to the person and once the smoke had cleared from that spot, Aralyn saw a tall, perfectly built, pale man. He could only be described as beautiful.

Vampires Don't Exist by Reyanna Vance

His hair was silver with black streaks and went down to his waist. He had two wings folded over his back, one was black and bat-like, the other white and angelic. His eyes, which never left Aralyn's, kept changing color, almost like a slide show, going from silver, to ice blue, to hazel green, to red, to brown, and then, finally to black. When they went black, his pupil's became tiny orange flames. But, his eyes were not what caught the most of Aralyn's attention. She could see his veins under the pale flesh of his body. They were glowing red; tiny rivers of glowing lava, coursing through his body magically. He smiled at her, a cold, sadistic grin, giving her cold chills, despite the suffocating heat.

"W- who are you?" Aralyn asked when she found the ability to speak again.

He chuckled, leaning against the rock wall, and crossed his arms over his bare chest.

"You mean you don't know?"

He grinned again, waiting for her to answer. She opened her mouth to respond and take a guess at his identity, but more screaming from the pools of lava cut her off. The man sensed her irritation at the noise. He raised a hand and the room became silent.

"There now. It's just you and me, beautiful," he said, smirking.

Aralyn looked at the people in the fire and saw that they were still screaming but no sound was coming from their mouths. He had actually muted the cave and turned all the sound off except for his and Aralyn's voices.

"Is this hell?" Aralyn first asked.

He laughed and nodded.

"Very good."

"So you…you're…"

"The one and only," he said, pushing off the rock. He coolly stepped up to her. "'Lucifer.' 'Beelzebub.' 'The

Dark One.' 'The First Fallen,' and the most popular, 'Satan.' I have many terms and names."

He was now only inches away from her.

"...So, what do you prefer?" Aralyn asked, in awe.

He smiled, a devious grin.

"No one's ever asked me that before."

"There's a first time for everything," Aralyn said, trying to keep her nerve.

The very presence of The Dark One was enough to strike fear into anyone, no matter how evil and arrogant they were. Aralyn was willing to bet almost anything that Aimeric would even be nervous under this demon's glare. Though she doubted he would show it.

"Yes...there is a first time for everything, isn't there?" he said thoughtfully. "Alright then, call me Angel."

The look in his eyes seemed to be almost daring her to question him.

"Angel?"

"Yes. Have you not heard that one before? I was an angel once, you knew that much, didn't you?" he asked.

"Of course," Aralyn said, not able to hide the annoyance in her voice.

"Angel" nodded his approval and moved backwards a few steps, away from Aralyn, but still held her gaze with his eyes.

"Do you know why you are here?" he asked after a moment.

Aralyn suddenly became angry, thinking of how she had been killed; her own sister had betrayed and killed her only moments after Aimeric had turned her. She hadn't even had the chance to enjoy, or even find out if she liked, her vampiric life. Claire had stolen it from her. If she waited long enough, she might be able to get revenge on her sister. Aimeric was probably furious and killing Claire now. Aralyn's sister may very well be joining her soon.

Clenching her fists, Aralyn nodded.

"Yes, I was killed."

"That's not what I meant. Aren't you wondering why you are here instead of above?" Angel asked.

"You mean Heaven?"

"Yes."

"I don't know…I haven't thought about it."

"Allow me to enlighten you?" Angel asked.

"Go ahead."

He smiled.

"You willingly chose the life of the damned and allowed yourself to be turned. You had sex with a vampire on many occasions, and you also were a part of changing the mortal life of an innocent child. These are all sins in the eyes of the Lord, so, you were sent to me," Angel said nonchalantly.

Aralyn grinned maliciously, thinking it all over.

"Yes, I did do all of those things, didn't I?"

Angel nodded, amusement shining in his, ever changing, eyes.

"So, now what?" Aralyn asked.

"Now, you have a choice. You can accept that you belong to me and become my true follower in which, one day, you may become a true demon and rank among my highest officers. Or, you can whine, say you don't want to be here, and I will turn you into a mortal soul where you will be condemn for eternity and thrown into a pool of fire…with them." Angel gestured over his shoulder to the bobbing heads of the screaming mouths still on mute.

Aralyn looked at them for a moment and then, looking back at Angel, asked, "Why am I being given a choice in the first place? Does everyone who comes here get to choose?"

"Because you died as a vampire, you get a choice. Unlike the mortals sent here who have just 'gone down the wrong path,' as some say, you have potential, as all vampires do, to becoming a demon warrior."

"I see," Aralyn mumbled, thinking for a moment.

She placed a finger over her lips as though trying to keep a secret in. She was coming up with a plan to get everything she wanted. She would have no problem with being Angel's loyal follower, but she wanted to get what she could out of the deal.

She bowed gracefully.

"I am yours. But first, allow me to request some things of you?"

"Tell me," Angel said.

"I will become your follower, but when the time is right. Allow me to return to earth to enjoy the life, in a manner of speaking, of the undead, which was stolen from me so quickly. To spend time with my husband and child, whom I haven't even met yet. While on earth, I will also recruit potential members for your demon army, in moderation, of course," Aralyn proposed.

"And?" Angel asked, grinning, knowing that she was keeping something else from him.

Aralyn smirked.

"And also, allow me to get revenge on my dear sister, if my husband hasn't already done the job."

Angel chuckled softly.

"That's what I thought."

He stared at her for a long while, and she held him, unafraid, not intimidated, and waited for his response.

Finally, Angel sighed.

"You know, Aralyn, normally, I wouldn't even consider letting one of my souls go back to earth, for fear of them changing their minds and turning to God, even as an undead creature; it's happened before," he said dryly.

"But?" Aralyn asked hopefully and smirked.

He grinned again.

"*But*, you were sired by one of my most evil creations," he said, thoughtfully.

"Yes," Aralyn agreed, excitement filling her insides.

"As long as you are with Aimeric, I don't believe I have to worry about you and, I must say, revenge is a good reason to let you go. I'm curious to see what it is you will do to poor Claire," Angel finished, chuckling softly.

"So am I," Aralyn said quietly, her anger rising again at the mention of her sister's name.

Angel eyed her for a few moments longer.

"Very well, Aralyn. I will send you back. For how long, I do not know. My decision will depend on your behavior."

"What do you mean?"

"If I think that, for even one minute, you might betray me and turn to *Him*, I will send my Death Riders after you and you will be brought here and cast into the fire," he said warningly, his tone strong and stern.

Aralyn scoffed sarcastically.

"You don't have to worry about anything. I want to be with Aimeric and my child; I wouldn't do anything to jeopardize my time with them."

Angel nodded.

"That's good. Are you ready then?"

Aralyn stepped forward.

"I am."

Angel smirked.

"Think happy thoughts," he said sarcastically.

She grinned.

Chapter Twenty-Four: Julian

"Aimeric! Did you see what she just did?" Morgan cried and ran to grab Claire off of Aralyn's body.

His face was pure fright, looking from Aimeric, to the body, and then at Claire as she bit and clawed at his arms while he tried to restrain her.

"Morgan, let her go," Aimeric said calmly.

Claire stopped struggling and both, she and Morgan, looked at Aimeric in shock. Aimeric was still holding his son, letting the newborn grasp his finger as he gazed into the baby's eyes. He didn't seem to care that Aralyn had just been killed by her own sister. He hadn't even flinched, out of anger, or surprise. Morgan let Claire go and he stood there, watching Aimeric in disbelief. He had expected Aimeric to go on a killing rampage throughout the mansion, starting with Claire.

"What…what do you mean by this, Master? Are you not angry?" Morgan stuttered.

Aimeric laughed softly.

"Why would I be angry?"

"She's killed Aralyn! The woman whom you turned so she could be your lover for eternity! The mother of your son!" Morgan yelled, still shocked.

"And why do you seem to care, so much, Morgan?" Aimeric snarled accusingly.

Morgan looked taken aback.

"I- I don't, I guess."

Aimeric smirked and then beckoned for Claire.

"Claire, darling, come here."

She started to shake her head in protest, but, as if coming to her senses, she smiled, and slowly stepped up to him, going around the bed and past Aralyn's body. She stood beside Aimeric and nervously looked up at him.

"Why did you do it?" he asked calmly, as though speaking to a child.

"I, uh," she stuttered, and looked at Aralyn's broken neck.

"You wanted to save her from me, right?" Aimeric guessed. He grinned, taking his eyes off of the baby finally, and looked at Claire.

"Or, perhaps you were jealous of Aralyn?"

Claire glared at him sharply.

"Why would I be!"

"I think you may have been jealous of our relationship, despite your claiming to prefer women. Tell me what your feelings are for me, Claire," Aimeric said.

She looked indignant, at first, at the insinuation that she had any feelings except for rage for him after what he had put her and her sister through. But then, her frown turned into a seductive grin and she placed her hand on Aimeric's arm.

"You're right. I *was* jealous of Aralyn. I wanted you, she had you. I never got the chance to have a child, she did." Pausing dramatically, a blood tear fell from Claire's eye and ran down her creamy face and then she added, "I thought that by taking her away, I would have a chance with you. I never realized how much I wanted you before she came along. Perhaps, I could be a replacement to you…and the child."

Smirking, Aimeric shifted the baby in his arms so he had a free hand. He grasped Claire's dark curls and pulled her forward, close to his mouth.

"If that's what you want," he whispered, lowering his lips to hers.

He kissed her for a moment and, when they pulled away, Claire smiled, surprised. She didn't think he would actually believe her. It had been a long shot. Surprise quickly turned to fear though and she gasped loudly when Aimeric yanked her head back.

"Do you really expect me to believe that, bitch?" he hissed against her lips. Pushing her away, Aimeric looked at Morgan angrily. "Take her downstairs. I'm sure Aralyn will want to have a few words with her when she returns."

Morgan hesitated, confused.

"Master? What do you mean?"

Aimeric rolled his eyes and sighed.

"Oh, Claire, don't try and escape. You must know by now that I have the power to keep you here."

She was closing her eyes, trying to disappear out of the room, but Aimeric was right; he had the power to overrule hers since he created her. As if prodded by an electric rod, Morgan jumped and grabbed the female vampire, by the arm, and held her close to his side. He stood there, keeping her still, and waited for Aimeric to explain.

"Tsk, Morgan, do you really think Aralyn is gone for good? You should know better. Now take her downstairs," Aimeric ordered, nodding at Claire.

Morgan nodded and, on shaky legs, pulled Claire along with him, out the door and down the stairs to the basement. She appeared to have given up on fighting him, knowing that she wouldn't be able to escape Aimeric now. She went away with Morgan without so much as a jerk of the wrist.

Once they were gone, Aimeric glanced at the body of his wife, still lying on the bed. Her eyes were closed and her neck still bent at an odd angle. The first clue to Aimeric that she was not gone for good had been that her body didn't turn to ashes; and there had been plenty of time for that. Also, Aimeric knew that, if she asked, Satan would allow Aralyn to come back to him. He wasn't sure how he knew, but he did.

Hearing the baby fuss softly, Aimeric glanced down at his nameless child and let him grasp his finger once more. The baby closed his eyes, one violet, the other ice blue, and kept his fingers wrapped tightly around Aimeric's. The child's hair was jet-black but Aimeric knew that, with time, it would change to silver once the immortal part of his blood had completely fused with the mortal portion. The vampires didn't really know why the half-breeds' hair changed to silver, but it usually did. There were rare cases in which the hair stayed normal, but not many. Aimeric knew that the baby, also in time, would form fangs, along with his regular teeth. He wouldn't need to feed from mortals as often as regular vampires, but he would need mortal blood, in addition to a human diet, every now and then. The only thing Aimeric wasn't sure of was when the child would begin to crave the blood of a mortal. For the first year, or two, of his life, however, Aralyn would be able to provide the needed substance, of this Aimeric was sure.

"Just go to sleep now, your mother will be back soon," Aimeric whispered, taking the baby to a bassinet, which was sitting in the dark corner of the bedroom.

The bassinet was trimmed with black and gold lace instead of the traditional white. The newborn didn't even stir as Aimeric lowered him onto the soft bed; he only made sucking motions with his mouth, as if eating. Aimeric pulled a light blanket over him and then he turned around to look at the bed, his blue eyes their usual icy glare.

He was waiting.

After a few minutes of deathly silence, Aralyn's body suddenly sprung up into a sitting position, instinctively sucking in a loud breath, even though she didn't need it. She heaved a few times and then glared at Aimeric, her eyes showing nothing but pure hatred.

"Welcome back," Aimeric said dryly, stepping up to the bed beside her.

"Where is that bitch?" Aralyn hissed.

Grinning, Aimeric held out his hand.

"There are more important matters at hand, my love. You can deal with your sister later; I have her locked up. For now, come and meet your son."

Aralyn hesitated at first, her raging expression softening, and then she took the hand offered her. Aimeric led her to the bassinet and she peered down thoughtfully at the tiny life that she had been a part of creating.

After a moment of observing, she said, in a hardened tone, "It's disgusting. Get rid of it."

She was violently yanked around to face an angry Aimeric. He was baring his fangs and his fingers dug into Aralyn's arms. She didn't flinch; all she did was smirk, daring him with her eyes.

"You better not mean that," he said, his voice a dangerous growl.

Her smirk widened.

"Of course I don't. I wanted to be sure of how *you* felt about him."

Aimeric's grip loosed and he scoffed.

"You have some nerve," he said, only half joking.

Turning back around, Aralyn sighed and gently touched her son's hair. As if sensing she was near, the baby opened his eyes and peered up at her, beginning to fuss. She reached down and picked him up, cuddling the newborn, kissing his head, and then went to sit on the bed to feed him. Her breast milk was anything but normal. Her new body somehow knew that the child needed more than milk so it had, somehow, produced a small fraction of blood mixed in with it. Aralyn would have to feed herself more often to replenish the blood but she didn't see that as a problem. While she was feeding him, Aimeric sat down next to her and they both gazed at the baby for a moment before Aralyn spotted a mark on his neck. It was a tiny birthmark, in the shape of a fang.

"What-"

"It's his mark, to show that he is half vampire," Aimeric answered before Aralyn could get the whole question out.

"Half vampire," Aralyn murmured thoughtfully.

Aimeric gazed at her a moment and then sighed deeply. He knew this was coming.

"You want to know about Orrin, don't you?"

"Yes," she responded.

Another sigh.

"He was my son. In the same way this one is," Aimeric began, taking the baby's small hand. "A little over forty years ago, I went into a slight depression and refused to feed off humans, strange as that sounds. I lived off of rats and other creatures, for a while, until I began to crave the Blood again. My desire for human blood was so great, at that time, that I wandered the streets…until I came across the first human I had seen in many months. A woman. She was in the park, pregnant, alone, and seemed distressed.

"I asked her what was wrong and if I could help her; I didn't want to take blood from her and risk killing her child, so I really *was* going to help. She said that her husband had already gone for help, but that she was in labor.

"The woman was becoming frantic, frightened from being in labor, alone, in the park, and also from my appearance; she knew I wasn't normal. I used my charm and calmed her down but after a moment, her blood became too intoxicating for me. I was starving, so I bit her."

Aimeric paused and Aralyn waited for him to go on, shifting the baby in her arms to make him more comfortable while he continued to drink.

"I had only intended on taking a little; I couldn't care less about the woman, but I've always loved children and didn't want to harm the baby, but I couldn't stop. Before I knew it, she was dying and so was the child. I did the only thing I knew to save them."

"You turned her," Aralyn said.

"Yes. She delivered shortly after, before her body died. Orrin was born, thus making him, partly, my son. Because of that experience, I knew how to do it this time," Aimeric said.

He kissed Aralyn's lips softly but she didn't respond. She was thinking everything over and trying to absorb it all. She also had a hint of irritation in her eyes. The baby finished eating and Aralyn pulled him up to her shoulder to gently pat his back.

"And I suppose this woman became your whore? Where is she now, Aimeric?" she asked harshly after a moment.

Aimeric chuckled softly.

"Now, now. Temper, my love. Are you jealous?"

"No," Aralyn snapped.

Aimeric looked skeptical, knowing that she was, no matter how hard she tried to deny it. But he didn't taunt her; he wasn't in the mood.

"She's dead. She became power hungry after only three years and foolishly started killing off vampires from other clans. She was killed," he said.

"And Orrin? When, and why, did he start hating you?" Aralyn asked.

"About ten years ago. His physical body was thirty years old, but he only appeared about fifteen, as was his mentality; the age when most children are burdened with questions. He asked me about his *real* father and blamed me for taking him away from him, along with his mother's death. He said it was my fault that he never knew either of them and that he wished I would burn under the sun and turn to ash," Aimeric said.

"And what did you do to him?" Aralyn inquired.

"I told him to leave and he did, though he used to tell everyone he managed to 'escape my tyranny.' He found a new clan that accepted him because they felt sorry for him; he's lucky I didn't kill him before," Aimeric said.

Aralyn looked at the ash pile on the floor, which used to be Orrin and, her voice hardening into a warning, she said to Aimeric, "I hope you do not intend on killing *our* son if he questions you."

Aimeric sighed, taking the baby, who was asleep again, from Aralyn's arms.

"This one will not be a disappointment," he said confidently and stood from the bed.

Aralyn followed him to the bassinet and watched as Aimeric laid their son, gently into the bed.

"He needs a name," Aimeric said, looking at her.

"Julian," she responded without hesitation, coming over to stand beside Aimeric.

"Why Julian?" he asked.

"Why *not* Julian?" Aralyn snapped, irritated.

Aimeric raised a warning eyebrow, but didn't say anything; he was waiting for Aralyn to correct herself without him having to threaten her. She sighed and secured a blanket around the newborn.

"Julian was my father's name. Even though we didn't get along very well in the last year that we knew each other, he was still important to me. And since he's dead now, I feel like I owe it to him," she responded quietly.

Aimeric turned her around and, kissing her forehead, said, "'Julian' is fine."

Aralyn smiled and he picked her up, taking her to the bed.

"Get some rest now, I will take you out to feed in a little while," he said, laying her down.

He started to walk away but she grabbed his arm. "Aimeric?"

When he turned back around, he saw that she had sat up on her knees, still holding onto him.

"What is it?" he asked.

She pulled him down to kiss his lips softly, barely touching them, and then she pulled away, smirking.

"I feel fine. I don't want to rest," she said in a low whisper.

"And what is it that you do want?" Aimeric asked coolly.

She let her body answer his question. Slowly, enticingly, Aralyn lifted the nightgown, tossing it to the floor, and then laid back on the bed, letting Aimeric's eyes roam her naked flesh. He appeared cool and unaffected on the outside, his expression dull, but Aralyn could read his thoughts and she knew that he wanted her. She knew that the very sight of her perfect, naked, body, lying there on the sheets was making him hard and she knew he wouldn't be able to keep his composure for very long. She arched her back to fully convince him and soon after, she had successfully overpowered him, and their bodies became merged as one. Aimeric was buried deep inside of her, touching her undead soul. They quietly made love, so as not to disturb the baby, and held in their cries of pleasure, thus making it all the more pleasurable to them; they felt like they were going to burst. Finally, as the sun started to rise, Aralyn released, soon followed by Aimeric.

Chapter Twenty-Five: The First Time

Aralyn was standing in front of Claire, who was chained to the wall in the basement. Since Aimeric had released the prisoners, they were the only two down there. She had risen only a few hours after she and Aimeric made love and, after feeding Julian again, she left the child in Aimeric's care, not able to wait any longer to confront Claire. Her hatred for her sister as a vampire was stronger than the love she had had for her when she was a mortal. *Way* stronger. She had been hurt that her own sister had killed her and that hurt had quickly turned to hate.

There Claire was, chained to the wall as Aralyn had been so many times before. Claire had allowed her to be chained by Aimeric before. Claire had left her and let her suffer for so long. As a mortal, Aralyn had forgiven her, but as a vampire, the grudge returned and Aralyn wanted to see her sister suffer as she had done. Claire's eyes widened when she opened them and saw who was standing before her.

Aralyn. The sister, whom, Claire thought, she had killed. With her arms crossed and her eyes glaring, those violet eyes, which used to be so kind, Claire saw how dangerous Aralyn appeared now. She was truly a creation of Aimeric's.

"H- how are you…"

"Alive?" Aralyn finished when Claire trailed off, in shock.

"Yes."

"Why, dear sister, wasn't it you who told me once that vampires aren't, technically, *alive*?" Aralyn asked snidely.

Claire frowned, annoyed.

"Yes, I did. But how did you return?"

Uncrossing her arms, Aralyn strolled up to her.

"What's the matter? Disappointed? Did I spoil your chances of taking my son? That's why you killed me, isn't it? You're jealous?"

Claire clenched her fists and rattled the chains.

"I am not jealous! I was trying to save you!"

Aralyn scoffed.

"Save me?"

"Yes! This is not a life! This is a curse. I figured you would really be better off dead," Claire snarled.

"And abandon my son? Or did you plan on killing him too?" Aralyn hissed harshly.

Claire remained silent, not answering her, and Aralyn knew then that she really had intended on killing the baby as well.

"You bitch," Aralyn hissed.

Claire raised her head and started to defend herself but was cut off when Aralyn backhanded her.

"Don't you dare!" she screamed.

"Aralyn! This is no life!" Claire repeated. "For you or the child! Orrin was right; you can stop it all! Kill Aimeric, Aralyn, please!"

"You want me to kill Aimeric?" Aralyn confirmed.

"Yes."

"You want me to kill my sire, my lover, and the father of my child?"

Claire nodded.

"And what will this accomplish?" Aralyn mused.

"You'll be free. At least, if you choose this life, you and your son can be free from his tyranny," Claire said.

Aralyn laughed loudly.

"You just don't get it, Claire! I couldn't be happier right now! Aimeric changing me was the best thing that could have ever happened to me. I feel like I have a reason to go on in this world now. I'm not depressed anymore! And now we have a child; we are a family." She lowered her voice to a devilish whisper and added, "I don't need you anymore. If anyone deserves to die, it's you."

"Then do it! Kill me! If this is the life you so foolishly choose, then so be it, but don't make me live it any longer!" Claire yelled.

Aralyn shook her head.

"No. You don't deserve to get off so easily; you deserve to suffer."

"Do whatever the fuck you want to me, but don't expect to get away with it," Claire snarled.

"And what does that mean?" Aralyn asked, annoyed.

"Orrin. Aimeric killed him. His clan will know shortly if they don't already and they will want revenge."

"What do they have to do with you? You aren't a part of their clan," Aralyn said.

"I was going to be!" Claire hissed.

"Let them come," Aralyn said, rolling her eyes.

"They will."

"And I'm *so* worried," Aralyn said, sarcastically. "Now," she said, walking to the surgeon's table, "what shall we begin with?"

She had never tortured anyone before, but she had seen Aimeric do it enough that she didn't think she would have any trouble.

"Aralyn," Claire began, shaking her head. "You don't want to do this. I only meant to save you before."

Aralyn smirked and looked at Claire from the corner of her eye.

"I thought you said, 'do whatever the fuck I want'? Were you bluffing? Did you not think I was serious?"

"No. I didn't. The Aralyn I knew would never hurt anyone," Claire said.

"That Aralyn is dead. You, of all people, should know how the blood changes a person." She paused. "I think I like me better this way."

She was going through the tools as she spoke; dull and sharp. She picked up a scalpel and examined it closely.

"Too common," she remarked and set it back down.

She scanned the tray longer and, seeing a razor blade, she smiled and picked it up.

"Good choice...for your first time," Aimeric said, coming up to stand behind her, kissing her neck.

Aralyn turned to him.

"What did you do with Julian?"

"Don't worry, Morgan is with him."

"Morgan?" Aralyn asked, raising her voice in disapproval.

Aimeric smiled, ignoring her tone, and kissed her.

"Yes, with Morgan. Julian will be fine; he's sleeping. I couldn't let you play with your first toy without me, now could I?" he asked quietly against her lips before touching them again.

Aralyn smirked at him and then, taking the blade, she went to stand in front of Claire, who was glaring at Aimeric.

"One day, you will pay for what you have done," Claire sneered.

Aralyn grinned at Aimeric over her shoulder and he wrapped his arms around her waist, from behind, and laid his chin on her shoulder, smiling evilly at Claire.

"I'm sure I will," he whispered sarcastically.

"But for now, it's your turn, *sister*," Aralyn added.

She placed one hand on Claire's forehead and pushed it back, taking the razor blade and sliding it, slowly, down Claire's forehead, over her nose, lips, and all the way down to her chin. Claire gasped and gritted her teeth, but refused to cry out as cold blood ran down her face.

Aimeric watched, and guided Aralyn along, for the next twenty minutes or so, while she placed cuts all over Claire's body. She even removed Claire's shirt and took great joy in drawing tiny pictures, with the blade, onto the flesh of her stomach and chest. Claire had only screamed once during her cutting and that was when Aralyn took the blade around her nipples, cutting deep. Aralyn did not feel the tiniest bit of guilt while putting Claire through this pain. She truly believed Claire deserved it for trying to ruin her happiness.

After a while, Aralyn noticed that the first of the cuts were already closed up. She sighed and tossed the blade to the ground.

"This isn't fun anymore; you heal too fast."

"What should we do about that, then?" Aimeric asked, nibbling Aralyn's ear.

She turned her head and kissed him deeply.

"Kill her and get pets that won't heal so quickly and also, get ones that will scream. Claire's boring," Aralyn said.

Aimeric smiled.

"I knew I loved you."

Aralyn licked his bottom lip and then turned back to Claire.

"Are you ready to go?" she asked with mock sympathy.

Covered in cuts and blood from her stomach up, Claire spat out, "You both will pay!"

"I don't think so!" Aralyn hissed.

She smoothed the dark mess of curls from Claire's face and licked away some of the blood.

"You're kind of bitter, dear sister," Aralyn said in a soft, girlish voice.

Aimeric chuckled behind her.

"Fuck you," Claire mumbled.

Aralyn glared at her for a moment and then jerked Claire's head to the side, exposing her neck. She stared at the flesh for a moment, hesitating, the tiniest bit of soul left in her body urging her to think twice before she killed Claire, her own sister.

"Go on, drink," Aimeric urged.

Coming out of her trance, Aralyn nodded.

"Goodbye, Claire," she said softly.

She violently sank her fangs into Claire's flesh. Claire moaned loudly in both, pleasure and pain, but mostly pain. A vampire's blood was not as satisfying as a mortal's so Aralyn was hardly high when she pulled away, leaving Claire totally drained of the blood she had in her system. She finished Claire off by breaking her neck. Letting her hang there on the wall, until she would turn to dust, Aralyn turned around to Aimeric. Her mouth was closed but blood dribbled down the corners. She pulled Aimeric down to her mouth and he opened his, allowing Aralyn to spill the blood onto his tongue, which she had been holding for him. They went back and forth, swishing the blood between their lips until it was finally gone.

Pulling away, Aralyn became serious.

"We have somewhere to go."

Aimeric nodded and agreed, seeing in her mind what she had planned.

Chapter Twenty-Six: The Battle

"There had better not be one hair out of place on his head when I return or you will be thrown into the dungeon!" Aralyn yelled, talking about Julian, warning Morgan, over Aimeric's shoulder as he tried to usher her out the front door.

"Yes, Mistress," Morgan replied dully.

He obviously didn't appreciate the fact that Aimeric had ordered everyone in the mansion to address Aralyn as Mistress from that time on.

"He'll be fine," Aimeric assured her as he closed the front door once they were outside.

He turned, with Aralyn, to face the small army that he had waiting for him. They were all residents of the mansion, in essence, *his* children, and they were waiting for their Master's orders. Half of the vampires, most of the strongest, had been ordered to fight. The other half was to stay with Morgan and guard the house. Aimeric had also ordered Wes to be Julian's personal bodyguard while they were gone since he knew Morgan wasn't much of a fighter.

The vampires were all dressed in black, from head to toe, so that they wouldn't stand out where the humans were concerned. It didn't matter how they were dressed as far as other vampires went because they would be able to smell them and know they were there.

Aimeric stood before them, with Aralyn at his side, a queen standing by her king.

"Remember what I said earlier! Do not fight until I give the order! Once I have given it, then you may do whatever you wish, as long as you *kill* them or *capture* them. Do not let any of them get away. If I tell you to stop, you had better do it immediately," Aimeric said in his authoritative tone. "Also remember to *keep them away from the mansion*. If my son is harmed, it will be taken out on each and every one of you," he warned.

The vampires all nodded and mumbled in agreement, knowing that Aimeric wasn't bluffing.

"Good. Now let's go. I can feel Terek. He's on his way here," Aimeric said dryly.

Taking Aralyn's hand, he led her through the small crowd and the vampires followed the two down the driveway and into the forest, heading towards the city.

"How strong is Terek's clan, Aimeric?" Aralyn asked.

"I don't know for sure, but they're weaker than we are," he responded, smirking.

"Haven't you fought them before?"

"We vampires make it a habit to stay out of each other's way. We've never crossed paths before with Terek's clan. I only know of him and his capabilities from what Orrin used to rub into my face before, when we met a few times during feeding. Usually, when vampires meet from other clans we leave each other alone without a word. But since I have killed Orrin, I have broken the mutual understanding between all vampires."

"But didn't Orrin break it first?" Aralyn asked.

"Technically, yes. But I am the one who took a life," he responded.

"Well he deserved it," Aralyn replied coldly

Aimeric chuckled.

"You really have changed."

Aralyn smirked, sliding her arm around his waist.

"And I have you to thank for it."

They shared a quick kiss before continuing further into the woods. They were getting closer to the outer edges of the city. The vampire army behind them was being quiet and stealthy, a surprise to Aralyn. She didn't think they would be useful. She figured they would only be in the way.

"You have never fought before so I want you to stay near me, do you understand?" Aimeric said as the two walked, followed by their clan.

She sighed, annoyed.

"Aralyn," Aimeric said warningly. "I mean it. I doubt if Satan would be willing to send you back a second time."

"Alright, fine," Aralyn replied, still annoyed.

Aimeric suddenly stopped and held his arm out so that she couldn't move any further. The vampires behind stopped also and were looking around as the forest fell deathly silent. Everything was eerily silent. The air, the trees, even the animals and insects. After a moment of looking around and sniffing the air, Aimeric took a step forward and called out to the unseen enemy.

"Terek! Why don't you just come on out so we can get this over with?"

One set of hands began clapping, breaking the silence further, and out walked a tall man, with a medium build, wearing a long, brown coat. He was a vampire, the one clapping. His face was as white as snow and his eyes the color of the blackest coal, a drastic contrast to one another. His golden hair was slicked back away from his squared jaw and the hands he was clapping had long, sharp, nails, like claws, which were painted black.

"Very good, Aimeric," Terek said smoothly.

"I'm surprised you know who I am," Aimeric sneered.

Smirking, Terek replied, "Orrin had many things to say about you…though I can't say he was bragging."

"I'm not interested in chatting. Where's the rest of you?" Aimeric asked dryly.

Terek smirked and nonchalantly snapped his fingers. Two-dozen or so vampires surrounded Aimeric's clan, stepping out from behind the trees and bushes. Aralyn was glaring hatefully at Terek, wanting to hurt him, sink her fangs into him and feel him writhe. The other vampires, behind Aimeric, were anxiously awaiting the order to fight.

"I'm sure you know why we are having this little confrontation?" Terek asked, keeping his eyes on Aimeric.

Aimeric grinned coldly.

"I guess I pissed you off when I killed Orrin."

The blonde vampire frowned, disgusted at Aimeric's nonchalance about the death.

"Indeed. Tell me, Aimeric, I know you two had your disagreements but how is it that you could kill your own son?"

Aralyn shot her violet eyes up at Aimeric, curious as to how he would respond, thinking of Julian. He didn't look at her, but kept his cold eyes on Terek.

"Orrin was *not* my son. He ran to you and decided he didn't want me. He tried to kill me, and he interfered with my wife and mine's business. He deserved to die."

Aimeric said the words without a hint of remorse.

Terek shifted his black eyes to meet Aralyn's.

"You. Aren't you the least bit concerned that this *thing* with you will do the same to the child you recently gave birth to? The child that Orrin died trying to save along with yourself?"

Without hesitating, Aralyn replied, "No."

"Why do you say that?"

Aimeric stood beside Aralyn, waiting for her to answer, but kept his cold glare on Terek.

"*Our* son will have no reason to hate Aimeric and therefore, Aimeric will have no reason to harm him."

"You are a foolish woman," Terek replied.

Growling viciously, Aimeric ejected a silver knife from his coat sleeve, catching it in his right palm, while raising his left fist into the air. That was the signal. Aimeric's clan, almost in perfect unison, pulled out their weapons, tipped with poison to ensure death to the vampires they would be fighting. Poison was harmful to vampires, unless they could drain and replenish their blood before it could kill them. They scattered and the battle began.

Aimeric went straight for Terek but the blonde vampire disappeared before he could reach him and Aimeric was soon surrounded by some of Terek's comrades, who had jumped at the chance to defend their leader. Aralyn unsheathed the sword on her hip and went to help him fight the others off. He didn't really seem to need it though. He wasn't having very much trouble at keeping the vampire fighters at bay. Dagger in one hand and a sword in another, Aimeric was slicing the throats of the vampires left and right, taking their heads off, as they came to him, almost as though begging for their undead lives to be taken away. The, once quiet, forest became filled with the cries, growls, and hisses of the children of the night; the undead. Vampire blood, some almost entirely black, spilled onto the grass and piles of ash began to appear as some of the bodies disintegrated.

Aralyn stayed with Aimeric to fight for most of it, but only since he had made her promise beforehand not to leave his side. But it seemed he was hogging all of the fight so she started to inch away slowly, unnoticed, until she was completely on her own. She wasn't as good as Aimeric or some of the others, but she was still able to keep herself alive and keep from getting hurt. She dodged several weapons nicely and even took the head off one of the vampires that tried to take hers. Grinning at her first success, Aralyn quickly looked around for her next target. She found a male who was fighting Sadie. Aralyn didn't like Sadie all that well. The blond had always avoided her as a mortal except for when Aimeric used her to punish Aralyn that one time. Sadie had always stuck her nose in the air when the two had passed each other in the hall and she also seemed to always be glaring at Aralyn when Aimeric wasn't around. Maybe she was jealous.

So, because of her feelings for Sadie, or rather, lack thereof, Aralyn wasn't at all upset when Terek's vampire took Sadie's head. Her body fell to the ground and immediately turned to dust.

"Ashes to ashes," Aralyn mumbled, a smirk tugging at the corners of her crimson lips.

She took the moment, in which the male had begun to rejoice his kill, as her opening to take his own head off of his shoulders. She leered in pride as his body floated away with the wind, along with Sadie's. Aralyn hadn't liked the girl, no, but she still appreciated using her as an excuse to kill the other vampire. Sensing someone behind her, Aralyn turned around and kicked a female in the chin before the girl could grab her, which was what she had been intending on doing. She was stunned for a moment and then went to pay back Aralyn with a punch to the face. Aralyn dodged, ducking just in time. When she came back up though, she was kicked in the back and pushed into the girl. The girl restrained her and another vampire, a male, who was the one who had kicked her, grabbed one of Aralyn's arms and covered her mouth so she couldn't scream.

Not that she would have. Aralyn laughed to herself, thinking it was extremely foolish of the man to cover her lips. If she had wanted to, she could have mentally called to Aimeric. But she didn't. She was curious and wanted to know where the two were taking her. They dragged her behind the trees, far away from the fight, to where Terek was waiting with his hands clasped behind his back. The two vampires shoved Aralyn forward and she hissed at them over her shoulder.

"Calm down. I ordered them to bring you to me," Terek said.

"What the hell do you want?" Aralyn snapped.

"First, we need to get away from here before Aimeric sees you with me," he replied, holding out his arm in a polite gesture.

Aralyn bared her fangs at him threateningly.

"I'm not going anywhere."

"I'm not asking you to leave him for good right now. I just want to talk," Terek assured her calmly.

She hesitated, thinking it over, before curiosity finally got the better of her and she nodded, taking his arm. They disappeared and flew through the rest of the forest, quickly, before they reappeared on a large hill, overlooking the city, far away from Aimeric.

"I want to tell you about vampires. I want you to be aware of what they are truly supposed to be before Aimeric can completely corrupt your young mind," Terek began.

"I don't need-"

"Please, just hear me out," Terek interrupted.

She crossed her arms and glared, but nodded, giving him the okay to continue. She may as well muse him and listen to whatever foolish things he had to say. If anything, she could get a good laugh out of it.

"Vampires are not supposed to be these greatly feared, killing machines as Aimeric seems to believe, and as fiction portrays us. We are supposed to only kill when absolutely necessary and *only* for nourishment, taking the lives of those who are evil in their own mortal skin, who have no hope for the future. Aimeric has taken our existence and turned it into some horrible nightmare to haunt believers' dreams."

Aralyn raised an eyebrow, pretending to be curious.

"What do you mean?"

"He has poisoned the minds of his clan. He has made most of them believe vampires are to be evil and he has convinced them that torturing a victim is normal for our kind. The only ones of his clan that he didn't convince were Orrin, Cora, and your sister, Claire."

"I have no sister!" Aralyn spat, still angry even though she had already gotten her revenge.

"You killed her because your mind is corrupted and Aimeric has made you believe that she didn't care for you and so you didn't even bother to hear her out."

"Aimeric had nothing to do with my killing that betraying bitch!" Aralyn hissed.

"Maybe not directly. But had he not made you so hostile, you would have at least listened to her reasons for killing you."

Aralyn turned her head and looked away, not wanting to admit that he may be right. She knew she would have forgiven Claire if she had still been mortal. But things were different now. She knew what Claire truly was; a betrayer.

"Aimeric has it all wrong, Aralyn," Terek said, his voice becoming softer and more sincere.

She didn't respond, still looking at the ground, a crimson tear spilling down her cheek.

"Vampires are not torturing, killing, machines. We are supposed to think of mortal life as a beautiful thing. Aimeric thinks of mortals as pests and playthings. He will kill anyone. He killed his own son for God's sakes! It doesn't matter to him; if they did him wrong, he kills them, end of story," Terek finished sadly.

She was still quiet a moment and then shook her head.

"If he's so wrong, then why has Angel, Satan, whatever his name is, not taken him back and stopped him?"

"Because he made a deal with Aimeric to send him back to earth and once back, unless another agreement was made, enabling Lucifer to take him back before his time, Lucifer can't directly interfere because he promised and that promise binds him."

Aralyn stood there a moment, taking all that Terek had said into consideration, biting her bottom lip as usual when she was thinking or when she was nervous; that mortal trait of hers hadn't left her. Terek waited patiently for her response, a glimmer of hope shining in his black eyes.

Finally, Aralyn looked up with sadness in her violet eyes with a watery crimson coating them. What if Aimeric *was* wrong? What if everything Aimeric had taught Aralyn was just his own pleasure and not the guidelines of vampirism? She remembered how terrified and disgusted she had been, as a mortal, with Aimeric.

"Maybe you're right. Maybe we shouldn't kill and torture for fun," she said softly.

Terek smiled, relieved, thinking he would get through to her after all. Aralyn returned his smile, only to mock him for actually believing she had been sincere in her thoughts. Her grin turned malicious.

"But, where would all the fun in that be if we only killed the 'evil' and killed to survive?"

Terek frowned deeply and opened his mouth to argue at the very same moment that Aralyn ducked and fell to the ground. A flaming arrow flew through the air and burrowed itself into the back of Terek's head a millisecond before his head exploded, sending a thin ring of fire to burst around his neck for another second. Had Aralyn not seen it, the fire ring may have caught her too. Propped up on her elbows, Aralyn laughed softly as Terek turned to gray flakes and fluttered to the ground before being caught up in the wind and carried off to somewhere unknown. Her laughter turned into loud, almost maniacal, giggles as Aimeric walked up to her, throwing the miniature crossbow he had used to the ground. He stood over her and offered a hand, which she took, still laughing girlishly.

"Are you alright?" he asked, pulling Aralyn to her feet.

She nodded and kissed him softly, nibbling his bottom lip until it bled. He let her take a few drops, his cold eyes looking into hers, before he angrily shoved her back into a tree. Her grin faded and she glared, not afraid, but angry by his sudden behavior.

"Why did you leave? I told you to stay with me!" Aimeric growled.

"I got bored!" she snapped.

"And look where it got you. You could have been killed, *again*! Terek could have easily overpowered you," Aimeric sneered. "You're not as strong as you think! You're still just a little girl when it comes to battle."

"I knew you would show up sooner or later," Aralyn said. "I wanted to see what he had to say."

"It doesn't matter! Don't be so stupid, Aralyn, he could have killed you the second he had you in his possession, *before* I could have reached you," Aimeric sneered.

"Nothing happened, lighten up, and *don't* call me stupid," Aralyn hissed back.

"Don't show your stupidity and I wouldn't have to say it."

His grip on her was tightening and he was pushing her further against the tree. She pushed back at him, though it did her no good, even though she was a lot stronger than she used to be, she was still no match for Aimeric.

"What do you want me to say?" she snarled.

"Say you were foolish and you won't leave my side again."

Aralyn smirked, mischievously, and picked up his hand from her waist, taking his finger into her mouth as an obscene gesture.

"I was foolish. I'll never leave you again, *master*," Aralyn said in a low, seductive voice.

Aimeric grinned his approval and then touched his lips against Aralyn's, their tongues dancing against each other. They were locked together in a short moment of passion and then, Aimeric pulled away, suddenly calm and gentle, and stroked Aralyn's face with his finger.

"What *did* Terek have to say to you?"

Aralyn smirked.

"He said that you were evil and that you have corrupted your clan. And he said you would corrupt me the same way."

Aimeric grinned, pulling her from the tree, and up to him, wrapping his arms around her waist, and nuzzled her neck."

"Do you believe him?"

She smiled, wrapping her arms around his neck as he began to place soft kisses on hers.

"Of course I do… Did you know that vampires are supposed to be forgiving and not torture for fun?" she asked.

"Not at all," Aimeric responded in a low growl, kissing up Aralyn's neck to nip at her ear.

"Did we win the fight?" Aralyn asked in between soft moans.

"We're not dead, are we?" he responded against her flesh.

"Mm, in what way?" Aralyn asked, laughter ringing in her voice.

Aimeric smirked and pulled her away, leading her back towards the forest and the mansion.

"Come. We'll go check on Julian and then come back out to feed…and maybe a little more," he added mischievously.

"I can't wait."

***

When they made it to the circular drive, they saw that the door was wide open and the scene of a fight was before their eyes. The two rushed inside to see that the first floor of the mansion was a mess. Chairs and tables were overturned and pictures hung crooked on the wall, some had fallen entirely and were smashed on the floor.

Morgan was there to greet them right away.

"He's fine!" he said and raised his hands in defense before Aralyn or Aimeric could start yelling and demanding to know where Julian was.

"What happened?" Aimeric asked.

"Where is he?" Aralyn demanded at the same time.

"He's sleepin' upstairs. Wes is with him," Morgan said first in answer to Aralyn's question. Next, he looked at Aimeric and said, "A few, five or so, thought the house would be mostly empty so they barged inside. Wes and the others fought them and immediately restrained them, but not before they could knock around the furniture a bit. Wes ordered that they not be killed though. He thought you might want to keep them around for a while."

"Yes, indeed," Aimeric said nodding.

Morgan beamed and clasped his hands behind his back as if waiting for something. Aimeric smirked.

"You should know by now that I don't hand out praise and 'thank you's,' Morgan."

The sniveling vampire's face dropped and he hung his head and walked away, looking hurt. Aralyn smirked. She still hated Morgan and loved to see his pride shot down, which Aimeric was good at doing.

"Where are you going?" Aimeric asked when Aralyn started to climb the stairs.

"I want to see my baby."

Aimeric followed her to their bedroom where Julian was sleeping in his bassinet.

"Are you back for good?" Wes asked hopefully, obviously tired of babysitting.

He was on their bed, looking bored. He didn't have a mark on him from the fight. He had obviously had the upper hand.

"No. But take a break," Aimeric said dryly.

"Thank you," Wes said and sighed in exaggeration, making a beeline for the door.

"I really hate him," Aralyn said, glaring, as Wes left.

Aimeric laughed, closing the door, and then joined Aralyn at Julian's bed. The infant had heard them come in and had started fussing so Aralyn picked him up to feed him before they would go out again.

"Come sit down, darling," Aimeric said, taking Aralyn's shoulders.

They went to the sofa at the bottom of the bed and Aralyn leaned into Aimeric while she fed Julian.

"How many did we bring back from the fight?" she asked quietly so as not to disturb the child.

"Three. The rest were killed," Aimeric responded, playing with Aralyn's raven locks, which had become streaked with blue since her turning, around her shoulders.

"Do we have to be concerned with anyone else?"

"No. Any other clans know not to interfere."

She nodded and sighed after a moment, gazing down at the life they had created together, even if it wasn't in the old fashioned way.

"He'll grow up happy, won't he? …He won't hate us?"

Aimeric kissed her forehead and touched Julian's soft hair.

"We won't give him a reason to hate us."

She smiled and the two, mother and father, continued to gaze at their son while he suckled Aralyn's breast with his eyes closed.

"I need to know something, Aralyn. And you must tell the truth so that I know it won't be an issue in our future together," Aimeric said after a while.

"Yes?" she asked curiously.

He pulled her hair from her neck thoughtfully, playing with it still.

"Do you feel any remorse at all for killing Claire?"

Aralyn's eyes grew dark and they narrowed.

"No. She deserved to die," she said, her jaw clenched.

Aimeric nodded.

"Good, my love. One more question."

She looked into his eyes and waited for him to go on.

"Do you regret, even a little bit, what I have made you and Julian?"

She instinctively let out a breath, relieved he had asked such an easy question; she had expected something much more difficult with how serious he had been.

Smiling, she replied, "Not at all. I love you and Julian. And I love who I am now. I couldn't be happier, Aimeric."

He smiled and they leaned forward, tasting each other's lips for a long, passionate moment until Julian began to fuss again, distracting them. He was finished eating, so Aralyn gently brought him up to pat his back, smiling.

"Aimeric?" she asked in a curious whisper.

"Yes, my love?"

"I think we should fill up your cages."

He smirked, delight filling his eyes.

"As you wish."

<u>Epilogue</u>

It was a few months later and Aimeric and his queen were walking the slick streets of the city on a pleasant, October night. The air was crisp and fresh from the rain that had recently covered the city and the clouds were still thick above. A gentle breeze, left behind from the thundershower swirled the two's dark hair around their shoulders.

"It's a beautiful night," Aralyn said thoughtfully.

Aimeric brought the hand he was holding up to his lips and touched her fingers gently.

"It is."

"Tonight was fun," she said mischievously and smirked out of the corner of her eye.

Aimeric chuckled.

"Indeed. You're becoming an expert at making them scream, my love."

"Thanks," she said grinning. "Will I ever get bored of torturing those poor souls?" she added sarcastically.

"I doubt it," Aimeric responded.

They had filled the cages in the basement and, almost every night, the mansion played the horrendous music of men and women screaming, along with Aralyn and Aimeric's laughter. Aralyn was always the loudest though. She had truly changed. She loved to hear her victims scream and then tried to drown out the screams with her laughter, simply to see if it was possible to make more noise than them. Aimeric had no complaints.

She sighed, snuggling into Aimeric's arm.

"I can't wait until Julian is old enough to come with us. I hate leaving him behind, especially with Morgan."

"I know you do, but it will be quite some time before he can be brought with us."

Morgan had become baby Julian's official caretaker when Aimeric and Aralyn left to feed, which he wasn't too happy about, but didn't dare argue with them. Other than that need, however, Aralyn refused to leave the child with anyone but Aimeric. She had become almost *too* protective of him and frequently hissed at the other vampires when they got too close or even looked at him.

Aimeric studied her a moment while they walked, seeing the far away look in her eye mixed with a certain sadness.

"I know what's bothering you," he said.

"What?" she asked.

"We've talked about it before... You know Julian will die one day."

She looked down and watched the pavement go by before answering.

"I just...don't know if I will be able to watch," she said quietly.

"Don't think of it right now. He still has a long life ahead of him, maybe two hundred years or more. And, as I promised, the day he leaves earth, we will go with him."

Aralyn smiled and they stopped long enough to embrace each other in a soft and gentle kiss. Aimeric continued once they had begun walking again.

"Since that is our decision, I am going to take you and Julian, when he is old enough, to see the world together before we leave it."

"I've always wanted that," Aralyn said, smiling.

"I know. And we will do it one day but for now, let's eat."

Aralyn looked up, hearing the lusty tone in Aimeric's voice, and smirked when she saw a young couple ahead of them, walking hand in hand, completely unaware of what was going to happen to them. In a half second, Aralyn appeared on the side of the woman and Aimeric stood next to the man.

"Hello there," Aralyn said, in a lusty whisper, licking her full lips.

"Shit! Amy, run!" the man yelled to the girl.

He took a swing at Aimeric and the girl turned and ran just as Aimeric caught the man's arm and threw him against a light pole. Aralyn grinned as she watched the girl run away from her. To muse her, Aralyn let her go for a minute and allowed her to think she would be able to get away. It was always more fun that way. Once she had gone far enough, Aralyn ran after her and knocked her back into one of the buildings.

"I always like a good run before eating," Aralyn hissed into the girl's trembling lips, elongating her fangs.

The girl's eyes grew wide and she whispered, terrified, "A vampire…"

Aralyn sneered as the girl reached into the front of her shirt and pulled out a silver cross on a chain. Her shaking hands held it out to Aralyn's face.

"Father, please protect me."

Aralyn took the fist that held tight to the cross and licked the silver, religious icon, slowly, mocking the girl to show her that it didn't affect her. Foolish humans, believing everything they saw on T.V. and read in books.

The girl gasped, frightened, a tear rolling down her cheek and Aralyn smirked again.

"Tsk, tsk, sweetheart. Haven't you been told? Vampires don't exist."

The girl's screams were soon cut off and she was only able to gurgle as Aralyn's fangs tore into her neck and assaulted the pulse underneath. Moments later, the girl was drained, her heartbeat becoming non-existent, and her body hit the ground, thudding on the concrete loudly.

And Aralyn's cold laughter echoed through the, otherwise, silent night.

The End?

So there you have it. Now that you've read the story, you can come to your own conclusion about my Aralyn. Did she *really* fall in love with Aimeric? Or had he succeeded in doing what he had threatened before? Which was making Aralyn believe she loved him until she actually did. Is a person truly capable of loving such a horrible being? Perhaps Aralyn had been driven crazy by the sad events in her life that she…just didn't care. Perhaps she believed Aimeric's control over her was a way for her to be taken care of for the rest of her life. Maybe she just stopped trying. I bet she was very frustrating to you no matter what, though.

And now, is she truly happy as a vampire? Was becoming a vampire really the best thing that ever happened to her? She certainly seems to think so, doesn't she?

Nevertheless, I hope you enjoyed my tale.

"Vampires Don't Exist"
March 17, 2005
By:
Reyanna Vance

In loving memory of
Felicia Ann Jewell
February 7th 1982 – November 5th 1997
You were taken far too young. Rest in peace

Reyanna Vance was born in Tucson Arizona to a military family. She has three sisters and one brother. She is now 21 years old and lives in Oklahoma with her family, who has since retired from the Air Force. Reyanna started writing at age 17 by writing fan-fiction role-plays with her cousin, father, and two sisters. She hates the sun and likes staying up until the wee hours of the morning, working on her novels, because that's when she works best. Reyanna has always had a fascination with vampires and fantasy since she was a small child.

Other titles to look for by "Reyanna Vance" in the not-so-distant future:

"Blooded Angel" (2006/2007)

"Dies Irae: Day of Wrath" (2006/2007)

Also, be sure to check out Reyanna's website:
http://members.cox.net/reyannavance/

5939847R0

Made in the USA
Lexington, KY
29 June 2010